Armageddon Rising

# Return of the Watchers

D.P. Bennett

I0640471

Printed in the United States.
Book Cover design by D.P. Bennett
ISBN 978-0-9986587-2-8
First Edition February 2017

# -Acknowledgments-

This book has been a labor of love; however, it would not be complete without the important and valuable contributions of others. I would like to acknowledge the Near Death Research Foundation (www.nderf.org) for being a valuable resource and hope to those who are lost in life. Additionally, the Esoteric Archives (www.esotericarchives.com) were an important resource and inspiration for some of my material. Finally, to the members of my family that encouraged me and took time to help put my book together, I thank you all.

# One

THE ALARM SOUNDED ON THE sequencing machine, and Dorian wondered if he would ever find the answers he was searching for.

"Can you stop that for me, Yuki?" he asked of his lab manager. The familiar beeping sounds coming from the equipment were accompanied by the sterile smell of the chemicals and reagents that permeated the air.

Yuki set down her pipette after withdrawing a small amount of liquid and walked towards the control panel terminal. After pressing several fingers on the touch screen interface (she could do this in her sleep), the machine emitted the affirmative whirring sound, signifying it was reset and prepped for another batch of samples.

Yuki was a young, beautiful, Japanese student with a slender body and long black hair. She spoke softly with an accent, yet her English was quite understandable.

It had been two and a half years since Dorian began as a researcher and associate professor teaching Molecular Genetics at the University of Michigan, and he was becoming impatient with his progress. The task of researching a cure for Huntington's disease was slow and arduous; things were not going as smoothly as he had expected them to, prior to undertaking this position.

"A fresh start, a chance to run my own lab," he'd thought back then. Only now he had to deal with lectures, budgetary issues, outdated equipment, grant proposals, and desperate students vying for a spot in his lab. At his last job, the pressure was immense, the hours were long, and the ability to research to his heart's desire was limited. It was not long after his discovery that he decided it was time to leave; management was becoming suspicious, and the idea well was drying up. Not to mention the fact that he was running out of excuses as to why he didn't seem to get any older with the passage of time. Sometimes the grass isn't greener on the other side; it's just a different shade of brown, and today was no exception.

"Dr. Lystad, we're running low on reagent, we only have enough for two more runs," Yuki said in a depressed tone. Running the lab was expensive, even with free labor from some of the students. Still, the reagent was something they could afford, and one person was in charge of keeping the stocks adequate.

"Engel?" Dorian called out to his junior researcher his in a sarcastic, questioning tone, looking over at him as if to say 'Why the hell are we almost out of reagent again?'

Engel acted like he hadn't been paying attention to their conversation.

"Something up?" he asked carefully, realizing he was on thin ice.

"I hope for your sake that Yuki is imagining that we're almost out of reagent and that you have some stashed elsewhere," Dorian replied.

"I'll look into it, but I'm pretty sure I ordered plenty this time," he muttered in an unsure voice.

Dorian glanced back at him. "You're killing me, man."

Yuki interrupted. "Dr. Lystad, after these last two runs I am going to leave early, if I may. I have some personal issues to attend," she stated, in her typical polite and formal manner.

"That's fine. I'll need the data compiled by Kasia before you leave; make sure you drop it off with her," Dorian said.

It was twenty minutes until two o'clock in the afternoon, and Dorian had to make his way over to the lecture hall in the medical science building. He grabbed a turkey sandwich from the shared refrigerator and choked it down while gathering his notes, then headed for the door. Just as he was walking out the door, he stopped in his tracks and turned back. "Engel...Engel!" he yelled, food flying from his mouth.

"He's probably getting drunk, as usual," Kasia quipped through the doorway of the computer office adjoining the research lab.

"Yuki, tell him I want a copy of the purchasing invoice for the supplies on my desk by the time I get back," he snapped in an angry tone.

Dorian barely caught the bus that went to the other side of campus. Fortunately, it had been delayed by all the snow they had been getting.

BACK AT THE LAB:

"Where's Dr. Lystad?" Engel asked, knowing Dorian was at a his two o'clock lecture.

"He told me to tell you that you need to get a copy of the invoice for our supplies on his desk before he gets back. He also wanted you to clean the lab up," Yuki said with a wry smile.

"Nice try, Yuki. It wasn't my fault this time. I went into Gregorovich's lab and found out they've been 'borrowing' (his hands gesturing quotation marks) "some of our supplies. Lystad is going to be pissed," he proclaimed in a triumphant voice.

"I will be leaving in a few minutes; I have already informed Dr. Lystad. Please take the samples out after the sequencer finishes, and give the data to Kasia for processing," Yuki said, in a loud enough voice for Kasia to hear. Kasia's small head slowly peered out of a cubicle in the adjoining room; lights were reflecting off her glasses.

"I heard you were out of reagent, so I just made plans to meet my sister for lunch. What the hell is wrong with you people?" she yelled. Kasia, as it turns out, was short for *Katarzyna* in her native Polish tongue; however, no one could pronounce it properly so she remained Kasia, and occasionally, Kathy. She was another PhD. hopeful, whose area of expertise was bioinformatics. Her short, brown hair, small frame, and thick, coke bottle-like glasses that hung near the tip of her nose were the characteristics of a stereotypical librarian. The three made up the full time graduate students in Dorian's lab. Yuki was the most professional amongst them; Engel the least. Kasia was somewhere in the middle, and often they would argue amongst themselves the way siblings do. Today was no different.

"Why do you always have to ruin my day?" Kasia whined at Engel.

"What are you blaming me for? I ordered enough reagent, it's not my fault someone's been swiping it," he moaned.

"Here's an idea—why don't you ask us before you go off making plans instead of assuming we're finished? That way you won't end up—" Her eyes widened as she interrupted him. "Why don't you drown in your beer mug? That way I won't have to do it for you by dragging you to the bottom of the river!" she snapped.

Several students in the lab laughed out loud at their bickering. Engel wasn't particularly accustomed to exchanging barbs. Growing up as an only child, he mainly thought of Kasia as an annoying little sister he never wanted to have.

At twenty nine, he appeared to be the oldest in the lab, even older looking than Dorian. That could be attributed partially to his drinking habit, and to his life spent on the road as a guitarist touring with a group known as the "SOES Bandits". He had that California surfer-dude look, complete with long, sandy-blonde hair, beard stubble that changed from week to week, loose, hole-infested jeans, Converse shoes, and well-worn t-shirt; the whole grunge-look of the 1990's. Fortunately, for the lab patrons, he didn't smell like the sewer he looked to have crawled out of.

While the two exchanged pleasantries, Yuki gathered her things and made her way out of the building, laughing at their bickering. She was quite accustomed to the noise of squabbling siblings; it made her feel more at home. Carrying herself like the gentry, she avoided participating in juvenile antics and arguments with other students. Her demeanor emanated an upbringing of class; one that implied she came from money. In fact, her family at one time had been extremely wealthy; her great-grandfather had founded Sukekuni Supply, expanding it into an international medical supplier that her father now ran.

With the downfall of the Japanese economy, however, her family had lost some control of the company through consolidation of shareholders, along with a great deal of their wealth. Not wanting to go into the family business, she had decided to pursue her passion for science and study abroad. Already on her way to earning her PhD. in Proteomics at twenty-four, she was a valuable asset to the lab.

She took the commuter bus to the student parking lot and began the slow drive over to metro airport. Arriving several hours later, due to the traffic and snow, she made her way through the terminal, passing through security without difficulty.

The plane was full despite the exorbitant cost of a ticket; mainly the result of many airlines going under and current oil prices.

⁓⁓⁓

HER FLIGHT WAS SHORT, ABOUT ONE HOUR TO JFK airport. A limousine driver holding a placard with her name on it was waiting for her.

"I hope your flight was acceptable ma'am," the driver said politely.

"It was fine, thank you," she replied softly.

"It's not very safe right now in New York, so I'll do my best to get us there in one piece," he said with a nervous laugh.

Yuki had only been to New York, one other time, as a young child, and was trying to take in as much of the sights as possible, but it was difficult to enjoy with her nerves on edge.

Part of her wished that she had never agreed to do this in the first place. Although she maintained some illusion of wealth in front of her friends, the truth, despite her father's unsuccessful attempts in hiding it, was that her family had accumulated a considerable amount of debt, and this meeting might provide an opportunity to get out of it. At least, her father thought so.

The winters had become more brutal with each subsequent year, and today was no exception. In early-mid December, the sun was barely shining. The sky was mostly overcast and looked as if storm clouds were forming, the perfect way to set the day off.

As they traveled to their destination, she witnessed various protests going on along the way; some were passive, with protestors beating drums, marching, and shouting through megaphones, while others were more violent, with bottles being thrown, tires set ablaze and windows being smashed. Picket signs with just about every political stance and ideology were on display, from anti-capitalistic and anarchistic, to constitutionalist, and libertarian. Police in riot gear and armored vehicles were lined up opposite the protestors; waiting for the opportunity to pounce on their prey.

As the limo continued on, they passed by long lines of people—many of whom had lost their homes due to the economy, waiting at the food banks and shelters. The splendor that was once New York City had been tarnished, the latest in a long list of major cities that had fallen into oblivion.

As the driver pulled underneath the covered awning of the hotel, she felt a bit of nausea and butterflies in her stomach. He stopped the limousine and opened the car door for her. Several heavily armed guards flanked the doorman, who stood at the entrance to the hotel holding the door open. Graffiti was being removed from the façade of the building by several workers outside, a seemingly endless task as the gangs were becoming more prolific than ever. She picked up her pace as the wind and snow whipped up, feeling pity for the workers who had to stand outside to open the door for guests as they entered. "At least they have jobs," she thought.

The hotel was opulent, with marble floors, soothing music, and elegant décor. She headed straight for the ladies' room to compose herself before meeting her host. Right now, she just needed some privacy, but she wouldn't get it here with the restroom attendant sitting nearby staring at her. She fixed her hair, adjusted her skirt and blouse, then took a deep breath. After checking her makeup and gathering her thoughts, she tipped the clerk and slowly made her way towards the door, all the while wondering what this meeting was all about. The more she thought about it the less comfortable she became. All Yuki knew about Theodore Dantanian was that he was the largest private venture capitalist in Europe, and that he was willing to pay generously for information.

IT HAD BEGUN TWO DAYS AGO, WHEN SHE WAS contacted by her sister Aki, who was at home in Fujinomiya, Japan, a short distance away from Mt. Fuji. Aki was also a student at the university, and the two of them shared an apartment in Ann Arbor. Aki was home for the winter break, visiting friends and family. Yuki was curled up on her couch in the apartment with her blanket and tea, having just booted her laptop, when the call came from her sister.

"Father called me to tell you to look at the email he sent," Aki said.

"What is so important that he needs me to check my email now?" Yuki asked.

"How should I know? He barely talks to me, let alone you. He probably wants to ask if you got the Christmas present he sent."

Ever since Yuki decided to pursue genetics as a profession, her father was disappointed that she chose another path apart from the family business. Her sister was another source of concern for Yuki's father; he feared that she might somehow influence Aki into avoiding her duty to her family as well.

"How is everything there?" Yuki inquired.

"Did you hear on the news? Mt. Fuji is having major tremors again," Aki said in a worried voice.

"I heard. I was reading about it on the internet this morning."

"I know we've seen this before, but this time I'm pretty sure it's going to go off and wipe us all out," Aki added, with surprisingly little concern that her prediction might come to fruition.

"Well, if that happens at least you won't have to worry about exams anymore." Yuki replied in a similar tone.

The last decade had so many disasters and deaths that most people were apathetic toward just about anything; a sort of global numbness had taken root. Scientists were under pressure not to cause mass panics, but that approach often led to significant casualties. The frequency of tremors and smoke coming out of the mountain was enough to have everyone on edge there, especially after the devastating eruptions in Iceland, Chile, and Indonesia.

"I think something bad might happen this time. I tried to convince father to prepare but he won't listen," Aki said, frustrated with her father's stubbornness.

"I'll have a talk with mother. Hopefully, she will persuade him to do something."

"Yeah, she'll persuade him to throw us into the volcano and sacrifice the two of us so they can retire in peace," Aki joked. They both laughed. Yuki said her goodbyes, then looked at the email letter that had the Japanese characters for "Important" in the subject line.

She opened the email and read the following message.

*"Yuki, there is something that I need for you to do for our family. I was contacted through a business associate of mine regarding a person of interest that you are working with. A wealthy European businessman has some knowledge of your research and the professor you are working for. His name is Theodore Dantanian, and he would like to discuss a proposal with you in person. From what I am told, he is a venture capitalist who has backed many companies in the past and is aggressively financing biotechnology firms. It may be a long shot, but this meeting could be a very important chance towards securing a good financial future for our family. I have the contact information for one of his personal assistants at the bottom of the email. Go see him and find out what he wants."*

Pondering the email for some time, she tried to understand what this was all about.

"Huntington's affects so few people that any discoveries made would pay back little if any profit. I would assume that with his resources he could easily find out what we have, and determine whether it's worth backing without me. We're not real close on anything right now, anyway. I wonder who this person of interest I work with is?" For some reason she felt a sense of foreboding about meeting this man.

There was barely any sleep for her that night, but when she awoke the following morning she had received another email from her father with the subject line "Did you call him?"

Sighing to herself, she got up, made a cup of tea and ate some breakfast. After a quick shower, she wrote down the phone number of the investor and headed out to clean off her car, which had accumulated a few inches of snow and ice from last night's flurries. The cold hit her like a thousand tiny knives, and she realized she wasn't dressed properly for being outside more than a few minutes.

"I should have taken a position at the University of Miami, or UC Berkley. I'm sick of snow," she complained. While sitting in the car as it warmed up, she reached for her cell phone and called the number given to her. The phone rang three times, and just as she was about to hang up, someone answered.

"Ah, Miss Yuki, Ohayou gozaimasu." It was a female voice on the other side.

"Ohayou," Yuki quickly replied.

"Allow me to introduce myself. My name is April Wind and I represent a multinational investor by the name of Theodore Dantanian. Mr. Dantanian would very much like to meet with you to discuss a business proposal that he feels you will find intriguing and beneficial to you and your family. Would you be willing to take a flight to New York tomorrow afternoon for a dinner meeting? All expenses will be paid, of course."

"What sort of proposal and where exactly will I be going?" she asked, somewhat skeptical and suspicious at the lack of details for the meeting.

"Well, it involves a person of interest at your work. Mr Dantanian will explain the rest. Let me tell you that your father had many questions himself before he even allowed us to speak with you," April replied with a chuckle. "We have a first-class flight reserved for a two-p.m. departure from Detroit to New York. A table has been reserved at the Ritz Carlton Hotel restaurant next to Central Park in Manhattan. After the dinner meeting you can stay the night at the hotel if you wish, or we can have you flown back later that evening. As a token of our appreciation for listening to our proposal, we will offer you ten ounces of gold to be sent to your residence in Michigan, or anywhere you would like."

After the collapse of the global economy, many people preferred precious metals over fiat currencies; too many of the latter had become mattress stuffing and fodder for the fireplace. The Euro was not faring any better, nor most of the other major currencies. There was talk about gold backed credits or GBC's becoming the new global currency, but most people still desired physical gold and silver, both of which were in very high demand. Ten ounces for just listening seemed too good to pass up.

"I will listen to your proposal tomorrow," Yuki stated formally.

"Excellent. Mr. Dantanian will be pleased; we look forward to seeing you. I can have the itinerary of your flight sent to your phone in just a few minutes. As I mentioned, a driver will be waiting for you at LaGuardia. If anything should come up, please call ahead; Mr. Dantanian does not like to be kept waiting as he is extremely busy. Is that acceptable?"

"This is acceptable," Yuki replied, unsure if she was making the right decision.

# Two

THE MOMENT HAD ARRIVED TO FIND OUT WHAT this mystery man Theodore Dantanian wanted from her. She made her way over to the restaurant entrance, and the door was opened for her by the maître d'.

"Hello, um, I am supposed to be meeting—"

"Here for Mr. Dantanian? Right this way, Ma'am," the maître d' said.

The restaurant was somewhat empty, with tourism and the economy being down. As she was being escorted to her table, she noticed the curious glances from the patrons in the dining room and had a terrible thought of them happily feasting upon her in place of their meals. The appetites of the rich are seldom satisfied. She felt a twinge of guilt for being here when so many others that were outside were going hungry.

There was a couple sitting next to each other near the back of the dining room that she determined to be Mr. Dantanian and Ms. Wind. They both stood as Yuki approached, and a waiter moved in behind a chair in order to pull out for her to sit.

"Konnichiwa, Miss Yuki," Mr. Dantanian stated, extending his hand to her. His appearance was that of an aristocrat, judging by his impeccably tailored navy-blue Armani suit and the fine Italian leather shoes he wore, along with the exotic watch that most likely had cost a mountain of money. His black hair was well groomed; short, with a bit of grey on the sides, giving him an apparent age of about fourty-five. Rounding out the look, he had three muscular bodyguards with matching black suits and white shirts sitting at the table behind him. April was sitting alongside him. She appeared to be about thirty years old, with curly, flowing, blonde hair and an hourglass figure sporting a black business skirt.

"Konnichiwa," Yuki replied in a very soft voice, barely making eye contact while gently taking his hand. She placed her coat on top of the adjacent chair and sat across from the pair.

"I trust your flight was satisfactory?" he asked politely. His accent did not reveal his country of origin.

"It was fine, thank you."

At that moment, several waiters arrived with trays full of sushi and other Asian appetizers.

"Seafood. How typical," Yuki thought.

"Please, enjoy," he said, mindful of his guest. "Care for something to drink?"

"Water will be fine, thank you." She was beginning to feel a bit more at ease, gaining her confidence.

"First, I must apologize for asking you to see me on such short notice. My schedule requires me to take advantage of opportunities in various locations around the world at any given time whenever they arise, which necessitates extensive planning of logistics by my assistant. I make sure she earns her ridiculous salary," he said with a slight laugh. April quietly smiled.

"You're probably wondering why I brought you here, so I'll get right down to it. Some time ago, a contact of mine at Primase, I'm sure you're familiar with them, had gave me some information regarding Dr. Dorian Lystad that piqued my interest. How well do you know Dr. Lystad?"

Yuki thought back to the first time she and Dr. Lystad had met in person, after exchanging emails across the planet. After joining the lab, she had spent the last two years working sixty-plus-hour weeks there, sharing many conversations and meals with him. He had dropped her off at her apartment once when her car wouldn't start, but they had always maintained a professional relationship. There was a mutual admiration and respect between them, and she hoped one day they might become more than just colleagues.

"To what extent are you aware of his research?" Mr. Dantanian asked, shifting his approach. An easy question; this was her area of expertise.

"I know everything about his research. Currently we're looking into creating a vector for correction of the point mutation of the Htt gene for Huntington's disease," she said with precision.

"I was not referring to that research," he replied.

She frowned and looked over at April for a second. "I'm not sure I understand what you are speaking of; this is the only research we are conducting at this time."

"As you know, Dr. Lystad was one of the top researchers at Primase who was working on a cure for cancer. According to those he worked with, he was quite a dedicated man. I was told he spent countless hours working in the lab, day after day without a single vacation or day off, and then one day he quits." Dantanian snapped his fingers. "Just like that."

Dantanian continued, "I am aware that he had some issues of conscience with the company. However, that doesn't quite explain his rapid departure and abandonment of his research. Also, the data he left was incomplete and appeared to have sections removed. Why would he do that?" Yuki was processing the information and was about to offer a speculative response, when he continued.

"To a corporate attorney, his actions could be construed as those of someone who made an important discovery and possibly took that discovery to a competitor, earning enough to drop out and start up again in academia." He stopped himself and held out his hand, as if to answer a retort to that statement.

"Yes, I am aware he signed non-compete and non-disclosure agreements, but with good lawyers they can be circumvented," he added, examining her facial expression to see what allegiance she had towards Dr. Lystad. The answer became obvious as her eyes narrowed with a sour look on her face. She knew Dorian enough to know that he was an honorable man, not motivated by making money or by grabbing glory and attention for himself; he was quite the opposite of that in her eyes.

"There is much more to the story than that, however. According to my contact, Dr. Lystad was very surreptitious, drawing suspicion from some of the other researchers. Despite his lofty position, the senior management issued a directive to monitor his activity as a result of his odd behavior. As you can imagine, the situation was rather delicate; Lystad was a Nobel Prize winner with friends in high places within the company. They didn't want to accuse him of wrongdoing without evidence, and yet they couldn't easily search through his work without alerting him and others not privy to the situation. There was also a concern they might have a bio-terrorist on their hands," he added, watching her closely.

Yuki thought to herself how absurd that statement sounded, but she kept her cool.

"Shortly thereafter, under video surveillance, he was observed placing some vials into a restricted refrigeration unit. The concerned party obtained access to the refrigerator and discreetly removed a bit of what it contained. It seems their suspicions were justified based on what they found."

Yuki felt a bit of shock, as if she was going to be told the man she knew and trusted was involved in something nefarious; the restaurant became a vacuum, devoid of all sound save the voice of Dantanian.

"It turned out to be a blood sample unlike any found here on earth. In fact, we're not even sure if it's human."

"What do you mean?" she asked.

"It had fourty-nine chromosomes with three pairs on the seventh and a whole new twenty-fourth chromosome pair," he said, glancing at April's notes. "Now, I don't know much about genetics, but the experts I consulted advised that twenty-four chromosome pairs belonged to our ancestors as well as primates." Dantanian looked over at April who pointed to a word on a document she had on her planner. "Yes, the—"

"Hominids, ancient humans," Yuki interjected.

"Very good, Miss Yuki, that's correct," he said, impressed with her knowledge.

"Three copies of the seventh chromosome in the sample have never been reported in a living organism. Interestingly enough, the extra twenty-fourth chromosome is different than the Hominid variety."

Yuki's mind was jumping ahead, wondering what this was leading to.

"Even with the chromosomal anomaly," Dantanian continued, "when the sample was provided with nourishment none of the cells had died, almost three years later. In addition, the immune cells contained within the blood sample fought off every type of disease we could throw at it." He looked at a note written on April's planner.

"HIV, the plague, ebola, MRSA, VRE, salmonella, typhus, tuberculosis, Legionnaire's, and so on."

Yuki was beginning to wonder if this wasn't an elaborate joke that everyone in the lab and her family was in on.

"So why is it I bothered to call you when we have this amazing discovery of monumental significance?" Dantanian inquired.

The saving grace to this absurdity, she reminded herself, was that she might get paid for listening, though by this point she was beginning to doubt it.

"As it stands, several weeks ago, someone broke into our lab and stole the sample we had procured, along with our research data—basically everything pertaining to this. Believe me when I say that we have tight security at the lab I am funding, and yet somehow, someone managed to get in there."

"So, then, you want me to find out where Dr. Lystad obtained it, or if he has more of it? Is that what you're asking me? Why not just go directly to him yourself?"

He furrowed his brow as if to say 'Do you think I'm that stupid?'

"Miss Yuki," he said slowly, closing his eyes then opening them to look directly in hers, "At first we did try to contact him with an offer, and he outright refused; in fact, he denied ever having placed any such sample in the cooler at Primase. Unfortunately, the security footage in our lab had some strange disturbance, so we couldn't identify who might have stolen the sample from us. The management at Primase assures me that no such sample currently remains, and there are no other researchers who would have used that particular cooler other than Dr. Lystad."

"So, you only had a small amount from the beginning? Why didn't you at least replicate the code and send it elsewhere?" she asked.

"The code," April interjected, "was unlike anything our researchers had ever seen. It was very difficult to replicate with accuracy, and the sample was getting smaller and smaller with each failure."

"There is no doubt Dr. Lystad knows about the blood, its origins and how significant it is, I'm sure of it," Dantanian said. "All I'm asking of you, Miss Yuki, is that you watch him closely and see if he's conducting any strange experiments or doing anything else out of the ordinary. Certainly, a sample or a source would be an ideal outcome; we can also use any data that he may have."

She felt heat rising in her face at the thought of spying on Dorian. No doubt, Dantanian had reason for divulging so much information to her about the nature of this blood; you don't become a multi-billionaire by making a habit of tipping your hand to your opponent. Noticing the hostile look she gave him, he approached from a different angle.

"I think we can both profit from this arrangement." A cunning look crept up on his face; the way a cutthroat would appear as he patted you on the back with one hand and readied the dagger in the other.

"I know for a fact that there are negotiations for the takeover of Sukekuni Corporation. Of course, such a maneuver would have to be approved by the board; however, I am aware that your father had to sell quite a few of his shares in the past, so that he now finds himself in the unfortunate position of having significantly less than a majority stake."

This was a soft spot for Yuki. Her father was still CEO and ran the company, but the board of directors were becoming impatient with him. Her family was the single largest shareholder; however, they did not have controlling majority, making them subject to the whims of the other board members.

"I may be able to save his company and give back majority control to your father. Wouldn't that be nice?" he asked, an offer that sounded too good to be true. Shake the family tree and collect the low hanging fruit; a strategy that seemed simple enough, except he wasn't expecting the fruit to be a nut, and a terribly hard one to crack at that.

Yuki got up and bowed her head towards the two in a polite manner.

"I apologize that I will be unable to assist you in achieving your goal. I am sorry to have wasted your time. I would like to leave now," she said, trying hard not to make eye contact.

He sighed aloud and gave her a cold stare of disgust.

"How disappointing. Very well, we're through here for now. I'm certain your father may have something to say about this. Give him my regards."

At that, Yuki bowed again and turned towards the exit. Dantanian's bodyguards looked at him like a pair of Doberman pincers, as if to ask 'do you want us to tear her to pieces?' He waved his hand and shook his head, declining their unspoken offer.

"Was it wise to divulge so much to her, Mr. Dantanian?" April asked in a tone of disapproval.

"Who is she going to tell?" he asked in a slightly raised voice. "If she talks to anyone in her profession, they'll most likely dismiss her as a fool or a liar. We have to be careful to a certain extent, yes, but I know Lystad has someone helping him. I'm not certain who they are or if they are working together; however, I would rather try this approach after the failure Evans had. Wouldn't want to disappoint the master like he did, eh?"

"Poor Evans. The fool," April replied.

THE DRIVER WAS WAITING OUTSIDE IN A secured lot across the street and saw Yuki come out of the building. He honked and waved at her, then pulled up alongside the curb where she stood and got out to open the door.

"Done already? That was a fast dinner. Where would you like to go, miss?" he asked.

"Um, back to the airport, please." She was still hot under the collar and needed to cool off a bit.

"I'll take the scenic route for you unless you are in a hurry; no sense letting a visit to New York go to waste," he said with a smile.

At this point Yuki's thoughts were swirling through her head. She didn't know what to make of all this; the veiled threat of a possible takeover of the family business and the strange blood sample Dorian might or might not have had. She calculated that Dantanian was most likely not given to flights of fantasy, and must therefore be some truth to his grandiose claims about the nature of the sample. It remained to be seen as to whether Dorian was playing a part in whatever was going on. If he was, why would he hide such a thing, something that could save so many lives? Who stole the blood from Dantanian, and what information was Dantanian hiding? The other question plaguing her was how was she going to explain this to her father? Despite her skepticism, she felt a bit hurt for not being trustworthy enough for Dorian to share this with her.

Cracking the window in the back of the limousine, she let the icy air hit her face to drown out the numbness in her head. The driver made it to the airport a bit earlier than she had hoped. She used the extra time to research some of the information about Dantanian's story.

WHEN THE PLANE TOUCHED DOWN IN Michigan, there was a sense of relief to be back. The last vestiges of daylight slipped away to night as the shuttle bus took her to the short-term parking lot where her car was parked.

It was about the mid-way point in her trek back to her apartment when she observed that a white van had been following her for some time. It was too dark to make out who was in the vehicle. Thinking that it wouldn't be a good idea to lead a potential axe murderer to where she lived, she decided to get off the highway at an earlier exit. After taking some turns down different streets, the coincidences proved beyond a shadow of a doubt that she was indeed being followed. Now, with her heart beating hard in her chest, she reached for her cell phone and tried to call Dorian for help. She found herself driving in unfamiliar territory and lost her way. Since her cell phone was also her GPS, she wasn't able to talk to him and get directions at the same time without stopping to figure out how to do it.

A light on her instrument panel came on indicating critically low fuel. The process of simultaneously dialing Dorian, checking her rear-view mirror, and looking for a gas station distracted her enough that she failed to notice the red traffic light as she passed through it.

This got the attention of the Ypsilanti Police, who were parked at a convenience store on a street corner, patiently waiting like a spider for its prey. The driver of the white van, seeing that she was about to get stopped, wisely made a right turn down another street.

The police quickly pulled right behind Yuki's vehicle, flashing their lights and letting her know she had to pull over. Driving to a nearby gas station, she parked off to the side, frantically unbuckled her seatbelt and opened the door while the officer was looking up her license plate. The slippery ground did not prevent her from running towards the officer, waving her hands in desperation.

"Get back in your car!" the officer shouted through his loudspeaker.

Tears welled up in her eyes as she did as she was ordered. She was starving and exhausted; her bladder was the size of a basketball, and she was now starting to hyperventilate. A few minutes later, another police car showed up to back up the first. A large, burly female officer got out. Both police officers headed up to Yuki's vehicle, flashlights blazing and their hands on their firearms.

"Can it get any worse than this?" she thought.

"Do you know why you were stopped?" the police officer asked. Famous words to which there are no correct answers.

Yuki just looked scared and shook her head. "I need your driver's license, registration and proof of insurance," the male officer ordered.

"Please, can you help me? I was being followed by someone in a van. A white van!" she begged, her voice straining under the stress. Tears were streaking down her face when she heard her cell phone go off. It was Dorian. She tried to take the call, but the female officer demanded she put the phone down.

The corporate police, many who lacked empathy of any kind, often harassed, instigated and escalated encounters with the people they stopped, especially the homeless, in an effort to either arrest them or take their anger and frustrations out on them. Savage beatings and outright murder were not uncommon on any given day across the country, even against people calling for help. Crime had increased so much that everyone was looked at with suspicion and disgust. Many people fought back with demonstrations, and retaliations, which often led to rioting. Even with public outcry, the system protected its own interests.

After Yuki had presented all the necessary documents, and the police officers had finished searching her and her vehicle for contraband, it seemed like an eternity for judgment to be handed down. She received a ticket for running the light, and they took a statement regarding the van that followed her.

The driver's door window had been down for so long her teeth were chattering. Right now, all she wanted to do was use the bathroom at the gas station, which unfortunately, had closed while she was being interrogated by the police. Not to mention she was also shaking from hunger since she hadn't touched the food at the luncheon/dinner meeting.

Her cell phone rang again. She quickly checked; it was Dorian calling her back again. "*Yattah!*" she shouted in a crazed voice, which is the Japanese way of saying 'I did it!'

"Yuki, is everything all right? You sounded upset on the phone and then you hung up on me," he said.

"Please come get me, help me!" she sobbed.

"Okay, no problem, where are you?" he asked in a calm, soothing tone.

"At a gas station called Marathon on Michigan Avenue. There is no other sign."

"That's a pretty long road, can you narrow it down a bit for me?" he asked, trying not to upset her.

"One second." A group of people on the corner were holding signs and warming themselves over an oil drum that had a fire going. She darted over to get an answer.

"Um, excuse me! Can you tell me what street this is?"

They pointed out where she was and she thanked them with some money then gave the information to Dorian.

"Please hurry, please!" she cried, sounding desperate.

"I will, but you'd better wait in your car and lock the door. It's not safe to be out on the streets."

There were plenty of people milling about at this hour, trying to stay warm from the freezing cold, as the shelters for the homeless were filled beyond capacity. People huddled together on street corners, pacing back and forth, while holding signs that asked any passerby for assistance, whatever they could spare. As if their misery wasn't bad enough, they still had to contend with the thugs in the gangs and the thugs in blue.

AFTER TWENTY MINUTES HAD PAST, SHE HEARD Dorian's familiar vintage Camaro rumbling down the road. He pulled alongside her car and got out to inspect it, thinking that she had been in an accident or something. Yuki rushed to his side, wrapped both arms around him and began crying, speaking in small bits of English and mostly Japanese between sobs.

He patted her on the head as she rested it on his chest. She instantly felt better, in an almost supernatural way.

"I have to use the restroom very much." she said, looking up at him the way a child does when they have already had a small accident in their pants.

"There's a 24-hour pharmacy up the road. We'll stop there."

As they made their way, Yuki started telling Dorian about her day, why she had to leave early, and everything that had happened, at lightning speed.

"Okay, slow down for a minute. We'll go in together, you take care of your business and we'll continue this conversation when you get out," he said, as he pulled into the parking lot.

Yuki was trembling from what appeared to be hunger, so he grabbed her a Snickers bar and some juice while she finished using the restroom.

When she came back out Dorian was waiting for her at the front with bag in hand. "Let's get you something to eat. You look famished," he said, handing her the candy bar and the drink. Yuki loved chocolate so this was a gift from heaven.

He opened the car door for her, and she got inside. The seat made a creaking sound from the aged springs. The heater in the car gave out stale, lukewarm air that added to the unique scent of old car mixed with chocolate, cheap bathroom soap from the pharmacy, and oranges.

Her energy began to return with each passing moment. Looking over at him, she became mesmerized by his luminescent white hair and his unusual looking eyes. A small slit of eerie glowing light seemed to occasionally show itself around the bottom of his grey iris. She dismissed the phenomenon as a trick of the light and her fatigue.

"It's kind of late so there won't be much that's open right now. Are you okay with Mickey D's?"

She was still a bit hungry after the candy bar and could eat just about anything. "*Hai,*" she replied; then remembering to speak in English, "yes".

The road still had compacted snow from what had fallen earlier that day, and snow flurries were just starting up again. The consequences could result in her car being snowed in, or towed if she left it at the gas station. They got the fast food and she ate as he drove back to retrieve her car. She followed him to another gas station that was still open at that hour, filled up, and the two made their way to her home.

It was now after midnight, and even though he had an early morning lecture, he offered to stay and keep an eye on her. Not wanting to be a burden, she reassured him that everything was fine and that they would discuss the day's events in detail later on.

# *Three*

DORIAN LEFT YUKI'S APARTMENT FEELING THE weight of the world on his shoulders. Yuki had spoken only briefly about what had been discussed in her meeting, but he knew it had involved him and his research at Primase. Various scenarios were running through his head concerning the questions she would undoubtedly have. The best course of action, he decided, would be to test the waters, see what she knew, and play his responses off of that. At least that way he wouldn't have to divulge anything unnecessarily.

The following morning, Dorian got dressed and headed off to the University. He asked Engel to set up the power point presentation for the section he was lecturing on for an immunology class at the medical school. His concentration was not fully given to the lecture as his thoughts were drawn to the impending meeting with Yuki; undoubtedly, she was already in the lab.

"That went well," Engel said in a joking and sarcastic tone after the lecture.

"I've got a lot on my mind today. Engel, do me a favor and take my 2:30 for me. It's pretty straightforward; all the material is on the slides. You already know this like the back of your hand," he said, looking tired.

"No problem, Chief." Engel was clearly happy to have an opportunity to get in his good graces. "Everything all right, Dr. Lystad? You seem a bit distracted."

"I'm fine; I just have a full plate today. I appreciate you helping me out. I'll see you later on."

He took the shuttle bus back to the medical science building to finish his earlier conversation with Yuki. When he walked into the lab the familiar sounds of the equipment running filled the air, along with Kasia's Polish music. He usually enjoyed the ambience; it would make him feel like he was somewhere else when he was having a stressful day. It wasn't working today, however.

"Yuki?" he quietly called while peering around the corner. Kasia was sitting at her desk, staring intently at her computer screen.

"She got a package and went into the conference room down the hall; didn't say much," Kasia said, without looking away.

Dorian felt troubled by this. "What package? Is she all right?"

"Relax," she replied, shifting her gaze to Yuki's desk, where the remnants of a bubble packed envelope were sitting.

"She's fine; it was a memory chip with a movie on it. 'Something Street'."

Dorian went over to Yuki's desk. The package had been sent from T.D. International corp.

"Oh, before you go, don't forget you have office hours at four," Kasia reminded him. He pondered on whom the package might be from and headed to the conference room. Yuki was sitting alone with her laptop, watching an old movie titled "Wall Street".

"What's going on?" he asked.

"I don't know. This was sent to the lab. For some reason it was addressed to me. I didn't order any movie. There wasn't an invoice, a note or anything in the package," she replied, with a slight worry in her tone. "I just started playing it. What does this mean?"

"Why don't we start from the beginning of yesterday," Dorian said, closing the conference room door behind him.

"Tell me what happened."

Yuki paused, gathering her thoughts and deciding what she wanted to say.

"I was contacted by my father, who told to me to go to New York and meet with an investor who had some questions for me about your research. I did not give it much thought, as there is nothing top secret about what we do and little opportunity for profit, so I agreed to hear them out since they were offering payment just to listen."

Dorian's face was expressionless; Yuki worried he might be upset with her.

"When I arrived in New York, I met a man named Theodore Dantanian and his assistant, April."

"Theodore Dantanian", Dorian thought. "Where have I heard that name before?" Yuki started to speak again and Dorian interrupted her with his epiphany.

"Oh, right, the corporate tycoon investor; wait, *that* Theodore Dantanian?" he asked with a shocked expression.

"Yes, at least that's who he claimed to be. I do not think he was lying about his identity. At least, I know my father checked him out. He asked me if I knew about your research, and when I told him what we are working on, he said that was not what he was referring to. Apparently, he thinks you are conducting some kind of secret experiment. Crazy, right?" she asked, half-joking and half-serious.

"Damn," he thought. He was in trouble; someone had found out and this wasn't good. The need to trust someone was always there; for too long he had been carrying this burden. On the other hand, getting Yuki involved in something that could be dangerous, especially with a big player like Dantanian on the trail, was not what he had in mind. The prospect of an ugly future was beginning to take shape.

"What else did he say?" he asked, avoiding her question entirely.

She looked at him as if she didn't believe what she was about to say. "He told me about a blood sample that was stolen from you at Primase and said that it had unusual properties; impervious to every kind of pathogen, cells that had an unusual chromosome arrangement, immortal, fire resistant. You get the picture, crazy talk. He told me that he had already contacted you for a deal, but you turned him down, so, he offered me a lot of money to spy on you and give him whatever data you had or a sample of this super blood."

Dorian sensed she was skeptical so he played into it.

"Yuki, yes, I was contacted by an individual from a company called Hermoni, but they wanted me to head their research department at one of their subsidiary biotech firms, investigating senescence or something like that. I told them I wasn't interested. I did have quite a few mutated blood samples at Primase that I was using for my cancer research, but if I had something on that level of significance I would be researching it myself," he replied, evading the truth without directly lying to her.

Yuki smiled and laughed. "For a while there I was thinking there was this great conspiracy going on, what with the offer from Dantanian, the strange van following me, and then this package. It is funny how the mind plays tricks on you," she said in a relieved voice.

"So, what did you tell him?" he asked.

"You really need to ask? I'm hurt," she replied with a pouty face.

"Okay, okay," he said, smiling with his hands up. "You going to watch the rest of that, or are we going to get some work done?"

The movie was playing with the volume muted.

"I didn't know what it was. I am done here." She folded her laptop and followed Dorian out of the conference room.

As she made her way back, some doubts still plagued her. She wondered to herself why Dorian feigned ignorance about Dantanian since she had been told by Dantanian himself that he had contacted Dorian already.

Not falling for his ruse, she decided to quietly, indiscriminately, and carefully observe Dorian for herself; not to report back to Dantanian, but rather to ease the lingering questions that remained.

BACK AT THE LAB, SEVERAL UNDERGRADUATE students were working under the direction of Engel, who was sitting on a stool looking over some papers. Yuki went to her desk to clean up and took the movie out of her computer, returning it to its case.

Dorian shut himself in his office on the opposite side of the hallway and heaved a sigh of relief. Reaching into his bottom desk drawer, he took out a bottle of one hundred proof whiskey and filled a small Styrofoam coffee cup (that had a bit of old coffee in it) halfway with the rotgut. His body processed alcohol so quickly that he was unable to get drunk, but the really cheap stuff at least made him feel warm inside as it went down. Putting his hands over his face, he smooshed his cheeks in a circular motion as if to remind himself he still had his job to do. Four o'clock was approaching and he had office hours for one hour, data to go over, payroll for the three TA's and journals to read. Grabbing his phone, he paged Engel to bring the invoice calculations that Engel was boasting about earlier to Dorian's office.

"I'll be there in a minute," Engel shouted through the hallway.

"Does anyone want this? I'm not sure how to return it." Yuki asked, holding up the movie that had been mistakenly sent to her.

"You're giving away of one of the greatest movies of all time!" Engel announced with astonishment and mock interest, prompting Kasia to roll her eyes. "You sure you don't want this? Gordon Gekko, the Darth Vader of investing, master market manipulator slash destroyer of companies and all around greedy bastard?" he declared, followed by him quoting lines from the movie. "Thanks for spoiling it for me, loser! I was going to take it," Kasia snapped, even though she had no actual desire to have the movie; her primary objective was simply irritating him. "How does a drunk, surfer rock, poser, wannabe researcher know so much about this stuff anyway? Isn't this about the establishment and all that?"

"Let's just say I used to day trade for a bit, so I know a thing or two about it," he replied, not convincing the others within earshot.

Yuki froze for a second. A chill went down her spine and her heart began pounding in her chest.

"Engel, tell me, what happens in this movie?" she asked in a worried voice.

"I'd be delighted to tell you all about it. Pull up a chair," he said, the others in the room chuckling amongst themselves. "Well, it starts with—"

"Just the short version, the main plot points," Yuki interrupted.

Engel was taken aback. "Okay, okay, sheesh, what's the hurry? Basically, this billionaire investor would use dirty tricks to make money, like having insider information to make stock trades, or he would buy up companies and then strip the assets and raid the pension funds—pretty much obliterate the company to gut it for money. There was this younger associate he hire—"

He stopped in the middle of his sentence when Yuki got up from her chair and ran out of the building, trying to get reception so she could call her father. She let it ring until his voicemail came on, then left a frantic message. Immediately after, she attempted to reach her sister, but there was no answer from her either. Her heart still racing, she ran upstairs to get to her computer and went to the web site for the Tokyo stock exchange, entering the ticker symbol for her family's company. Sukekuni Corp. was up a considerable amount. She pored over the news headlines.

"Hermoni Corporation gains controlling stake in Sukekuni Company." Another read, "Hermoni positions itself as a global leader in healthcare."

She felt ashamed at the loss of her family legacy. Tears welled up and began trickling down her cheeks, and she regretted getting involved with the scoundrel who had done this. This wasn't an accident; TD International on the package she received was Theodore Dantanian's company, it had to be. It was a message being sent to her. Play ball or face the consequences.

Her sister sent a text message: "Mt. Fuji went off for the family today. Father is in the hospital, he had heart attack, mother is fine. Will call when I know more. Luv Aki."

Yuki started to come unglued. She went back outside and grabbed some snow on the ground and rubbed her face in it so she could feel something to take away the pain in her heart.

"What the hell is going on with Yuki? One minute she's asking who wants the movie, the next she's running around hysterically crying and whatnot. I don't understand women at all," Engel said in a dazed voice.

"And you never will," Kasia retorted with mock condescension.

Engel walked over to Dorian's office to give him the invoice numbers. He handed Dorian the paper, and whispered that Yuki was crying about something.

"Give me a moment, I apologize," Dorian said to the student who was in the office with him. He went out into the hallway where Engel was waiting.

"What's this about?" he asked, hoping it had nothing to do with the events of yesterday.

"Beats me," Engel replied. "One minute I was giving Yuki a synopsis of a movie, and the next minute she was running around like a chicken with its head cut off."

Dorian peeked his head into the lab. "Yuki?" he sheepishly called out.

"I think she's outside; her coat and purse are still here. She's probably trying to make a call. She was really upset about something," Kasia replied, while staring at her screen.

The other students in the lab were quiet, murmuring to each other about the commotion they had just witnessed. Dorian went back into his office.

"I apologize; we seem to be having a small crisis of some sort. I'm going to have to cut this short for today, but I'll have office hours again on Friday. Don't worry about your test grade. The final will be curved, so just make sure you go over what we talked about."

His student packed her books in her bag and gave him a dreamy smile. As soon as she had left he locked his office and went down the stairs to go outside, where he saw Yuki sitting on the steps of the building. Her hands were red, her face strewn with tears, and she was trembling amidst sobs.

"Yuki," Dorian said softly. "Let's get you inside." He gently put one hand under her elbow and the other around her waist, and the two of them walked into the building. They went into the conference room and she sat down; tears were running down her face. Dorian motioned he would be right back. A moment later, he returned with a cup of hot chocolate and a paper towel. After handing them over, he waited a few minutes until she was composed, rather than peppering her with questions.

"My family lost our company today and my father had a heart attack. I have to return to Japan," she said, amidst a renewed crying spell.

"I'm so sorry, Yuki. I hope your father is okay. Is there anything I can do for you?"

"Help me get to the airport. I need to book a flight." She slowly got up, dried her face and blew her nose. There were several student onlookers rubbernecking as she made her way into the lab.

"Yuki, can I help you with anything?" Kasia asked solemnly.

Knowing that she was bound to ask, Yuki decided it was best to just come out and tell her.

"My father had a heart attack. I will be going back to Japan for now." The news shocked everyone within earshot. Yuki conducted the bulk of the main research in the lab; her shoes would be difficult to fill.

BY SOME MIRACLE, YUKI MANAGED TO FIND A flight that was leaving close to three hours from her present time. It cost a small fortune, but no price was too high for her family.

Dorian got his coat and the two walked outside to the bus stop. He followed Yuki back to her apartment and waited outside while she packed. An empty feeling washed over him with the knowledge that she was possibly leaving for good, or at least for a long time, along with a sadness for the pain she was burdened with.

They didn't say much to each other on the way to the airport; he didn't want to add to her troubles.

"I will see you again, won't I?" he asked softly.

She put her head on his arm as he drove. "Of course you will." They continued their conversation in Japanese for the remainder of the journey. Over the past several years he had gone so far as pretending to learn her native language in order to make her feel special, despite the fact that he was already quite fluent.

Every now and then he would purposefully mispronounce some words, or use incorrect sentence structure, so she could correct him. It helped break up the monotony of lab work, and she respected him even more for it. In Yuki's eyes, he was learning Japanese for her sake, which explained in part why she was so loyal to him.

"I'll call you when I get there, and let you know that I arrived safely. I don't know what's going on for sure, but I think that Dantanian was behind the take-over of our family's company. He tried to pretend that he would help return control to my father, but he was obviously giving me a veiled threat. He must really be serious about you. You should be careful, who knows what he is capable of."

Dorian felt heat rise in his face and his hand gripped the steering wheel tightly. "Yuki, when we meet again, there is something important I need to talk to you about."

With that said they didn't speak much more. Dorian dropped her off at the terminal, he hugged her goodbye, and she smiled and waved as he drove off.

On the way back to the University he decided it was time to put his research into high gear and learn as much as possible while he could. His mother had warned long ago that if anyone discovered his secrets he would end up as a lab rat. She was the only one alive who knew about him, aside from his biological parents, whom he had never known. That was the reason he had become a genetic researcher in the first place; if he was to go under a microscope, it would be his eyes looking through it.

The radio was tuned to a news station as he was driving back. With his schedule, it was difficult for him to find out what was going on in the world, so he turned it up to listen. A talk radio show was discussing the record high unemployment and how the global economy was in the beginning of the second great depression. One of the hosts mentioned that as a result of cities going bankrupt, police forces were diminished, leading to uncontrolled crime. That was followed by discussion of the riots taking place in multiple cities and states around the country, as well as the international trouble with China and the chaos in Europe. In addition, there had been a tremendous increase in natural disasters that year, causing increased financial strain. The consensus was that the world seemed to be coming apart at the seams.

"More depressing news," Dorian thought. This was all that seemed to be on the radio, television, and internet anymore. Looking out the window while he waited at a red light, one could see the desperation people were facing; even in these frigid temperatures there were two to three people at many intersections, their signs in hand, each with their own heart-wrenching story asking for assistance. He felt his spirit ache for them and wondered where the world was headed.

All this brought him back to the reality of the situation: Funding for his research was all but spent. Up to this point he had been able to provide for the majority of it from the sale of several patents, in addition to the money he had received from winning a Nobel Prize in Medicine. But as a result of the out of control spending and government debt, research money was scarce. With the pressure he was facing from Dantanian, he would have to put his secret research more in the open in order to find the answers he was looking for.

What made him different? Why was he not getting any older? Why had he never been sick a day in his life? Why was he able to run five times faster than the average male his size, and why was he so much stronger?

"Am I some kind of alien?" he occasionally thought. At a young age he would read comic books in his bedroom and try to see if he had super powers like his heroes did. Would he have X-ray vision like Superman? Or could he control the weather like Thor? Or use the force like Luke? To his dismay, he was unable to perform any of those feats. He could run very fast, but not *super* fast; he was very strong, but not quite *super* strong; and he had no other observable abilities -aside from not getting sick, but who wants that power when you're a child? His mother would often remind him to take it easy when he played sports with other children, so as not to draw attention to himself, or hurt anyone.

As he got older he became interested in genetics to find a logical, scientific explanation for his gifts. His aging didn't really appear as being unusual until he reached about forty-five years and it seemed suspicious that he still looked twenty-five or so.

Up till now, he had been able to discover everything that Dantanian had and then some. The blood sample that he had carelessly left in the cooler at Primase was his own, and undoubtedly Dantanian would be back to find the source. Unfortunately, Dorian wasn't sure what he was looking for. He knew that the makeup of his blood was of a similar make up to that of the early humans, with some exceptions. Something else was driving him, though; compelling him to look further. He was close to a discovery. It was a feeling he had, a guiding force; one which would seemingly take him far beyond his understanding to discern a greater mystery.

# *Four*

AFTER TAKING YUKI TO THE AIRPORT, DORIAN decided to get some Chinese carry out, then returned to the house he owned in Ann Arbor. It was a large, old, two-story, historic home that had seen many previous owners over the years, and that had been through several renovations and restorations to bring it back to its former glory. It had a nice, carved stone fireplace that he would occasionally park himself in front of on nights such as this. The crisp air outside, along with the smell of burning logs from the homes in the neighborhood, made him feel alive, bringing back memories of his adolescent years in Colorado. Curling up on the couch in front of the fireplace, he ate while sorting through his mail.

He turned on the television for all of two minutes before it depressed him enough to shut it off. "Another tsunami kills thousands; what in the world is happening to this planet?" he said.

That night he dreamt of being trapped in his house, only it was filled with garbage and junk piled from floor to ceiling. It wasn't the first time he'd had this strange dream, and he wondered why it kept repeating.

The following day began with a bit of shopping and laundry before going to the lab a bit later than usual.

A gathering of about four hundred people were braving the colds outside the medical science building.at the university. They were holding up protest signs against genetic manipulation, suggesting things were about to go bad for Dorian and for anyone else involved with the lab. One protestor held a megaphone up while shouting in unison with the crowd, "Leave our DNA alone!" Dorian had been so preoccupied with his work that he hadn't noticed the growing public resentment towards people who worked in the industry.

Genetic engineering had become fashionable, as those with the means were able to have designer children. One could choose the sex of their child, the height, eye color, hair, even their dexterity. This practice was extremely controversial at first; so much so that it was not in the United States until after it had been used elsewhere.

It had originally gained popularity in China, where the population was so out of control to begin with. Well-to-do parents wanted their progeny to be exactly what they wished for at the start; no need to rely on chance. From there the technology moved to India, where for decades many female babies had been killed in the womb, or in secret after birth by their parents, or given up altogether because of the desire for a male child. Parents in the west took notice and began going overseas for custom in vitro fertilization and paying big money for it. Governments, being the starving elephants they were, decided to tax and regulate rather than let business leave their country. Dorian's research had nothing to do with enhancing children; quite the contrary, he was trying to save lives from a terrible disease. It didn't matter, however. In these desperate times, people had become more zealous and polarized. Many considered what was going on in the world, with the economy, crime, depravity of humans, and natural disasters, to be a sign of the end times, and they felt that evils such as genetic engineering were one of the spokes in the wheel. Perhaps they had a point; however, Dorian thought it best to avoid confrontation, so he found his way into the lab through the adjoining building that shared access from the lower levels.

By the time he managed to get to the third floor, protestors were in the lobby, pushing their way onto the staircase as the security personnel held them back. He made a bee line straight for his office, when he saw that his office door was ajar. Folders were strewn across his desk and on the floor, all the desk drawers were open, and papers were scattered everywhere. "Who are you to play God?" was sprayed across the wall-mounted cork board that held recently published research articles. His cell phone rang at that moment. It was Kasia.

"I don't know if you're going in the lab today, but if you're planning to you might want to find something else to do," she said in her happy-go-lucky tone.

"I'm here right now. Someone's ransacked my office. Are you in the lab?" he asked, fumbling for his key to the lab door.

"I was just outside. Now I'm in the hallway to the adjacent building, making my way through the back," she replied. The echo of her footsteps reverberated through the phone.

Dorian inserted his key and turned it to unlock the door, but it was already unlocked. At first glance, nothing appeared to be broken, but he wasn't taking any chances. After looking around in the dim daylight, he had gone back to turn on the lights when Kasia opened the door, almost smacking him in the face.

"Easy," he said, stopping the door with his foot before any damage was done.

"Sorry, I didn't know you were there. What the heck is going on? No one told me we were this popular," she said, seeming a bit excited by all the commotion.

"Get that, will you?" he asked, nodding towards the bank of light switches. "I'm not entirely sure this is about us; there's six other researchers in this building alone, and it could be any one of us they're protesting. Someone managed to get into my office. I found graffiti sprayed on one of the walls," he said, stepping over piles of paper and trash.

As he was talking, Kasia went over to her desk and began examining it to see what if anything, had been removed, then booted up her computer. Dorian was checking the cabinets and the sequencing machine when he noticed the cooler door was ajar.

"Aw, you've got to be...Damn it, they left the door wide open. Well, there goes weeks of work down the drain. Great! Most of the tube racks are empty. I'm beginning to think it wasn't these protestors; some amateur thieves, maybe students, probably hired by Dantanian. This is ridiculous," he fumed.

"Who is Dantanian? Sounds like some kind of gangster name. What have you gotten yourself into? Is this because of a gambling debt? Did you give someone's child two left feet or something at your last job?" Kasia asked with excitement.

"He's some businessman, and no, I didn't give someone's kid a duck bill or anything of the sort," he huffed.

"At this point, I don't give a rat's ass who did it, I'm just happy that my data is intact," she said, as if she was the only one that mattered.

He breathed a small sigh of relief; first, for the fact that the data was still there, and second, for the fact that Kasia's apathetic nature did not encourage lingering questions.

After spending some time cleaning things up, they went about their work. Since he was now aware of his carelessness at Primase, he decided from here out to only work with a fresh sample, and to destroy it after each successful run. This was the seventieth trial for sequencing. He labeled the test tube Esme70, after his birth mother's name, the only thing he knew about her.

Sequencing his entire genome was very difficult to process accurately, which is why he had to complete it in bits and pieces. If all went well, this could be the final run for him. The genome would be complete and he could analyze the data in the hopes of finding out more about himself.

He placed part of the sample in the sequencing machine and began the final trial run. While that was running, he went back to his office and sorted through the paper strewn everywhere until he heard the familiar sound of the machine indicating his sample was completed. It was a success.

Gathering all of the data from his previous runs and this current one, he gave it over to Kasia for her to compile into one common data set.

"This is going to take at least a few days to finish, and I still have four other experiments to compile and sort," she whined.

"Make this a priority if you can, and if you observe anything unusual, please keep it discreet," he said, carefully choosing his words.

She gave him a sly smile. He looked at her with his eyebrows raised, as if to say "No, I'm hiding anything on some illegitimate child of mine!"

He left for the day and returned home, carefully looking around to see if someone had broken in and was waiting for him. Nothing was out of the ordinary, so he went to bed, taking extra precaution by keeping a baseball bat at his bedside. That night it was the same repeating dream again with a twist; now he was stuck in a landfill with trash everywhere around him.

MONDAY MORNING ROLLED AROUND AND HE eagerly went to the lab to check on the progress of the data.

"Well, you're full of surprises, aren't you?" Kasia chirped as she saw him coming down the hallway towards his office.

He quickly unlocked his office door and motioned for her to step in. She looked like the cat that just ate the mouse.

"What do you mean?" he asked nervously.

"Did you find an alien or something? Is that what all this cloak and dagger is all about?" she asked, trying hard not to laugh.

"What are you talking about?" he asked in the way he knew best, feigning ignorance.

"Keep your secrets then, fine by me. Here's the data you asked for." She handed him a small fob and left him alone. Plugging the fob into his laptop, he opened up the software that he and Kasia (well, mostly Kasia) had designed, for analysis of genomes.

The program began comparing his blood to that of an ordinary human to see what differences there were. It would most likely take another day to complete. Deciding not to take any chances, he took the portable computer to his two o'clock lecture that afternoon.

After his lecture, he called Yuki to see if everything was all right with her father. She didn't pick up, so he left her a text message wishing them well.

Later that day, he received a call from an old friend who asked to meet him at The Blind Pig for drinks at seven. He reluctantly agreed. Since the program crunching his data would take the rest of the night, he could afford to unwind a bit.

As the day's work came to a close, he put his laptop into a closet to continue running, locked up the lab and headed over to First Street to join his friend. It was necessary to move quickly to get there; the sun was setting and the streets were not safe anymore at night, even in a college town. He could always get a ride back afterwards, provided his friend didn't have too much to drink.

AS DORIAN CLIMBED THE NARROW, SNOW-COVERED steps of the club, the familiar scent of beer and muffled music greeted him at the door. The sound of the band rushed to him like a tidal wave as soon as he walked in. He looked around and saw his friend sitting at the bar, nursing a whiskey of some sort.

"How you been Roy?" Dorian asked, patting him on the shoulder.

"Hey, Dorian, good to see ya," he replied, extending his hand. Roy looked like a fish out of water. Dressed in an exquisitely tailored navy blue pinstripe suit, with fine leather shoes and expensive wristwatch to match, it was clear he represented someone with money in a predominately blue-collar club. Sitting next to him was another fish out of water in a grey colored Armani suit; twenty-something, give or take, ostentatiously scratching his ear to show off his high-dollar watch. He held a lit cigar in one hand and a mojito in the other. These two contrasted with Dorian, who was dressed in a brown tweed sports jacket, blue jeans, olive colored t-shirt and casual loafers.

"Dorian, this is one of the junior attorneys at our firm, Trevor Maslin. David, this is Dorian Lystad." Trevor was partially looking at the band and partially at Dorian. He had a slight grin, the kind you could easily imagine seeing on a billboard with the word "Injured?" below it.

"How's it going?" he asked, offering a limp-wristed handshake. Dorian grasped his hand firmly.

"Roy's been telling me about your earlier years and the odd jobs you two had," Trevor said. "It's hard to believe you both went to high school together, you look about the same age as me," he said, a hint of jealousy in his tone.

"I guess it's in the genes," Dorian replied coolly, a line he had used hundreds of times in the past. He took up a chair to the left of Roy, ignoring Trevor, who seemed to be more interested in looking around to see who was looking at him.

"How long are you in town?" Dorian asked Roy.

"I'm guessing we'll get a settlement by Wednesday, so most likely a few more days. You enjoying Ann Arbor? Met any nice college hotties here?" Roy asked with a smile, elbowing Dorian gently.

"It's not too bad, just a lot of headaches. My lab was broken into a few days ago, and my primary research assistant just went back home, possibly for good. I've had a crazy mob protesting in front of our building the other day, student issues, et cetera, you get the point. It's a different kind of pressure cooker from Primase, but I'm still simmering in a pot none the less. What about you? I figured that since you made partner, you'd take it easy and swim in the pools of cash you squeezed from big pharma."

Roy set down his drink and shot an angry look over to Dorian.

"Easy there, pal, I'm not on trial here," he said pointing a finger with the same hand that was holding his drink.

Roy's profession and what he represented was somewhat of a sore spot for Dorian. Even though Dorian wasn't part of any drug company, he still felt some association with the researchers there. From his perspective, he understood what it took to get a treatment to market; a lot of money and luck. Unfortunately, some of his fellow researchers were caught using unethical tactics, such as fudging data to get medications out of the pipeline, only to discover later that those medications had major safety issues. All to keep the gravy train rolling. Those bad apples made it difficult for everyone else.

In these times, you couldn't win any sympathy for drug researchers; people were unemployed and viewed anyone who achieved success with distrust, or suspecting that they had dodged the rules, cheated, or used some other illegal activity outside of hard work and sacrifice. Additionally, many of the mass public shootings were attributed to the effects that certain anti-depressants or psychotropic medications had on fragile minds; effects that had been either willfully ignored or purposefully hidden in the name of profits.

It was no wonder that people were resentful of the whole medical establishment; like many other institutions, it had failed to keep the public trust. Thus, a large part of society regarded them as a source for easy money. It didn't matter if you truthfully experienced a side effect of a drug, just find a doctor who would go along with the scheme and sue for millions.

Now, having sent many corporations into bankruptcy, the vampires were running out of victims to bleed. Dorian figured Roy wasn't directly implicit in scamming the pharmaceutical companies, but he also knew that Roy was able to ask rational questions and draw reasonable conclusions about the veracity of his client's claims.

"Sorry, man. I've been under a lot of stress lately," Dorian said in a muted tone.

"No problem," Roy replied, still miffed at Dorian's innuendo.

"How's your mom doing?" Dorian asked.

"Well, she's down to about eighty-five pounds now, cancer eating her alive," he responded, as if he was discussing his golf handicap, a matter of minor significance.

"How you've changed Roy," Dorian thought. His friend used to be one of the nicest, most caring, give-the-shirt-off-your-back kind of people whom Dorian admired growing up. When the union at the bottling plant where Roy's father worked went on strike, the company closed down in Colorado and moved the jobs to Florida. His family fell on hard times and his father had a stroke not long after that. Roy felt cheated by the world and blamed the company for their misfortune. That's why he had decided to become a lawyer; so that he could make companies like the one his dad worked for pay for their misdeeds. Dorian had thought Roy would be a force for good and fight against those who would take advantage of the little guy. Money, however, tends to corrupt those even with the best of intentions. Roy, who used to loathe executives at the top, had ironically become one himself.

"I'm sorry to hear that, tell her that I'll be praying for her." Dorian replied in a somber tone.

"You're not drinking?" Roy asked.

"Not tonight, thanks," Dorian replied, doing a double take at the stage. "I don't believe it, Engel, you're pretty good."

Roy looked puzzled, "You know him?"

Engel was playing a guitar solo with the band on stage. The bass drum read "Flat Pop", the name of their techno-rock band.

"He's one of my grad students; a bit laissez-faire in the head, but not without potential. I forgot that he toured Europe in a band a while back."

They continued with some idle chit chat about Colorado, the people they knew growing up and times that made them both laugh. Dorian started to see shades of his old friend amidst the fog surrounding his spirit. Saying their goodbyes, Dorian left, embraced by the bitter cold night.

IT WAS LATE, AND AS DORIAN MADE HIS WAY TO one of the few operating bus stops, he noticed a pack of five adolescents following him. He endeavored to stay on lighted streets to avoid giving them an opportunity to attack, feeling that the best course of action would be to avoid any confrontation if he could. The group mustered enough courage to run up from behind, forming a half circle around him. One of the jackals produced a small handgun. Another one had a knife.

"Let's have it. Give me the money or you're dead," the one with skulls tattooed on his forehead said, with his hand out.

Dorian edged his way to the wall of the building next to him so that no one would be able to strike from behind. The thug holding the knife made a stab at Dorian's abdomen. Dorian grabbed his wrist, snapped it, and pulled back, causing a compound fracture. The attacker with the gun had already started to pull the trigger when Dorian moved faster than the gunman could see; in fact, Dorian himself could scarcely believe how fast he moved. He kicked the gunman on the side of his leg so hard it shattered the bone, causing the man's leg to fold like a card table. Before the gunman could fall, Dorian grabbed a hold of the gun while twisting the man's wrist, crushing the bones together.

The gunman howled in pain as blood spewed from the fractures. The attacker with the skull tattoo took a swing at Dorian, who easily sidestepped it and returned a blow to his diaphragm that caused him to collapse, gasping for air. The two remaining thugs decided not to press their luck and took off, knowing the others were sure to be arrested.

Everything had happened in a blink of an eye. Dorian was feeling very strange at this point. He could *feel* the heartbeats and movements of each of the three men on the ground, a sensation that made him feel more awake and alive than he ever had before; as if a switch had been thrown and every sense was heightened tremendously.

When Dorian was a boy he was attacked by some bullies. At that time, however, he simply ran away—faster than anyone could catch him. At this moment he decided he was no longer going to run, but instead, stand his ground and fight.

A passing police cruiser shone its light on his face and flashed the lights on top just as he was reaching into his pocket to call them. Dorian stood where he was as several more police units were called to the scene, as well as an ambulance. The police cuffed him on the ground, then started peppering him with questions.

"I need to speak with my attorney before I answer any questions," he told them. He reluctantly called Roy and told him what had happened and asked him to meet where he was.

"Don't say anything to anyone," Roy commanded. "Wait until I get there."

Dorian was concerned because he knew the Ann Arbor Police were not known for their patience. They had no problems throwing out both the baby and the bath water. Roy showed up a few minutes later with Trevor; apparently, they had not driven too far away from the bar.

"I'm his attorney, we'll be happy to answer any questions you may have, just give me a few moments with my client," Roy said to the police officer in charge.

"Are you sure about this, Roy? You're not a defense attorney," Dorian said.

"You called me, remember? Besides, they don't know that. I've got a basic understanding of criminal law, so why don't we start with what happened?"

Dorian filled Roy in on the details and Roy gave a pretty convincing explanation to the police, complete with Dorian's position at the university, accolades, and so forth. They decided it wasn't worth charging a professor who most likely had been attacked, even though he showed no signs of damage to himself; not even his hand was bruised.

"Thanks, Roy. I can see why you've become so successful at winning cases. You have a way with words," Dorian said.

"Anytime, my friend," Roy replied.

"By the way, since when did you learn to fight? You took on five guys and thrashed three of them. Two look like they've been hit with a steel pipe. Didn't think you were capable of something like this. I better remember not to get you upset."

"Come on, man, you know me, I hate this sort of thing. I don't know what happened there; probably the flight or fight response, my body went on autopilot. I hope those guys are okay."

"Don't worry about that garbage. You did society a favor. If more people fought back, we wouldn't have as much crime as

we do. Let me know if they try to sue you, I'll have their attorney
wetting his pants in no time."

After saying his goodbyes again, Dorian went home for the
night. At about one a.m., as he was pulling into his driveway, he
received a text message from Yuki letting him know that her
father was improving, and that she would try and call him around
nine a.m. later that day.

# *Five*

IN ANOTHER PART OF THE WORLD, THEODORE Dantanian met with several advisors from Hermoni regarding the recent acquisition of Sukekuni Corporation. Afterwards, he boarded his private jet for a flight to Japan to meet with the Sukekuni executives to discuss their options of continuing operations under new leadership, expansion, or dismantling the company through forced liquidation and buyouts. He addressed the Board of Directors in a closed meeting shortly after his arrival.

"What happens from here all depends on the outcome of a meeting I have with someone closely involved with the company," Dantanian said to the board members, referring to Mr. Sukekuni, Yuki's father.

One of Dantanian's assistants handed a sealed note for Mr. Sukekuni to Hiroshi Sato, one of the senior managers at the company.

The meeting ended and the board adjourned for the day, leaving the board members puzzled as to why Hermoni would have them on their radar and what advantage they could give such a large company.

After leaving the corporate office, Hiroshi drove to Mr. Sukekuni's estate, where Mr. Sukekuni was recuperating from his heart attack. Hiroshi was greeted at the door by Aki, Yuki's younger sister, who led him through the courtyard towards the main living quarters of the pagoda-styled mansion.

"How is he feeling?" Hiroshi asked with trepidation.

"He is regaining his strength quickly. Father had a mild heart attack, but the doctor feels he still needs to take it easy for a while and not get too stressed," Aki replied, glaring at him with those last few words.

Hiroshi laughed nervously. "I don't want the Chief to be stressed; I have a note to give him, that's all." He held out the sealed letter.

"A note? What note? From who? Let me see it!"

Yuki, who silently approached from the adjacent hallway, stepped in and held Aki's wrist just as Aki was about to grab the note, reminding her to mind her manners towards guests in the house.

"Forgive her Hiroshi-san; she's been a bit emotional since all that has happened. Is this a matter of great importance?" Yuki asked politely.

"I believe so. I was at the board meeting in place of your father and one of the assistants of a Mr. Dantanian asked me to deliver this with urgency. I didn't ask what it was about and they didn't tell me."

"I see. Follow me, then." She led him to the main living room, where her father was in a bed reading a newspaper with the television playing in the background.

"Ah, Sato-san, good to see you," Mr. Sukekuni said in a weakened, gravelly voice.

"It is good to see you also, Chief. We all hope your health is getting better. I did not wish to disturb; however, I was asked to give you a note from a Mr. Dantanian, whom I believe you are acquainted with," he said respectfully.

"Hand it to Yuki, please. Thank you, Sato-san."

Hiroshi pulled out a very large "get well soon" poster from the folder he was carrying. The poster was signed by everyone in the company—all four thousand four hundred of them, give or take a few. Aki's face lit up when she saw the enormous number of well-wishers.

"Aww, that's so nice. Arigato, Hiroshi-san," she said with a flirty smile, changing her disposition towards him. He handed the note to Yuki, said goodbye and departed. Yuki opened the note and read it aloud.

"*I would like to discuss a final opportunity for you and your family. Make sure Yuki is present. Six p.m. tonight in the executive conference room. —TD.*

Yuki looked furious. "Is he crazy? Doesn't he know you just had a heart attack? What is with this guy?" she yelled.

"Calm down, Yuki," her father said, having been roused out of his feeble state. "Aki, I need you to do me a favor. Look up this Dantanian fellow and tell me what his relationship is to the Hermoni Company."

"Yes, father," she replied with feigned enthusiasm.

His assistants had already completed preliminary legwork before Yuki had her meeting with Dantanian; however, he wanted his daughters to take more interest in the family business. It was because of the business that he had been unable to spend much time with both of them when they were growing up. Now that they were older, it was his dream to get them more involved with the company in order to get to know them more. Yuki might be a lost cause at this point, but it wasn't too late for Aki. Several minutes later, Aki returned with some answers.

"Theodore Dantanian owns TDI Corp, and they own many other companies, including Hermoni," she said. His face looked strained upon hearing this.

"I did not have an opportunity to speak to you about the meeting with him. What happened?" he asked Yuki.

Trying not to upset her father, she carefully worded her response. "I met with Mr. Dantanian as you asked, but I could not provide him with the information he was looking for. He seemed to think the Professor I am working under has some secret research going on. I believe he is wrong and now he is trying to force me to spy on Dr. Lystad."

Her father put down his paper and turned his head towards her with a very stern look. "Is that all he wants from you? What harm is there in giving him some information? Do you see what he's done? He's going to destroy us if you don't cooperate! Give him what he wants, Yuki. You can always work for the company if you lose your position there."

"You tell me to calm down, look at you! You're going to end up back in the hospital!" she shot back. "I will go to this meeting and in your place Hiroshi can come with me. You're not well enough to go."

He looked back at her with consternation. "Get Aki to set up the camera and I will attend the meeting by video conference. I need to speak with this man myself," he huffed with shortened breath, as the stress of their conversation began taking its toll.

SOMETIME LATER, A DRIVER TOOK YUKI AND Hiroshi to the company headquarters in Tokyo. The two of them discussed the upcoming meeting and shared some small talk on the way. They arrived a bit early, giving them enough time to set up the equipment and make sure everything worked properly.

Five minutes before six o'clock, Theodore Dantanian and his assistant April arrived, along with several of his bodyguards who inspected the room prior to standing at their posts outside.

"Miss Yuki, I'm happy to see you again. I see that you received my message," he said, as if they were old friends.

"What message would that be, Mr. Dantanian? The one for this meeting, or the one you delivered by taking over our company?"

He responded in Japanese: "Touché, Miss Yuki. I didn't want things to have to come to this, especially since Sukekuni is such an old, stagnant company; it wasn't something I really wanted to acquire. Since I had to deliver a message, I felt it should be one that you would pay attention to this time."

Yuki shot an icy glance at him.

"Now that you know how serious I am, I will give you one final opportunity before I dismantle this company and four thousand people lose their jobs. I need you to convince Lystad to give up the source.

You can tell him what he's up against, and let him know that once I'm finished with you I'll move on to someone or something else he cares about," he said casually.

"Mr. Dantanian, why are you involving us like this? If you need something from him why don't you just go to him yourself?" Yuki's father asked.

"As I told your daughter, we went through that phase already. Now I'm giving him more of an incentive to cooperate. If he gives me what I want, I'll turn over all my shares to you, giving full control to you once again. I believe that is a fair and equitable exchange."

"And what if he does not give you what he wants? Why do my workers have to pay the price?"

"That sir, is what we refer to as collateral damage," Dantanian replied, with a slight grin.

"Call him, Yuki, now!" her father ordered.

"I told him I would call at around nine a.m. their time. I'm sure if Dr. Lystad understands how serious you are, he will do his best to cooperate. I will contact you at the conclusion of our conversation. Is that acceptable?" Yuki asked coldly.

"That will be suitable. April will give you a number where we can be reached. I'm happy that I have your understanding and full cooperation. If Dr. Lystad refuses to give you a sample, then I'm going to have to come up with another way to persuade him that will be far more... unpleasant."

She bit her tongue to avoid screaming at him.

Dantanian and his troupe departed, leaving Yuki, Hiroshi, and her father in the conference room sitting in silence. Her father spoke first.

"Yuki, this man is trouble, and I don't like him any more than you do, but what other choice do we have? It's not just the family we have to be concerned about; we have to think of all the employees here that could be affected."

She could hear the weariness in his voice and see it in his face. It pained her to see him like this. "I understand that, father, but how can I give him that which does not exist? I do not even know if what he is after is something Dr. Lystad has or is aware of. Perhaps someone else at Primase was conducting some strange experiment. I don't know; I'm at a loss for words right now. Why is this man putting pressure on us if he wants something from Dr. Lystad? Why go through all this trouble just to get me to act? With this man's power, he could just hire someone to get the samples, or just threaten Dr. Lystad directly. This makes no sense. Hopefully I'll get something that Dantanian wants so we can move on."

"Yuki, you have to understand, some men with power like to control others. He doesn't care who he has to step on to get what he wants. We are in agreement; I cannot see why it should be necessary to go to these lengths to extract something from the professor," her father said as he reached for his oxygen.

"I think this man believes this is all a game to him," Hiroshi remarked. "So maybe that is why he is not having a thug or gangster attack your professor directly. Maybe it is beneath him. That is my guess."

BACK IN ANN ARBOR:

The familiar ringtone of Dorian's cell phone echoed in the hallway of his house as he was upstairs brushing his teeth. He peered through the adjacent bedroom and looked at the clock on his nightstand. It was nine a.m. and he had completely forgotten Yuki was supposed to call him at this time. Running downstairs with toothbrush and toothpaste foam in mouth, he managed to answer the call just before it went to voicemail.

"Just a sec," he gurgled into the phone while running over to the kitchen sink. He poured a small glass of water and quickly swished and spit. "Sorry about that, I had a mouth full of toothpaste," he said cheerfully. "How is everything—is your father well?" he replied, changing his tone to a more somber one, in case she was delivering dreadful news of her father's health.

"My father is getting better, but he is still under quite a bit of stress that is affecting his health. Dr. Lystad, Dorian, I need your help and I don't know what to do."

"Of course, Yuki. What can I do for you?"

"Do you remember when you were taking me to the airport and I told you that I thought Theodore Dantanian was responsible for taking over my family's company?"

Dorian paused. "Yes, I seem to recall that. Why?"

"It turns out that he did take it over through one of his subsidiaries. I met with him again, only this time he was not asking nicely. He told me that if I do not get some sample from you, he is going to break apart our company and everyone will lose their jobs. This would affect over four thousand workers. Is there something you are hiding from me? Please tell me, I need to know what is going on."

"I am so sorry to have brought this on you and your family, Yuki, I had no idea things would get so far out of control. If Dantanian wants a sample, he can have one. I don't want innocent people to be caught up in this. I don't think we should say anything further over the phone, but I will be happy to talk to you in person."

They agreed to meet in Honolulu, Hawaii, on Monday evening and he would fly back on Tuesday afternoon. Dorian still had commitments to the University, so arrangements were made for personal time off.

IT WAS A TIRING FLIGHT TO CALIFORNIA, AND the connection to Hawaii made the day seem really long. After arriving at the airport in Hawaii, he took a shuttle bus to the hotel and checked in. It was four p.m. and he was to meet Yuki at his hotel in three hours and give her the sample, which he had to draw up from the supplies he packed.

He sat down on the bed in his room and proceeded to fill a small vacuum test tube with his blood and then placed it into a cooler. Afterwards, he called Yuki and told her he had the sample with him and was ready to meet with her.

Seven p.m. arrived and Yuki entered the hotel lobby. She was wearing a yellow flower print skirt and a white short sleeve button down blouse. Dorian was sitting in a lobby chair with the cooler in his lap and sunglasses on top of his platinum-white hair, his grey eyes fixed on her. He smiled as she caught his glance, and despite her extreme stress, she felt a peace

"How do you want to do this?" he asked.

"I have a driver outside waiting for us; we're going to meet Dantanian at the Arizona Memorial at Pearl Harbor."

Dorian looked puzzled. "Ah, isn't the park closed now? It's after seven."

"The monument is a popular tourist spot, so people will still be congregated there. I wanted a public place; I just don't trust him," she said, as if they were venturing to a back-alley drug deal.

They went outside together where a limo was waiting. The driver was holding the door open for them and they got inside. Dorian looked over at Yuki.

"Okay, I'm not exactly sure how the process of share transfer works, but I'm not giving him anything until I have confirmation," he said.

Dorian's thoughts were swimming in a sea of scenarios. What if Dantanian backed out of his deal? What if something went wrong, and of course, how was he going to explain all this to Yuki?

"We have several bodyguards to ensure our safety. They're in the vehicle behind us and another one is in the front seat next to our driver as well. I'll have my father on the phone and he will verify with his lawyers and executives that the transfer of the shares has gone through. You still have some explaining to do," she said with a glare at him. They made eye contact and he looked down.

"Of course, but right now we need to get this over with. Afterwards, I'll fill you in on the details."

They pulled into the parking lot of the memorial, which was mostly devoid of cars apart from what looked like a limousine and several large SUVs parked over to the far right. The sun was making its descent and there was a slight breeze outside.

Yuki's limousine and bodyguards pulled up in an empty spot with the front of the car pointed towards the exit in case they needed to make a quick getaway. Her guards got out first and surveyed the situation, then signaled for Yuki to get out. Dorian followed after Yuki and they made their way with the sample over to the limousine that Theodore Dantanian was getting out of. Before Dantanian could get a word out of his mouth, Dorian made his demands.

"First, before I hand this over to you, you're going to transfer the shares over to the Sukekuni family. You can have one of your assistants check the vial if you need assurance," Dorian said.

Dantanian had a slight grin on his face. "That won't be necessary; I'm quite certain it's genuine." He nodded to someone in his limousine; it was unclear who it was, as the glass was too dark to see through.

"Miss Yuki, I think you will find that the share transfer is complete," he said coolly.

Yuki had her father on the phone for confirmation. "We have the shares, Yuki, everything is in order, you have done well," he said, over the distant shout of excitement from her sister in the background.

"Is everything good, Yuki?" Dorian asked.

"Yes, my father confirms the transfer."

He handed the cooler over to Dantanian. "Here, take it. I don't ever want to have to see you again. I'm not sure what you are planning to do with it, but you obviously want it really bad. Let me give you some advice. There are some things in this world that should just be left alone."

At that moment, he began to feel very strange inside, as if a terrible evil was emanating from Dantanian's limousine, closing around him with a sense of death and foreboding.

"Wise words, Dr. Lystad. Allow me to add some of my own. You may think I have gone to great lengths for something that can be easily attained, but I assure you, you have no idea the lengths I will go to if I find that this is what we've been searching for. So tell whoever this belongs to that they should enjoy their freedom while they can," Dantanian said with an evil look.

Dorian felt his face go red. Did Dantanian know his secret, or was that just a reference to something else?

"Well, if we are finished here, we will be leaving now," Yuki interjected. Her bodyguards were looking intently at their surroundings. Dorian didn't say anything. Just as he was turning towards their ride, his senses started picking something else up in the same manner they did when the muggers attacked. He could feel the electrical impulses coming from everyone around him; their heartbeats and their movements.

There was something different about the occupant of the limousine, and about the man walking a dog at the far end of the parking lot. He couldn't quite put his finger on it. The dog walker appeared normal, with long, brown hair, an olive complexion, and a scruffy shaven face, but Dorian sensed a different energy emanating from him. At that moment, the man dropped the leash, turned, and within a second had run almost one hundred fifty feet up to Dantanian, who was still holding the cooler, and had snatched it out of his hands. The stranger then looked over to Dorian.

"Run!" he shouted. Dorian and Yuki both looked astonished, as did the bodyguards, but not Dantanian. In fact, he appeared as if he was fully expecting it.

"I was wondering when you were going make your move," he said nonchalantly to the stranger. "You were the thief who took the last sample. Looks like someone has something to hide. No matter. My master will deal with you," he said, stepping back.

The stranger smashed the Styrofoam container, then grabbed the sample with his hand and destroyed it. The door to the limousine opened. The stranger turned to Dorian and Yuki once more.

"What are you waiting for? Get out of here!" he shouted.

An ethereal voice pierced Dorian's head and he felt a horrible sense of doom and dread come over him, as if he were losing his grip on reality. Yuki, dazed herself, shook him, grabbed his hand and pulled him towards their car. Her bodyguards, trembling in fear, drew their weapons and started to back up towards their vehicles, unsure of what they were witnessing, or what to do.

The tall figure got out of Dantanian's limo. She was wearing a long coat that seemed almost alive as it wrapped tightly around her body, leaving nothing exposed. It was some type of translucent material that shimmered with different colors, like one of those undersea creatures that live in the deep. Her face was radiant and her skin had an amber glow to it, both terrifying and beautiful. Her eyes were bright, as if illuminated from behind, and her hair was a lime-green color that sparkled like chrysolite.

A bright light surrounded her hand and suddenly the hand transformed itself into a claw, glowing like molten metal.

The stranger holding the vial observed her display of power with a stoic expression, as if preparing himself for a confrontation.

Dorian's heart was moving much faster and he felt a despair and doom like he had never felt before.

Dorian and Yuki jumped into their limo and both shouted to the driver to get them out of there, leaving the stranger to deal with the extraterrestrial-looking woman.

"Did you see her face? What the hell was that? She looked like some kind of alien. What in the name of all that is holy is going on here?" Dorian asked. Yuki didn't answer. She was still in a bit of shock, wondering if it was some sort of hallucination.

As Dorian and Yuki's limo sped away, several stragglers leaving the memorial witnessed the confrontation between the woman and the dog-walker, who had himself produced a weapon made of light seemingly out of nowhere. It appeared to be himself—a blade that was part of his forearm, glowing like molten metal, similar to his opponent's claw.

"I am Onoskelis," the woman proclaimed, her voice sounding as ten speaking in unison with slightly different tones, producing a harmonious effect. The words were uttered in an unknown language which seemed to be laced with a spell. The stranger was able to understand and withstand it.

"Your Ka isn't going to work on me!" he yelled. As soon as the words left his mouth she was upon him, grabbing him by the neck with one hand and lifting him off the ground. His concentration broke, causing his weapon to disappear; both of his hands were on her one arm, desperately trying to get her to let go. She moved his head near hers.

"I sense Gavri'el in you. I don't care if you're his offspring, if you get in my way I'll destroy you!"

The stranger managed to break her grasp and jumped back, surprising his attacker. There were more onlookers that had gathered in the parking lot wondering what was going on, and a few of them appeared to be making phone calls.

"Master, we need to go. We can get another sample from him later," Dantanian said confidently. She flashed an angry look and got in the limousine. The stranger glared at the two of them and ran off quickly in the direction Dorian was traveling. Sirens could be heard approaching the area from the distance.

DORIAN AND YUKI DROVE ABOUT TEN MILES from the harbor, not saying anything until the car pulled into the parking lot of a diner.

The bodyguards traveling behind them pulled alongside their car, got out and went to the parked limo.

"Okay, what just happened there?" Yuki demanded.

"I have no idea; one minute I'm giving him the box, the next I'm in a *Star Trek* episode. Who or what was that? I'm beginning to wonder if this is some kind of caught on camera thing going on, but I can't fathom how. No special effect I've ever seen looked *that* real."

"I was thinking the same thing the first time Dantanian was telling me about this fantastic blood sample. What is the story behind the super blood? Is everything true? Where did you get it? What is it? What is going on?"

Dorian grimaced, then took a big breath and let it out.

"Okay, this probably isn't going to come as much of a shock after what we've just experienced, but here goes. The blood I gave him does seem to have some unusual qualities."

"Such as?"

"So far, I know of no pathogen that can negatively affect it. The immunology is quite remarkable. It seems to have a chromosomal anomaly, as well as no shortening of telomeres over time. I have the full genome at home; I just finished sequencing it and compiling the data, but haven't had a chance to do a comparative analysis. My computer's running a program for that as we speak. That's pretty much it."

"You left out one big detail. Where did it come from?"

Dorian decided he might as well get this all out in the open. "The sample belongs to me."

Yuki looked confused. "I know it was yours. Are you saying that the test tube had your blood in it? That you—," She stopped herself and paused for a moment, pondering his proclamation.

"I suppose that makes sense; I see," she mused aloud, piecing together the clues that supported his statement. There was the fact that the man beside her who was forty-nine years old barely looked twenty-five. She remembered him responding to one of his colleagues who questioned his youthful appearance. "Must be in the genes" was something she'd heard him say several times before. She also recalled the incident when everyone in the lab and most of the building had caught a bad case of the flu when one of the researchers using live virus didn't follow proper handling protocol. Everyone was sick except Dorian. It still didn't seem possible to her.

"Yuki, I know this may be hard to believe, but I need you to forget about this and go back to Michigan, for your sake and the sake of everyone you know."

"It's too late for that, I'm already involved!" she shouted. "Look what happened to my family. They'll be coming after you now, I'm sure of it! If what you say is true, your blood is worth more than I could imagine, just considering your immune system."

"I don't think this is about money anymore Yuki," he said in a depressed voice.

"Why didn't you tell me in the first place? But I suppose you wouldn't want anyone to know, especially the government."

She paused and looked at him, her mental wheels were churning.

"What is going on? Why is he after you? Why go to all this trouble to get some blood from you?"

"I really don't know what is going on, Yuki. I wish I did, believe me. You're right, things are not adding up. For one, why go through this whole elaborate scheme to buy up your family's company stock to use as leverage against me? Why not just threaten me directly? I don't get it; it doesn't make sense. Also, what are they planning to do with it? Some kind of biological warfare?"

"So, they're not after money, certainly curing infectious diseases are counterproductive to profit oriented entrepreneurs. The immortality part I can see of being high importance. We can clone blood, but we can't alter the genome to any appreciable extent," she mused.

"With the exception of designer babies, no, not really," he replied.

She sighed and rubbed her eyes and Dorian did the same.

"We probably shouldn't stay here for too long, I'm guessing that Dantanian is going to be looking for you again," she said. "Who was that guy with the dog? It seemed like he was trying to help you. Did you see how fast he moved? Please tell me I wasn't hallucinating."

"Not unless we both had the same one. I can move quite fast myself, though I'm not sure if I'm as fast as he was, but that woman—if that's what you want to call her; wow, that's on a level I can't comprehend."

"It seemed like he was trying to prevent them from getting your blood, which means he must know about its properties. Dantanian did say someone broke into his lab to steal the blood he took from you," she said.

"There's a lot more going on here than what we know about," he replied.

Yuki smiled slightly. "So what else can you do? Can you fly? How about breathing underwater? X-ray vision? What color is my underwear?"

"Now you're beginning to sound like Kasia! No I can't fly, breathe underwater or microwave dinner with my eyes. To answer your other question, you're wearing white with purple flower panties," he said with a grin. She started to blush and crossed her legs.

"Relax. You got in the limo before me, remember? Your underwear went above your skirt line."

She playfully smacked him on the arm. "Baka!" she yelled, which was Japanese for 'idiot'. There was a tapping on the glass from two of the guards outside, who seemed to be in serious discussion about the events they witnessed. Yuki lowered the window.

"Excuse me, miss, we really should leave the area. This island is very small and we really aren't equipped to handle the supernatural," the guard said, only half-joking.

Yuki peered over to Dorian. "I don't think we should go back to the hotel. Let's get to the airport and return to Michigan."

Dorian frowned in confusion. "You aren't going back to Japan? What about your father?"

"My father will recover just fine; he had a mild heart attack. Now that he has controlling shares in our family company, he'll want to get back to work as soon as possible. Also, Aki is there, she'll take care of him. I'm more concerned about you," she said, looking at him, then down, embarrassed by her confession.

"Yuki, I'm not so sure you should get involved any further. Things could get dangerous. All I wanted to do was get some answers about who I was and where I came from. I never knew my biological parents, so research was my way to find out something about myself."

She smiled at him. "I'll be fine; I have you to protect me, right? Besides, who else is more qualified to help you find out about your family background?"

He was still hesitant. "I may not be able to go back to the lab after all this. For all I know, my house is burning to the ground right now. You have a future and an education to finish. For now—."

"For now, I'm coming with you, because if I go back to the lab, who is to say Dantanian or this alien lady won't come looking for me in the hopes of getting to you?"

A defeated look formed on his face. "I have a feeling we may end up seeing them again one way or another," he replied. It was becoming apparent his immediate fate was joined to Yuki's. Dorian sighed. "Okay, okay, we'll need to find a safe place to work from for the time being."

She smiled, feeling scared and excited at what the future might present.

"I suppose I can request a leave of absence from the university and inform Engel and Kasia. I had better check on my mother to make sure she's all right. My return flight doesn't leave until tomorrow, so let's find a new hotel for the night. We can have your driver drop us off at one near the airport. Call your sister and see if she can book you a flight to Michigan."

Yuki looked confused. "I thought you said we need to get to a safe house or something?"

"I left my laptop running in the lab; it has all my data on it. I can't just leave it there," he replied.

She looked outside at the guards standing by their SUV. "Let's get out of the limousine. We'll ride with the other guys."

The two got out and instructed the bodyguards to drop them off on the sidewalk near a strip of hotels not far from the airport. Once they found a decent enough looking hotel, they checked in for the night

They had a single room on the seventh floor that had double beds, and windows overlooking the ocean. After getting situated, she ordered some Thai food and had it delivered to the room. Yuki called her sister in Japan and told her to book them both tickets with their father's credit card, just so they could stay together.

"Should we be getting a disguise and fake ID's?" she playfully asked trying to lighten the mood.

"I think saw an advertisement in the lobby for authentic-looking fake ID's, I'm sure we can have them before our flight leaves. Besides, if they really want to find us they will, so you might as well give up on the whole cloak and dagger bit," he said, deflating her balloon that was filling with fantasies of a couple on the run.

"If anyone asks, we're a pair of highly trained counter-terrorism experts. My expertise is biological weapons and yours is field operations. That sounds pretty exotic," she said, staring off into space the way she sometimes did on occasion, undoubtedly daydreaming about a romantic drama involving the two of them.

"Yes, because that's the sort of thing counter terrorism experts tell people when they want to know what they do. You're better off saying we're architects or something," he said, laughing.

"It's my story, get your own!" she yelled back, sticking her tongue out at him. He started to get the idea she was enjoying this bit of excitement in her life. It didn't surprise him; years of study and boring lab work brought out the hidden adventurist in Yuki. Even Dorian felt a bit more alive after recent events.

They couldn't go incognito for long; he had a considerable amount of time and money invested in the lab. Then there was the matter of this stranger who had shown up out of the blue and helped them. Was he being followed? How else would this stranger have known of their meeting time and place? What were his intentions? The lingering questions kept Dorian from getting any sleep.

# Six

THE FOLLOWING MORNING DORIAN TOOK A quick shower to help him wake up and the two-headed downstairs for breakfast. A breaking news story was being broadcast on the television overhead. Terrorists had struck simultaneously at the New York Stock Exchange and the NASDAQ building in New York, killing about one hundred sixty-nine people. Both attacks involved armored cars that smashed through the front door and detonated explosives. Authorities were stating it was an act of domestic terrorism, as evidenced by a website on which a group known as 'Starve the Beast' claimed credit for the attack.

"Wow, that was a big one. I wonder what the fallout from this will be. I'm guessing Engel is glued to the TV right now," he said, sipping his orange juice.

"I was just near there last week. I can't believe this is happening," she replied with a gloomy look on her face.

They finished up and took a nearby shuttle bus to the airport right away, since security was going to be extra tight after the attack in New York.

DORIAN FELL ASLEEP ON THE FIRST FLIGHT AND
had a dream where he was in a battle with about seventy others,
attacking another group of about three hundred beings. He
looked like an alien himself in a supernatural way, as did many
of his comrades in arms. There were loud crashes and flashes of
light and thunder all around him. He awoke with the shaking of
the plane on touchdown at the Los Angeles International
Airport. Yuki looked over at him and noticed that he was griping
the arm rests tightly. He had apparently crushed them during his
tumultuous dream session. The plane wheeled around and stayed
put on the tarmac. A bomb threat had been called in to the
airport, one of many they regularly received; however, after the
attack at the stock exchanges everything was being taken very
seriously. They waited on the plane for almost an hour until the
Captain received the green light from the flight tower to proceed
to the docking station.

On the second flight, Dorian fell asleep again and had a
dream of armies of immeasurable count gathered for a war. He
saw beings that looked like a mixture of human and animal in
the battle lines.

The dream had become more like a replay of future events;
as if someone was fast forwarding a movie, stopping for a
second and then moving forward again. At one point in time, he
felt a terrible loss and the pain and sorrow associated with it. The
face of the stranger had become familiar; Dorian understood a
mutual respect and friendship between the two. Conversations
took place with people and beings he had never seen before. All
this flashed before him when suddenly the vision moved to a
scene of three mountains and a river of blood that moved up and
down over the tops of the mountains, into the valleys and onto
the plains, going past modern buildings that transformed into the
shape of X and Y chromosomes. The river formed a moat around

the seventh building, the fourteenth, and the twenty first building. His visions began to fade and he awoke to Yuki wiping away the tears he had shed.

"You were crying in your sleep. It must have been some dream, are you all right?" she asked, feeling sorry for him. He yawned and rubbed his eyes.

"I had this terrible sadness at one point in my dream, more than any I've ever experienced. It seemed so real. Thanks for not making me feel embarrassed. It's not often you'll see me get emotional."

A SHORT TIME LATER, THE PLANE LANDED AND they disembarked. After reaching the corridor that lead to the terminal, the icy cold air and dull, grey sky snapped them back to the bitter reality of a Michigan winter.

It was about ten days before Christmas and Dorian did not have time to even think about the holidays. His only thought right now was to get to his house, grab his bug-out bag and some clothes, and make some phone calls. It was finals week at the University and he had exams to give.

They grabbed some drive-thru fast food on the way and ate in the car. There were no lights on and no cars were in the driveway of his house when they arrived. The front door appeared to be closed and he could not see any sign of break-in. He handed the car keys over to Yuki.

"Wait here; I'll only be a moment. If you don't see me come out in ten minutes, take the car and find some place safe to go," he said while getting out of the car.

She didn't know what to say, except, "Be careful."

He quietly made his way up to the front door and unlocked it. Nothing seemed unusual, so he opened the door and went inside where everything was dark and quiet. The house was so cold he could see his breath, having turned down the thermostat too low before he left. After checking out the kitchen, he went upstairs to the master bedroom where his bug-out bag was stored. Grabbing the bag, along with some cash and a taser, he had in his nightstand, he turned around to leave. Then, out of nowhere, two beings appeared in front of him. One was the huge woman from before in Hawaii, her face unmistakable; the other was a very tall male with long black hair and ash-colored skin. His eyes were similar to hers, and he had black markings like sigils on his skin. She clutched Dorian by the neck as the other being put his hand on Dorian's forehead. Dorian was unable to move.

"What the hell are you people? Let go of me!" he demanded. They ignored him.

"This could be the one, but it's hard to tell; his Shi isn't active so his blood would be useless to us," Onoskelis said to the other in an alien language that Dorian somehow was able to understand.

"What do you want from me? Just tell me and I will try and help you." His captors continued to ignore him.

A small device materialized in the woman's hand. She placed it on Dorian's neck. He could feel it penetrate his skin and begin to drain him of blood. A loud humming noise followed by vibrations in the device began increasing in intensity until the woman's expression became fearful. She pulled away just as the device was destroyed. The two beings looked at each other in astonishment.

"That has never happened before. Salami'el, what do you make of it?" Onoskelis asked, gripping her hand in pain.

Salami'el motioned with both hands, chanting something which caused a symbol to appear as a 3-D hologram in a flame. The symbol fizzled out within a few seconds.

"I do not know. Perhaps Phanu'el has marked the boy. I will have to research this," he replied, looking intently at Dorian.

"I feel more confident with this one, especially after the Nephilim I encountered. We won't bring him to Belial unless we're sure, I have witnessed many of these turn out false. Salami'el, put a Shemzol on him and let us be away," she said. She waved her hand over a small box she held in her other palm. It became bright, forming a moving sigil on the ground in a circle around all three of them. Salami'el grabbed Dorian by the back of the neck and chanted something. Dorian felt a slight tinge of pain with some pressure. Salami'el released his grip, dropping Dorian to the floor. Someone was heard making their way up the stairs slowly.

"Is everything all right?" Yuki asked in a cautious tone. Before Dorian could say "Run", the two beings disappeared in a flash of light, causing a power outage. Yuki walked over to the bedroom where she saw Dorian lying on the floor and she ran over to help him. "What happened?" she asked. Dorian had a vacuous expression on his face.

"I can't move; my body is numb. They were here, Yuki; the woman from before and a male one like her. They did something to me. I can't move." Yuki lifted him from behind under his arms and dragged him to the bed, leaning him upright against it, then wrapped him in a blanket to keep him warm.

"One of them put something on my head. Reach behind my neck and let me know what you feel."

She did as he instructed and felt around the nape of his neck. "There is something attached. It feels hard with a raised surface, almost like a button. Does it hurt when I touch it?"

"There's just pressure, and I feel a bit dizzy when you run your finger over it. I hope someone can tell me what the heck is going on. They wouldn't even answer or talk to me, like I was just a piece of meat or an object to them," he said, slowly twitching his fingers.

"It looks like you're beginning to move again. That's a good sign. At least they didn't give you the standard anal probing you usually hear about," she said with a laugh, trying to raise his spirits.

After about twenty minutes the feeling in his arms and legs returned, and he was able to move again, albeit in a slow, groggy fashion. She helped him to his feet, and the two of them dragged his bug-out bag to the stairs and slowly slid it down each step while he held tightly to the handrail. Whatever was on the back of his head was giving him a bit of vertigo, causing his balance to be a bit off, so the process was tedious. They made it down in one piece and he sat at the kitchen table, somewhat exhausted from the ordeal.

"I've never felt this way before; these are new sensations for me. Do me a favor and run into the bathroom. There's a hand mirror in the top drawer; can you bring it to me?" he asked, while gingerly touching the foreign object on the back of his neck. "You don't happen to have a small mirror in your purse, do you?" he asked.

"I think so," she said. She made her way into his bathroom and returned with his mirror. "Here's yours. Now let me see if I have one." She went outside to get her purse, returning a moment later with the lid to her makeup case.

"Hold this up for me please," he said, positioning the smaller mirror in the front. "I have a flashlight attached to the bag, on the side, right there; grab that for me, will you?"

She aimed the light so that he could clearly see the object on the back of his head. It was metallic, made of what appeared to be pure gold, with a strange symbol of an arrow pointed to the right with two small circles above the tip on the left side and one on the right, bearing a resemblance to a crop circle image. It appeared to be fused to his skull and any attempt he made to pick at it caused a great deal of pain all over his body.

"This thing isn't coming off without help. I have no idea what this symbol means; have you ever seen anything like this before?" he asked.

"No, maybe in a movie once, but not in real life. Do you need to go to the hospital to have it looked at?"

"Part of me wants to, and part of me thinks that if a surgeon tries to remove it I'll suffer some horrible effect that they won't be able to predict. Things just keep getting stranger by the minute," he replied with exasperation.

Yuki sat down next to Dorian and held his hand in hers. "What happened up there? What did they say to you?"

He told her everything that had happened and they sat quietly for a moment afterwards.

"By the way," he said in an annoyed tone, "I thought I told you to wait in the car and take off if I didn't come down in ten minutes."

"I'm sorry. I heard you yelling and some loud humming noise and ran in to see if you were all right. When I got in I heard a strange voice talking and saw a bright light. I figured you might be in trouble."

"So, what were you planning to do, rescue me?"

She looked hurt. "I didn't know what was going on; I couldn't just leave you."

He smiled then kissed her hand. "Fair enough, thank you. Let's get out of here."

They left to get his computer, which was locked in a closet at the lab. It was early morning Wednesday and as they drove they noticed many military vehicles on the roads—quite an unusual sight, considering there were no major military installations in Ann Arbor, let alone Michigan.

"I wonder what's going on?" Yuki asked, thinking of the recent terrorist attack in New York.

"It could just be precautionary, judging from what happened at the stock exchange." he replied.

She looked over at what he was doing. "Um, I don't think it's a good idea to touch that while you're driving. If you have black eyes or get dizzy we are going to crash."

He laughed. "I think you mean blackout, not black eyes."

She lightly punched him in the arm. "So my English isn't perfect. I'm going to give you a black eye if you don't watch it, mister!"

THEY ARRIVED IN FRONT OF THE MEDICAL science Building and Dorian waited in the car while Yuki left to retrieve his computer. All the while he wondered what this thing on the back of his head was, and how he was going to have it removed. It was a strange feeling to him, knowing that aliens (or what he thought were aliens) actually existed. What was in his blood that these beings wanted?

Yuki approached the car with a box in her arms and a worried look on her face. She opened the door and got in.

"I just realized that thing on the back of your neck might be some kind of alien embryo implant like this movie I saw. We should get it x-rayed just in case, to make sure it does not cause your head to explode or something," she said in her half-joking, half serious tone.

"I'm glad this is providing amusement for you, Yuki. My life could be in jeopardy here."

"Let's get going to the safe spot. Where is it, by the way?"

"In Norway, near Bergen. My mother went back there to retire," he replied, as he placed the car in gear.

"Norway? I didn't know she lived there. Ooh, how awesome!" She beamed and clapped her hands together in delight.

"We have a vacation home we used to visit during summer when my father was alive. Mom keeps it for the memories and in the hopes that someday I'll have a family to bring there. It should provide us with a quiet place to work. I'll get the tickets for the flight. We can stop at your place so you can grab whatever else you might want to bring."

Yuki was getting excited at the thought of traveling to Europe with Dorian, and as usual she was in fantasy land, smiling with the occasional blush thrown in.

Dorian called Kasia, who was usually up at this hour.

"Ah, there you are," Kasia answered in a disgruntled voice.

"Hi Kasia. I don't have a lot of time; my battery is about to go on my phone. Listen, I need a favor or two from you."

After Dorian had finished making arrangements with Kasia for his exams, he and Yuki traveled to Yuki's apartment to gather her things and chart out their next course of action. He booked their flight for the following day while Yuki packed for the trip and made some phone calls to her family.

They had some time to kill before his scheduled office hours so they headed over to the lab. Yuki did some searching on the internet for the symbol, but she was unable to find a match.

Dorian began the arduous task of sifting through the one hundred fifty-plus emails he typically received on a given day and noticed one that stood out from the others. The subject line read "Esme", his birth mother's name.

His pulse quickened and he wondered who else knew about her and what new calamity this would bring.

Just as he opened the email there was a knock at the door. The first student had arrived; his email would have to wait.

AFTER EVERYONE HAD LEFT, KASIA DROPPED BY before leaving for the day. She stood at the doorway with her hand held out. "Where is the gift you were supposed to get me?" she asked, with a toothy grin.

"I'm going to be traveling to Europe in a day; I promise I'll pick you up something," he replied, in a pathetic attempt to appease her.

"You just got back from Hawaii, and now you're headed to Europe? Must be nice. I better get something good from you. I like jewels, gold, and chocolate. In that order; good luck," she said with a laugh.

"I have the perfect thing in mind," he replied with sly smile.

"By the way," she said as she was walking down the hall, "You might want to turn on the TV. I think the President is going to have a speech or something to do with all hell breaking loose here."

He went into his office and shut the door behind him. Logging back into the university mail, he opened the message with his mother's name as the subject.

*"Dorian Lystad. Since the time of your birth we have been keeping a close watch over you, and have been very gratified with what you have become. Though the odds have been considerable, you have succeeded in many ways, but you have not begun to reach your full potential. The answers you have been searching for and more are within your grasp if you would hear our words. Therefore, we invite you to take a small journey where we can discuss the events of the past, present and possible future; the end of the human experiment, as well as information about your parents. If you would be willing to trust us, then trace your hand along the ground following the outline of this sigil and say the words "PETA BABKAMA LURUBA ANAKU", then we shall discuss things in more detail. No harm will come to you."*

He re-read the message to make sure he hadn't missed anything, and stared at it for some time, trying to make sense of it all. The notion of chanting some bizarre incantation was contrary to everything he knew as a scientist, and the only reason he had not deleted the message as asinine drivel was due to his recent experiences. He took a deep breath and called Yuki to his office to ask her opinion.

"Take a look at this," he said, turning his computer monitor towards her.

"Take a look at what?"

"The message in the email," he replied, checking his screen to make sure he wasn't missing something.

"What email? There's a blank page," she replied in confusion.

"You're not messing with me, are you? There's a paragraph right there." He read the message to her, apart from the incantation—or what he believed to be some type of incantation—to her.

"I think I saw this in a movie once. You say the words and then you'll be transported to some castle in the sky. Or was it another planet? I don't remember. When do we go?" she asked nonchalantly, in a way that suggested she didn't believe him.

"I have no idea who or what these people are. For all I know they're going to do something horrible to me. The only reason I haven't deleted this is because they seem to know something about me that only I and my adoptive mother know. Which reminds me, I should call her and make sure she's okay." He reached for his cell phone. "Yuki, could you please excuse me for a few minutes? Grab your stuff; we're going to be leaving in a bit."

She bowed slightly and exited the room, closing the door behind her.

He dialed the number for his mother in Norway, letting it ring several times before she answered the phone.

"Hallo," his mother said, in a sleepy voice, with her heavy Norwegian accent.

"Oh, mom, I'm sorry, I forgot the time difference. How are you?"

"Dorian, my baby! Oh, it's so good to hear your voice. Let me turn down the TV," she said, as the sound of some local news program got louder and then became inaudible.

"How have you been, darling? Are you well?" she asked, switching from English to Norwegian.

"I am well, mamma. I called because I was concerned about you. How have you been? Has anything unusual happened recently?"

"Well, I am fine, but everything around the world is in chaos. I don't know what to make of it. We have a lot of recent refugees from Iceland after all the volcanoes went off there. I'm sure you heard about it. I was thinking of letting a family stay at the cottage, unless you are planning to visit."

"As a matter of fact, I am coming, and I'll be bringing a friend. Actually, she's a researcher in my lab—from Japan," he said, wincing for the impending reaction.

"A woman? Oh, how nice! Is she married?"

"Okay, Mamma," he interjected. She ignored him.

"I bet she is pretty. Those Japanese women are beautiful."

"Mamma, please. We'll be leaving tomorrow morning and we'll reach there sometime around midnight or one a.m. Friday. Don't worry about picking us up, I'll rent a car at the airport. Just get the spare room ready for her; I can sleep on the couch. We'll go to the cottage on Saturday. Sound good?"

"I can't wait. I'm so excited, I'll make some torsk for us and we can have some potetstappe, I'll make lefse, and we can have—"

She was carrying on when Dorian interrupted. "Mom, there's two of us, not an army. I'm looking forward to seeing you. I'm going to have to go now. I'll call when we get to Amsterdam. Love you."

"Okay, I will see you tomorrow, bye-bye. I love you too. Bye-bye. Love you." She managed to squeeze in a few more before he hung up.

"Well, at least she seems to be all right. That's a relief," he murmured to himself. He looked at his monitor again and tried to highlight the text in order to figure out how he could see the message that Yuki couldn't. 'What did they mean by human experiment coming to an end?' He rubbed his hand over the strange implanted disc on the back of his neck. "I wonder if any of this has to do with all that has been going on in the world?"

Writing down the words from the email, Dorian traced the image on the screen to his paper and put it in his pocket. He got up from his desk chair and went into the lab to look for Engel.

"Has anyone seen Engel?" he asked the nearby students, who were having a conversation about the recent protests.

"I think he went—he's right behind you," Carol, the pre-med student, replied.

"Engel, you got a minute?"

"Sure. I got your voice message by the way. What did you need?"

Dorian handed him an envelope.

"What's this?" Engel asked, holding it up to the light.

"It's a small Christmas bonus and a bit extra for helping me out. I need two favors. First, I need you to cover my office hours tomorrow. It shouldn't be a big deal because I had a small lecture today with most of the students who care about their grade, so tomorrow should be just a few stragglers, if any. Second, I need you to proctor the exams for my classes. That's what the bonus is for. You won't have to grade them; it's going to be a multiple-choice exam that the computer can grade. They can take the exam from home if they want to, but I just need you available in case something goes wrong."

"By the way, nice playing. I saw you performing at the Blind Pig," Dorian said with admiration.

Engel perked up with the mention of his band.

"Thanks. We've been playing together for about six months now. I wrote most of the songs. I'm writing one about the recent attack on the stock market. By the way, have you seen all the military vehicles around here lately? What's up with that?"

"I'm not sure what is going on, I don't like the looks of it," Dorian replied.

"Anyway, yeah. Uh, no problem, I can cover your office hours and proctor the exam. I'll get with Kasia and see what I need to do. Where are you going this time? Is everything okay?"

"I need to check up on some things. I'll be gone through the break. Keep an eye on the lab for me. I'm leaving you in charge."

Engel gave him a strange look. "Isn't Yuki staying? I figured since she was back she would—," he stopped as he noticed Kasia giving him the throat-slash sign with her finger. "Right, then. I'll make sure the lab doesn't blow up while you're away," he said, grinning.

"Oh, I see. You give him a present but not me. So that's how it is," Kasia said, with her usual mock derision.

"And here I thought you'd already left," Dorian sighed, and walked over to her desk. "I would never forget about you," he said, handing her an envelope.

"I was only kidding, but I'll take it anyway. I need the money. I have lots and lots of things to buy with it."

"You have my number; call me if anything comes up. Have the grades submitted to Blackboard and I can post them on Monday. Have a Merry Christmas and a Happy New Year everybody," Dorian said.

He turned to leave and the students in the lab wished him Merry Christmas and said their goodbyes. Yuki followed him out of the lab and Dorian handed her an envelope also. She looked a bit sad, as if she was still just another employee to him.

"It's only fair that I compensate you, especially after what you've been through and what you're doing to help me. It's not Christmas yet," he said, an off handed suggestion that something of a more personal nature might be in store. She smiled and her mood improved.

"Well, our flight isn't until tomorrow, so if you have things to do or catch up on, I can come pick you up in the morning if you want," he said, trying to be polite. She smiled and bumped into him with her hip a bit.

"I shouldn't leave you alone. What if something happens and I'm not there? Or what if someone comes after me? I won't have you there to protect me," she said with a grin.

"Okay then, we'll head to your place and you can pack what you need to and then we'll grab some dinner and go to my place," he replied.

THEY LEFT THE BUILDING TOGETHER AND WENT to her apartment. When they got inside, he could smell the faint aroma of Asian cooking in the air along with a lemon air freshener that was past its prime.

The apartment was very clean and organized; sparsely decorated with a few plants here and there along with a hodge-podge of furniture. Adorning the walls were a few pictures of Yuki and her family at various vacation spots. One picture showed her and her sister wearing skiing outfits with a mountain backdrop.

"I didn't know you skied. I grew up in Colorado, and I love skiing. We have some nice slopes in Norway, maybe we can find time to go," he said, happy that they had something else in common.

"I would very much like that. My sister and I have skied Mt. Fuji since we were little; that picture was taken in Switzerland."

He continued to look about her apartment. Apparently, she was fond of rabbits, because she had rabbit slippers, rabbit stuffed animals, rabbit pajamas, bunny earmuffs, and other similarly themed accouterments strewn throughout the place.

"Would you like something to drink?" she asked politely.

"No, thanks. I see you're fond of rabbits...and romance novels, judging by that stack over there," he said.

She smiled and laughed a bit. "Well, not *all* of them are romance novels, just the top seven or so. I also like romantic mysteries, murder-romance, vampire-romance, and science fiction novels." Dorian began to see where she got her vivid imagination from.

The sound of keys rattling could be heard outside of the apartment, followed by a bang at the door. A second later it opened and Yuki's sister stumbled across the threshold with an oversized suitcase in hand. "Careful!" Yuki shouted.

"Here, let me help you with that," Dorian said, reaching for the suitcase. Aki smiled at him.

"Who's the cute guy?" she asked in her native tongue.

"That is Dr. Lystad, the Professor I work under. He is fluent in Japanese by the way," she replied. Aki turned a slight shade of pink and smiled.

"Hi there, nice to meet you," Dorian said, offering a handshake. "You two probably have a bit of catching up to do, I'll be back in a few minutes."

"Where are you going?" Yuki asked impatiently.

"I'll be back in a few minutes, keep packing. Oh, and don't forget to pay your traffic ticket," he replied.

"Says the man who normally needs to be reminded of everything," she shot back.

He laughed. "Okay, you got me there."

At the flower shop down the street, he stopped and picked up a dozen roses along with a bunny balloon. He returned about ten minutes later with the gifts.

"I figured this might brighten up the apartment a bit. I know we're leaving tomorrow, but I wanted to say I'm sorry for all that you've had to go through," he said, handing her the flowers and balloon.

"Oh, it's so cute. Arigato gozaimasu," she said, bowing with a huge grin on her face. Aki was gushing over the gifts as well and seemed a bit jealous.

Dorian had obviously made her very happy with his gesture, which might have been received as something more than what he intended. He had never found the time for romance in his life; his father passed away when he was seventeen, requiring him to work two jobs to help support his mother, sacrificing much of his adolescent years. His mother, once a world-renowned concert pianist, continued to work by teaching at the local university and to children in the neighborhood, but it didn't pay all that much. Still, they managed to keep the cottage in Norway, and when his mother retired and moved back she was able to purchase a small house with assistance from Dorian. By then, his focus was on his work, which consumed much of his personal time and prevented him from forming any relationships.

# Seven

IF THE FLOWERS AND BALLOON WEREN'T enough to send Aki over the edge, the revelation that Yuki was going to Europe with Dorian certainly did. After the two sisters had argued for some time Aki closed herself in her room to sulk while Yuki and Dorian carried the bags to the car.

"You have your passport, right?"

"Yes, sir. It's getting quite full. Might need another one soon, depending where we go next," she laughed.

They stopped at a local grocer to pick up a few supplies and headed towards his house. Making a quick glance in the rear-view mirror he noticed a white van with several occupants was following him. The roads were far too icy for him to attempt any evasive maneuvers. Yuki noticed his serious expression as he silently looked in the rear-view mirror.

"Is something wrong?"

"Well," was all he managed to say before she checked to see what was holding his attention.

"The white van! That's the one that was following me before. Do you know who they are?" she asked in a panic.

"Not a clue. Don't worry, I have an idea," he said, turning down a road away from where he lived. There was still a bit of daylight out so he decided to head towards a busier section of town. He brought the car to a halt at the side of the road and the white van pulled behind them.

"Stay here," he said. He put the gear in park but kept the engine running.

"What are you doing? Get back here!" she shouted as he got out of the car.

Reaching inside his coat pocket he felt for the handle and trigger of the taser he had on him, just in case things got out of control. As he made his way toward the van he made eye contact with one of the two occupants. One of them was an older woman, most likely in her late sixties or early seventies; the other was a middle-aged man who was at the wheel. They were talking to each other as Dorian approached, almost arguing.

He stood alongside their vehicle and motioned for the driver to roll down the window.

"Hi, there," Dorian said politely. "Is there a reason why you've been following us? Can I help you with something?" He looked inside to see if they were about to use some type of weapon against him.

"Are you Dorian, son of Esma?" the woman asked across the window.

"Esme," he said, correcting her. "How do you know that name? Who are you?"

The older woman and driver both started to speak at the same time. Just as the driver realized his mistake, the older woman smacked him across the chest. "Be silent!" she snapped, giving him a dirty look.

The old woman got out of the van and approached Dorian carefully, as if she had not seen him in many years and was trying to remember his face. Her hair was long and grey, pulled back to expose a birthmark in the shape of a moon on the side of her face, and she wore a long wool coat. Judging from her accent and skin tone she was of middle-eastern descent. The woman walked with a limp over to where Dorian stood waiting on the sidewalk. The driver was thin and homely-looking, balding on top, with a sour expression, as if he was perturbed by the whole affair.

"My name is Mahin Zadeh. I am pleased to meet you," she said, extending her gloved hand toward Dorian. He cautiously shook her hand with a bewildered look.

"That is my useless son Shahin in the van over there. I'm sorry if we frightened you and your woman there. I was not sure how to approach you. I know what I'm going to tell you might sound crazy, but I am what you call a Seer, or what some refer to as a Prophet. I can see the future. It's the truth," she said with a grim expression. "You must be wondering what all this has to do with you?"

Dorian could sense she meant him no harm so he relaxed his guard somewhat. "You might say that, yeah," he replied with a slight smile.

She began to look him over. "Hold out your hands," she said, holding her own out. He held out his hands as she instructed.

"Turn them over for me." He did as she said, wondering what was going on. Yuki observed the scene from the car. She shut off the vehicle and cautiously walked over to see what was going on, keeping a bit of running distance between her and Mahin. Dorian looked over towards Yuki.

"That's fine, she can listen," Mahin said to him.

"Who is she Dorian? What does she want from you?" Yuki asked, looking nervously at Mahin as Dorian flipped his hands around for her.

"She says she's a Seer, right?" he said, looking over at Mahin.

"That's right, young one. I do not mean any harm." She glanced over at Yuki. "Hello, dear. I am Mahin. I am sorry if we frightened you before, I did not mean to. I was explaining to your friend here I had to give him a message. I am sorry to delay you." She turned back to Dorian.

"When I was about twenty-three, that would be right around the time you were born, I had a vision about you." Dorian's eyes widened.

"Do not look so surprised young man; I know you are not as young as you look," she said with a grin. "I was instructed to deliver the message to you from a higher power, so that you would know what to do when the time was right. Now, did you have anything strange happen to you recently?"

Dorian was running out of patience.

"Listen, I think this has gone on long enough. I'm a scientist, okay, I don't want to be rude, I showed you my hands; they're fine, see?" He was holding them up, flipping them around back and forth.

"Show her the back of your head, Dorian," Yuki piped in.

"What is on the back of your head?" Mahin asked. Dorian shook his head.

"Fine, then; have a look at my button. I'll give you fifty bucks if you can take it off without killing me." He turned around and pointed at the back of his head.

"Okay, it's okay," she said trying to calm him. "I think I see what we have here. This was what I was looking for. I saw this object in my vision, you see, but I did not expect it to be there. You have the mark of Hermoni on you. He is one of the fallen. This cannot be removed by my hands. No, mmm, it cannot," she said shaking her head.

"Herman who?" he asked.

"Hermoni. A Grigori. One of the watchers. Did you not receive the message?"

"What message would that be?" he asked.

"I don't know what it said, but it should have a mark that looks like an oval with three wavy lines in the middle and some lines coming of the sides. Do you remember seeing that anywhere?"

He reached for the message in his pocket that had the traced sigil from the email that he received.

Like this?"

"Yes. That is it, that is the one. You are going use that sigil, but you should know that you face much danger ahead. In my vision, I heard a voice and saw a figure standing before me those many years ago, and it frightened me to my bones. The voice was like an ocean and a great many voices all in one; and the being I saw—may God have mercy." She placed her hand over her heart.

Dorian and Yuki stood there listening, mesmerized. For some reason the words Mahin spoke touched his spirit; he could feel a stirring in his heart.

"Her face was the most beautiful and terrifying thing I have ever seen in my life; I cannot describe it with words; it's not possible. Her eyes were like emeralds and lightning, and her hair was like living fire if such a thing could exist. She took my hand in hers, and I felt an amazing sensation, as if I was flying and happier than I could possibly be. I saw her home and the love of her life. She showed me her transgression and her punishment to come and I could hardly bear it. I felt her pain, her sorrow at what happened." Tears began to run down Mahin's face. She had one hand on her mouth and held the other out, waving it back and forth to try and contain her emotions.

"I saw you as a baby and as a young boy, and then I saw you as you are here today, and how you will be in the future from now. Young man, you have no idea how important you will be for us.

"She looked at me and told me this: 'Three notes make the chord; three instruments are required to play. The music is read with the aid of the stand. The mighty ones shall be your reward.' That is all she said to me and then I was back in the world. I was instructed to give you the message in this year and month.

"I'm sorry, but I have no idea what any of that means. How did you find us and why did you follow her?" he asked, while looking over at Yuki, who stood silent.

"My visions," Mahin said, gathering her thoughts, "are difficult to describe. They have a feeling along with a picture, almost like a memory. I knew you would be at the place near the gas station that night, I just didn't know exactly when. We saw the police and decided it would not be a good time to approach you. The spirit left and returned today when we were on the road; I could feel your presence, and I knew it was you. As soon as I saw your face," she said, getting emotional again, "I knew I could finally fulfill her wishes for you."

Her son's eyes widened.

"I've been in a hotel for almost the whole month waiting for her to finish this thing so we could go home. Now, mother, are we done? Can we go now?" he asked impatiently through the driver's side window.

"You do not speak now! We will go when I say we are done; do you understand?"

Shahin gave sour look and rolled up the window.

"Is there anything you wish to ask me?" Mahin asked.

"Well, for starters, how the heck do I get this thing off of me?" Dorian asked, pointing to the mark of Hermoni.

"Go to a quiet place, one where you won't be disturbed. Take the message you have and follow the instructions. They will help you remove it. That is all I can say about that," she replied.

"What is all of this about? Really, what am I? What is going on here? Are we really not alone? Is this some kind of alien takeover of our planet or something?"

"Like War of the Worlds?" Yuki chimed in.

Mahin looked surprised at them. "You really have no idea what is going on? Have you not read the prophecies concerning the end times? It is not surprising there is so much darkness in this world when even the chosen are blind," Mahin said with disdain in her voice.

"Esme, you mentioned her name. How do you know it? What do you know of my mother?"

"She told me that you were the son of Esme. I said it incorrectly before. I don't think I am permitted to say anything else," Mahin replied.

There was a pain in his heart, and the hair on his body stood up as a chill came over him. He had a lost feeling, as if he was in some sort of nightmare, the kind you have when you take an exam and have no idea what you're being asked, or how to answer any questions.

"Mahin, please, I need some answers, what is going on?"

"There is an unseen war going on. Can you not tell by what is happening all over the world? Remember the message I gave you. I waited many years to give it to you. I must leave now. May God be with you." She turned and gave Yuki a slight smile and made her way back to her van and got inside. Dorian looked over at Yuki, who looked back at him in silence. The van started up and drove away, leaving him with more questions than answers.

The two made their way back to his car without saying anything. They sat for a moment in silence, then Dorian started the car. Yuki put her hand on Dorian's. "We will figure this out together," she said with a worried smile. Dorian didn't say much aside from the growls that came from his stomach. Yuki laughed, and he quickly put his hand over the cantankerous organ.

"Well, that's embarrassing. We should be at my house soon, barring any other surprises. I'm looking forward to dinner," he said with a less somber look than he had earlier.

A SHORT WHILE LATER, THEY MADE IT BACK TO his house in Ann Arbor. He parked the Camaro in the driveway and they slowly got out of the car. They cautiously approached the front door, all the while looking about the place for anything out of the ordinary. After checking the house for aliens, they headed inside and set about unpacking the groceries. Afterwards, he showed Yuki the sparse utensils and cooking pots he had that were worth using.

"You haven't taken your coat off, are you cold?" Dorian asked.

"You're not? I see no reason to have a refrigerator running when you could just leave everything sitting out. I doubt anything would spoil."

"All right, all right, I'll turn up the heat so we don't slide on the ice forming on the ground," he replied, laughing out loud.

Yuki began chopping up the vegetables, and after several moments the sounds of frying were coming from the kitchen, along with the delicious aroma of her cooking.

"I'll get a fire going. You need any help in there?" he asked, placing four logs in the fireplace.

"I'm fine. What are you doing?"

"I figured we could eat near the fireplace, so I'm just getting it set up for us." As soon as he said that she began fantasizing instead of paying attention to the task at hand. A few moments later, she realized their dinner was overcooked.

"Is something burning?" he asked.

"Ah, er, no, everything is fine," she said, as she doused the blackened onion and celery with water. She quickly chopped some more and started frying again, reminding herself to be more focused.

"Do you like wine?" he asked.

"That sounds wonderful," she said, doing her best not to get distracted again.

He had finished setting up the wine glasses and place settings by the time Yuki brought the plates into the living room.

"I got this wine as a gift from an old professor I studied under when I won the Nobel. I never opened it, because I didn't have anyone to share it with. Now's the perfect time; I just hope it hasn't gone bad," he said, wiping dust from the bottle. He poured a pair of glasses and they set about their meal.

"Cheers," they said in unison while clanging their glasses together.

"The food looks amazing, Yuki. Thank you, for everything. I'm not sure how I would be able to cope without you in all this," he said. She smiled and glanced into his eyes, then looked away. They finished eating and sat on the couch together to discuss the day's events.

Yuki looked over to the piano in the corner. Getting up, she walked over and sat down on the bench in front of the piano and started playing 'Twinkle Twinkle Little Star'.

"Do you know any good songs?" she asked.

"I just learned this one recently, you might like it." He sat down next to her and began to play Liszt's B Minor Sonata, with exaggerated movements, hamming it up further with an occasional maniacal gesture that made her burst into laughter. Dorian's piano playing skills were quite remarkable, the result of his extraordinary reflexes in addition to the superior training he had received from his mother.

He played several more until it started getting late.

"I am speechless, that was incredible. Why didn't you become a professional pianist?"

"Piano wasn't my destiny. I had too many questions that needed answering and I sacrificed a lot to try and find those answers." He got up from the bench and sat on the worn, tufted brown leather couch near the fireplace. Yuki joined him.

"Um, that message you read to me, what are you going to do with it? Do you think it's a good idea to do what the old woman said?"

"At this point, I can't make heads or tails of anything. The message Mahin gave was obviously coded with my musical upbringing in mind, so whoever came up with it knew of my adoptive mother and her background. 'Three notes make the chord; three instruments are required to play. The music is read with the aid of the stand. The mighty ones shall be your reward.' Nope, I haven't got a clue," he said.

"Well, at least the mystery surrounding the white van was solved. I should have told Mahin she cost you a ticket from the police," Dorian said with a laugh.

"What do you think she meant when the old lady said we were in a war? She mentioned something about a prophecy. Also, that mark on the back of your head, she said it was Amaros or Hermoni, one of those. I will see if there is something on the internet about it," she said. She walked over to her pile of luggage to search for her tablet.

"Good idea, let me know if you find anything useful." He gathered the dishes and brought them to the kitchen while she searched.

"Wait a minute. I remember the name Hermoni when I was at home in Japan. That's the name of the company that took over our company. Didn't you say that they offered you a position there?" she asked.

"Yeah, that's the company, but I somehow doubt this is their way of getting back at me by turning them down. I can't imagine how they could be involved in all of this nonsense. Let's see how deep the rabbit hole goes on this. Keep looking and let me know what you find."

She began pouring over multiple pages, following numerous links to different websites: Biblical, mystical, alien, conspiracy, Free Masonry; the list didn't seem to end.

Sometime later, Dorian joined her on the couch. He quietly sipped from his wineglass and stared into the dying fire. After placing a fresh log on the fire, he began to stoke it with a poker, releasing a concentrated aroma of hickory into the living room.

"Well, what have you found out so far?"

She was still searching, switching between multiple pages at a rapid pace. The silhouette from the backlight of her tablet met with the flickering of the fireplace on her face.

"According to the legend, 'Hermoni' was one of twenty leaders of a group of two hundred fallen Angels or Grigori. That's the word Mahin used, wasn't it?" she asked, looking over at him.

"Yes, I believe she did use that word. Was there anything else?"

"So, from what I discovered on the religious side of things, Hermoni left Heaven and came to Earth with his brothers after making a pact to have relations with human women. It says that he also taught men the 'resolving of enchantments', or how to 'raise spells'. I suppose this would mean magic of some sort, or perhaps science so advanced it would almost seem like magic. I also read that he had some teaching in the making of hallucinogenic and psychedelic drugs. It goes on to say that he was bound and imprisoned with the other leaders of the rebellion.

"Now, as for Hermoni the company, it was founded back in 1948 as an archeological excavation firm with permission granted by the Egyptian government to excavate around the historical sites. They also had underwater salvage companies under them that assisted with preserving and maintaining antiquities. It seems their transition into healthcare was accidental. They opened a tomb of an ancient physician and discovered medical journals that contained very precise methods for obtaining an extremely rare herb thought to be able to heal all ailments. The flower was said to have grown in a valley which they believed to be located in northeast Egypt. There is no explanation beyond that as to why they stayed in healthcare or if they ever discovered this rare flower, or why they have been investing in genetic research over the past twenty years. Also, there were some pages with rumors about who the financial backers of the company originally were; from the descendants of John Dee, to the Illuminati, or the Freemasons or the remnants of the Nazi Party. I'm not sure why so many people think the company is up to no good, given the fact that they mostly purchase other companies that make products to help with disease and illness."

"Since Dantanian is involved with them," he replied, "I'm willing to bet they're not entirely innocent. In fact, I think there's definitely something to whet the appetites of the conspiracy theorists out there. Knowing that they started out digging things up in Egypt, who knows what they found, or what they were looking for. Certainly, there's a plethora of wild theories and such when it comes to ancient Egypt. What can you find out about Dantanian? What's his background?"

"I did some research before I met with him in New York," Yuki said. "There isn't much to say. It seems he had a very private upbringing, and where he currently lives is unknown to the press.

Here is a section from an article written about him: '*His name first surfaced about twenty years ago, when he single-handedly brought a major investment bank to its knees by purchasing billions worth of credit default swaps against banks heavily leverage in real estate. At that time the global economy contracted and the real estate bubble burst, allowing him to reap an enormous windfall. It has never been published how Dantanian obtained the financing for the swaps, nor who may have assisted him. From that point onward, he has remained in the public eye as a financial backer of multiple biotech, excavation and salvage firms.'"*

Dorian checked his watch again. "It's getting late; we should get some sleep. Do you want the spare bedroom or the couch?" he asked.

Yuki set down her tablet, sprawled across the deep couch, and proceeded to wrap herself up with blankets like a tamale.

"I suppose that answers that," he said. He went to the closet and grabbed a spare set of pillows and threw them her way.

"We need to be out of the house by six a.m., so set your alarm. The bathroom is down the hall to your left. I'll be upstairs if you need me. Here's one of my phones, it has a paging function. Press this here and we can talk," he said, demonstrating its use. He handed her the phone she looked at him and smiled like she was home and happy. He held her gaze and smiled back at her.

"Ok, get some sleep," he ordered.

"Yes sir," she replied while mock saluting him. He leaned over and kissed her on her forehead and turned out the light, then made his way upstairs to his bedroom.

# Eight

THE FOLLOWING MORNING DORIAN AWOKE TO the sound of Yuki's alarm on her tablet. Unsurprisingly, it was rabbit-themed, complete with dancing and singing bunnies on the screen.

They quickly dressed, grabbed their baggage and left to catch their flights. It didn't take long to arrive and soon afterwards they were in the security line.

Everything seemed to be going smoothly until the security screeners at the airport detected the object embedded in his head. Dorian managed to make up a convincing story from something he'd read about implantable devices for Parkinson's disease, allowing him to pass through without incident.

It was going to be a long day of traveling for the pair; Yuki decided to use the time to try and find out more about the characters involved and solve some of the mystery.

"Take a look at this," she said, showing her computer to Dorian. It was a picture of the same image found on the object that was attached to his skull. "It's the sigil for Hermoni, one of the fallen, no mistake."

"Who were these watchers?" he asked.

"I told you before, they were these Angels who came here and did some pretty bad things. They had children with humans that supposedly became giants. There is also mention of these beings called the Nephilim, although it's not exactly clear who they were; some documents say they were the Watchers themselves, some state they were their progeny."

"Ok, so far we have a billionaire mystery man who wants my blood; a pair of angel/watcher/alien types who put something on the back of my head with a sigil of this Hermoni guy who is another of their kind, possibly imprisoned somewhere; an old Caribbean lady who pops up to give me this cryptic message saying something about me being important to her cause, whatever that is, and some vague Biblical references. Oh, and let's not forget the bizarre email message I got from the mystery group with a bunch of hocus-pocus nonsense intermixed. What's next? Obi Wan is going to materialize and tell me that I need to find Yoda?"

"Relax," she said. "Remember Occam's razor. Right now, we can assume for the sake of argument that these beings are real. We know that Mahin lady wasn't hostile and obviously had an important message she had been holding onto for a long time. We also have the unknown helper from Hawaii who destroyed the sample and prevented that Dantanian man from getting it. Clearly, your blood has some significance to this 'war' that Miss Mahin was speaking of. It may be somewhat safe to assume the ones who sent the email are not partners with Dantanian, but it could be a trick. I think we should concentrate on looking at what we can understand about your genetic makeup."

"I've been going over the data and let me tell you it's going to take some time. When we get to the cabin we'll split up the work to try and sort it all out," he said, rubbing the back of his neck where the object was embedded.

THEY LANDED IN AMSTERDAM AND TOOK THEIR connecting flight to Bergen. It was almost midnight before they got their rental car. It took some time for Dorian to adjust to driving on the Norwegian roads, especially in the dark, but he managed to acclimate quickly.

"It's been about ten years since I've come home, and it's still awesome. I miss the mountains, the water. Every time I come back I want to stay. Colorado was the closest thing I had to this, growing up, but there is no comparison; Norway is far more beautiful," he said, taking a deep breath, as if he was trying to absorb the essence of the land and become one with it. Yuki was silent at this point and feigned attention, but in actuality she was starting to go in and out of sleep.

He pulled off the side of the road to get out and admire the silhouette of the aurora borealis reflecting off the waters in the fjords down below. Looking back to the car, he noticed Yuki fast asleep, so he enjoyed the quiet moment by himself. No doubt his mother was up at this hour, waiting with bated breath for him to arrive, so he didn't tarry too long. Her house wasn't far from the airport, located in the settlement of Starefossen, overlooking Bergen to the west, way up on the mountainside.

Even though they spoke regularly on the phone and several times through videoconferencing, he was very excited to see his mother for the first time in almost six years. Pulling up in the drive, he felt ashamed for waiting so long to come home, especially considering he didn't just come here to see his mother; his primary reason for visiting was to find a quiet place where he could conduct some research and hopefully not be noticed or bothered by Angels, demons, leprechauns and the like.

A light was on in the living room, and he could see his mother peering through the curtains to see if it was her son who was outside the house. Dorian gently shook Yuki awake and proceeded to pull out some of their luggage and bring it to the threshold. The front door opened and his mother stood at the doorway, beaming as she saw her son in the flesh.

"*Hvordan har du det,* my darling?" she said in a quiet tone so as not to disturb the neighbors.

"Mom, it's so good to see you," he said embracing her barely five-foot slender frame with a long hug. His mother was seventy-four years old and looked to be about sixty, with long, golden and silvery hair pulled up on top of her head and wearing a thick, navy-blue sweater and grey stretch pants.

Yuki extended her hand. "Hello, Mrs. Lystad, I'm Yuki."

"What's this hand stuff? Come here," his mother replied, extending both her arms and embracing Yuki. Yuki smiled and patted his mother on the back, looking slightly uncomfortable.

"Call me Iduna, my students call me Mrs. Lystad," his mother said.

The aroma of freshly baked pastries hit them through the vestibule, along with the scent of air freshener.

"Come in, come in. How was your flight? Are you hungry? I have plenty to eat, here," she said as she quickly made her way back to the kitchen counter, producing a plate of cakes.

"Have a hjortbakkel. Would you like?" she asked, gesturing over to Yuki.

"We're fine, mamma. We need to get some sleep; it's been a long day. Do you have the guest room prepared? What am I thinking, of course you have everything ready," he said, knowing how attentive his mother was. He put his arm around her and she wrapped hers around his waist.

"I've missed you so much. I'm so happy to have you home," she said as tears fell from her eyes.

"Mom, shhhh, don't cry," he said, hugging and rubbing her back. Dorian looked over to Yuki with a 'Sorry about that' look on his face. Yuki looked like she was going to burst into tears herself.

"Ok, let's cheer up," he said, then kissed his mother on the forehead.

"I'm going to get the rest of the bags. Mom, can you show Yuki to the guest bedroom?"

Iduna finished wiping her tears and grabbed one of Yuki's bags. "Right this way, my dear," his mother said, gesturing to the hallway on the left. Dorian returned with two more bags and closed the door behind him. There was slight murmur coming from the hallway followed by the sound of the guest room door closing. Iduna came through the hallway with a happy look on her face.

"She's beautiful, and very polite. Oh, you look tired. Here, I have your room ready; we can talk in the morning. There is an extra blanket on the bed and fresh towels in the closet where we always keep them," she said quietly.

He took a suitcase with him and made his way to his old room that he used when he visited. The familiar smell, along with the sight of some of his belongings that his mother refused to give away, brought back distant memories. Right now, he was too tired to reminisce about the past.

"Good night, I'll see you in the morning, love you," he said, slowly closing the door.

"Good night, my dear," she replied in a chirpy tone.

That night he had a terrible nightmare about alien-looking beings who were contorted and vicious, furiously pounding on some type of barrier. They were in a cavernous dwelling, screaming demands to be released. One of them looked at Dorian and pointed.

"You, you're the one who did this! We are going to tear you to pieces!"

He awoke in a sweat, just as the monsters were upon him.

A murmured conversation was taking place in the background coming from the kitchen. The sounds and smells of cooking permeated the air. His head was in a fog, as if he'd been drugged. The object on his neck felt very painful to the touch and was ice cold. He rubbed his face and looked around the bedroom. The few hours of daylight Norway received during winter peeked through the curtains, inviting him to take in the view. Obliging the window's request, he opened the curtains enough to see the sun shining off of the white snow that garnished the rooftops. The view of the city below was as spectacular as he remembered it.

After taking in the scenery for a bit, he formulated a plan for the day, deciding it would be rude for him to just take off for the cabin without spending some time with his mother. The weekend would be hers, and on Monday he and Yuki would depart. After putting on some clothes, he made his way into the kitchen where Yuki and his mother were enjoying a cup of tea along with their breakfast.

"Good morning, everyone," he said, smiling

"Here we say 'God Morgen' for good morning," Iduna said, looking over to Yuki.

"We say 'Ohayou' in Japan," Yuki replied.

"I see; ohhiyo. Oh-hi-yo," Iduna said, repeating it several more times.

"I was wondering when you were going to join us sleepyhead," his mother said with a wink. A startled look came over her face. "Whoa, what is—"

"Everybody outside! Move!" Dorian shouted as the house began shaking.

Glasses were clanking together and several pictures on the wall fell down, along with a few of the ornaments on Iduna's Christmas tree. The three ran outside where several of the neighbors had already gathered, standing in the street and looking bewildered. The shaking lasted for about a minute and then stopped. Smoke was rising from the city in a few spots, but no buildings seemed to be destroyed. Sirens began blaring all around and most of the neighbors on the block were gathering together to discuss the earthquake they had just experienced. Dorian, Yuki, and Iduna stood outside for a few more minutes and then ventured back in when it seemed they could not tolerate the cold any longer in their pajamas.

The house was in minor disarray, so they began to put everything back in its place and straighten up.

"We've been getting a lot of tremors lately. I hope this settles down soon," his mother said.

"That was way more than a tremor, mom; it was about a minute long. Turn on the television; I want to see what's going on," he said.

Iduna turned on the local news channel that was displaying an emergency alert for all of Norway. Pictures of the fires in Oslo, as well as demolished buildings and emergency vehicles scrambling to and fro filled the screen, switching back and forth.

"It looks like it hit Oslo pretty bad. Eight point seven! They're saying it was an eight point seven about ten kilometers east of Oslo," he said, astonished. His mother had both of her hands on her checks in disbelief.

"I've got to call Berjit and Nada," Iduna said, reaching for the telephone. Dorian stood still looking at the television as Yuki started picking up some of the books from the bookshelf that had fallen over. The house did not seem to have suffered any apparent structural damage, just a bit to the contents that had been tossed around inside.

"Here, let me help," he said, bending down to assist.

"She's not answering. There's no answer," Iduna said, dialing again. Yuki looked over to a picture that had fallen off the wall.

"Was this your father?" It was a picture of his mother, father and himself in front of a mountain waterfall.

"Yeah, that was a good day for us. We were visiting family in Sweden and took a day to hike a trail. It wasn't long after that my father started showing symptoms. Unfortunately, he passed away a few years later when I turned seventeen. He was one of the reasons I entered into the profession myself. He was a good man; very patient, caring. I miss him very much."

Iduna walked over to him, clutching the phone in her hand.

"I miss him as well," she said, putting her arm on Dorian's shoulder. She looked over to Yuki. "When Jorn passed, my world was shattered. I had a house in Colorado that wasn't paid off, two mouths to feed, medical bills and funeral expenses. His life insurance did not pay a whole lot, and poor Dorian had to work several jobs so we could make ends meet. I was concert pianist, but by then I was unable to perform to that level after going through the ordeal of Jorn's passing. I still managed to teach though," she said looking over at the piano taking up most of her living room. Several framed photographs taken from afar of with her performing solo at large concert venues adorned the walls.

"I should try calling Nada again," Iduna said with a sad look on her face. Dorian went to the kitchen and cleaned up the few things that had fallen and fixed himself a sandwich.

"I'm going to hop in the shower before the world comes to an end. Do you need to take one?" he asked.

"I already did while you were sleeping. What are we going to do today?"

"I was hoping we could spend the day in Bergen, see the sights, eat at a restaurant or two, but after this, I'm not so sure," he replied as he walked into the bathroom.

After washing up, he joined his mother and Yuki in the living room. They were having a conversation while watching the news on television.

"Dorian, look at the television. Downtown Oslo is in ruins. I haven't been able to reach my cousin, nor any of my friends," his mother said in a worried voice.

"There's nothing to be gained from panic. I think we should all head to the cabin in case there are aftershocks or another big one. It doesn't seem to have affected the area near Sognefjord," Dorian said.

"I'll pack us something to eat. You get your things and we can leave together," Iduna said, somewhat shaken by the day's events.

THEY PILED INTO THE CAR AND HEADED ABOUT eighty miles northeast to their cabin, which was nestled at the bottom of a fjord that ran alongside several mountains. The cabin itself was a small three-bedroom cottage about sixty years old. His father had purchased it just after Dorian arrived so they would have a special place to enjoy memories. There was a swinging bench in the back that hung from a tree which overlooked the water. Iduna would often sit there while reading a book or having a cup of tea in the summer. In the midst of winter, it wasn't a place you wanted to be for long before you froze to death. They spent many summers there fishing, skiing, and making friends whom they had lost touch with through the sands of time.

The surrounding scenery was breathtaking, and Yuki was taken aback by its beauty. The cabin had been vacant for some time, so it required a bit of cleaning up and dusting. The three of them traveled into town to pick up some new bed sheets and blankets, along with cleaning supplies and toiletries. Upon their return, they ate lunch and Dorian went out back to gather some old firewood that was piled up behind the cottage and got a fire going. It was getting dark out due to the shortened span of daylight during wintertime, so Yuki and Dorian decided to try and get down to deciphering the data that was compiled from his genome and how it compared to normal human DNA.

"I know this may sound strange, but I've had some unusual dreams and visions involving the seventh, fourteenth, and twenty first chromosomes. It's as if someone or something is trying to tell me something, so I think we should start there," he said.

"I'll take the seventh, you can look at the fourteenth," she replied.

They sat next to one another on the sofa and worked while Iduna watched a news program on the television in the spare room.

He copied the data from his chromosome and sent it to Yuki's computer. They both spent the next four hours in silence, poring over the information. It was getting late, so he checked up on Iduna, who had fallen asleep in her chair with the television on.

"Mamma, wake up, you don't want to be up all night," he said, gently shaking her. She rubbed her eyes and yawned.

"Oh, how long was I out?" she asked, as she stretched a bit and got out of her chair.

"It's about nine. Come. Let's all have some dinner," he said softly, as if they were in a library.

DINNER CAME AND WENT AND HIS MOTHER asked what they were working on. Yuki looked at Dorian, waiting for him to come up with an answer so she wouldn't have to lie to his mother.

"Were trying to find out what is in my blood that makes me different and why some people would be after it," he answered, to Yuki's dismay. His mother sort of snapped to attention with a shocked look on her face.

"It's okay, she knows about it," he said, looking at both his mother and Yuki. "I suppose that statement applies to the two of you. Of course my mother knows about me being different, but she obviously doesn't know about the recent events we've experienced," he said to Yuki.

"Mamma, don't worry. I trust Yuki; she's one of the few people I know that can help me sort through all this and make sense out of it," he said with a smile, as he looked at Yuki.

"Arigato," she said, with a humbled expression.

Iduna, however, did not have a peaceful look on her face.

"Are you going to tell me what you are talking about?" she asked, sounding short of breath.

He spent the next half hour explaining all the events that had occurred over the past several weeks and showed her the object fused to his skull. His mother's expression turned dour, as if she could scarcely believe what she had heard. Suddenly Iduna's eyes widened.

"Oh....I completely forgot about it until now. This must be what she was talking about. I think it's time, then," Iduna said to him.

"Time for what?" Dorian asked.

Iduna got up and went to the bedroom she was staying in.

"It is a good thing we came to the cabin. I had forgotten I left it here," she said, her voice muffled. The sounds of shuffling and furniture being dragged were heard coming from her bedroom. Several minutes later, she returned with what looked like a piece of metal in her hand, about the same thickness as a credit card, in the shape of a heptagon. It was a bit bigger than a standard postcard and shimmered with a translucence similar to the garment worn by the alien that he had seen in Hawaii. She scrunched it up in front of them, then set it on the table and it returned to its natural shape.

"What is it?" Dorian and Yuki asked in unison.

"I have no idea. I had forgotten about it all these years. I left it in the cottage a long time ago when we first started coming here. She just told me to give it to you when the time was right, that I would know when. At first I carried it around everywhere we went, thinking something was going to happen, but nothing ever came of it, so I stored it away and completely forgot about it until now. I always knew you were special Dorian; I knew from the moment she gave you to me," Iduna said, looking uncomfortable.

"Umm, mamma, who are you referring to? Who told you to give this to me? Are you telling me the representative from the adoption agency here in Norway gave you this alien-like object and handed me over with some cryptic message about knowing when the time was right? Or is there something you haven't told me?"

"You were not brought to us from an adoption agency Dorian."

"What? What are you talking about?" Dorian asked.

"Your father and I decided it would be best not to tell you, out of fear you would leave us or say something to the wrong people and end up like one of those lab rats," she said with a look of shame on her face.

"I thought that all you knew about my biological mother was her name. What are you saying? That she dropped me off?" he asked in disbelief.

"I don't know if it was your birth mother, dear. The person who handed you to me was not like anyone here on this planet that I have ever seen," she said, lowering her voice. "She was much like the one you described earlier; a head full of fire, almost alive, but no heat. Her eyes were terrible and powerful; radiant. I cannot put it into words. We thought she was an angel. The sound of her voice was comforting, as if many were speaking at the same time in harmony. Somehow, she knew I wanted a child, but was unable to conceive. She said that she had watched me for many years, and that I would be a good mother for you. Your father was there also; otherwise I think he never would have believed such a crazy story. We were both petrified. She handed me this object and told me to give it to you when the time was right."

Dorian and Yuki looked at each other in bewilderment.

"We had no idea what you were going to be like, you know, like Superman or something," Iduna said with a laugh. "It almost seemed like that story. You are not that different from the rest of us; perhaps a bit stronger and faster. Well, that and of course your hair and those eyes of yours. You still look the same after all these years. Honestly, I'm just grateful you didn't have a tail, or could disappear. Who knows what mischief you would have gotten into then huh?" she said smiling.

"Your eyes?" Yuki asked.

"Custom full eye contacts. Worn them since I was a child. Not that I need them to see, but you can imagine what someone might say if they saw this," he said, pulling the lens away from one eye to reveal its glowing green color, which almost appeared to be illuminated from within. Yuki just put her hand to her mouth in amazement.

Iduna continued, "Anyway, this belongs to you." She placed the object on the table. "It doesn't appear to do anything apart from returning to shape when you crush it," she said, once again demonstrating its remarkable ability.

Dorian slowly brought his hand over the object and picked it up.

"Aaaaagh!" he shrieked with a terror-stricken face.

Yuki and Iduna were stunned.

"Just kidding," he said with a devilish smile.

"Oh, you! I'm going to give you a big hurt for that," Iduna said, reaching for the wet dishrag on the sink and hurling it at him.

"Whaaaat?" he asked, in mock protest. "Lighten up, everyone, sheesh." He focused his attention on the object once more. Holding it in his hand he began to see faint symbols light up on the object.

"There's definitely something there, can you see it?" he asked holding it up for them

"I see nothing there, dear, where?" Iduna asked.

"Right here," he said pointing to the symbols on the object.

"I don't see anything either," Yuki said, straining her eyes to see what was there.

"What does it say?" she asked.

"In the common tongue it reads 'One ring to rule them all, one ring to find them, one ring to bring them all and in the darkness bind them', he said, smiling again.

"Can you take this seriously for once?" his mother said, her patience wearing thin.

"Okay, okay. It just reminds me of that, the way the symbols light up on this thing when I hold on to it. I can see dots along one of the edges in groups, and the next edge has symbols. On the next edge are other symbols that are different. Each edge has a different set of symbols. Below the set of dots are more dots, different in number; then to the right below the first set of symbols are different symbols but similar in their manner, and so on. Yuki, do you have any paper? I'll copy them down."

She handed him some paper from her calendar and he started to trace the symbols as they appeared on the object. He flipped it over and found more dots, symbols and such like those on the front. After about four hours he managed to finish writing everything down.

It was getting late and he was tired from the day's events, coupled with the jet lag, so they all said goodnight to get some rest.

THAT NIGHT HE HAD ANOTHER NIGHTMARE which was more real than the last one. Once again, he saw the same beings trapped or imprisoned in a cavern. It was as if he was being forced to watch their suffering and suffer with them. He awoke to Yuki shaking him. "Get up, sleepy head, we have work to do," she said, pressing down on the mattress and generally annoying him.

"What time is it?" he asked, rubbing the back of his neck where the ice-cold imbedded object was.

"It's almost noon. We've been up, ate breakfast, talked and walked. I thought you were going to sleep the day away," she said, looking frustrated at him.

"I can't help it, Yuki. Whatever this thing is on the back of my head, it seems to have an effect when I sleep. I saw these beings howling and shouting at me, mixed with this terrible feeling of dread and gloom. It's been getting worse each day. I don't think I can take much more of this. I'm going to have to try and get this thing off somehow."

She put her hand on the back of his neck where his hand was and touched the object.

"Ow! It's freezing cold. How can you stand it?"

"Believe me, it's very painful. There's something going on here, I wish I knew what," he replied. He went into the bathroom to warm up some water and soaked a washcloth in it, using it to heat up the object on his neck. It seemed to help lessen the pain a bit, so he continued by taking a shower until all the hot water was used up.

"What are we going to do today?" Yuki asked through the bathroom door once the water stopped running.

"I need you to try and scan a copy of what I wrote down last night so I can email it," he said.

"Who are going to send it to?" Iduna asked in place of Yuki.

He opened the door wearing a towel around his waist as steam poured out of the bathroom.

"I'm going to send it to the linguistics department at the University of Cambridge and see if any of the symbols represent any known languages. We don't have a scanner here in the cottage so you and mom may have to go into town," he said.

"What are you going to do?" Yuki asked, feeling left out.

"I've got to try and get this thing off of me. Mahin mentioned the people behind the strange email might be able to help. If that doesn't work—well, I'm going to saw the damn thing off."

Iduna walked over to him and gave him a hug. "I hope you know what you are doing, dear."

"I don't have a clue, but I have to try something. Yuki, could you come here for a moment?" he asked, still wearing nothing but a towel. She felt heat rise in her face and followed him inside the room. He closed the door behind them. Water droplets were beaded on his muscular chest.

"If anything happens to me I want you to promise that you'll leave this all alone and go back to the University. I don't want your life getting ruined for no reason. You have my permission to use my blood to research whatever it is you want, just don't go looking into my longevity. Believe me, it would end up being far more trouble than it's worth."

"Hai," was all she could say.

"One more thing," he said, drawing her body close for a passionate kiss. She held him in her arms and pulled closer, absorbing every ounce of the moment. He ended with a smile and gently brushed aside her hair from her face. She smiled in return, feeling somewhat dizzy from the whole event.

He opened the door to the room. "Mamma, take Yuki out so she can try and get this paper scanned. Have some lunch while you are at it." He felt it was best for them not to be there for what he was about to do, in the event that something went wrong.

# Nine

SHORTLY AFTER YUKI AND HIS MOTHER LEFT, Dorian finished dressing and closed the door to his room. After retrieving the email he had jotted down back in his office, he sat down on the bed and looked it over.

"I can't believe I'm going to follow this nonsense," he said, letting out a sigh. "Ok. It says to trace my hand like this and say 'PETA BABKAMA LURUBA ANAKU?'"

As soon as the words left his lips the objects in the room stretched, and he felt a tremendous rush of force pulling him through what looked like a tunnel in space. It did not appear to be outer space in the way that he was familiar with; this was altogether different. It was as if he was riding along a river or stream of consciousness that ebbed and flowed with thought, memory, and understanding.

With a thunderclap, he arrived at his destination, quite disoriented, yet feeling incredibly alive. It was like being awakened from a very long slumber; everything was more real here than in the world from which he had come. There was an inner peace he had never experienced before, along with a feeling of weightlessness.

Above was what looked like a view from an otherworldly planetarium, somewhat similar to the outer space he was familiar with. Colorful lights flashed and flickered across the expanse, their silhouettes resembling some of the Hubble Telescope images of gaseous clouds he had seen in the past. Below, on the ground (if you could even call it that) was a solid surface, flat, shimmering with different colors and adorned with symbols and markings along a routed pathway. Several towers, each about the height of a standard skyscraper, loomed in the distance. There were no plants, trees, birds, animals or insects of any kind.

Before him stood a tall figure, roughly fourteen feet in height with a body glowing like molten metal, dressed in a white robe. He appeared humanoid and male; his face was somewhat androgynous, with snow-white hair and deep blue eyes that had what appeared to be lightning flashing inside of them. In the distance Dorian could discern the shapes of other beings similar to the one before him.

"Welcome, Dorian, welcome. I see that you have chosen to come here out of necessity, as it appears you have been afflicted. We shall address that later. I am known as Amprodias, the guardian of the eleventh gate, from which you traveled to be here with us. I sense that you have many questions, so I will indulge your desire for knowledge. What would you wish to know?"

Dorian was in a state of shock and awe from the sensations he was experiencing and the sights around him. Indeed, even his own visage had changed, as evidenced by the reflection from the shimmering surface below. His hands were translucent, unlike those of the stranger before him, and his eyes seemed to be like those of a marble statue, devoid of life. His hair was similar to his Earthly hair, just translucent. He stood approximately eleven feet in height, floating above the surface below. The clothing he had on in Norway was reproduced in a silhouette that resembled a negative photograph.

"Yes, your appearance," Amprodias said. "What you are looking at is your Baltu spirit form; different from that of a human and one of the two spirit forms ones such as we possess, the other being the Melammu form." He stared at Dorian for a moment and muttered softly, "Yours would undoubtedly be very unique, given your heritage. You will have to wait until your Shi is awakened before you can progress towards your higher form."

Dorian's eyes opened wider. "Am I dead? Is this the afterlife?"

Amprodias smiled, "No, your flesh remains intact. I have placed a protective spell around you for the time being, as a result of the Shemzol."

Dorian looked puzzled. "Shemzol? I seem to recall hearing that word somewhere. What exactly is it?" he asked.

"A Shemzol is a device used to follow energies in both spirit and flesh form. It may be something small that joins *to* the flesh and *with* the spirit. It is a sigil marked upon the light form. In your particular case, I will leave it for another to explain."

"I think I understand. It's that object that is on the back of my neck," Dorian said. To his surprise, he discovered the object was nowhere to be found on his head.

"Where are we? How did I get here? What is going on?"

Amprodius smiled. "We are in another dimension of reality; you traveled through a black hole in space to get here. The area about and outside of us belongs to what you may refer to as a fourth dimension, which as you can observe has meaning and significance here, but is impossible to equate to the world in which you are accustomed to.

"This plain on which we stand is known as Verdes Seventeen, and is known by this sigil," he said. He gestured with his hand at the surface below, and an enormous pattern that looked like three intersecting triangles placed at their ends within several concentric circles in a turning pattern brightly emerged on the ground.

"You arrived here via an opening in a space time continuum, created via a spin-wave-controlled neutron tunnel. The tunnel was sealed to your voice pitch frequency and a semi rough approximation of your hand gesture in the shape of a circle with three wavy lines. In other words, when you said the phrase and motioned in the way that you did, a gateway was opened and attached to your spirit, your light being, much like a lock and key. In this plane, you and I are composed of dense particles of light that are tangible matter. Ah, I see he approaches. I will turn you over to Matthias for further instruction."

Amprodias nodded towards Dorian before turning to depart. In the far distance a figure was approaching rapidly. It was difficult for Dorian to determine how far away the figure was, but it was moving at tremendous velocity. Dorian was still captivated by the amazing surroundings and his sense of heightened perception. He could feel the surface below without touching it and it was as if every molecule around him was sharing information in some unique way. Breathing was not required, yet he noticed his light form still possessed a nose; for what purpose, he could not ascertain. Perhaps it was involved in the extra-sensory perception he was experiencing.

"The fourth dimension is an amazing thing is it not?" the figure approaching asked.

"Hello there," Dorian said with a small wave. What is this place?"

"It would be rude of me if I didn't introduce myself first. Greetings to you, I am Matthias," the being standing before him said. His appearance was similar to Dorian's with a few minor differences. Of note, he had a slightly shorter stature, about nine or so feet in height. His general countenance was similar to that of an ordinary human with regular hair and clothing, but with a translucence to his whole being. He extended his hand in a familiar way of greeting on Earth. Dorian took his hand and information was shared between them. Matthias presented a sensation of goodwill towards him.

"Yes, it is quite different from a normal handshake. I recall the first time I came here, also; I was very much like you, totally taken in by the whole experience. The reality of Earth just doesn't seem to compare in any meaningful way. Don't misunderstand me; the Earth certainly has some beautiful places; however, the fourth dimension adds many different elements not found there. Come, we have much to discuss," he said gesturing as he began to move towards one of the towers in the distance. Dorian attempted to follow by walking as he would on Earth, which felt like he was walking in place.

"I don't seem to be moving," he said with a laugh.

"This is your first lesson, how to walk. You need to imagine your being advancing and will it to be so. Slowly."

Dorian began to focus on willing his body to move; however, the instinct to move his legs was still present, resulting in him float-walking.

"Well, it may look awkward, but you're moving. You do not need to move your legs," Matthias said, observing Dorian struggling with his movement. "You'll learn to control it. Anyway, as Amprodias indicated, this space we are in is Verdes Seventeen. The best way for me to describe it that makes sense to you would be to say it is like an airport that consists of various facilities for conferences, a sort of exposition center where beings gather. There are thousands of such places in this dimension, and each one is different from the other in various ways. This particular breece, as we call it, is specially designed for training light beings in their use of Shi. It is an ancient word meaning or referring to the soul, similar to Chi, or Chakra, words you may have heard before on Earth. For now, we don't need to give it much attention; suffice it to say that we train our spirit energy here," he said, as Dorian was trying to keep up with Matthias.

"The fourth dimension is connected to the third dimension via Pilsu, or what you would call a black hole."

At that moment, a group of about seven beings, very thin and tall with elongated heads, were passing by. They were unlike Matthias or Dorian in that they seemed to be composed of something resembling solid matter. Dorian was startled by their appearance. Matthias uttered something in a strange language to the beings that were fixing their attention on the one staring at them. Whatever it was Matthias said, they went back to communicating amongst themselves.

"You will see many types of beings here as these facilities are for more than just ones such as us. In truth, you happen to be considerably different from me. In fact, I would say you are one-of-a kind, but I don't want to get ahead of myself."

Dorian was bursting with questions, overwhelmed by his newfound sensory stimulus almost to the point of having a panic attack. Matthias touched his arm and Dorian calmed down a bit.

"Be at ease, we will address all of your questions in time."

Dorian felt better at his touch and was surprised that someone else shared his ability. Matthias noticed his astonished look.

"You took my hand earlier, we exchanged information and I could sense your Shi fluctuating towards dalhu, which prompted me to draw off and release a portion to maintain a balance," Matthias said with a smile.

"Oh, is that all?" Dorian asked.

Matthias chuckled. "Patience, my friend. We will allay your concerns."

"Are you the one that we saw in Hawaii who—," Dorian began.

"No, that was not I. You are referring to another whom you will undoubtedly meet. We will head to the Pessipone. There we can discuss additional details in private. Come, let's see if you can gather some speed," he said, moving far ahead of Dorian.

It took a bit of concentration on Dorian's part, but once he could command his spirit form to move he was able to catch up and keep pace with Matthias.

They approached a very large tower that appeared to be constructed of many different types of materials and construction styles. Some parts resembled a modern skyscraper with glass, and other parts were very alien in appearance; liquid metallic surfaces with unusual symbols everywhere. Beings of various types were coming and going in a constant steady stream. It seemed that the effect of gravity was not the same as it was on Earth, so that they simply floated along the surface of the side of the tower effortlessly.

Matthias reached his desired location and said a few words, motioning with his hand in a pattern not unlike the one Dorian had been required to use to get to his present location. The surface of the tower began to glow brightly with a bluish light, and suddenly they were in a large open space with a blue sky, similar to the one found on Earth. Several familiar-looking trees were embedded into sectioned areas of soil. The ground was similar to the area they had just left, appearing almost plastic with a pearl-like translucent sheen. Towards the back of the room were four expansive sitting areas that resembled something you would find in a well-to-do lodge or clubhouse, as well as a large pit that had several steps leading down to the lower level, as if it were an area for a speaker or for demonstrations. The whole area was slightly larger than a modern-day earth-built stadium for a sports team. Matthias moved to the back and settled in one of the sitting areas. He gestured for Dorian to sit opposite him.

"Now we will talk for a while. You have many questions and I think this has been quite an ordeal for you, so we should start at the very beginning. Why are you here? I should explain some basic things first, and then we will address that question. You are different from the normal humans on Earth; undoubtedly you are aware of that fact, correct?"

Dorian nodded.

"It would seem you are still unaware of your heritage, however. Since you have made it here, I believe my convincing you will be a bit easier than if we were on Earth. You are the result of a union between a Dumuzi, that is a son who is life, and an Anunnaki or *Angel* as they are known on Earth."

Dorian's eyes narrowed. Matthias continued speaking.

"The Dumuzi were the progeny of Celestial Spirits and human females and are of Earth, immaculately conceived, whereas the Angels are not of Earth and are not a hybrid race. From the beginning of time itself, the Angels have overseen the inhabitants of countless planets and galaxies formed ages ago by The Creator, The Ancient of Days. Benevolent in nature, they were created with a purpose and a higher function than any other being in all the cosmos. It was this way up until almost ten thousand years ago, when the unthinkable occurred. One of their kind, The Bringer of Light, conceived a plan to overthrow the Ancient of Days and set up his throne above all. He did not wish to be subservient to mankind; he desired their adoration and worship. You may have heard this account from various religious texts found on Earth. A great war was fought, leading to his expulsion from the upper dimensions, along with many of his followers. This was the largest of several insurrections that changed the course of human history.

"Humans, as they exist on Earth, are avatars: flesh forms that house their true selves, their spirits. Human spirits are immortal, everlasting entities; some created from the beginning of the universe, some after, and others currently coming into existence. Each of them has a bit of The Creator inside them, The Source of everything; yet they still are in their infancy, even the ones created from the beginning of time. They are all inextricably connected to each other in a spiritual web or fabric, yet while they wear their human avatars the majority of them are unaware of this fact. In the spiritual dimension, there is no hatred, anger, jealousy, or malice. There are no negative emotions, and so a separate dimension, the physical dimension, was created containing countless galaxies and worlds for all of the spiritual beings to grow and develop; a school for spiritual growth where one could experience both positive and negative emotions. The Earth school is just one of many like it.

"As the Earth had been formed many years prior to the arrival of humans, it served as a proper test environment for human life, with lower human life forms thriving in many areas. Different beings across different galaxies have been made to allow for different amounts of spiritual growth; some beings have much higher growth and development and therefore they have been reborn into bodies capable of expanding their potential.

"A proper analogy would be the sport of racing. One who is a complete novice might begin with the most basic devices for locomotion, perhaps a skateboard or a bicycle, eventually moving to a motorized kart. From there perhaps they get a faster kart, then an automobile. When their skills have progressed over time with the automobile they may attempt a beginner race car, gradually moving up in speed and complexity. It is the same with spirits and avatars: As they advance in development they reincarnate into higher life forms.

"Yes, all sentient beings re-incarnate. It is an integral and fundamental component of existence. The human spirit has to undergo sufficient trial and tribulations to give it strength, much the way human athletes use weights to strengthen their muscles; so it is with the soul. For some, they are born and live for a time to give sufficient strength to others, as a gift to bring them towards the light. This is decided beforehand; the spirit that is strong may be born again to help train the spirit forms of others.

Some who pass before their spirit has been trained will undergo a rebirthing to give them an opportunity to advance towards the light. Also, a spirit in need of further training may be re-born with a new set of difficulties, such as a disease or birth defect to strengthen and help them achieve the light.

"To assist them along the way, humans have spirit guides assigned to them. These are what some refer to as Angels, performing functions similar to what is done for other sentient beings. The spirit guides help humans with their tribulations in a variety of ways; they can bring their petitions to higher powers of the Angels, they can prevent a mishap from occurring, and they can assist with fending off many of the corrupted spirits inhabiting the Earth."

"Evil spirits? Really?" Dorian asked incredulously.

"I shall explain," Matthias said. "When a human being dies their spirit travels through the light gate to one of the planes of Heaven for a determination, or judgment. If they have a sufficient vibration, a positive energy trait, they may stay or be re-birthed to help other human spirits attain a higher vibration state. Once re-born, their memory of any previous life is removed, but their life begins with a stronger spirit. Just as there have been some terrible humans among Earth's inhabitants, so too have there been great ones.

"If a human spirit is found to be towards darkness or a lower vibration they may be given another re-birthing to strengthen it. If they have been corrupted beyond a human re-birthing they may be sent back as a lower life form for more basic spiritual growth. In some cases, they are sent to the place the fallen Angels inhabit as their spirit condemns itself. They will still be able to redeem themselves, should they accept the light which is always available to them.

"Humans are certainly not at the top of the spiritual ladder, so to speak, yet they are not at the lowest either. There are some beings who are so much more evolved that they would recognize humans the way humans recognize ants—as significantly lower life forms.

"If we go back in time, we can see that the Earth was formed long before humans came about. It had many types of creatures that grew over the millennia, including small, ape-like creatures that eventually began to change, or evolve into upright walking mammals. This is not information you don't already know. These mammals did not possess the same spirits that humans do; theirs were animalistic in nature, yet they were advancing over time to where their bodies would be able to accept a human spirit, albeit a poorly developed one.

"Homo Sapiens were an engineered species originally designed to house a human spirit. Their design was not too different from the Homo Erectus living at the time, with the exception of their spirit. The first two, known as Adam and Eve, were prototypes for others who, after a time, were placed all around the planet to help populate it. The region of Earth where they were placed was unique and special; I think you are aware of the ancient story of the Garden of Eden and the forbidden fruit. It was Gadre'el, one of the Satans, who deceived Eve into eating that which she should not have. There were lasting consequences for this action. For one thing, she was now able to produce offspring that were corrupt. Cain was one such offspring and his descendants still roam the Earth. As time went on there was an intermingling between Homo Erectus and Homo Sapiens, producing unnatural results, corrupting the gene pool. In that era, another insurrection from Heaven took place," Matthias said, observing Dorian's reaction.

"I don't mean to interrupt such a fascinating lecture, but I've been here a while, and I don't want to worry my loved ones," Dorian said, checking for a watch that wasn't on his wrist.

"Oh, you need not be concerned over the time you've spent here. Time in this dimension is offset significantly from that of Earth. One Earth year spent in this dimension would only show the passage of sixteen days of time there. You have only been here for about five minutes, and no one is at the cabin where your body is now. We are currently monitoring it for your safety," he said putting to rest Dorian's concern.

Dorian paused and sighed. "All right, continue then."

"Very well," Matthias replied. "Now, where were we? Ah yes, the insurrection. A long time ago by Earth standards, a group of two hundred and twenty Angels travelled to Earth in an effort to take human wives for themselves."

"How did they get to Earth? Did they fly over in some kind of alien spaceship?" Dorian asked.

"Not using a craft. At the time of the original arrival on the planet, multiple gateways were left around the surface to allow for faster travel to and from their home world. The gateways could transport light beings; however, other objects could not be transported by these means. The invader's corruption and betrayal was unexpected and had devastating results. As it was, the progeny of human and defiled Angels did not provide suitable inhabitants; many, but not all had unusual mutations that made their cohabitation impossible. The first sets of offspring, the Nephilim, were gigantic in stature; spawning the fables of the Titans. Other offspring were more human sized. The Nephilim gave rise to the Elioud. In addition, the fallen Angels educated their offspring, including the humans, in many things that were outside of the intentions of The Creator."

"Such as?" Dorian asked.

"Forbidden subjects, such as the use of weapons and armor, the use of magic, enchantments, astrology, writing, and so on. From a casual perspective it would seem that knowing such things would not seem unreasonable; however, the evil and corruption within them was unleashed by this knowledge, becoming more rampant as their resources dwindled. The giants consumed everything in sight, faster than the land could sustain, while the humans were unable to control their lust for power. The two began to turn on one another.

"There was much bloodshed on the Earth at that time and The Creator, Elohim, decided to cleanse the Earth of it. A plan was placed in motion to purge the land of almost all of the Earth's inhabitants. The fallen and their leaders were captured and imprisoned within the Earth, while almost all of the giants and Nephilim were destroyed by the angels. Your mother was one of the Archangels that fought and imprisoned them.

"Afterwards, the great flood was unleashed and the remainder of the world's inhabitants were destroyed. I'm sure you've heard the account of Noah.

"The spirit forms of the giants were left to remain on the Earth, as well as many of the Nephilim. As for the humans, the few that were not too corrupt were given a rebirthing."

"What happened after that?"

"Everything on the Earth was destroyed, but not everything within it was. At that time, there were seven human females who had had an immaculate conception; that is, they all had a child without a human father. All of them were chosen because they were righteous women and those special children we call the Dumuzi. There were seven before the flood and five after. The original seven who were of Angelic origin were as skilled as the Angels themselves, but did not share their knowledge with humans. That is when Anidon came into existence."

"I'm sorry, Anidon?" Dorian asked.

"It is the home for beings like us, our sanctuary. Your father was one of the original seven who found the dimensional space within the Earth. He along with the other six and their families found Anidon as a safe haven during the great flood, and it is still in use to this day.

"So now you have a basic understanding of the course of human history and why humans are on Earth," Matthias said.

"Thanks for that, but what does all of this have to do with me?"

"Today we face unprecedented numbers of the fallen and their agents. There is not a single government on Earth that has not been infiltrated by them, and events are leading to a worldwide takeover. In addition to human weapons and technology, all the advancements of the Angels are at their disposal as well. They have infected various governments on this world and on others in an attempt to gain control and ultimately, we suspect, to use the humans' spirit energy to attempt a takeover of Heaven again. Another great war is approaching as multiple prophecies are coming to fruition. If we do not have all of the support we can possibly get, all will be lost. We simply do not have the numbers to contend with the opposing forces. Will you at least consider joining our cause?"

Dorian was overwhelmed with the amount of information he had been given and it was becoming unbearable. "Okay, this is too much. I feel as if I'm losing my mind here. Thirty days ago, I was writing a grant proposal for my research and final exams for my students. Now I'm caught up in some end of the world scenario with alien Angels and demons. I thought it might be nice to know about where I came from and why I was given up for adoption. But this—this is beyond my wildest imagination.

"Listen, you don't need me. I'm pretty sure the Angels can take care of themselves, right? They won their war before, I'm willing to venture they can do it again. Besides, what can I possibly offer? I'm just a researcher. I don't think I would do very well on a battlefield or anything like that."

Matthias could see that he might have overestimated Dorian's ability to take in all of the information and remain rational. "My apologies. I see that I've upset you and you have every right to be upset. To give you all this information about your birth parents and the history of Earth—I suppose it was too much."

He started to move towards Dorian to rebalance him and Dorian recoiled.

"I'm fine. It's okay," Dorian said holding his hand up.

"Very well, as you wish," Matthias said in a diminutive voice.

"You work your whole life to save up for a place, get a few things along the way, have friends, family. I suppose none of it matters., It's all an illusion, as you say. It's bad enough the humans are tearing each other apart on a regular basis and destroying themselves. What's going to be left after all is said and done? Isn't there enough death and destruction already?"

Matthias looked at him with gentleness. "Dorian, even though the world of Earth may be changing does not mean everything is coming to an end. It signals the dawn of a new beginning. The material things you had on Earth were there to give comfort to the hardships that all beings face while training their spirits. They are Earthly things, and as such will perish with the Earth. You are not of this Earth, and your future lies beyond your imagining."

"Matthias, I see the desperation in your message and the situation, but I'm not sure what use I'm going to be for your cause. I have no real skill set apart from a specialized knowledge that I very much doubt would be of any benefit to your needs," Dorian pointed out.

"You have a great power within you that lies dormant. We can show you how to use it. The knowledge we have gained from our leaders and experience over the millennia can be yours if you would allow us to instruct you. I'm sure you've noticed the events taking place on the Earth of late; the wars, earthquakes, floods, hurricanes, volcanic activity, murders, thievery, and the overall corruption. These are a direct result of the actions of the fallen Angels and their accomplices. They have been poisoning the humans and searching for a way to free their brethren, events which have been foretold long ago by some. You have already been caught up in it, as seen by their attachment of the Shemzol to your head. There is more good you can do with us than with your research, and I believe there are others on Earth that you care about; others worth fighting for. We will need everyone on the side of light to help us fight the darkness or we are lost.

"Whether you join us or not, war is coming to you and all whom you hold dear. Please consider carefully, Dorian. Our future, everyone's future, is at stake. If I may entreat you with a small request, I would like to introduce you to a few others of our group. Would you be willing to meet with them?"

"I'm really not interested in joining your cause, but I will consider it on one condition," Dorian said with indifference.

"What do you require?" Matthias asked.

"That you remove that thing from the back of my head."

Matthias smiled. "Of course, we can assist with that. We will need to prepare you in advance for removal. Come, let us go to meet the others," he said. They had gotten up from the sitting area and moved towards the back of the room. Dorian followed him to the place where they had arrived. The next moment they were both outside the Pessipone. Dorian paused and looked over at Matthias.

"Why did my parents abandon me? Where are they now?"

Matthias tilted his head with an uncomfortable expression. "Your father will seek you out when the time is right and explain, whereas, I cannot speak for your mother. Rumor has it she has been imprisoned. Your father has asked that I not reveal to anyone else who she is, so it is vital that you do not think about it when we arrive at our destination. As far as the rest are concerned you are the son of Urieth and a human mother, and therefore an Elioud like me. Although your appearance is similar to mine, that may not be the case when we activate your Shi. Also, be advised there are some who can read surface thoughts.

Until you are instructed on how to block this, do not think about your birth mother. Do you understand?"

"Yeah, I got it, don't think about it, no problem," Dorian replied.

"Follow me," Matthias said, moving towards the entrance. They travelled to one of the platforms used to disembark the breece

"We are leaving Verdes Seventeen and will be traveling to a secure location on Erustian Prime. There we will meet with the others and discuss removal of the object from your head. The travel sensation will feel similar to the first time you journeyed here. Prepare yourself."

They both stood together on the platform. Matthias said some words and instantly the two of them were bathed in a bright light. Once again, Dorian found himself whirling through a tunnel with flashing lights that twisted and contorted around him, then suddenly stopped.

IT TOOK A MOMENT FOR HIS SENSES TO ADJUST to the new surroundings before he discovered they had been transported to a large room with about fifty beings of various shapes and sizes. The room itself was, like everything up to this point, unique. The beings inside were moving about making gestures in the air, uttering sounds that could be perceived as language. He couldn't understand most of them, except for a few that looked human. Clearly, there was technology far more advanced than anything on his Earth.

The matter in the room appeared to be floating in place, giving the impression everything inside would disappear if a switch was thrown. Each of the walls, including the floor and ceiling (if that is what one would even call them), were like a giant window to various other-worldly places and dimensions, continuously changing. Each view was completely different, much the way video surveillance cameras would switch and

Dorian wondered if he could walk out of the room and into the world beyond the window.

"Aye, you can," A humanoid female composed of light said to Dorian as he was observing his surroundings with amazement. Dorian looked over at Matthias, unsure if he was the one whom she was speaking to.

Matthias smiled. "I believe my friend may be responding to a question you asked yourself. Allow me to introduce you to Yelnisha, one of our operatives in our special operations group, the *Avavago*. Some privacy please, if you don't mind?" Matthias asked with respect.

"Of course, Matthias," she replied, smiling coyly at Dorian.

"Is everything all right Dorian?" Matthias asked with concern, noticing Dorian appeared bewildered by all the sights around him.

"Ah, no. I mean, yes, yes; everything's fine. Everything is fine," he replied softly, still absorbing his surroundings like a newborn baby. His heart began to feel light with excitement at the thought of learning and knowing so much more than he had ever thought possible.

"Matthias, you return so soon?" one of the beings asked as it approached the two of them. It had an amorphous body that shifted into a humanoid form. Dorian observed its tentacles transform into arms, elongating into hands and fingers that extended towards Matthias.

"Ah, I see then," the being continued as the two exchanged information through touch.

"My apologies, Dorian; this is Zazu," Matthias said.

"Greetings, Dorian, we have eagerly anticipated your arrival," Zazu said, extending an appendage towards Dorian. Matthias smiled, holding in his laughter as Dorian sheepishly looked over to Matthias as if to ask '*is it okay*?' He touched Zazu, which felt a lot like exchanging greetings with Matthias.

"I will leave you to your tutelage, Matthias. Dorian, until we meet again, *Shadom ni ana*," Zazu said, returning to the area in back.

Dorian turned to Matthias with a stunned expression.

"Their kind are known as the Distrogan; obviously, they are not from Earth or one of the Angels, but from a distant planetoid in another galaxy not too far off from the Milky Way itself. They were used over the millennia for their skills in espionage and subterfuge, due to their unique ability to rearrange their molecular structure at will. Unfortunately, most of the Distrogen were hunted or enslaved by those who feared what they could do or who exploited them for their abilities. Very few remain, and they must return to their home world every year to renew and replenish themselves from the source of their life—the planet itself. Zazu has been with us for over a thousand years now, and I consider it a good friend."

"It?" Dorian asked.

"Yes, well, they are not male or female as we are accustomed. Now Yelnisha over there, whom you previously met, is one of the Elioud, an offspring of the Nephilim.

"One of her many unique abilities, as you may have already surmised, is thought capturing, or mind-reading, in simplistic terms. We can teach you how to close off your thoughts to others, including her,"

Matthias said as he moved about the room.

Dorian was following him, partially paying attention to what he said and partially to his newfound surroundings.

"I was wondering to myself if you could just walk through these walls to the places we're looking at. Apparently, you can, according to her. Hey there's the cabin!" he shouted, as one of the walls in the room switched to a view of his body lying on the bed where he had left it.

"Well, only beings of light can walk through. Many of our bodies are also in secure locations on Earth or other areas and are being monitored just as yours is," Matthias explained.

"This place we are in is one of our bases of operation, where we monitor the activities of those like us and the agents of the fallen."

"Sounds like the CIA for celestial beings," Dorian mused out loud.

"Well, we are not funded by any government; we operate within the order of our society of Anidon. Our numbers are very small, less than seventeen thousand in total, and not everything involves operations on the Earth. We mainly observe their activities, but occasionally we do have some direct contact with the enemy. It is usually limited, due to the risk of being observed by ordinary humans, as well as the risk of capture by the enemy in order to learn our whereabouts and numbers.

"I think we've covered quite a bit for today. We should conclude things for the time being and continue on another occasion. What do you say?"

Part of Dorian didn't want to leave; this was all too fantastic and every new sight left many questions. "I understand, Matthias, but we still need to have that thing removed from the back of my head," Dorian replied.

"Ah, yes, the Shemzol. I had almost forgotten. In order to remove it we will need to go over some things. No doubt Amprodias mentioned that the device binds to the flesh and with spirit, correct?" he asked. Dorian nodded.

"It is used to track spirit energies and sends a signal to the sigil holder when the Shi is active. It was originally designed by the fallen Angels to monitor and track the Nephilim, as a sort of homing beacon.

"They've been using them more and more lately on ordinary humans or on humans with latent Shi. Anyway, in order to remove it we will need to teach you how to awaken your Shi energies. The problem, however, is that the device will send a signal to the enemy that your Shi is active, along with your precise location.

"Because you do not possess active Shi, it would seem they are unsure if you are a person of interest to them. For what purpose I cannot say for certain; however, based on past events, it seems that they are interested in the blood of a specific individual. It may be you, it may not be. I can only assume that they do not even know you are a hybrid, but awakening your Shi will remove all doubt, as hybrids have significantly different Shi from ordinary humans. Another point worth mentioning is that some have awakened their Shi to discover latent abilities, so you will undoubtedly experience some changes."

"So what happens if I don't have this removed?" Dorian asked.

"If you were not a hybrid, as you are, eventually it would fall off and turn to dust. In your case, I do not believe you would come to harm, but I cannot be certain. The pain could become quite intense," Matthias said, noticing Dorian's look of concern. "You have questions, ask."

"So, if I have this straight, we're going to 'activate' my Shi? Then what? It's going to fall off, or start beeping? Hopefully not explode?"

Matthias laughed. "No, it will not explode. At least I do not believe it to be so," he said with a slight grin, observing Dorian's worried countenance.

"This is not funny, you know," Dorian shot back, looking around as several others within earshot were chuckling.

"More important is the act of awakening your Shi. It may be quite uncomfortable. I should warn you right now, your life as you know it will be completely different from what it is now on Earth. You will sense things that you never had before— heartbeats, electrical impulses from others, thoughts and unexpected phenomena."

Noticing that Dorian wanted to say something, Matthias paused.

"I already can. Or at least I have on a few occasions recently. It more or less happened on its own, but was a very strange sensation. Does that mean my Shi is active?"

Matthias was taken aback by this revelation.

"Indeed, you are an interesting one. It would seem that you may have tapped into your Shi without realizing it, but it is not active; we would all feel it and you would know. In addition to those things I mentioned, you may also be able to see celestial beings in your flesh form; spirits of various origin as well as spiritual energies surrounding flesh beings. In time, it may be possible for you to learn how to make light energy into solid matter. You may also be able to penetrate the thoughts of others and the abilities you have in your flesh form will be magnified greatly. These are some of the things you may experience, and some things unexpected as well, since..."

He stopped his sentence short when it became obvious others were listening. Some of the ones eavesdropping stared more intently at Dorian.

"Finally," Dorian thought to himself. "I'm going to become a superhero." His thoughts brought extreme laughter from several beings nearby.

"Okay, get out of my head!" Dorian shouted as he cringed with embarrassment.

Matthias chuckled. "We're going to have to make that your first lesson when your Shi becomes active—how to block your thoughts. Now, in order to keep the enemy from knowing your Shi is active and learning our location, we will have to perform some preparatory spells."

Matthias looked over to the room where the others were working. No words left his mouth, yet six of them stopped what they were doing and moved over to where Dorian and Matthias stood. Yelnisha stood facing him.

"Dorian, I will need you to concentrate and focus on one thing. Picture one thing, an object, in your mind and tune everything else out. Remove all other thoughts that occupy your mind." she said.

Yelnisha positioned herself equidistant from the others who had already formed a circle around Dorian. The seven then placed their hands-on Dorian and did not speak as all sound in the room began to dissipate. The walls, the objects in the room, everything including the seven, disappeared and Dorian was floating in darkness. An icy chill filled the air, and some voices could be heard; mostly muffled, some with a panicked tone, some shouting. Then silence. A terrible, foreboding feeling washed over him as he was trying to concentrate on one thing— Yuki's smiling face.

The voice of a multitude spoke in the darkness. "The time of our imprisonment is nearing its end. We will find you no matter where you are, no matter where you run. Come willingly and free us, or be destroyed!" the voices boomed in unison. The sound was so loud it was crushing. A faint light formed in the distance as a clawed hand in the darkness reached out at him. The light began to grow, pushing back the darkness. Dorian heard Yelnisha calling out to him.

"Dorian! Focus on the light. We almost have you!"

All at once a series of sensations hit him, as if he was smelling, seeing, and hearing for the first time. Only he wasn't doing anything different. The darkness quickly faded as loud shrieks could be heard dissipating. A great weight was lifted as the terrible emanating evil passed.

The seven were all staring at Dorian with shock and terror themselves, after what they had just witnessed and struggled against, and what they were now beholding.

Dorian's hands were bright, much like Amprodios's, and his eyes appeared as if they were emeralds; sparkling and glistening a deep green color, with a glowing light that emanated from within. The top of his head was covered with what looked like a living fire, moving and flowing like a river, flowing down past his shoulders. His new form stood approximately fifteen feet in height. The clothes he'd had on in Norway were not to be seen, instead he was adorned in a material that moved with almost a will of its own, a bioluminescent material that shimmered with an array of colors and enveloping him like the robes in a Renaissance painting.

"Please stop it!" several being cried aloud. "I cannot survive this," another shouted. Dorian looked confused as he was washed in newfound power. Tremendous energy emanated from him.

"Dorian, quickly, you need to."

Before Matthias could finish his sentence Yelnisha grabbed him by the arm and pushed the two of them into the wall with the cabin in view and Dorian felt his spirit slam into his body in a very uncomfortable fashion.

# *Ten*

A COLD SWEAT CAME OVER HIM AS HE TRIED TO acclimate himself to all the new sensations he was feeling. After having adjusted to being back his body, he found it difficult to keep up with the newfound sensations. Sounds were coming from all over the room—voices, as far as he could ascertain. As he was looking around for the source of these noises, a wave of fear hit him. There was no one else in the cabin, and yet sounds filled his head, as if twenty radio stations were all playing simultaneously. In addition to the noises, he could feel a squirrel outside foraging for food, its heartbeat, its movements, as well as its thoughts. It was struggling to live, as if it had been forced underwater, leaving him with a very disconcerted feeling as the squirrel suffered. He could also feel the presence of several birds also struggling to live, and he wondered what was going on. Instinctively, he tried to move a hockey puck in his room with his mind, reaching his hand out to test out a childish theory. Nothing happened.

"Well, I don't have The Force; that's no fun," he thought. "I suppose this means I can't fly either," he said aloud this time, trying to will himself to fly. Again, nothing happened.

He reached for his cell phone before it rang. "How did I?" he thought, as he answered the call.

"Know it was going to ring?" a voice with an Irish accent said on the line. "You've read far too many comic books for your own good," the female sounding voice said to him.

"Ok, I give up. No wait," he said pausing to focus his thoughts. "Yelnisha. Somehow, I know it's you, but your voice is completely different. How did you know my, never mind. Oh, boy, what else did you look at in there? You know that's not right. A person's mind is their own private place!"

"Shut your gob, listen to me! You need to do exactly as I say, or you're going to end up killing a lot of people without realizing it. The spiritual force you have is too great to leave unsuppressed," she said with urgency in her voice.

Dorian glanced out the window and noticed birds dropping to the ground around the house. He could no longer sense the squirrel and noticed its lifeless body outside where he had last felt it.

"Whoa, what's going on here? What do I have to do?" he asked in desperation, knowing his mother and Yuki could be returning at any moment.

"You need to calm your mind and imagine that you have something like The Force, only it's coming from all over you. Now, imagine how you tried to move that hockey puck and pull it towards you. You need to pull the energy inside you. Bring it in."

"How do I know if it's working?"

"You'll feel pressure build up and your energy level will increase."

He set the phone down and sat on the bed, trying to concentrate. There was too much sensory overload. He couldn't focus.

"It's not working! Help me!" Dorian shouted in desperation.

"Aw, bollocks, relax! You're going to have to calm down or people are going to die. Listen to me. Shut everything down and take a deep breath. Take slow, deep breaths and imagine a large clock ticking. Tick tock, tick, tock, tick tock. There's nothing but you alone in space. Tick tock, tick tock. Pull it in Dorian. You're calling yourself home. Bring the energy back. Feel it returning, and imagine your power building. You're filling up an empty container."

He concentrated on her words and could feel his internal power growing along with his sensory abilities increasing in amplitude. The sound of the rental car was approaching and he could hear it pull into the driveway.

"Focus, Dorian!"

He tried with every ounce of his might to concentrate, but he was picking up their heartbeats, thoughts, movements, and it was overwhelming him. His focus was shifting, and with that, he could feel his mother and Yuki both attempting to get to the cabin door. They both were gasping for breath.

"What's happening? There's no air! I can't stand! Yuki, help me," Iduna said, reaching out to her as she dropped to the snow-covered ground. Yuki was on one knee, struggling to get back to the car.

"Bloody hell, I don't have the ability to get to you! I'm sorry!" Yelnisha said, tears in her voice.

Panic and anger raced through Dorian. He stood and concentrated, willing his spirit into himself. As the pressure mounted, incredible energy filled him. A feeling of weightlessness accompanied by strength engulfed him, and his thoughts moved much faster than ever before. It was working, somehow. This was like drinking a megaton of caffeine. He truly felt invincible, and had to remind himself to remain focused.

The sound of the rental car engine came to life, and he could feel Yuki's racing heartbeat. He ran outside the door and saw his mother's lifeless body in the snow, face down. There was nothing coming from her body; no life could be observed save the spirit-energy he felt coming from the bright light that was visible above her. A large being, an Angel he suspected, was standing aside the light and seemed to be opening a portal.

DORIAN FILLED WITH RAGE.

All of his emotions were on overload. He let out a yell so loud that many of the windows on the street shattered. Multiple avalanches began forming on the mountain peaks around them. Yuki was terrified and Dorian immediately realized he had made a terrible mistake. His mother's death was one thing, but he couldn't bear to be responsible for the deaths of other innocents.

The loud rumble of snow filled the air, almost as loud as Dorian's cry. Instinctively he ran to the base of the mountainside to try and stop an avalanche all by himself, even though he had no idea how he would accomplish such a feat. Without realizing it, he was moving at incredible pace, augmented by his spirit energy.

Even with his unthinkable speed, he made it to the bottom of the mountain only to behold an awesome sight—an entire legion of Angels was at the base of the mountain, stopping him dead in his tracks. In an effort to contain the avalanche they superheated the snow to the point of evaporation. This was also taking place at the other mountain bases, creating a large amount of fog and a bit of precipitation.

A large, fifteen-foot-tall angel appeared before Dorian. It seemed obvious to Dorian by the way the others attended this being that it was their leader. His countenance was soft and his face was glowing with radiance. His eyes were similar to Amprodias's, only his hair was much longer, and he looked terrifying. Dorian could not penetrate his thoughts, but he sensed a peacefulness and a connection with this angel. The armor the angel was clothed in shimmered with translucence, and had a gigantic sword affixed to his waist that was sheathed glowing white-hot scabbard.

"My thoughts are my own, Arrai'el. Consider this miracle a gift, young one. You must learn to control yourself. Although you are known to all of us, it is not my place to speak to you at this time," he said, with his head turned slightly towards Dorian while supervising the cleanup and repair. The other Angels were buzzing around like worker bees quickly going about their appointed tasks; some on cleanup and some were affecting the few onlookers with persuasion of the events that had transpired. The witnesses would come to believe this was the result of an underground fissure of molten magma that opened up and evaporated the snow; a side effect from the events in Oslo. A few of them were observing Dorian with cautious curiosity and seemed to be whispering to each other.

He looked up at the powerful being, and his thoughts returned to Yuki and his mother. Without a word, he turned and began to make his way back to the cabin, albeit considerably slower as many onlookers were now out in the streets. As he rounded the road the cabin was on, he saw Yuki leaning over Iduna's lifeless body.

No longer could he see the angel that presided over his mother's spirit-energy; however, he was able to see another standing near Yuki that seemed to be comforting her. The angel peered over at Dorian with an expression of surprise and apprehension at his presence. He could sense the heartache coming from Yuki, and yet somehow his pain at the loss of his mother was attenuated. He also began to hear random thoughts, causing a bit of sensory overload

"I will miss you mother," he said softly while kneeling to caress her face, trying to maintain composure. He went into the cabin to retrieve something to wrap her with and found her favorite blanket on a chair inside. He gently rolled her onto the blanket while Yuki remained silent, in a state of shock. Slowly he carried her lifeless body towards the car, holding her tightly, embracing her small body. Yuki quickly got up to open the passenger door and Dorian gently laid his mother in the seat.

"I am so sorry," she said, putting her hand on his arm. "I don't understand... As soon as we got out of the car it was as if we were in outer space. There wasn't any air. What happened? Did one of those aliens do this to get back at you?" she asked, dried eyeliner streaks covering her face.

"No... this was my fault," was all he could muster without losing composure.

Yuki put her hand on his shoulder. "You look so different now. What happened? What are we going to do?"

"I suppose I'll tell the police she collapsed when she saw the avalanches happening all around us. I'm not really sure what happened to her. All I know is I'm responsible."

"What are you talking about? We were outside and felt this immense pressure, and it was very hard to breathe. What did you do?"

"I'll fill you in on the details later. Right now, I just want to get my mother to a proper place. I need to call this in to the authorities. You go ahead inside. I'll be back in a while."

AFTER PLACING A CALL TO THE EMERGENCY line and explaining that his mother had passed away, he drove Iduna's body to the local hospital. The county coroner met with him upon arrival, along with a police detective who asked Dorian some basic questions. It was difficult for him to concentrate on the words of the authorities, due to all of the static noise emanating from them, and it was becoming uncomfortable. After a cursory exam, the coroner advised Dorian that his mother may have had a stroke, but it was too early to tell. Dorian heard some of their thoughts amidst the noise, and he knew they were suspicious of him.

He left the facility with a heavy heart, questioning himself as to why he hadn't broken down after what just happened. Instinctively, he reached for his phone that he somehow knew was about to ring. A familiar voice was on the other end.

"Dorian... I'm so sorry about your mother. There was no time. If any of us thought this was going to happen we would have taken greater precautions. Honestly, we had no idea this was going to be the outcome, it was totally unexpected," Yelnisha said.

"I don't understand. How could you not have known? Doesn't this sort of thing happen every time? What went wrong?" he asked, sounding on the verge of tears.

"Just who the bloody hell are you? You didn't look like any Elioud I've ever seen, and you certainly had way more power. We've never awakened someone with Shi like yours before. Most of us have brought out half-breeds or less and all of those without exception were very easy. No one had the spiritual energy after first awakening to harm a mouse, let alone a human. That typically takes years of training, and only a handful of us are capable. Honestly, Dorian, I've never felt such immense spiritual energy before, and I had to make a quick decision. You were hurting the others back on Erustian Prime. I hadn't a crazy notion what was going to happen, but I had to do something. Listen; that's not all."

"What do you mean? What now?" he asked.

"The Shemzol removal was another disaster, and I think the enemy is going to be coming after you. I called to tell you you're not safe. Whoever put that on you is really bad news. It took everything we had to keep them from getting hold of you. I think they were trying to trap your spirit during the awakening process, which is why everyone was in a panic. I don't know for sure who they were, but they have some serious juice behind them. You need to be careful, Dorian. We never had the time to show you, but you need to learn how to suppress your spiritual energy and close off your mind, otherwise you're going to be found pretty easily. Until we can get you to a safe location, you need to do exactly what I'm about to tell you."

"Where's Matthias at?" he asked.

"His spirit remains on Erustian Prime, but his body is elsewhere.

"Judging by your accent, I'm guessing you're Irish. Is that where you're at, Ireland?" he asked.

"You're lucky. If you had said I was from England or Scotland, I might have taken offence to that.

"Listen, we don't much time. There's a small village near the center of Sicily, called Villalba. You need to get on a plane and head there right away."

"What? Sicily? I've got to take care of my mother. I can't just leave her here!" he snapped.

"I'll explain later, just do as I say and don't dawdle. I know you just lost your mother, and I'm really sorry about it, but you're going to have to put something together for her by tomorrow. If you don't get out of there soon, you risk a lot of other innocent people getting hurt. The enemy obviously wants you for some reason, and I don't think it's a good idea for us to wage war when we don't know who or what we are dealing with.

"Villalba is almost in the middle of Sicily, so there will be some driving to get there. I've got some preparations I need to do myself in order to make the trip as safe as possible for all of us.

"Now, here's what I need you to do: First and foremost, do not let any spiritual energy out when you're flying. I shouldn't have to explain to you why you don't want to do that. You don't have the necessary control to bring it back in, so I need you to remain calm and focused. Remember what I told you back at the cabin when you were in trouble? I need you to be focused like that the entire plane ride. You can't let it go, Dorian, so stay focused. Right now, your Shi is in check, but I have no idea how long you can maintain that. Don't risk everyone's life by getting distracted. Second, you need to know how to control your thoughts, because you can be read pretty easily. Essentially, you're like an internet connection that's broadcasting everywhere without any security in place, so we need to act fast.

"My mentor explained it to me like this: Focus your Shi around your mind and place an imaginary shield around it. You have to be able to feel someone trying to access your thoughts.

"Remember that handshake you had with Zazu? Now, imagine that in your head, but you're not letting anyone in. I'm guessing that you're probably getting a lot of static because everyone is broadcasting their thoughts to you at the same time. You need to learn how to tune it out by focusing on either your thoughts, or one specific thought from someone else. I don't have any more time, Dorian, so call me at this number when you get to Sicily, and I will tell you exactly where we're going to meet. I'm really sorry about your mother."

"Wait, why are these beings after me? What did I ever do to them? I still don't understand what's going on."

"We can talk about that later. For now, just take care of your mother then get to Sicily." She disconnected the call, and Dorian was left feeling empty inside.

Normally he would be the one comforting others, but now, who was there to comfort the comforter? He didn't have a spirit guide as far as he could tell, now that he could see them quite clearly. Yuki would have to fill the void.

DRIVING BACK TO THE CABIN PROVED difficult, as he was trying to remember Yelnisha's words and focus on them.

As he made his way through the town, he could hear the thoughts of the passers-by in his head. It was quite disorienting, as if someone got hold of the radio and started rapidly changing channels. He began to focus on his thoughts only and attempted to tune out the others, but it was so difficult that he instinctively muffled his ears, causing him to almost lose control of the vehicle.

Approaching the cabin, he could see the faint glow of lamp light from within that extended, forming a silhouette of the window panes in amber on the snow-covered ground. Through the window, he saw Yuki pacing and biting her nails. Dorian sensed the worry in her thoughts and the mounting questions she had for him. Her focus shifted when she heard the car pull into the driveway.

Dreading the inevitable conversation that had to take place, he forced himself with heavy heart to the door. His emotions were welling up inside, culminating with a terrible pain in his heart.

Yuki was standing at the threshold when he opened the door and immediately embraced him. Closing his eyes, he could feel himself letting go and began to weep. She gently stroked the back of his head and held him tightly, standing on her tippy toes as Dorian leaned over her. Several minutes went by, and he let go to wash up. Yuki went into the kitchen and prepared a cup of hot chocolate for him. A few minutes later, he returned and collapsed in Iduna's favorite chair; her scent still on the blanket draped over it giving the illusion she was still there.

A moment later, Yuki joined him with beverage in hand. He sighed and began to tell her everything that happened. Initially she was at a loss for words and just sat there, unable to decide on what to say, while Dorian was trying hard to focus his thoughts enough to get some peace in his mind.

"So that-," she started.

"Yes," he interjected, knowing her question before she was able to verbalize it.

"You did not let me finish. I suspect these aliens that have been after you are probably looking for revenge. What I don't get is why they just let you go when they had you in the house. Why bother to put that thing on your head in the first place?"

"I can only speculate, as I'm in the dark as much as you, but I think they may not have known for sure who they were looking for. I seem to recall one of them saying something to that effect. I'm guessing it's because unless someone's Shi is active, they can't tell. At least that's my working theory," he said, cupping the drink between his hands and staring at the wall, lost in thought.

"If my birth mother had something to do with their imprisonment, maybe they're wanting to use me to gain their freedom? Or revenge? I don't know. Maybe I'm not even who they're after. All I know is that I need to take care of my mother's funeral before anything else. We'll head back to Starefossen in the morning. I'll have to make a lot of calls and let everyone know what happened. Let's try to get some sleep. It's been a long, horrible day."

They said their goodnights, and he headed to bed, unsure how sleeping was going to play out. This was his first night with an awakened spirit, and he was afraid he would end up doing something terrible in his sleep, or that the fallen Angels would be coming for him. Sitting on the bed, he focused in a meditative state by concentrating on Yelnisha's words. This allowed him to have greater control over his spirit and shield his thoughts.

"I should have asked her about sleeping; now I don't know what to do," he groused, unsure if he should stay up all night or not. The meditation was taking its toll, and he was feeling more relaxed. Sleep came without him realizing it.

THAT NIGHT HIS DREAMS WERE MORE REAL than any others he had experienced before; it was as if he had been transported to another plane of reality again. All of his senses were intact, and he was fully aware of his surroundings. He was in his spirit form, standing atop a grassy hill that overlooked a large body of water, much like the ocean on Earth, with the exception of the violet-colored water and silver-colored grass. As he bent down to run his hands across it, he heard a familiar voice.

"No, you're not imagining it. The grass really is silver."

Quickly turning, he observed a man who was also in spirit form, standing roughly fifteen feet in height, with sandy-white hair that stretched down to his upper chest, and clothed in a loose-fitting shirt and baggy pants. His face looked familiar to Dorian, yet he could not identify this stranger who was standing before him.

"Well, I can see where you get your good looks from; definitely your mother, and not from me that's for sure," the stranger said telepathically, as he stretched his hand towards Dorian.

"Urieth," Dorian thought, as they met their hands together. Urieth extended an expression of good will towards Dorian, who was feeling whipsawed by all the sensory, emotional, and traumatic events that had recently transpired. Meeting his father for the first time was not something he had prepared himself for, and this particular moment was not a good one. They studied each other for a few moments before Urieth broke the silence as he turned towards the sunset on the cliff on which they stood.

"I was made aware of Iduna's passing. My sincere condolences, Dorian. She was a good mother to you; Esme'el chose well. If it were up to me I would have raised you myself, but we wanted you to try and have a normal life. Your mother did not know she would give birth to a male, and seeing that she already had broken her command by having a child with me instead of with an ordinary human, we felt it best to have you live with Jorn and Iduna. No one except Matthias knows who your birth mother is, and I kept it a secret for a reason. She has quite a few enemies because of what she did and who she is.

"You have some questions, I'm sure, but before we get to anything else I want you to know that I've watched over you over the years, and I'm very proud of what you've become. Sin has a way of corrupting those who are like us more than it does ordinary humans; it's remarkable that you've turned out so well. It gives me hope for the rest of us."

Dorian looked over at Urieth, who was gazing at the sunset. "Do I have any siblings?"

"None that are alive. I had a son and a daughter from another that were both killed by a flood many years ago. Since then I have remained unattached. To my knowledge, you were the only one that your mother birthed. She sought me out almost fifty years ago, although I had known her ages before that.

"From time to time she would visit me over the centuries; perhaps out of curiosity, or perhaps it was love. They are very unusual beings, the Angels. Matthias explained everything to you, I presume?"

"As much as I could handle at the time. He mentioned that Esme was one of the Archangels who fought against the fallen. He also mentioned a coming war," Dorian replied.

"Yes, that is correct, on both accounts. I still cannot fathom why she chose me or why she wanted a child. It went against her station."

"She didn't tell you why she wanted to have a child with you? That's kind of odd, don't you think?" Dorian asked.

"It wasn't like that between us. Esme'el just didn't ask lightly, she was very persuasive. I wasn't even there when she gave birth to you, but I did get to see you shortly afterwards, just before she sent you off. I don't believe she was prepared for the reaction her superiors had, but who knows, she may have foreseen everything. Her conception was not like you are accustomed with humans; we merged our spirit essence, not just our genetic code. She had to take a flesh form for the birthing, and the result was an entirely new being altogether," he said, as he created flying swine with a motion of his hand in this imaginary world of his. Dorian looked over and chuckled inside at the irony of the moment. He would have believed this encounter a month ago, when pigs fly; now, it seemed, they were.

"Does any of this have to do with what is happening to the planet? There's more natural disasters now than ever before; people are going crazy, killing each other for no apparent reason. We've had asteroids fall, animals and fish dying everywhere, famines, plagues, wars and endless violence. It's like the Earth is going through death throes," Dorian said.

"All that is taking place points to the coming war. The biggest of all; the end of the humans and beginning of a new world. The fallen and their followers are not going to go out quietly, that much is well known. The enemy is trying to free those that were imprisoned in the Earth. There are others bound elsewhere also. As I understand it, they are looking for your blood in order to help break the spell that holds the barrier in place. They found out about your mother's confinement and know she had a child. That's why they're looking for you, Dorian; your mother, along with six others, bound the lock with their spirit essence, the same essence that makes up who you are. They cannot get to her, as only a few actually know where she has been exiled." he said grimly.

"Well, I wouldn't exactly say no one knows about it, because there was someone who was in Hawaii that knew about my blood. At least I presume so, since he grabbed the sample I was handing over and destroyed it," Dorian said.

"That was my doing. Also at Primase, where you worked before the University. As I said, I've been watching over you all these years."

"How did you manage to watch me there? I've never seen you before Hawaii," Dorian asked with some skepticism.

"I was able to observe in spirit form. Once I saw what you were doing, I had to keep a close eye on the others around you. Some spells can be worked to fool security cameras and open doors."

"So, this Hermoni Company—who is behind it and who is Theodore Dantanian? As I understand it, Hermoni was one of the fallen, correct? I find it hard to imagine he's running a multi-billion-dollar organization while being imprisoned at the same time," Dorian said.

"Theodore Dantanian's name has changed throughout the centuries. He is a Nephilim and his father is Hermoni—one of the fallen. Dantanian has spent years trying to find a way to locate and free his father. The company was formed as a front in a discreet attempt to discover the location where the fallen are interned. Unfortunately, we don't know much else of what he knows and who he is working with. That woman who was in Hawaii is also one of the fallen. Her name is Onoskelis; she was not one of the retinue that came to Earth to have children with humans. She, along with several others like her, are searching for Asa'el, the leader of the two hundred, who was bound and placed in the desert of Dudael. Asa'el was imprisoned alone, whereas the others were placed together in separate locations. To my knowledge, they are being held in thirteen prisons in total.

"If the prophecy is correct, he will be freed. There can be no doubt he will unleash hell on Earth."

"Did you say Dudael? Where exactly is that?" Dorian asked.

"In truth, I do not know the exact location myself. Your mother did not tell me, and I would not want to know. Some say it is below the great pyramids in Egypt; others say it is in the Nubian Desert at Nabta Playa. I suspect it is a place where the air is foul and there are no signs of life. Wherever he is entombed, it will not be his final resting place. As for the others, I am unaware of their whereabouts as well," he said bleakly.

"It sounds like there's nothing we can do about it except prepare ourselves," Dorian replied.

"That's exactly what you need to do, my son—prepare yourself. Yelnisha is somewhat experienced and can teach you how to hone your spirit energy. You will need to part ways with the woman who is traveling with you. She will not be of any use from this point forward and will only serve to become a liability."

Dorian looked despondent. He knew Urieth was right, but could not bring himself to part from Yuki. Not after all they had been through.

"It's for the best. If you have any love for her, you know it is the right thing to do. In this matter, I can speak with assurance; I've lost far too many loved ones over the millennia to lead you in the wrong direction."

Dorian's life was spiraling out of control. What had begun as an escape to check up on his mother had led to her death and a situation that was becoming a life-changing event. There was no doubt he had to take a leave of absence from the university and try to get a handle on things, but he knew in his heart that leaving the university meant he was leaving everything, and there would be no going back.

A few scant weeks' prior, none of this would have seemed possible—and yet, here he was, facing otherworldly beings in an end of the world scenario. A part of him wanted to walk away and get back to his normal life, but something stirred inside him: a feeling of duty, responsibility; a sense of destiny that overpowered his personal desire for normalcy. This was the greatest cause he could undertake. Billions of humans in the world were all consumed with their individual lives, but this was about everything—his whole purpose and theirs. If this was his greater calling in life, then he would face it head on, with courage and determination. The world was rapidly changing; why should his life be any different?

Urieth smiled at him. "I will join you and Yelnisha in Italy so we can begin your training. Finish up in Norway as quickly as you can. There is still much you have to learn. If you find yourself either out of control or under attack, simply speak my name and motion two fingers as I am doing, and you will find me," he said, demonstrating the maneuver. "You will need to use your spirit energy to accomplish this, so hopefully I won't be needed prior to Italy. It has truly been a blessing to finally meet you and for us to talk my son. I look forward to our next encounter. Take courage," he said as he extended a hand to Dorian. They looked at each other a moment and their surroundings began to dissipate. Dorian was slowly fading into a dreamlike state, falling fast asleep.

# Eleven

THE NEXT DAY HE AWOKE WITH A FOG IN HIS head, feeling as if he could sleep for another week. That, along with the monumental weight of the tasks that lay ahead, made his body scream in protest at the notion of getting up.

Forcing himself upright, he began rubbing his eyes when it dawned upon him that he had forgotten to tell Urieth about the strange object he possessed, in addition to the cryptic message that Mahin had given him. It would have to wait. It was Christmas Eve, and he needed to make some calls to his relatives on short notice.

From behind the bedroom door, he could hear the sound of dishes and pots clanging, along with the sound and aroma that accompany frying, coming from the kitchen. Moving his mind to Yuki's thoughts, he saw that she was desperate to try and make this day go well for him. Her surface thoughts revealed nothing else to him, so he got dressed and made his way out into the kitchen where Yuki had breakfast waiting on the table.

"Please, sit," she said, motioning with her hand. She had a worried smile on her face. The breakfast was a nice gesture that served as a brief respite to take his mind off of his mother's passing.

"I looked up some of the Norwegian recipes and hopefully this does not taste too bad," she said, preparing him for potential disaster.

"Yuki, this could taste like dirt, and I would be thankful. But it smells wonderful and looks every bit as Norwegian as my mother made it," he said, peeking into her thoughts. He remembered when Yelnisha looked into his mind and decided it was best not to pry; Yuki's mind was her own private sanctuary.

"I also looked up several funeral homes in Bergen and spoke with them. I wrote down the details. You can call when we're finished."

They gave thanks for their meal and proceeded with the cleanup. Dorian began by placing phone calls to the funeral home that had held his father's service, to Iduna's church, and to all the relatives and friends of his mother and father. The service was going to be held in the evening, as he did not want his relatives to have their Christmas day celebration, what little there would be given all that had happened, on the same day as a funeral.

THE CHURCH WAS VERY ACCOMMODATING, given the short nature and timing of Iduna's passing; however, there were many other casualties as a result of the earthquake, and their time was limited. White flowers and lilies adorned her casket and surrounded the aisles. She would be laid to rest next to her husband and their family in a centuries old cemetery that was not far from where they had first met. A picture of Iduna and Jorn together was brought in by her close friend Berjit, who, along with several of her other close friends, mourned her loss.

After many hugs and stories shared amongst Dorian and his relatives, they said their goodbyes. All the while Yuki stood by his side as a pillar of support. After everyone had left, he had a moment alone with his mother. Saying a final farewell, he simply hoped she had achieved her purpose in the life she lived.

When they reached the house in Starefossen, there were multiple cards, candles, and gift packages left by her students and friends in the community; a gesture that helped raise his spirit a little.

The two ate their dinner, and afterwards, Dorian turned on the television in an effort to help take his mind off all that had happened, in addition to the concerns he had over the future that lay before him. He had not yet told Yuki of the meeting he'd had with his father, nor had he decided on how to handle their inevitable parting. The journey to Italy would be made alone; the risk was too great and he couldn't bear the loss of another at his expense.

Yuki looked at him with a worried expression. She could tell something was on his mind, but she reconciled those thoughts with the understanding that Dorian had just lost his mother. "Is there anything you want to talk about?" she asked gently.

"We can talk tomorrow, Yuki. I have a lot on my mind right now, and I need to do a few things before I go to bed. You should get some sleep, you look exhausted," he said, looking quite fatigued himself.

"Hai," she replied, slightly bowing her head with glassy eyes. She was turning towards the hallway when he called out to her.

"Yuki."

She turned and looked over at him with a sad expression on her face. Dorian could sense that she was hurt.

"Thank you so much for everything," he said, rising from his chair. He walked over to where she stood and wrapped his arms around her, then gently kissed her forehead. As he held her tight in his arms, he could feel the love in her spirit grow.

After she closed the door to her room, he sat down for a moment to catch a glimpse of a breaking news story involving the US dollar. The newscaster announced it would no longer be accepted by almost all the oil producing nations. It seemed to overshadow the major earthquake, and panic was setting in around the world as European and Asian markets were tanking. Interest rates were skyrocketing, and it was apparent the United States was in big trouble. China had positioned itself well for such a situation; almost too well, and some pundits on television were stating their back-room deals amounted to "acts of war". The market would be closed on Christmas day, but Tuesday was going be a global catastrophe, Dorian surmised.

Taking a deep breath, he opened his laptop and decided to book his flight to Italy for the day after Christmas, as all flights were booked to both major airports in Sicily. Now all that was left was to figure out a way to tell Yuki.

ELSEWHERE AT THAT SAME MOMENT A HUSHED conversation was taking place at the Elmamoura Planet Garden, in the ancient city of Alexandria, in Egypt.

"I'm telling you the truth, Jizam, we all felt it. There is no doubt, this event was shown from the Picatrix." Samir said.

"And the order?" Jizam asked.

"What of it?" he replied with a raised eyebrow.

"They're just going to let you call upon Malik?" Jizam asked incredulously.

"The order is not sanctioning this action; there was quite a bit of concern which took a lot of convincing. They will not help me; however, they are not going to interfere. I have made several talismans to conceal my purpose from prying eyes. I do not intend to hold him for long, just"

"If—Samir, if you can even hold him at all. Most likely you'll die horribly or have your spirit removed from your body. This is a major affront, and I do not believe this will end well for you. I beg you to reconsider the consequences of even attempting such action."

"Jizam, my friend. I have known you all my life, and I do not wish to die just yet. The conjuring will not be done alone, I have others who have agreed to assist, although they are not from the Rosae Crucis; mainly individuals who have an interest in shaping the future."

"Who are these individuals? You need experts to have any hope of survival, not amateurs. This isn't something that should be under taken lightly. You could upset the balance. I would be very suspicious of anyone who wants to call upon Malik, and to be honest, I'm not convinced your motives are clear either. As far as the entombed fallen are concerned, let them rot where they are. If the Creator thought that they needed guards for their prison he would have appointed them. Perhaps there already is sufficient security in place. Knowing where they are isn't going to keep you or any of us safe," Jizam said in a hurried voice.

"Don't you think I am aware of that?" Samir snapped, his patience wearing thin.

Jizam looked around cautiously. "Shh; keep your voice down."

Samir observed his surroundings and lowered his voice.

"You do realize what's been happening lately? Look around; things are getting more tense by the minute. As I said before, we all felt it, the wakening of a mighty one; another prophecy concerning the end times is coming to pass. Several of the other watchers that were not imprisoned here are desperately looking for their brothers, and rumor has it they've found a few of them already. Once they discover where they are at, it's over for us."

"They've been searching for thousands of years. What makes you so certain they're any closer now than before?" Jizam asked skeptically.

"Have you heard nothing I've said? Why do you think I mentioned the awakening of the mighty one? My sources say he may be the key to unlocking their prisons. They are going to be coming for him or her or whomever they are. That knowledge is power. It's leverage. It's one of the few things that can save us. We're going to need all the leverage we can get. I don't want to upset the balance any more than you do; I simply want to be able to protect the ones I love and what I have."

"And what makes you think your sources are the only ones who know about this? Perhaps the enemy is also aware as well and are searching for the awakened one. Do not cling so desperately to this world, Samir, for it will surely pass away and everything in it. You would be wise to stand on the sidelines and put your faith in in God."

Samir took a deep breath, rubbed his face with both hands and sighed. "Who knows; perhaps all that will come of it is that I may cause Malik to smile."

"I very much doubt that my friend," Jizam replied.

IN THE REMOTE DESERT, JUST SOUTH OF AYN Qazzam in Algeria, thirty-nine men were working late into the night, digging into the Earth with heavy equipment. The deep blue night sky gave way to the lights emanating from the In Guezzam airport, about five miles to the north. They had reached a depth of approximately one hundred twenty meters when several of the workers began shouting.

"All work is to cease immediately. All workers are to report to the command tent for further instructions. I repeat, all workers stop what you are doing and report to the command tent," the site foreman announced over his handheld loudspeaker after the discovery.

A faint, glowing, blue color could be seen radiating from down below, and a low frequency, seventy Hertz hum could be heard as well. A chill swept over everyone in the camp, with the exception of a few who were making their way to the edge of the pit. Three of them stood tall, their faces shrouded with linen. The eerie glow of their eyes shone through the slit in their wrappings as they walked forward. The spirit guides of the workers took notice, many out of curiosity as they were unaware of what had been discovered. What they were aware of was the unmistakable presence of evil emanating from the three beings who were casually striding towards the anomaly.

"Mr. Cassi. You and the others, wait for me in the tent. I will be along shortly," the fourth one said to the foreman, as he observed his brethren making their way towards the pit. Cassi meekly nodded in acceptance and made his way inside, his spirit guide glaring from a distance at this being who stared back in defiance.

Inside, multiple tables were set up holding an array of computers and technical equipment. Maps of various design were laid out, some very ancient, depicting long lost cities which many of the locals viewed as dubious, since no such landmarks existed where they were displayed. Dry erase boards stood in the back, listing the worker's names and job site listings for the day. Outside, several tents belonging to the workers were pitched around the main tent, a short distance away from a cluster of vehicles. Local music blared on a small portable radio sitting outside, competing with the rattling sound of the portable generators.

Several minutes passed as the workers began pouring into the tent in small groups, and within short order they were all accounted for. Acrid body odor combined with the local cuisine filled the air inside the tent, mixing with the fumes of diesel exhaust that permeated the surroundings outside. The workers began talking amongst themselves as to the nature of the discovery; some thought it was an alien craft, while others believed they had stumbled on the dwelling of a Jinn, as local folklore would tell. There was a general feeling of uneasiness amongst the workers, as they had been told their purpose for digging the hole was to search for ancient artifacts. Discontent began brewing amongst them.

As the site foreman made his way inside, along with his two assistants, he caught the eyes of the workers, who were visibly upset. Mr. Cassi nervously looked over the group of men and wondered how he was going to ease their concerns, as the discovery was just as puzzling to him. The tall, covered figure entered the room, and all eyes focused their attention towards the menacing being. The spirit guides of the workers arraigned themselves in a defensive formation.

"Is this everyone?" the tall figure asked, looking down on Mr. Cassi with his softly glowing eyes. All Mr. Cassi could muster was a nod in the affirmative to the question asked. The tone of the speaker's voice was quite eerie, and Cassi wondered what land would produce such an accent. The presence of this being caused a shiver to go down his spine, as well the others nearby. Cassi had dealt with other project managers and assistants of his boss, not nearly as mysterious nor as foreboding as the one standing before him. Dantanian had phoned in advance and advised of the stranger's arrival; still, this was not what he expected, and with their precipitous discovery, Cassi's imaginations and fears began to take hold of him.

Several individuals in the back of the group did not seem to be affected as much as those standing closer to the glowing-eyed being, and they began shouting their disapproval.

"What is going on here?"

"What in the name of Allah are we doing here?" a sweaty, bearded man, covered in grease and dirt asked.

The tall stranger's eyes narrowed, his face still shrouded by the dark shemagh wrapped around his head. Beneath the wrapping his skin barely showed, but from what little could be seen in the dark it appeared scaly and leather-like. The sound of grinding teeth and what could only be described as leather being pulled tight exuded from him. Several men nearby gasped, and all fell silent as the tension in the air became palpable.

The exit to the tent was enticing many of the men as fear began to lend wings to their feet. The spirit guides were warning their hosts to run and raised their Shi in unison. The light they created was blinding to those capable of witnessing it, yet the dark figure was not even moved in the slightest.

Suddenly, the air became much cooler, to the point of frost forming on the computer screens. Terror filled the hearts of most of the men, yet their bodies would not comply with their demands to run. All they could do was to watch what they knew in their hearts to be the inevitable. One of the spirit guides began to open a portal to call reinforcements, but was too late.

"You have all done well," was the last thing they heard. A brilliant light filled the tent, as well as the harrowing sound of thirty-nine bodies dropping to the ground simultaneously. A purplish-black light was faintly glowing from the tall being's outstretched hands that held a large sword. The hilt had numerous markings and symbols on it, and its edge was emitting a bright white light which was slowly turning black. From a distance, it appeared as if it was made of obsidian. Upon closer inspection, the blade displayed various flashes of lightning, along with a misty gaseous apparition of changing colors.

"But none as well as you, Alal," the profane being said, admiring the work of his demon blade. He focused his concentration on the sword, and it seemed to be swallowed up into another dimension, leaving just the hilt, which wrapped itself around his hand like a glove.

Making his way outside the tent, he saw his three companions standing at the edge of the pit staring at the scene below. The worksite was a bit quieter now, with only the sound of a few generators off in the distance, the wind, and the mesmerizing tone coming from the pit.

"It has finally come to pass, the event that I promised long ago. I knew I would eventually find it, and thus I have," Vassago said triumphantly.

"In truth, a mere six thousand nine hundred ninety-eight years later. Were it not for the ring and the blade, we would still be waiting," Ornias said with slight condescension.

"What that I could give for Solomon to see this day, and moreover, yet be in throes; it would impress this one to bid him dig every hole in our pursuance and take great pleasure in seeing him humbled thusly," Kludun stated with a smile, her sharp teeth exposed beneath the wrapping of her head.

"Five grasshoppers loosed him of his stature for the ravishing Jebusaean, and he possessed much greater wisdom than all who dwell upon this plane now. Our victory is wholly assured, once we release the others," Vassago said, looking at Kludun who was staring down into the pit.

"Do not be promiscuous with conjecture, Vassago. Our triumph is yet to be realized. Had Beelzeboul not caused the humans to destroy the temple, you would still hold fast the pillars. Underestimate our condition at your peril; we have yet to meet their forces in battle. Come now, our repose must be hastened; even with the sword thus infused with the power of the ring, the spirits within stir."

With his last proclamation, Bernael leapt into the pit with his sword drawn and plunged it into the wall. An enormous eruption sprang forth as the spirit energy of the humans and their spirit guides was released all at once, disrupting the barrier of the prison. The other three remained at the top and peered down. Darkness filled the pit as the blue glow faded into nothingness, and the humming had dissipated. Many glowing eyes shone through the darkness below, as loud shrieks of unnatural origin filled the night sky. Eighteen would be added to their number this night. At that moment, a large earthquake in the Red Sea shook Egypt, Sudan, and Saudi Arabia, causing massive infrastructure damage and devastation, leading to untold numbers of casualties.

TEN HOURS LATER:

"What's the current situation?" Dantanian asked Dina, one of the fallen deceivers.

"Kokav'el and Barak'el were recovered, along with sixteen others, which adds three leaders and thirty-three followers in two prisons. Unfortunately, the captured Hashmallim of Rapha'el's regiment could only give us the Amangeldi District site in Kazakhstan. Vassago was quite auspicious with Algeria and he delivered, although Vassago would argue his skills discerned the location. Therefore, I have appointed him to assist Kokav'el and Barak'el with the next site. Kludun believes the signs of the constellations may reveal one additional site. So far, we have Algeria and Kazakhstan as our two reference points. Ar'tekif points out that if a Pentacle of binding was used, it would need equidistant points. He has provided possible options for the location of the others, and has calculated seven, possibly eight sites in total.

We also have several teams dispatched to capture Lystad, now that his Shi has been awakened. After consulting Ramt'el, signs indicate he may in fact be the one we are searching for.

"While we count on that to materialize, my recommendation is to wait for the global destabilization effort. The templates for the new currency have been completed and await your final approval. The European campaign is underway in Germany and Mullah Xul's name is being spread there. I expect things to pick up momentum in the near future.

As you know, Nivel has his operatives in thirteen cabinets amongst the nations that rule, and they are sowing discord among the humans. With the attack on the New York Stock Exchange, along with the Chinese manipulating their currency to crush the US, large scale war is imminent, so we should seize the opportunity to unify the nations under our command.

"Also, a fortuitous event occurred with the earthquake in Egypt: The Egyptian government is blaming the earthquake on the fracking in the Red Sea by British and US oil companies. We can use this to our advantage. With the Iranians and Iraqis forming a unified coalition, along with Turkey, Libya, Egypt, Lebanon, Yemen, Oman, and now Saudi Arabia, the tension against Israel can easily be escalated," Dina noted while flipping through her holographic screens.

Dantanian was smiling as he signed the documents his assistant April was handing to him. "I like the way you think. Temple Mount?" he asked.

"Precisely. The destruction of the Dome of the Rock and the Al-Aqsa Mosque would be the perfect spark for the tinder. We have procured multiple short range ballistic missiles that should level the area. Our operatives are positioning backups in the event the Israeli military shoots one down. We should be ready by the New Year," she said.

"Right when the clock strikes twelve would be the best time, I should think. Make it happen," Dantanian ordered. Then he asked "How goes the training?"

"Byleth has her legions prepared, although we will have multitudes of new recruits when flesh forms can be restored to the spirits who walk the earth. For that Asa'el will have to be freed," she said.

"Find Lystad," he ordered.

"It is assured," she replied.

# Twelve

THE FOLLOWING DAY, DORIAN AWOKE EARLY; his thoughts about the past events, along with his looming future, kept him from getting adequate rest. No sounds could be heard save the occasional creaking and howling of the wind outside. It was still dark outside, allowing the aurora borealis to take the stage, casting an eerie glow over the frozen valley onto the lake. He looked over his surroundings in the room. Yuki's Christmas present was sitting in a box that had arrived at the doorstep the day before, along with his mother's gift. It was a snapshot of life's simple rituals that grounded him in the previous reality he had comfortably enjoyed.

After quietly going through his mother's bedroom to find something to wrap them in, he returned to his bedroom to finish the task, despite the fact his heart was not invested in the undertaking. Afterwards, he sat upright on the edge of the bed to attempt a meditative state, in an effort to gain greater control over his newfound abilities.

Willingly opening his mind to his surroundings, he began to pick up thought-feelings of neighbors engaged in various activities. Some were just waking up to Christmas day with concerns over whether gifts would be appreciated, some were feeling stress over their food preparation, many had feelings of fear over world events, and plenty of siblings were bickering over one trivial issue after another. The thought crossed his mind that the attitude and mood of the people around could somehow be projected onto his so he decided not to push his luck. He had enough baggage of his own right now and he didn't need the weight of other's concerns added to his. Instead, he chose to focus on Yuki's gentle breathing and heartbeat. With this came an inner peace that had been sorely lacking, and he relished the feeling.

Several hours later, Yuki awoke to the sounds of Dorian clanking pots and pans in the kitchen as daylight began to slowly creep in the house.

"Good morning and Merry Christmas," he said, with a smile that seemed a bit distant. "Please, sit."

The smell of breakfast filled the air as he removed a fresh potato cake from the pan onto Yuki's plate. Shuffling over to the table like a zombie, she sat down and muttered something inaudible in Japanese akin to 'thank you' and 'good morning' rolled up into one word. The chair attempted to drain what little energy remained inside her until she sipped the cup of tea he had prepared, which seemed to bring her back to life. They both ate without speaking until Yuki broke the silence.

"Thank you for breakfast, that was nice. Merry Christmas," she said, with a weary look on her face. The phone began ringing shortly thereafter with neighbors and family members wishing Dorian a Merry Christmas and offering continued condolences over the loss of his mother. Yuki took the opportunity to get dressed and bring out his gift while he was tied up on the phone.

After about an hour he was finally able to get a moment's respite from the well-wishers. He sat down in his mother's chair and turned on the television, randomly flipping channels as he was primarily using it for background noise. He didn't want any of the cheery, feel-good Christmas music or programming, so he settled for a history channel that was documenting World War II. Yuki was fiddling with her tablet, texting her relatives and making a few calls of her own; mostly to keep her sister and parents abreast of her current whereabouts and well-being.

Dorian walked over to her, holding a small package. "I'm not into it this year for obvious reasons, but I would like you to have this," he said, extending a package to her.

Setting down her tablet, she took the gift from him and said a solemn thank you with a slight bow, so perfectly that one would think she had rehearsed it for months. As the opportunity presented itself, she handed him a neatly wrapped gift. The rabbit mug and chocolates he had bought her brought her spirits up a bit, making him feel a bit relieved.

He opened her gift to reveal an unusually carved metallic disc with a slender triangular slot cut out. It had a dark patina, which gave the appearance of it being very old. Carved on top was a scene of cranes standing at the water's edge which were inlaid with gold. Accompanying it were a pair of small, golden, ornamental figures, of a horse and rider, which had posts on their back to fit into something.

"That is a tsuba and these are called menuki. They are parts of a katana that the samurai wore," she said, unsure if he knew what it was.

"Yes, I'm familiar with their history. They're quite beautiful. They look very old," he replied, studying their design.

"They belonged to my grandfather, many generations back. The shape that you see is of our family crest. A samurai would carry his sword everywhere he went. It is said that the soul of the samurai is one with his sword. I hope you find it acceptable," she said politely.

Dorian felt a bit embarrassed at his comparatively paltry gift, but he was happy that she had shared a part of her family history with him.

"Are you sure you should be giving me this? It seems like a valuable family heirloom," he said, with a concerned expression.

"Of course, it is fine. We have many other items from our past. I want you to have it," she replied with a gentle smile.

"I meant no insult—believe me, it's awesome, I will treasure it always. Thank you so much." He got up from his chair and hugged her tightly for some time, and she patted him on the back. As they embraced, he stared at the pictures of his parents on the wall and wondered if they were sharing a moment like this.

They cleaned up the mess, and he sat back in his chair, thinking about how he was going to tell her that he was leaving without her. There was a pit in his stomach and an ache in his heart; he needed her more now than ever, so how could he say goodbye?

"What are we going to eat for dinner?" she asked.

"Um, well, we could...," he started. "Damn," he thought to himself. There had been no planning, given recent events, and his mind wasn't on his stomach since it wasn't growling at the moment. He checked the refrigerator in the back, and sure enough, his mother had prepared in advance for Christmas dinner. There were pork ribs wrapped in paper from the butcher, some lutefisk along with a bowl of cloudberries and ingredients for riskrem. Yuki was unfamiliar with traditional Norwegian Christmas dinners; however, with the help of the internet they managed something palatable.

After eating, they sat down together in the living room with the television in the background. Dorian was still avoiding the inevitable discussion he would have to face. They both sat quietly watching the espionage tactics of the Axis and Allies from WWII, not exactly the most festive of programs.

"...*With the development of the Enigma Machine at the end of World War I by German engineer Arthur Scherbius, espionage was taken to new heights. It saw widespread use by Germany before and during World War II. The subsequent reverse engineering of the device by the Polish Cipher Bureau with the help of French Military Intelligence had a significant impact on the war effort. The device itself employed a combination of mechanical and electrical parts that consisted originally of three movable rotors between two fixed wheels. Over time, subsequent revisions increased the rotors to five. The basic function of the machine utilized a poly-alphabetic substitution cipher that helped obscure messages from being detected by opposing forces. It was not long...*"

Dorian was staring intently at the television, his eyes widened as epiphany struck both of them simultaneously.

"Are you thinking what I am?" he asked.

"Do you suppose?" she asked with widened eyes. Her pulse quickened. "Where is that thing your mother gave you? The strange, metallic scrunchy thing?" she asked. She got up and began making room on the kitchen table.

"I'll be right back. I don't believe it. If this is what I think it is...," he said. He ran back to his room to get the device as well as the deciphered diagram he had written. Running back from his room with both in hand, he set the object on the table for the two of them to examine.

"Do you see this?" she asked, pointing to the dots on top, then to the symbols down below. "There are three rows of dots set up in some kind of pattern. This one has one dot on top of another on top of another, three single dots in one column. Look to the right. There is one dot on top of another, which is on top of two dots side-by-side. The next has one dot, then two side-by-side, then one dot."

Dorian was staring at the document when something peculiar just occurred to him. "These symbols, down at the bottom of each set of dots; I know what they are. That's 'tu' and that is 'ka', and this one is "un". These are letters of an alphabet, and these at the end are numbers zero through nine. That's strange; I didn't recognize them the first time I copied all this down," he said, looking over at Yuki, who appeared to be counting.

"It probably has something to do with your spirit awakening," she replied. "Look; there are sixty-four sets of dots which correspond to the sixty-four symbols, and ten of them are numbers so that leaves fifty-four for the alphabet."

"Hold on, five of them repeat. There are forty-nine letters in this alphabet. This thing is some kind of Rosetta Stone. Something is missing though. There are sixty-four sets of dots that have three rows with up to four dots. Eight times eight is sixty-four. Sixty-four...," he said continuing to stare at it.

After about fifteen minutes of them contemplating and thinking, Yuki broke the silence

"The message!" she shouted.

Dorian snapped to attention.

"The one from the old lady. How did it go? I wrote it down on my tablet," she said.

"Something about three notes make the chord, three instruments and something else. Glad you wrote it down. I've practically forgotten it," he said as Yuki flipped through her tablet to find the saved message.

"Okay, I found it. 'Three notes make the chord, and three instruments are required to play. The music is read with the aid of the stand. The mighty ones shall be your reward'. Three notes and three instruments. Well there are three rows of dots. Three instruments; maybe there are more devices? Try looking at it closer maybe?" she said, unsure of how to piece the clues together.

Dorian picked up the object and scrunched it a few times. Each time it returned to its resting shape. He began flipping it over and scrutinizing it closer, hoping to find something that would shed more light on the subject.

A moment later, he had another revelation.

"I can't believe we both didn't see this earlier. I don't think this message is just about my musical upbringing; I think it's talking about my background in genetics. It's starting to come together. These three rows of dots represent a codon. Look, there are four of them that have the same number of dots in all three rows. There are sixty-four possible combinations for the four amino acid bases. I kept having dreams about garbage and the strange dream about the seventh, fourteenth, and twenty first chromosome. Junk DNA! It has to be. These dots represent specific codons which when translated give these letters. There's something in those three chromosomes, I'm sure of it. Three notes make the chord or codon; three instruments are required to play; the three chromosomes. The music is read with the aid of the stand—this thing," he said holding the heptagon up.

"I'm betting part of the answer to the riddle is in the seventh, part in the fourteenth, and part in the twenty-first. Three instruments playing together to make the chord. Some kind of message or something else," he said.

"I wonder why Urieth never mentioned anything to me," he thought, suddenly remembering his encounter with him.

"Okay, but even if we translated the non-coding portion of those three chromosomes and wrote some program to turn those into the letters of this alphabet, it would be billions of letters jumbled next to each other. How will you find any message in it? It could take years, no?" she asked.

"Good question. That's what I need you to do for me, figure out a way without taking years to do it," he said with newfound vigor, realizing that this was his opportunity to send her off with less risk of harm coming to her.

"Listen," he continued, "there's something I have to tell you. I met with my father a few nights ago. My biological father. He wants me to head to a remote location for some training; spirit training. He told me that everything that's been going on in the world, all of the disasters, the floods, earthquakes, wars, riots, all of it—is leading to some kind of war. I don't want you to get hurt, so I think it would—"

"—be a good idea for me to go home. Is that it? I get it. So, this is your way of getting rid of me?"

"Yuki, look, you're twisting it into something else. I couldn't bear to see anyone else I care about end up... Look what happened to my mother; and that was because of me. I wasn't even trying, and I almost killed the two of you. I have no idea what I'm going to be facing, or if I stand any chance against it. I just want you to be safe; I'm not trying to get rid of you. How about we join forces again once I know more about what's in store, and at least that can give you some time to solve this mystery? I'll write down all of the symbols' meanings, and you can see what you can come up with. I have faith in you, so I could use your help if you're still up for it," he said with a pained expression.

She stared off into space for a few moments, taking it all in with a sour look on her face. "I suppose I'll head back to Japan, then. I may need Kasia to help me come up with a way to find a hidden message in all of that data. You better not forget about me or leave me out of this. We are in this together, right?"

"Of course, Yuki. I appreciate everything you've done and gone through for me. Thank you for understanding," he said with a slight smile, grasping her hand in his. She looked depressed as she picked up her tablet to try and book a last-minute flight home.

"What was it like to finally meet your father?' she asked.

"Not what I expected, of course, especially the setting; he visited me in a dream." Just as she took her eyes off her tablet and was about to say something, Dorian interjected. "No, I didn't imagine it all. It was just as real as you and I sitting here, believe me. We spoke about the past, and he told me some things I needed to hear."

"So where are you going then?" she asked.

"Somewhere in Italy. Sicily in fact."

"Who are you going with?" she asked in a peculiar tone.

"I'm going by myself, but I'm meeting Yelnisha and my father there. I have no idea who else will be there. Is everything all right?"

"That Yelnish woman, what's her name? She is the one who called you, correct? Why is she helping you, I wonder? Remember what the old lady said, not everyone is who they seem. I wouldn't trust her, Dorian," she replied, her tone glazed with a bit of envy.

Dorian played along so he wouldn't fan the flames any further. "Thanks, I forgot about that. I'll keep my distance, for sure. There were a number of beings that I met when I made my journey. I'll have to remind myself to be on guard.

"I still don't know what to do with the University; if I don't return after the break, I'm going to lose my position there, along with everything I've worked for. I just want to go back to my old life; I really don't want to deal with this Armageddon craziness, but I have more questions now that need answering, so I suppose I can't walk away just yet," he said, pausing for a moment. "How difficult would it be for you to complete your thesis in the next three months?"

"I don't know. With me helping on this it would be difficult, but I can try and get it completed. Why do you ask?"

"How would you feel about taking over the lab for me? I know the University will want to hire someone from a pool of candidates, but I can give you a glowing recommendation. The death of my mother may serve as reasonable excuse for me to take an extended leave of absence, provided you can cover exams and such for me. That can buy you enough time to finish your PhD. I know that's a huge burden to throw in your lap, but I would rather have you in charge than someone else. What do you say? Are you willing to give it a try?"

She looked at him with reverence and bowed slightly. A small smile formed on her face, something Dorian wasn't expecting. He returned her smile in kind and breathed an inward sigh of relief.

"I'll set up access for my grading software as well as any passwords you might need. I have a business account set up for the funding, so take what you need out of that. Thank you so much, Yuki, this makes me feel a lot better about leaving.

"Before I forget, here's the fob with the data we compiled on my genome. Do the best you can, but if you can't figure it out, don't worry about it. I don't want you spending all your time on it, just whenever you can spare the time. Your degree and the lab come first, okay?" he said, handing her the fob.

"Arigato sir!" she replied with her tongue sticking out. Dorian just shook his head.

"Did you find a flight?"

"Yes, leaving tomorrow afternoon," she replied.

"Good, we can go to the airport together. I'll get to work writing down the translation of those symbols and put some of them together into words that might allow a program to detect them faster. It's going to be a long night," he said, as he got up to make a pot of coffee. Opening the cupboards, for some reason, brought his mother to his mind, and he said a silent prayer for her, hoping she had found peace and thanking her for being a good mother to him. He couldn't allow the events of his life to cause him to forget her, but at the same time he couldn't allow his grief to relax his focus. Guilt was settling in for not having seen her for as long as he did. Pausing a moment, he looked over to Yuki, whose spirit guide suddenly appeared and seemed to be whispering something to her. Yuki got up, made her way to

Dorian and put her arms around him. He smiled at her spirit guide as they embraced.

THEY SPENT THE NIGHT AND INTO THE EARLY morning working on the riddle. Dorian was typing word translations for the symbols and arranging the dot configurations, while Yuki looked over websites with information on how to crack ciphers. She eventually fell asleep on the couch, while Dorian continued working. A few moments later, Yuki's spirit guide appeared before him. She was dressed in a beautiful set of robes, shimmering with a multitude of colors that would be hard to describe to mortal minds. Her face glowed with a brightness, and her expression was very loving. They looked at each other for a moment; then Dorian attempted communication telepathically, not certain how else to proceed.

"Hello there. My name is Dorian, I'm a friend to Yuki. You probably already know that. Who might you be?"

"Peace be with you. I am Hadriel. I have been with, and watched over Yuki since her birth. It seems we both love her very much," she said, as she moved closer towards him.

"I know you have important things to do, but should anything come to harm her, please let me know. I haven't learned how to move my spirit form yet, but if you are able to connect to me somehow, I would be grateful," Dorian said.

"The enemy; they are searching for you, Arrai'el. We have been trying to obscure their vision so you would remain hidden to them, but they will find you here eventually," she said. Hadriel reached out her hands and took hold of his. He could feel her love, which was overwhelming, unconditional, and full of peacefulness; so much that he did not want to let go.

"We now have a special bond that connects us with Yuki," she continued. "Should something happen to her, you will feel your Shi fluctuate and you will know," she said, as Dorian was almost melting in blissful peace and tranquility.

"Thank you. If you should decide to visit for any other reason, you know, so we could hold hands like that, I would be fine with it," he said, half-joking, half-serious. Hadriel smiled and laughed.

"Until we meet again," she said, fading into nothingness.

He smiled in return. "Until we meet again."

BY SOME STROKE OF LUCK, DORIAN MANAGED to get a few hours of sleep without any disaster befalling him. Groggy, but awake, he cooked up a few potato cakes and poured some juice, saving some for Yuki. Afterwards, he began prepping the house and packing his important belongings, selecting a picture that he wanted to remember his parents by, as well as a small square of his mother's favorite blanket to keep with him. Yuki was up and had her bags packed and ready to go when the taxi arrived to bring them to the airport.

They arrived at the airport earlier than anticipated, so Yuki used the opportunity to continue her research into solving the code, while Dorian was looking at the news on the monitors which showed the stock exchange in New York. It had not yet opened; however, it was already experiencing immense premarket selling pressure. These losses meant many pension funds would go broke, undoubtedly forcing some retirees to require the services of food banks. The Norwegians were much better at handling their resources than the Americans, and there didn't seem to be any sense of panic in the streets, even after the huge earthquake they had suffered.

The time of Dorian's departure approached. "Here is my house key, take it. If you want to stay there you're more than welcome to. Your sister can stay there also; I have plenty of spare bedrooms. Call me as soon as you get to Japan, or text me. I'll do the same when I arrive in Italy. I'll be keeping in regular contact with you to monitor your progress whenever I can. I want to thank you from the bottom of my heart, Yuki, for all you've done. You've been a blessing to me, and I want you to know that," he said wrapping his arms around her. Amongst the other passers-by, he noticed Hadriel standing in the back and smiling at him. He caught her smile and returned it in kind.

"I will miss you," Yuki said, putting her hand on his face.

He leaned in and gave her a kiss. "I will miss you also."

# Thirteen

APPROXIMATELY TWO HOURS AFTER THEIR planes had departed, multiple vehicles approached Iduna's home. Several tall figures wearing grey cloaks got out and quickly made their way to the entrance. Some of the nosier neighbors witnessing the scene began to call each other, wondering if Dorian was in some kind of trouble with the authorities.

"Not here; hold fast," Arita'el said, as he held his hand up to the door. Grasping the handle, he caused it to unlock, then stepped inside to search for Dorian's aura among the objects in the house. A strong residual remained on his mother's blanket. Arita'el picked it up and took with him.

"I can sense his presence moving to the south. Let us be away," he said to the others.

DORIAN HAD TWO STOPS TO GET TO THE airport in Palermo and didn't arrive until late in the night. After getting his luggage off the carousel, he found a rental agency that had a suitable vehicle to get him to the town of Villalba.

He called Yelnisha's number as he had been instructed to, but there was no answer. Not wanting to wait around in the airport, he decided to just head to the town and hope she would return his call by then. The GPS in the car showed about an hour and a half drive to his approximate destination, which would end up being closer to two hours to get there.

At that same time, another airplane was in pursuit.

"His traveling speed has slowed considerably. It appears his aura is shrouded; he is being assisted by others," Arita'el said.

"What should I advise the pilot?" Lahash asked.

No answer was returned as Arita'el concentrated. A minute later, he spoke. "Continue heading south. I will travel in astral form to improve our search. Do not disturb my meditation," he said, looking at the others on the plane.

IT WAS ALMOST TWELVE A.M. BY THE TIME Dorian reached the small town of Villalba. He was getting concerned, as Yelnisha had not returned his call. The thought crossed his mind to attempt contact with Urieth, but he decided against using that method without dire need. A pub was still open, the Oasi Di Territo, midway down an old cobblestone road surrounded by travertine buildings and timeless architecture. It was a rustic and cozy place, the kind that rarely served outsiders, especially foreigners at this time of night.

As soon as he walked in, he sensed an uneasiness from some of the patrons. There were about nine people inside; twelve if you counted the staff. Looking about the place, he decided to read their thoughts in an effort to discern if he was in any sort of danger.

A peculiar oddity struck him as he noticed a spirit that was trying to quench his thirst with the other barfly's drinks—a pitiful scene which took an unusual turn as one of the living patrons passed out and the thirsty spirit managed to hijack the body of the drunk man by climbing through the top of his head. Perhaps, Dorian surmised, the state of passing out rendered one susceptible to possession of sorts. This particular spirit must be in a type of self-created hell, a slave to the vice he had undoubtedly attained as a living soul.

Dorian was starting to channel surf through their thoughts one at a time: angry at the world, spouse abuser, merry maker, and one very unusual man he was unable to read.

"That's strange," he thought. Was he like Dorian, or something else entirely?

The man appeared to be of advanced age, with a long, grey beard and soft eyes hidden beneath his bushy eyebrows and winter cap. Dorian casually looked over to the stranger, who not only lacked a spirit guide, but his aura was hidden also. All of the other people in the tavern had various colors emanating around them, a kind of electromagnetic radiation out of the visible spectrum, for those with the gift to see. There was something about this man that Dorian felt drawn to; a familiarity that he couldn't quite place his finger on. The man beckoned Dorian to join him, at which point Dorian began looking around, unsure if the man was waving at him or someone else.

"Yes, you," the man said with a smile, pointing at Dorian. "Come, have a drink with me."

"That's odd. He seems friendly enough; wonder what this is about?" he thought, as he made his way across the room towards the inviting stranger.

He smiled and sat down casually with a "Hello", situating himself across from the man at one of the small tables in the back. A barmaid came by to get Dorian's drink request: a double whisky, straight up. Dorian looked over at the old man, who had no drink.

"What would you like?" he asked.

"Oh, I'm quite fine at the moment, thank you," the man replied.

The waitress looked at Dorian like he had two heads and muttered something under her breath. Just as he was about to peek into her mind to see what that was all about, the old man spoke.

"I would be more cautious if I were you. That skill tends to get one in trouble more often that you would think," he said. Dorian was suspicious at this point, as it was clear this was no ordinary human. The old man had a peaceful smirk on his face, yet Dorian could sense no malevolence from him, nor any heartbeat or electrical activity for that matter. It was as if he wasn't there. He checked his surroundings to see if anyone was watching the two; however, it was obvious that no one was paying them any attention.

The waitress returned with Dorian's drink, telling him in Italian that this was the only one he was getting, which seemed to bring great amusement to the old man who bellowed out in jovial laughter. No one in the bar seemed to notice the man's outburst which led Dorian to suspect they could not see this being. The man composed himself and cleared his throat while Dorian took to drinking his entire glass all at once. His face went red immediately and he felt the room spin a bit.

"What's happening to me?" Dorian thought. Had he been drugged? The typical warmth that came with alcohol lasted much longer than usual, but he was also feeling woozy; his thoughts clouded. Was this the sensation of being drunk? He had no idea, but he thought that somehow the old man was involved with his predicament.

"Alcohol can have that effect on a person, you know. I can see now, why your limit is one drink," he said, bellowing out again in jovial laughter.

"Who are y-you," Dorian asked, his speech slurring a bit. He peered over at the other patrons, making sure they weren't privy to his conversation.

"Well, that's a good question, my boy. I have many names—too many, in fact. I should like to have fewer. I think having one name above all is special, don't you? The first and last name needed. Take, for example your name. Dorian, from the Latin Dorianus and Greek Dorieus; meaning of the Dorian tribe or of Doris, which refers to one of the four tribes that defeated the Athens and eventually settled in Sparta," he said, speaking in a soft, almost mesmerizing voice.

"The Dorians had their own dialect and musical mode named after them, which I understand is the reason Iduna named you thusly. An interesting people, full of art, music, culture... and warfare," he said, his eyes gazing off in another direction to some untold place and time. A bit of sadness seemed to adorn his face. A moment later, he snapped back to his discourse. "The last name, Lystad, from old Norse *Lýsa, meaning* the shining one, and *staðr, or* dwelling. There is power in a name, you know. The power of Love, Arrai'el; above all, more than anything."

"How do you know my name? Did Yesh-Yeshnila, what's her name send you?"

"No young man, no one sent for me. I've been keeping my eye on you for a little while observing your progress, in a manner of speaking." His eyes shifted, piercing Dorian's soul in an indescribable fashion. The man took his spirit across time and space an experience which seemed to last an eternity or a microsecond, he could not say which; it was beyond his comprehension. Time had no meaning where he was, and Dorian was paralyzed as he experienced the journey.

Without speaking, the old man proceeded to give him information that he was unable to recall. Coupled with his drunkenness, he thought he might also have been under some hallucinogenic substances.

Then it was over. Dorian sat for a moment in shock and disbelief.

"Right, sir! Well, aren't you a fine thing? No time to be gettin' langered. Settle up, so we can get going," a woman with an Irish accent said, with an impatient tone. She was standing next to him, looking him up and down.

His lucidity returned all at once, and he was stunned for the moment, trying to make sense of everything that just happened.

"Do I—Yelnisha?" He asked with trepidation. She was tall and fit; with a slender, muscular build and a bushel of red hair that was pulled back. Their features were similar enough to that she could almost pass as his sister. Dorian looked around for the old man, who was no where to be found.

"You were expecting someone else? Now, if you don't mind, we're not particularly safe here, so we need to move along."

Dorian paid his bar tab, and the two of them left. The waitress muttered something under her breath that caused Yelnisha to burst into laughter.

"I seem to be a source of amusement for everyone tonight," Dorian groused. "How did you know where to find me?"

"Two sheets to the wind, are you? You sent me a text message with the name of the pub, remember?"

He checked his cell phone, and sure enough, he had texted her the name of the bar; only he had no recollection of having done so.

"Wait a minute. I have to tell you about this old man in the bar," he said, having sobered up almost instantly.

"Yeah, how does that joke go?" she asked with a slight smile as they walked to her car.

"I'm serious! Here, read my mind, you'll see what I'm talking about," he replied in desperation.

"You're letting on, yeah? You bought the old git a drink, and he was full as a bingo bus on a Friday evening. Then his relatives came and got him. You need to get out more laddie. Any other stimulating conversation topics you want to share?"

Pausing for a moment, he wondered if it was all imagined. The answer was without a doubt a resounding 'no'. It was not imagined, yet it didn't make a lot of sense that Yelnisha would have seen a different set of events in his mind. Whoever he was, the old man's power was great.

"Yeah. Hmmm... I guess you're right," he replied, letting it go for the time being.

"We're going out of town, so we'll need to drop off your rental car. It's about twenty minutes to Spoto Angelo. You can follow me there," she said in a chirpy tone as they walked to their parked cars.

"By the way, I hope you don't plan on going back to America any time soon. Probably ever," she said, getting into her car.

"Why, what do you mean? What happened?"

"Besides the attack on the stock exchange, there was a major earthquake in Yellowstone. They're saying it could go off any moment. Let's just say there's some serious rioting going on all over, and not just America. Let's get a move on."

Dorian stood for a moment wondering how bad it was and how Engel and Kasia were faring. He said a silent prayer for the two.

THIRTY-NINE MINUTES LATER, OVER Barcelona, Spain, an airplane carrying several otherworldly beings was circling back. There were many impatient stares at the meditative body of Arita'el, hoping for a sign of their quarry. Suddenly, he returned from his trance. "Turn the plane southeast towards Sicily. He's there."

Lahash immediately got up and went to the cockpit to instruct the pilot to change their heading. A few of the corrupted Nephilim looked at each other with some skepticism, but were cognizant of the fact that Arita'el was an ancient fallen, while most of those present were either demons inhabiting humans or lesser beings. Arita'el's power was extraordinary, and questioning his abilities could easily prove disastrous.

BACK IN SICILY:

The next half hour went by uneventfully as Dorian and Yelnisha drove to the larger city to drop off his car, then made their way to the tiny village together. As they traveled, he could sense her pulse quicken when she talked to him. "What is she nervous about?" he wondered, or was something else afoot? Perhaps she was excited by the idea of the two of them working together. To anyone else besides Dorian, it was obvious she had a bit of interest in him. She smiled several times, along with a few nervous laughs while catching a glance his way. He sat quietly, focusing his thoughts, so she would be unable to read his mind.

"So how long have you been doing this?" he asked, trying to get to know her better.

"Doing what exactly? You mean assisting the Avavago? I've been with Urieth and Matthias for twenty-eight years, since I was ten. Well, now you know how old I am, so don't be calling me no 1690, or I'll bust your cranium!" she replied with a burst of laughter while driving the car through the winding roads.

"A what?" he asked.

"Sixteen from the back, and ninety from the front; 1690," she replied with a smirk.

"Ah, right then. You look pretty good for thirty-eight. I would have guessed about twenty-two, give or take a few," he replied.

"Thanks. You know how to make a lady feel special. Actually, I'm aging a bit slower than most ordinary humans, but not like some of the other Elioud or Nephilim."

"Yelnisha isn't an Irish name, right? Where did you get it from?"

"Right. My dad named me after winning a bet with my mom. Have no idea where he got it from."

"Where did you get your abilities from?"

"Well, my dad was an Elioud, like me. From what little he told me he was the sixth generation from a Nephilim, but he didn't know who he was descended from. I had no abilities before he died, so I really thought he was just making up some fancy talk about our ancestry.

My mom was an ordinary human who had no idea what my dad was; apparently, he kept it hidden from her. I was only eight years old when a truck on the highway rolled over on top of his convertible, killing him and my twin brother. The trauma of that event must have awakened my Shi. After that, I started seeing all kinds of things—spirits, auras, angels, dark spirits, fallen ones...you get the picture. Then the sounds started popping in my head; you know, random people's thoughts, all that noise.

My mom took me to every kind of doctor she could afford; psychiatrist, neurologist, internist, gynecologist—anything ending in 'ist'. Nothing showed up on any of the tests or the psychiatric 'evals', of course. They said it was all just an 'Overactive Imagination'.

"After the so-called experts said I was making it all up, my mom started beating me any time I would point out a spirit, so I kept quiet about it. Anyway, eventually I figured out how to tune out the noise and focus on hearing the specific thoughts of others whenever I wanted. It was kinda cool at first."

Dorian looked over at her with a frown. "I want the cool part. It's just giving me a headache most of the time," he said in frustration.

"Aw, cry me a river. This is my story, so kindly shut your gob and listen," she said, letting out another batch of giggles.

"Whoa there, sheesh. By all means, continue," he replied with a raised brow.

"The headaches will pass," she said, smiling and sticking her tongue out at him to prove she wasn't trying to be mean. "Now where was I? Oh yeah; so I started using it to my advantage," she said.

"Let me guess, poker?" Dorian interjected.

"At nine years old? What am I going to win? Lunch money? Get a clue, boy. Back to what I was SAY-ING. Once you go down the pathway of reading other people's minds it becomes second nature; almost an obsession. So, in school I would read my teacher's mind and know exactly what to say, but it just made the other kids hate me for being a know-it-all. By the way, my teacher—Mr. Connolly; he had such a dirty mind; had to keep both my eyes on him. The girls I thought were my friends; well, let's just say they were a bunch of mean, rotten apples. They made me become more socially withdrawn. With my mom, it was worse, because any time we argued I would call her out on any lie she made. Thing is, if you can read someone's mind you know when they're pissed off and what not to say, or so you think.

"Eventually, she started to figure out there was more than an overactive imagination going on and began to believe the things I was saying all along; you know, about the spirits, Angels, dark ones and stuff.

"Anyway," she chuckled, "she thought I was possessed, so she calls in this priest to 'exorcise' the demons in me. Oh man, was that crazy! He was talking with her in the other room and then he comes in to ask me some questions. In case you haven't noticed, I have a hard time keeping my trap shut.

"So, he looks me over, and I take a peek inside his head, and he's actually wondering what I would look like without my clothes on. So, I asked him, "Why do you want to see what I look like naked?" she said, bursting into laughter.

"My mom looked mortified because she couldn't tell if I was telling the truth or not. Well, that caused the priest to start shaking real nervous-like. He's thinking to sort me out, so he's quoting Bible verses and holding his crucifix in front of my face, right? Then he gets the holy water out, and I figured since my mom is paying for this, I might as well put on a show. So I start playing along, right? I'm grunting and growling, hootin' and a hollerin,' saying stuff like 'She's mine!' and he's thinking in his mind 'Sweet Jesus, she really is possessed!'" she bellowed, proceeding with a fit of giggles.

"Anyway, this goes on for about ten minutes until I finally couldn't hold it in anymore, and I started laughing so hard I was crying. The priest was very embarrassed; my mom was so upset! She apologized over and over to him and went into the kitchen to get a rolling pin to beat me to death. That's when I grabbed my coat and ran out."

Her expression became serious. "When I came back about four hours later I found her in the bathroom. She'd had enough apparently. Enough of me, enough of trying to make ends meet, enough of disappointment in life. Even being able to read her mind, I never looked long enough to see that she was in a lot of pain.

"After her funeral, I was placed in foster care for a bit. The worst part of it was, I saw her wandering spirit. She was always around me apologizing, over and over. It was like she was this shell on auto pilot or something. I just about lost my mind, believe me. I prayed to God, to the angels I saw, over and over. I only wanted her to find peace. And then I saw him."

She turned off the engine. "We're here."

"Go on, finish your story," he said, sitting still in the passenger seat of the car, the cool air permeating the vehicle.

"Another time. But that was fun," she replied with a sly smile.

He sighed and sent a nasty telepathic comment to her. "You get that?" he asked. She smacked him across the chest.

"Hey, you earned it. Can't leave someone hanging like that. Where the heck are we anyway?" The moonlight shone across the adjacent mountainside, and he could hear the sound of a nearby river running. The car had travelled down a deserted road that led to a small, barely noticeable outlet amidst a thicket of trees that formed a privacy wall alongside a series of small mountains. A very high-tech fence with an even more advanced control pad that looked like it didn't belong on Earth, let alone the rural countryside, was blocking the way ahead. At that moment, Yelnisha's cell phone rang.

"Janey Mack! Right. Coming in now," she said, then put her phone away.

"Surprised you get reception out here. Everything all right?" he asked, observing the shift in her aura.

"We've got company headed this way. Got to get cracking."

She got out of the car and waved her hand over the device and muttered some words, causing the gate to slowly open. Returning to the car, she started it up again, and the two proceeded through. The narrow road stopped at a dead end, yet they continued travelling over what looked to be gravel and boulders, heading straight into the mountain itself. She looked over at him and smiled. "Pretty cool huh?"

Dorian was intrigued by the camouflaged entrance, but after what he'd seen recently it did not shock him the way Verdes Seventeen had.

"What is that, some kind of hologram?" he asked.

"Way more than just a machine with lights and mirrors I assure you. This next part is going to be a bit trickier."

OFF IN THE DISTANCE, SOME TWENTY kilometers away, a group of three large vehicles traveled with haste towards the little village of Villalba.

"The link is becoming stronger. His Shi is not concealed here; we are close. He may not be alone. Tell the others to prepare," Arita'el said to Ehasar, the driver of their vehicle.

As the group approached the town, Arita'el began to bounce his spirit energy off the few villagers still awake who had darkness in their spirits, in a futile attempt to see how many were traveling with Dorian. A couple of pub patrons were heading back to their cars, and he was able to see Yelnisha in their recent memory.

"He travels with one other, possibly more. We are close. Turn down that road."

YELNISHA'S CAR WOUND AROUND THE ROAD AS if they were descending deep into the ground. Further and further down they drove until almost twenty minutes had passed. Lights floated in place on both sides of the road with an ethereal, greenish-grey hue to them. The tunnel itself had alien symbols carved into the rock every so often—either some sort of warning to would-be unwanted guests, or travel markers. The symbols also glowed with an unnatural light that reflected off their faces as they made their way inward. She checked her wrist and looked up, then suddenly stopped the car.

"Whoa, that was close. Ana Harrani Sa Alaktasa La Tarat Talamu Enir," she said, with both hands forming a triangle. The road ahead disappeared. Instead, a trail led to a large open area on the left and a set of double doors of immense size on the right.

"It's a unique lock. You only learn the combination as you leave, and it only works for that person. All those symbols in the cave are part of the lock."

She waved her hand over her wrist, and a dozen symbols appeared, glowing with bright colors that matched the ones on the ceiling.

"If I didn't get out at the right time we would be traveling down that road forever. It can trap you if you don't pay attention. So, when you leave and plan on coming back you're going to either use what the road shows you, or wait for someone who left the sanctuary to bring you back in. This is going to be your home for the next several months. Are you ready?"

Dorian did not answer as he was still wondering who had created such an elaborate entrance.

She pulled the car up alongside the double doors and got out.

"Okay, give me your hand. They need to see what's in our minds, so you'll have to open up to them, otherwise we're not getting in."

She took his hand in hers and whispered something while placing one hand along the door. A faint glow of amber surrounded her.

"All right, here we go. You can let go now—that is, unless you don't want to," she said with a flirty smile. He smirked and shook his head in disbelief at her carefree personality. The doors didn't move at all. Instead, Yelnisha walked completely into one until she was not seen. A few seconds later, her head poked through to face Dorian, who was standing at the doors, unsure of what to do.

"Grab your stuff, c'mon," she said, disappearing back into the unknown. He picked up his bags and proceeded to walk into the adjacent door, which he quickly discovered was quite solid; knocking him on his butt. She peeked her head through the other door again, trying to contain her laughter.

"What the bejabbers are you doing? This is no time for a lie down ghost-post. Get in here! This side, ya plonker, the other one's just for show."

"NOW YOU TELL ME! Arrgh, I'm going to… Oooh you...you...," he grumbled, seeing a vision of her being thrown into a lake.

After rubbing his head where he had run face first into the door, he picked up his bags and used his foot to make certain the other door wasn't solid, which (thankfully) it was not. Stepping through, he immediately felt a pulling sensation similar to when he was sucked into the black hole on his travel to Verdes Seventeen. It lasted a couple of seconds, then it was over.

THE GROUP OF SUV'S CAME TO A STOP AT THE unusual gate at the foot of the small mountain. Several of the fallen with their grey cloaks left the confines of the vehicle to inspect the unusual lock as Arita'el approached it with caution.

"Sa Belet Ersetim Ki'Am Parsusa Amelatu Peta," he said, waving his hand over it. A moment later, it began to shine with a dark red light.

"It is finished. The opening is masked with Magick. Lahash, I feel his Shi in that mountain. A spell has obscured my vision; cast a reveal so we may continue our pursuance," he said to the tall being with long white hair and olive skin.

"A simple task. One moment," Lahash replied. He paused for a moment, mumbled something inaudible, then clasped his hands together, causing thunder to rumble in the distance.

"I will lead us through. The opening is just beyond those rocks, which are nothing more than an illusion. Come, we tarry no longer," Lahash said, moving back towards the vehicle.

They all climbed inside their transportation and carefully made their way over the wide path through the obscured opening until all vehicles were inside. Arita'el looked over to Lahash with concern.

"The entrance lacked a circle of protection; this troubles me."

"Perhaps this is not the entrance to their lair; we may have yet to see it. There can be no doubt they are aware of our pursuit," Lahash replied to everyone with radio communication.

They continued their journey down what they thought was the same path their quarry had travelled for almost ten minutes until the road forked. They followed the fork on the left for another ten minutes before stopping at the request of Arita'el.

He paused for a moment, concentrating on Dorian's spirit energy. "We are undone. I do not sense his Shi; a faint resonance lies within, as if it were before me but out of reach. These symbols that we have ignored; I suspect they are the requirement for entrance. We can only hope to return from where we came from, yet I have my doubts," Arita'el said over the communicators to the group.

"Are you certain, Arita'el? We have only travelled for twenty minutes. The trail is still shifting; perhaps we must continue further down," Ehasar said, his glowing grey eyes piercing the darkness within the vehicle.

"We are trapped, my friend. I suspect this was their intent from the outset. It is pointless to continue. You have done well, Lystad. When I have finished destroying you, I will polish your skull ever so bright as a reminder of your cunning."

# *Fourteen*

WHEN DORIAN REACHED THE OTHER SIDE, there were approximately fifty or so beings of various sizes, shapes, and origins to greet him and another two hundred or so in the vicinity going about their business. Advanced technology was on display everywhere around him, well beyond anything currently on Earth, yet somewhat dissimilar from that which he had seen on Verdes Seventeen and Erustian Prime.

Daylight appeared to be coming to a close; the sky was beginning to display a beautiful panorama of an unknown galaxy highlighted by a pair of moons, one yellow, one crimson. Colors danced in the atmosphere, not unlike the Aurora Borealis, bathing the enormous city in the distance with their ethereal light. A grassy knoll stood nearby, covered with amazingly beautiful flowers. Dorian could sense a sort of greeting coming from them, a feeling which he found slightly unsettling. The trees also gave a positive energy of welcome, as did some of the smaller life forms. One thing was for certain—he would never look at plants the same way again.

About a dozen or so beings were in floating chairs at a designated covered security area off in the distance, with screens that also floated all around them. Uniformed security patrolled the area, in addition to what looked like small flying vehicles.

There were no spirit guides to be found there, which struck him as odd. He was able to pick up some of the surface thoughts from those going about their business in the distance, but nothing from the group standing before him.

The majority of the beings appeared human; there were about four in the group of fifty that had human bodies with animal-type heads, and two that were composed of light, which he surmised were of celestial origin.

It was difficult for him not to stare, given the unusual life forms present, so he focused on the human faces to avoid insulting his hosts. Yelnisha stood off to the side, smiling. A tall figure with an olive complexion and grayish-brown hair pulled back into a ponytail moved forward. Dorian recognized him from his vision as his father Urieth, who was accompanied by two of the angelic beings. Urieth was dressed in a loose-fitted burgundy shirt with black pants and tall boots.

"Welcome, Dorian. We all welcome you to our sanctuary, our home, Anidon," Urieth said with a smile, while putting his hand on Dorian's shoulder.

"*Shadom ni ana*," the group said in unison.

Dorian stood still, astonished by his newfound surroundings.

"Thank you," he replied, feeling like a piece of meat on display. "I wasn't expecting all this.... Can anyone tell me where we are?"

Everyone in the group laughed.

"We are standing in an extra-dimensional space on the Earth, or more accurately, within the Earth," Urieth answered. "There are several dimensions of reality, and Anidon is located in the second. We are not on a planet, rather a large piece of land that stretches out with its own atmosphere and gravity. It is a self-contained country where we create our own food, have our own schools, library, and government. There are several lakes and rivers here, as well as many parks, theaters and sporting arenas. In addition, we have multiple training facilities throughout the city, which you undoubtedly will become acquainted with. As you can see, we use various methods of transportation that are significantly different than what you find on present day Earth. There is much to see and do here.

"Now, I think it's time for some introductions. Standing over to my left is Commander Yelnisha Reid, whom you are already acquainted with; she will be your introductory instructor on the fundamentals of Shi mastery. Assisting her will be the twins, Tiddi and Osokas. Standing next to her is Sargent Simon Newell. There he is," he said, pointing him out as Simon peeked his head through the crowd and waved.

"Standing to my left is one of our advanced trainers, Eshri'el, and to my right is Caphri'el." The two beings resembled Amprodius, with white hair and glowing amber bodies standing close to seven feet in height. The entire group stood apart from them, in a sort of reverence to their stature and significance. They both were wearing loose fitting clothing over their bodies, which had an iridescence about them. They gently smiled at Dorian. "They will be your advanced instructors when you reach the appropriate level of understanding.

"Our head of security is Zeracon, over there. Raise your hand Zeracon," Urieth said with a smile. One of the mixed humanoid beings roared very loudly, making Dorian freeze with a shocked look on his face. Zeracon had the head of something close to a lion and a body resembling that of a muscular human, with the exception of fine fur and claws. His eyes were yellow and slightly glowing. Everyone, including Zeracon, laughed out loud and Dorian just shook his head and muttered "You people," under his breath.

"Mishka," Urieth said, pointing to a dark-haired ruddy boy standing behind him, "will show you to your quarters and give you a tour of the city after you've had some rest.

"Last, but certainly not least, the people you see standing behind me represent a small part of our elite field operatives, warriors, and experts in Magick and science, known as the Avavago. They will be your brothers and sisters, guiding and helping you along the way.

"Welcome home, Dorian," he said, followed by applause from the group. Dorian smiled and nodded uncomfortably, and they slowly began dispersing.

Urieth walked over to him after the introductions.

"It's good that you joined us here, Dorian. This is where you belong. We have much catching up to do, but I know you've had a long journey, and recent events have been unkind, so I think it best you get some much-needed rest. We can talk tomorrow. Good night, my son," he said with a smile, patting Dorian on the shoulder.

"Oh, all right, good night then," Dorian replied.

A young boy about the age of twelve walked over to Dorian and touched his wrist. Warm greetings emanated from the lad. Dorian attempted to return the same, causing Mishka to giggle with laughter at his poor attempt.

"Okay then. Apparently, I've got a lot to learn. Mishka. Isn't that Russian for 'mouse'? Is that where you're from?" he asked.

The boy tried to speak with his hand and grunted; more like pushed air through his mouth with a guttural effect. Shaking his head as if to say 'no', he pulled down his scarf to reveal a large scar across his throat. Yelnisha was standing a short distance away, talking with some of her friends. Dorian looked her way with raised eyebrows and a smile, hoping to get her attention.

She noticed him looking her way and knew what his concern was about. "It's all right, he can speak to your mind. You just have to open up to him. Don't worry, just keep your thoughts clean, okay? We don't need any bad influences corrupting him," she said with a devilish smile. He gave her a mock frown and pursed his lips, causing her to laugh out loud.

As Dorian opened his mind, the boy was in the middle of communicating to him about where they would be traveling to. Dorian interrupted Mishka so he could start at the beginning.

*"Sorry about that, Dyadya. We will drop you off at your house and then we can look around the city tomorrow,"* Mishka said.

Dorian's eyes widened, and he moved his head back a bit. "My house? My house is in Michigan, very far away from here. You mean where I'm going to stay tonight?

*"Come, I will show you. Come,"* Mishka said, motioning with his hand. The boy led Dorian towards a platform that was some kind of lighted force field. It was orange in color and floating a few inches off the ground. They both stepped onto it, and the boy waved his hand around the center in a peculiar fashion, moving his lips but making no sound. The platform raised itself off the ground with the two of them onboard, forming a small enclosure to prevent them from falling out, along with several seats that enveloped them. Looking back at the remnants of the disbursed crowed, Dorian watched several of them wave goodbye as the two sped off into the unknown.

THE FLYING VESSEL WAS QUITE FAST, AND Dorian held tight to the seat as it whisked them around the outskirts of the city towards the sections that contained the living quarters. Several other flying platforms could be seen in the distance moving about with occupants on board.

From their height above, he had a better vantage point to view Anidon in all its splendor. Off to the east, an enormous crystal lattice sphere floated in the air, shimmering with light.

The lights from the structure produced a dazzling array of colors on the adjacent buildings and the sky. There were many floating signs near buildings that seemed to advertise various businesses of some sort or another, not unlike billboards found on Earth. The architecture was quite futuristic to his eye, and he felt as if he was in a science fiction movie come-to-life. As they travelled away from the heart of the city, he could see the housing communities lit up with people moving about.

They began to slowly descend as they came closer to the vast series of structures that housed the residents of Anidon. Most were composed of astounding materials of various kinds; some were made of onyx, some of diamond, others of emerald, sapphire, gold, pearl, and unusual substances found outside of Earth. A few were arranged side-by-side in gigantic spherical, obelisk, and pyramid shapes; while others were freestanding, similar to castles and other Earth dwellings. It was truly a spectacle to behold.

In the distance, separate from the main housing section, three large structures stood apart from the rest. Equally unique in their construction, they were seemingly comprised of the elements themselves.

The first had the appearance of solid crystal with lightning arcing about it. The second was the most unusual of the three. It appeared to be composed entirely of black fire; there was no color in the flames other than black with a faint grey silhouette within that danced and flicked about. It was quite striking in its appearance. The third structure was simply made entirely of light, a brightness and beauty that shone all around itself spectacularly. Despite its incredible brightness, it did not seem to illuminate anything beyond its immediate area, which he thought odd until he observed the dwelling with the black flames consuming the light that radiated outwards. It was as if the two buildings were designed to hold each other in check.

*"The Hashmallim live there; that area is forbidden. They frighten me; I mean, they are kind, but their power is terrifying. Eshri'el has watched over me though; I like him.*

*We are almost at your house. I think you will be happy with it,"* Mishka said as he piloted the platform while scouting ahead.

The area they were moving towards was separate from all the other housing communities. They passed over rolling hills that stretched across a meadow, culminating atop a hill that overlooked a forest surrounding it from all sides.

There appeared to be a large fire off in the distance.

"Hey, you might want to call the fire department. What do you people use to put out fires here? Looks like something is burning," Dorian pointed out while trying to see exactly what it was that was on fire.

Mishka smiled and laughed a wispy grunt. *"That is your house, Dyadya. Do not worry; I brought some marshmallows and hot dogs."*

"Everyone's a comedian," Dorian replied with a sigh.

They casually approached the giant structure in the shape of a castle that was completely engulfed in flames. The fire itself looked like the fires seen on Earth, but with more reddish hues to the flames. From afar, there wasn't any visible damage to the structure.

Floating lights, similar to those in the cave he and Yelnisha had travelled in, lit up a walkway that led to the threshold. The walkway itself was made completely of cut chrysolite and emeralds with incredible luster and beauty. The surrounding landscape consisted of an array of tropical flowers and plants that were not be found in Sicily, or Europe for that matter, as well as an unusual assortment of trees from all over the world. Nothing seemed out of place or overdone; it was simply perfect in its beauty. Flames roared off the house with all of the sounds that would accompany an actual fire, yet there was no heat at all, which he found quite remarkable. No source for the flames could be observed, yet they enveloped the entire structure.

The two disembarked from the platform and slowly proceeded towards the entrance.

"*Well, what do you think?*" Mishka asked with a smile.

"Takes cozy fire to a whole new level. I hope everything isn't burning on the inside also," he quipped. He slowly put his hand out and touched the flames that made up a supporting pillar. "Aaaaaaghh!" Mishka's face went blank for a moment, and his eyes widened like saucers as Dorian quickly pulled his hand away, holding it gingerly.

"*Oh my! Are you—what happened? Are you injured?*" Mishka asked in shock.

"Got ya, didn't I? Hahaha," he replied, pointing his 'burnt' hand in the shape of a gun at Mishka.

"*That was pretty good. I can usually tell when someone is trying to fool me,*" Mishka replied with a smile and a slight giggle.

"I've been practicing a bit. Can't have that Yelnisha reading my mind whenever she wants, you know. So how do we get in? I don't see any door handle, or do we just walk into it?" he asked, feeling around for a mechanism to enter.

"*Like this. Put your hand up and bend your last two fingers. Like I am, see? Now put it toward the door and say whatever you want to say to get in. It will only open for you. I cannot open it. You try now,*" Mishka said, stepping back.

"Okay, does this look, right? Just put my hand out and say whatever I want? All right then, open up." The door was unchanged. He looked over at Mishka who simply pointed at the entranceway.

"*Go in now.*"

Not taking any chances, Dorian used his foot to feel if the doorway gave way after remembering the prank Yelnisha had played on him. It went right through the burning door much the same way as he had entered Anidon for the first time. He slowly slipped through the wall of fire to the other side and found a large open space adorned with all sorts of curiosities.

"Mishka, are you coming?" Dorian asked, as he peeked his head through the door, having a sense of déjà vu.

*"You have to invite me in or tell the house to let me in,"* he replied.

"Oh. Sure, come on in." He slipped back inside as Mishka followed through.

*"Wow, Dyadya, this is so cool!"* Mishka exclaimed with amazement, stamping his feet in place as if preparing for a jog.

"So, you've never seen something like this before?"

*"I have seen a holovision program about this kind of place once, but I've never seen one in person. Let us look around."*

The interior was well lit throughout by soft white light that did not seem to have a source, yet the brightness illuminated everything perfectly. There were no wall switches of any kind that Dorian could see; the walls themselves appeared solid with a shimmering luminescence to them. Dorian approached a wall and touched it, lighting up a display that conveyed the status of the dwelling, including the number of occupants, where they were, options for climate control, hydration, sleeping quarters, food sources, in addition to personal messages, travel, entertainment and many other useful items as well. It was as if the entire house was a living butler.

*"Try walking through the walls. You just have to tell it to let you pass,"* Mishka said, while running about.

Dorian looked straight ahead and said "Pass" and he was able to walk through a wall to an adjacent room that was completely empty

"All right, nothing to see here. Pass." Closing his eyes, he slowly slipped through the way he came, returning to the main entranceway

*"You can change the color of the walls and what they look like. Tell it to turn into green watermelon,"* he said with excitement.

"So, what do I do? Just say 'walls turn in to green watermelon'?" As soon as the words left his mouth, the surface of the walls transformed themselves just as Dorian had pictured it in his mind. He touched the wall and the texture was that of watermelon skin, including its fragrance.

"Incredible. Wow, I don't know what to say...except...I don't want to live in a house full of watermelons, so walls turn back please." A second later, they returned to normal.

*"The house will become whatever you want. If you want a pond over there it will make one. If you want stairs made of balloons it will become balloons. You will have to decide what you want. I have to go home now, so I will let myself out. Goodbye, Dyadya, it was nice to meet you."*

"Oh, all right, I suppose it's late; thank you, Mishka. Hey, before you go, how do I call you if I need help? I have so many questions."

*"Don't worry, you will figure it out. The house will do everything for you. Goodbye,"* Mishka said, and slipped out the way he came in.

Dorian let out a sigh. "Great, where is the bathroom? I really have to go. House, where is the bathroom?" Instantly, he was surrounded by a small enclosure where he stood. A floating holographic screen appeared before him asking what function he would like to accomplish. It had a myriad of options, including showering, bodily functions, oral hygiene, music, preferred air scent, seating, infotainment, even food choices which he found rather unappealing.

"I would like to pee. How do I tell it I want to pee? Do I press this or what? Urinate. Number one. Are you listening? Comprendo?" The screen disappeared and a small, flower-shaped cup appeared out of the ground with an energy tube attached that extended to the floor.

"I'm supposed to make it in that? Hope this thing comes with a maid, because my aim isn't that good."

After he had completed his business, the option to wash his hands came up. Placing his hands into the receptacle, he felt a rushing of water, micro-scrubbers, drying, and emollient application within seconds.

"Well, that was pretty cool, I have to admit. I'm done, exit. Let me out of here," he said, flailing his hands about the holographic screen before him. The small enclosure disappeared, and he was back where he stood earlier. Picking up his bags, he began shuffling about looking for the bedroom.

"House, where's the bedroom?" he asked aloud. A screen appeared on a wall with a layout of the house and a map showing 'you are here'. Once again there were multiple options, from joining rooms into one, to configuring the layout, or dining, or other option too numerous for him to go into at this late hour.

"There's a room on the left in the back. Let's see if I can sleep there," he said, shuffling towards the general vicinity of the room the map had shown him. Colored lines appeared on the ground leading the way to the nearest room, as if the house had read his mind and knew what he was looking for. The door opened before him, or more accurately the door allowed him to pass through it, and he stood inside a completely empty room.

"Great, no bed, no closet, no chair…fantastic. House?" A holographic screen appeared before him with the question, "What would you like to do?"

"I need a bed, a dressing chest, and a chair or two. Know where I can get them?" A virtual catalogue appeared with an enormous selection of sleeping chambers; some were of the traditional type with mattress and box spring; some were of the Asian variety, futons, hammocks, water chambers, sleeping bags. He chose one of the zero gravity chambers.

"Can I have a chair to sit on?" The catalogue switched to chairs. He picked a couple of rustic-looking leather chairs and finished things off with an antique chest for his clothes. When he finalized his selections, much the way someone would check out from an internet purchase, he began to hear a faint humming sound which became more of a vibration, increasing in intensity until he noticed chairs literally coming up out of the floor, along with the wooden chest and the anti-gravity chamber.

"I don't believe it," he said, feeling around the chairs and chest to see if they were in fact really there. "Okay, I'm stumped. How did they... pull that off?" he asked, still touching and smelling the very real and quite sold chest. Changing into his bed clothes, he turned his attention to the large black cylindrical-shaped object that had come up. The surface was satin smooth and had what appeared to be black-green flames beneath its outer shell. A faint humming sound was emanating from it. It appeared to be made of some kind of stone; perhaps obsidian, or some alien material, it was not clear which.

"How does this thing work?" Another screen appeared before him. An animation demonstrated how to open the chamber and get inside. Waving his hand in front of the flashing light as instructed caused the large chamber to slowly open, revealing a pillowy, padded interior. Once he stepped inside, the device closed and a soft light illuminated his surroundings. The cabin became pressurized and a screen appeared before him with options for climate, lighting, sounds, scents, scenery, and more. Once he finished his selections the device began to lift him into weightlessness and he fell fast asleep.

THE FOLLOWING DAY HE AWOKE WHEN THE lights inside the chamber slowly increased, and the gravity gently brought him back to the ground. A scene of a perfect morning sunrise over a lake displayed all around him as if he were there. As he was acclimating to the gravity change, a screen appeared before him with a live view of Yelnisha outside his house and the option to engage in conversation. Rubbing his face and yawning, he selected to speak to her.

"How're the onions?" she asked in a chirpy tone. She was wearing makeup and a dress, which caught him by surprise.

"What's that?"

"How's the form? How's she cutting?" A sly smile crept up onto her face.

"I'm sorry, what exactly are you asking me?" he said with a chuckle.

"How are you? There, that better?" she sighed. "We'll make a proper Irishman out of you yet. Are you going to stand there staring at me or are you going to let me in?" she asked with a wink and a smile.

He sighed and rubbed his temple. "Yeah, sure, come on in, I guess."

"Wrong answer!" she shouted. "Your first lesson is to get your home security under control. Don't let anyone in here unless you absolutely know who's there."

"I already know it's you. I don't think anyone else would annoy me this much."

She gave him the two-fingered salute.

"Are you, or are you not Yelnisha?" he sighed.

"Maybe I am, and maybe I'm not. How're you going to be sure?"

"I don't know. I could have a code word, right? Like copper top, or in your case Irish Ham?"

"Keep it up, ya numpty. We're going to have sooo much fun together in the training I have planned for you," she said, massaging her fist.

"Okay, okay, sheesh. I suppose I could have the house scan you? Make sure you're not some sharp-tongued android or something," he replied while making his way out of the gravity chamber.

"You're getting warmer. What else?"

"I could share a picture between our minds; so, if we decide to make it a rabbit then that's what you would use. What do you think?"

"Yeah, you want to use a mental picture. It could be anything really, but I would have to plant it in your mind, and you would have to know. So, are you ready? I'm going to put an image in your mind that you will soon never forget. I know I didn't," she said with a laugh.

"Hey, wait a minute, awww, oh God, that's disgusting. No way, get that out of my head, you!"

"Te hehe hehe. Well, I happened to walk in on my granny and grandad flapping parts together, so I figured why shouldn't I share this precious moment? Certainly traumatized me as a six-year-old, let me tell you."

"Find something else, Yelnisha. I mean it. I don't want that image in my head again!" he yelled, pointing a finger at her.

"Oh, all right, then, how about this?"

"Better. I like..." he said as she interrupted him.

"Shush. Don't say it out loud. Now, are you going to let me in?"

"Hmmm... I don't know. I just don't know. How can I be sure you are who you say you are? You might not have been Yelnisha all along and just used this as a ruse to have me let you in," he said with narrowed eyes.

"Oh, just shut up and let me in dammit!"

"House, what do you say, should we let her in?"

The house responded with a question mark and a statement saying it was not responsible for making decisions.

"Well, I suppose we could let her in for the time being. Be ready to eject her on my command," he jokingly stated, causing the house to frantically try and interpret his statement.

She walked through the door and up to Dorian, who was wearing a grin on his face. Catching him unaware, she darted quickly behind him to deliver a blow to a nerve center at the back of his left leg and another at his right arm, leaving him temporarily paralyzed in those limbs long enough for her to form a light-energy weapon, a type of blade, under his chin.

"Ow! What the hell, Yelnisha?"

Alarms went off in the house, and tubes of energy instantly formed a cage around her.

"Crap, I forgot about that," she said in a defeated tone.

"House, find the nearest body of water and throw her in it," he said, rubbing his arm and leg.

"Hey, I was just trying to prove a point. You always have to be on your guaaaaaaaaaaaard!" she screamed while being catapulted outside. He followed her trajectory on the video screen as she flew across the meadow, splashing down into a nearby pond. He fell on the floor laughing.

"House, can you save a copy of this and send one to Urieth and Yelnisha?" The house responded with an affirmative.

"Hope she doesn't hold a grudge. I think I'm beginning to like you." The house showed a picture of him with hearts showering down all around.

"We have to come up with a new name for you. Can't keep calling you house all the time. Hmmm, well, I think Uchi will work."

The home screen changed to the phrase 'My name is Uchi. I am happy to serve you.' Hearts continued to shower around his image on the screen.

"Glad you like it Uchi. Can you talk?" he asked while looking through some of the menus. Instantly a catalogue of voices popped up offering an array of choices—cartoonish, male, female, robotic and the like. There was a customizable option that he could choose from his own memory. He immediately selected it and thought of someone while placing his hand on the screen, and within a few seconds he heard Yuki's voice asking him if she sounded acceptable.

"You sound just like her—amazing... and creepy at the same time. Okay, Yuk, ah, I mean Uchi, where's the kitchen?"

"Follow the trail on the floor. What would you like to eat?"

"Is there any food? What am I saying? I bet you can make amazing food, am I right?"

"Searching for food called amazing. Found two thousand fifty-eight dishes with the title amazing. Please narrow down your query."

He laughed. "It was an expression, Uchi, I'm not looking for a dish called amazing. How about some simple buttered toast with eggs and coffee?"

As Dorian made his way over to the unusual looking kitchen, Uchi prepared what he had asked for, as well as some tables and chairs to his liking. After finishing breakfast, he cleaned up with an instant shower over where he stood, comparable to the experience of washing his hands in the bathroom.

He checked his appearance in the mirror, staring at his face for some time. "Well, I suppose it's not necessary for me to wear these here," he said, removing his contact lenses. The light shone from his eyes with a glowing emerald green hue that seemed as if they were illuminated by a source from within his head. It was a strange sensation going without them for the first time. "I can be myself here."

A feeling of happiness began to slowly creep in at the thought of being accepted for what he was, without fear of being viewed as a freak. Just as he was about to start making a few calls to get his tour of the city, Matthias popped up on his screen. He engaged the communicator.

"Matthias? Is that you?"

"Greetings, Dorian. Yes. How are things so far?"

"Fine. Still getting used to it here. Are you in Anidon?"

"Yes. I live in the southern district of Shem; however, most of the time I am out and about. Coming from Earth, I can tell you that life here will take some amount of adjustment before you are accustomed to it. Take your time becoming familiar with everything, there is no rush.

"Now, to the reason I called. I have been made aware that Yelnisha is to provide you with Shi training along with Tiddi and Osokas. To further enhance her tutelage, I can provide you with instruction on the basics of warfare, as well as espionage, tactics, and subterfuge. Some of what we cover will be conceptual and some will be practical. We—that is, your father and I—believe these to be necessary skills in order to survive encounters with the fallen or other spirits working alongside them. Having been educated as a scientist, your disposition towards such precepts may undoubtedly be considered hostile or dismissive. I can only ask that you consider such education as being necessary for your own survival and possibly that of others as well. In fact, one could argue that your scientific education will be an asset, allowing you to consider possibilities that defy conventional wisdom. So, with that said, I would implore you to take a small journey with me to the first series lecture hall at the Obelisk of Enlightenment, where we will explore these and other concepts. What say you?"

"Well, I suppose since I've come this far it would be impolite for me to decline such an offer. How will I get to this lecture hall and what time will we begin?"

"Currently the time as observed in Anidon is eleven a.m. And my class will begin in approximately two hours. The house that you have been given is equipped to instruct you with directions as well as a means of transportation to the lecture hall. I have sent the schedule to your house already. Simply be ready to receive transport around that time. I look forward to working with you and expanding your education. See you soon," he said, ending the transmission.

Just as that call ended, another one came through. This time it was Urieth. Dorian answered to see him laughing.

"I don't know what happened between you two to cause her to be thrown into the pond, but that was one of the funniest things I have ever seen in my many years of life. I know she can be a bit of a pain sometimes, but try to put up with her for the time being for the greater good. Heaven knows she's probably thinking up some elaborate way to get her revenge, so I would be on my guard if I were you. Anyway, the real reason I called is I wanted to try to catch up with you later on, perhaps a couple of hours after you are done with Matthias? I would like to introduce you to some friends of mine and show you a few sights around Anidon. Are you up for it?"

"Sure, sounds fine, where, how do I contact you?"

"The house has a portable communication device everyone carries with them. Just ask for it," Urieth replied.

"It's quite remarkable, I have to say. I've never even conceived something like that existing. Someone could bring that technology upstairs and change the world," Dorian opined.

"Technology this advanced would unfortunately end up destroying the world above. Matter convertors, when controlled by the wrong group, would leave the humans in perpetual servitude and bondage. No, my son, the humans have quite a way to go before they have evolved enough spiritually to allow such devices to be used freely. In actuality, this science does not originate on Earth or Anidon; we have been fortunate in that our extra-terrestrial allies have graciously bestowed this gift upon us to utilize for our purposes," Urieth said.

"I suppose that makes sense. Well, at least I'm getting some use out of it. This seems like an enormous treasure though; I'm not so sure I deserve something this elaborate, Urieth."

"Everyone on Anidon has access to some type of matter convertor, either for sustenance, or for their general living. The one your house is equipped with is far more advanced than what

most citizens have access to; they are very limited here in
Anidon. I know you have demonstrated responsibility in the
world above, and to those who use well what they have been
given, even more shall be given. So, do not worry that you are
unworthy to accept such a thing; you are more than worthy. On
that note, I will end our conversation and we shall speak over a
fine meal at the conclusion of your studies. Unfortunately, I will
have to ask you to wear your eye covers outside and from now
on. We must keep your heritage a secret for the time being.
Farewell," he said with a smile, ending the communication.

Dorian sighed aloud. "Someday I'll be able to go without
them, oh well."

The next few hours flew by quickly as Dorian made
additional customizations to his new house and discovered the
Anidon news, its infrastructure, history, and 'internet', all with
the aid of Uchi.

THE TIME APPROACHED FOR DORIAN'S instruction
with Matthias. Uchi informed him to step outside onto the
waiting platform, which would take him directly to the lecture.
Approximately five minutes later, he reached his destination.

The landing area was atop a gigantic white obelisk that
stood at two thousand one hundred feet. There were numerous
other platforms on that side of the obelisk that led to various
floors within the structure. Hundreds of people were coming and
going, and he had to quickly get out of the way to avoid creating
a traffic jam. Once he disembarked the vehicle, it shrank into a
miniaturized form, allowing Dorian to take the semi-sentient
Uchi EL-84 module with him. It floated alongside as he was led
to a small lecture hall on the ninety eighth floor where he
observed Matthias standing at a podium giving instruction to six
other students.

"Ah, Dorian. Please come inside and be seated. I was just
explaining to your fellow classmates that you would be joining

us. Allow me to introduce you all to Professor Dorian Lystad, son of Urieth." Everyone in the class turned their attention towards him.

"Over there on the far left is Sasha; next to her is one of our field leaders, Sergeant Simon Newell; to his right we have Josiah; behind him is Emerelda."

"Emma," she interrupted.

"My apologies. Continuing to the right is Xui Mei, and finishing up the lot is Juan Velazquez." Most of the group turned to greet him, or at least look at him, with the exception of Emma.

Dorian paused; the truth of the situation struck him for a moment. Here he was in an alternate dimension of Earth's reality, standing in an auditorium in a giant obelisk in order to learn about supernatural warfare. Not more than four weeks prior could he have possibly imagined all that had transpired and how much his life had changed. For a second he wondered if he was in a coma in a hospital somewhere after some terrible accident, and that all that he experienced was one big hallucination or dream.

"Dorian? Is everything all right?" Matthias asked.

Dorian was staring ahead with a blank look on his face.

"What are you, some kind of idiot? Sit down, so we can get this over with," Emma barked, scowling with disgust.

"Miss Emma, if you would be so kind as to refrain from speaking in that manner, I would greatly appreciate it. Professor Lystad has been through a great deal of difficulty very recently, and I am sure he is just adjusting to his surroundings," Matthias said gently.

"Forgive me, Emma, everyone. Pleasure to make your acquaintance. Please, continue Matthias," Dorian said, fitting himself into a seat that conformed to his body. The others looked at him and gave off various emotions; mostly curiosity, slight indignation, a bit of lust, and a touch of jealousy. Dorian refrained from reading their thoughts, as being called out on it at the present moment could become embarrassing for him.

"Currently, the class is into its seventh week, and we have much material yet to cover. For today, all I ask is that you listen and not concern yourself too much with mastering the information. My wish for everyone is to understand the greater concepts and how they apply to what we do here. I will send the materials to your house computer for you to get up to speed on what we have been learning. With that said, let us continue," he said, turning his attention to a floating screen with an animation of the topic he had most recently discussed.

It was no surprise that their educational methods were superior to those that were employed on Earth. If a student had a question or was unsure, Matthias would simply touch them and 'transfer' the correct way of thinking about the matter at hand. Dorian remained quiet for the two-hour lecture, and at the conclusion he waited for all the students to disperse before approaching Matthias.

"I hope you found my discourse educational, or at least somewhat enlightening," Matthias said.

"It's not exactly a subject material I am familiar with, but I think you presented it well enough for me to get the basics of what was being discussed. You all take this very seriously it seems," Dorian replied.

"Yes, and with good reason. Over the centuries, the citizens of Anidon have tried to influence and counteract the infiltration of the enemy imbedded in human affairs, with mostly disastrous results. There are very powerful forces at work among them, and we believe they have laid the groundwork for a significant and dramatic action that is nearing its fruition. Their skills are quite superior to ours in many ways, yet we have advanced to the point where I feel that we have a fighting chance against them. Your father can give you more of the specifics of what we are up against. Suffice it to say it is far beyond conventional human warfare."

"I see. I will try to take it more seriously then. I have to admit, I am a bit envious of your presentation skills and ability to transfer information through thought-touch. Tell me, why don't you just give them everything they need all at once? Is that not possible?"

Matthias smiled. "The visual examples I gave, coupled with the conceptual and practical, helps cement the ideas. As to your query posed about thought transference—that method works best when in Baltu form. The human brain, and that includes higher forms of human, is incapable of absorbing too much information at one time, and thought transference can lead to identity issues in those who have not mastered their Shi. We tend to use it sparingly for helping to clear up misconceptions and misunderstandings. Your Shi is quite powerful; however, it is vital that you learn to control it to a greater degree before experimenting with matter manipulation, light gathering, and thought transference. Yelnisha, ahem, will be your guide for that," he said, looking past Dorian.

"Thaaat's right," a familiar voice coming from behind said slowly and somewhat malevolently. Dorian grimaced and winced while Matthias looked puzzled.

Dorian casually turned towards Yelnisha while keeping the two of them in his sight. "Ah, about what happened earlier. Listen, I had no idea that was going to happen. I didn't think the house was going to literally throw you into a pond. I was just as surprised as you were. Believe me—"

"Oh, I believe you all right. Believe me, I won't let you make that mistake again," Yelnisha replied through gritted teeth.

Tiddi and Osokas, her two subordinates, were standing next to Yelnisha, using every ounce of willpower to avoid bursting into laughter.

"What brings you here?" Dorian asked.

"Oh, I just came to bring you the good news. I just spoke with Urieth, and he wants you to begin training with me tomorrow, five days a week. I can't wait for us to get started," she said with narrowed, sinister eyes. "I've sent the information to your house pet, so I expect you won't be late," she said, then brusquely walked out.

Dorian looked over at Matthias. "Sounds like she's going to hold a grudge. She's not a vengeful person, is she?"

"I have known Yelnisha since she was ten years old, and in that time she has consistently demonstrated herself to be vindictive towards those who have crossed her in some form. I suspect considerable repercussions for this act. Good luck my friend. A word of advice, she likes puppies."

"Puppies? Great, one loves rabbits and the other loves dogs. I had better think of something by tomorrow. Thanks for the lecture, Matthias, and the advice. When do we meet again?"

"Just so you are aware, this class is held three times a week. I've sent the schedule to your house computer to remind you. Until the next time my friend." Matthias waved goodbye and left.

Dorian walked out of the classroom, a bit disoriented by the unfamiliar surroundings and the pace at which his life was transforming. Xui Mei was standing outside and made eye contact with him as he walked out. She smiled and they both started laughing.

# Fifteen

AFTER WALKING BACK TO THE AREA WHERE HE had arrived, Dorian asked Uchi where he was to meet his father for dinner. There were still two hours remaining, so he decided to walk around the city to do a bit of sightseeing. Making his way outside to the terminal platform, he climbed aboard his semi-sentient mobile home and proceeded to get the grand tour of the city in daylight. Thousands of people were moving about to various places, some flying, some walking, some with ground transportation. Going over the main city, he spotted a coliseum or stadium of sorts that looked to be hosting some type of sporting event. He moved in for a closer look, where he observed banners hanging up top of the stadium that were advertising for the current year's cooperation events. Holographic videos of players engaging in the sport were all around the front steps, along with immortalized statues of what he surmised were famous players.

Continuing around the town, he heard loud crashes of thunder and sounds of explosions that rumbled in the distance.

His heart began to race, wondering what it was all about, so he followed the noise until he came to an outdoor training facility.

About two hundred people of various sizes and origins were sorted into different groups; one on one, two vs two, five on five, and so on in an area about the size of twenty football fields. About two hundred of them were off to one side doing some type of physical training with several instructors leading them in smaller groups, much like a modern day martial arts class. Some of the pairings were moving so fast it was difficult to follow. Flashes of light, loud crashes, impact shockwaves, and explosions took place in the air and on the ground.

The intensity and speed at which these combatants moved was incredible. They seemed very focused on their training. There was no laughter or playing around amongst them, with the exception of a small group that looked very much like the ones in the class Matthias just finished up with. Spectators' were gathered to watch them practice in designated areas all around the training facility. Many displayed a look of awed reverence on their faces, almost as if the combatants were some sort of chosen ones. Five minutes later, the melee had ceased for the combatants to take a break. A few moments later, the field began to repair itself with multiple floating disk shaped devices that Dorian suspected were a type of portable matter generator.

Uchi reminded Dorian that the time to meet with Urieth was approaching. He departed, and a few moments later arrived at The Whispering Wind, an enormous circular building with flashing multicolored-lights on the exterior. The venue was much larger than Dorian expected. Hundreds of people were coming and going, making it seem like some type of concert or media event. As he approached the entranceway, he observed multiple holographic sentient beings similar to Uchi managing the seating assignments for the guests.

"You may proceed inside, Dorian. Your father's table has already been prepared and he is waiting for you. Follow me," Uchi said.

The interior of the Whispering Wind, like much of Anidon, was unique. Floating lights similar to the ones that lit up the tunnel and the front of his house were lined up all along the walls. The walls themselves utilized the same technology found in his house, allowing for a fully customizable appearance. Patrons had the ability to customize three walls in their section, the table and seats, in addition to the floor and ceiling.

The visitors seemed to be trying to outdo each other with elaborate and creative designs, which obviously was part of the allure and charm to the place. Some used pre-made templates that they brought from home, some set up their space on a whim, and others had the computer randomly customize their surroundings. Everything from snowy grounds with a campfire, sandy beach settings with tropical plants, stone castle walls with ornate fixtures, solid ice bars, Asian outdoor spas, otherworldly-looking settings, gothic designs, and so on were on display. Many people were milling about, looking at all the different creative deigns.

The customizable spaces were all along the walls, and in the center of the giant facility chefs were preparing food alongside of performers that were engaging in different forms of entertainment. Dorian was overwhelmed by the sights and felt sad that the world above was not able to enjoy something this magnificent.

Uchi brought him to Urieth's section, which was done up exactly like Dorian's living room in Ann Arbor, complete with his fireplace, aged tufted leather couch, his tables, and even the pictures on the walls.

"I see you made it here, excellent. I thought you could use some familiar surroundings, so I hope you don't mind me taking the liberty of making it up like this," Urieth said.

Dorian stood at the precipice admiring the realism.

"Please, be seated," Urieth said with his hand extended. Dorian sat down and felt the leather on the couch, which was almost identical to how his own felt.

"The only thing missing is the freezing cold temperature I've been accused of keeping in the house," Dorian said with a laugh. Urieth smiled.

"How is this possible?" Dorian asked.

"We call them matter converters, which is a basic description of their function. Once we have the molecular makeup of something we can determine its atomic structure, and from there it is simply a matter of rearranging things to transform it into something else. With this device, I can take a mound of dirt or sand and turn it into a turkey sandwich, or a shirt, or whatever I want. It's quite amazing to say the least, and it's transformed our society. There is no want for anything; everything created is for all of us to enjoy. When you can have whatever you want whenever you want it takes greed out of the equation. The focus shifts from a materialistic society to a more spiritual one," Urieth said.

"And here I was under the impression the major human incentive to succeed was driven by greed," Dorian said. "The desire for nicer things and a better way of life drives societies to advance and produce. When people can get whatever they want whenever, as you say, don't they lose their drive for life?"

"In a society where greed is rampant, your assessment is correct; when the need can be satisfied on a whim the effect of gathering things to impress or get ahead of others is lessened and eventually becomes meaningless. What then is left for the greed driven individual? To look within and to recognize that the most valuable commodity was already before them all along; each other. When we see that what is most important is not things that we can gather up and look at, but rather caring for and loving one another, then we have realized our true purpose for this existence.

"What was once about the self is now about the other self. We are all connected, you, me, and everyone in this room, this world. We are all part of the source of everything and we all originate as one; and therefore, that person over there and that one there are as if brother and sister to you and I.

"Greed, however, does not necessarily reflect an attribute for only those desiring material things. Selfishness can be in the form of laziness, of being unwilling to do what it takes to help your fellow brothers and sisters out.

"I have witnessed societies that tried taking the approach of shared wealth, but they did not flourish as greed prevailed, either through corruption of their leaders, laziness of their populace and general apathy. The same downfall can be applied to democratic societies as well.

"A wise man once described the cycles a nation goes through—From bondage to spiritual faith; from spiritual faith to great courage; from courage to liberty; from liberty to abundance; from abundance to complacency; from complacency to apathy; from apathy to dependence and finally dependence back into bondage. I have lived for many thousands of years and have seen all forms of governance on Earth and several on other planets. There is yet to be one lasting form that all can rest comfortably in.

"Forgive me, I did not intend to become so overbearing with my opinions. It's just that I feel pity for humans; after having lived so long humanity still cannot get it right," he said with sadness in his voice.

"You won't get any argument from me," Dorian replied.

"Anyway, here in Anidon, we have, for the most part, channeled our drive towards creative endeavors. Even though we use matter converters, they still require a blueprint; if none exists, then we must create one. All of the amazing things you have seen here are a result of the creative spirits within that have applied their skills for the betterment of all. Some here do not possess the intellectual or creative capacity to create; however, most here have found something that brings them some form of happiness that contributes towards the greater good."

"Everyone seems happy. I suppose what you have going here is a good thing." Dorian replied.

"It is not all without strife. There are those among the council and their followers who have more radical ideas towards ruling and our role in combating our enemies. Many citizens, the majority I would say, are in uniform agreement that the agents of the Light-Bringer need to be dealt with. Only the methods we employ seem to be contested. Indeed, there are those on the council who would like to see me expelled from Anidon because I voice my concerns too loudly and disagree with how some would have things done here. But that is for another discussion. Today we should celebrate this occasion where father and son are reunited, and enjoy our time together.

"As I have chosen our seating environment, I think it only fair that you decide on what we shall eat. Several friends will be joining us shortly that I should like you to meet, so I suggest you choose wisely; two are fellow council members and two are part of my intelligence gathering team," he said with a wink at Dorian.

"I should also remind you not to mention or think anything about your birth mother; that stays between us and Matthias," he added.

Dorian looked over the menu options, which were too numerous to decide; he played it safe with Italian. The selection was made, and a couple of punk rocker-type girls skated over the table to prepare the settings for their meal. In actuality, they used a portable holographic screen that everyone in Anidon was fond of to select the place settings. A moment later a robotic servant brought them over. Dorian instinctively started to get up to help make the room more inviting for the anticipated guests.

The girls smiled. "Have a seat, relax. We'll take care of it," the pink haired one said, sizing him up.

"I keep forgetting this isn't my living room," Dorian replied with a laugh.

All sorts of smells filled the air, and in fact part of the fun of walking around was to see what other people were eating. While Urieth seemed to be interrupted by his subordinates checking in, Dorian took the opportunity of letting his mind sift through the thoughts of those around him for a few moments. He didn't pick up anything significant until he heard a female voice telepathically in his mind.

"*You are being watched. Be on your guard, especially your thoughts,*" she said.

"*Who is this?*" he asked, peering around to see if the messenger was in his visual field.

"*A friend. Be wary of councilman Ashmus Terharax; he is not who he seems. I will say no more,*" she replied, then abruptly ceased communication.

"You would be wise to exercise caution using that skill. You don't know who might try to poison your mind," a tall figure standing in front of the living room said. He was completely bald with an ashen-colored skin, much like the fallen watcher Dorian had encountered at his home in Ann Arbor. The markings on his skin were similar as well, as if they were branded, and the resultant scars formed sigils that were licorice colored. His eyes were glowing with a yellowish hue, and his teeth were blackened and pointed. Dorian looked at his aura which was a deep violet. The feelings given off him were warm and inviting, which contrasted greatly with his appearance.

"Your countenance suggests you have seen an apparition," he said to Dorian while glancing over at Urieth. Urieth smiled and stood up to greet him.

"Sonra'el, my friend, I am warmed at your presence," Urieth said, grasping Sonra'el's forearm in his. "Please, I would like to introduce you to my son, Dorian."

"It is my honor to meet the son of Urieth. We have all heard so much about you," Sonra'el said, extending his hand to Dorian, who received it. A feeling of greetings was exchanged between the two. Suddenly, out of nowhere, Dorian had a flash of Sonra'el's past from ancient times, many thousands of years ago. Before his fall from grace he was a beautiful angelic being that shone brightly with the light of the creator. His fall disfigured him as he was seen now, and the vision changed to a battleground of a major war. At that time, his brother, Salami'el joined with the Morning Star and fought against the forces of Heaven. Dorian saw that Sonra'el had also been one of his followers, but through a turn of events he betrayed the other fallen Angels, including his brother. Using very powerful magic, he managed to open a dimensional rift to escape their wrath; however, his form remained unchanged. The next several thousand years flashed before Dorian's eyes in an instant, and he witnessed the trials Sonra'el had faced over the millennium. A cold sweat formed on Dorian's forehead and his skin turned pale.

"Are you well, my son?" Urieth asked.

Dorian slowly pulled his hand away with a blank expression on his face, staring at Sonra'el.

"Yes, I think so. I think. Did you just?" he asked, looking at Sonra'el

Sonra'el looked at Urieth and then back at Dorian.

"What is it, Dorian? Did something happen?" Urieth asked.

"I'm not sure if I should...I had some kind of vision. You were an angel of light. I saw you in the war of heaven, the first meeting of the two of you, your struggles, the death of your family. It was as if I was there—I felt what you felt, everything," Dorian replied, unsure of why he was able to view Sonra'el's past with such clarity. Sonra'el and Urieth looked at each other with astonishment.

"You have witnessed what very few have then. And if what you say is true, then you have shared the pain of my existence since that fateful day. I would not wish that upon anyone, my friend. Are you well?"

"I'm not feeling the greatest, no. I thought you sent that vision to me; I have no idea how that happened. I'm still learning to control things. Looks like I have a long way to go," Dorian replied, holding his hand over his forehead.

"It would seem you have been blessed with many gifts," Sonra'el replied. "One can only wonder what else is in store for you. Come, let us not relive the past, but enjoy each other's company while we are able.

"Urieth, I should mention, Gregory informed mc hc will be late in his arrival," Sonra'el stated, appearing slightly shaken by Dorian's confession.

Urieth paused a moment while he looked over at his son with concern, then back at Sonra'el. "That is no surprise. Gregory is typically late for most social gatherings. Jasmine and Marcus should be here shortly. I see them now, actually," Urieth said, waving at the council members to join them.

The two made their way over and fit themselves on the couch.

"Ah I see everyone's here except Gregory, as usual," Jasmine said. Her face appeared to be much younger than her voice and demeanor suggested. Her skin was coco-olive in color, and she wore a dark blue and gold appointed turban and large gold earrings, along with a gold-woven dress; all in all, she was a remarkably beautiful woman who garnered much attention from those passing by. She smiled at Dorian with her exceptionally perfect teeth and lips. Dorian smiled back nervously, having a difficult time maintaining his focus after his disturbing vision.

A tall, dark man wearing a futuristic-looking grey suit moved in behind Marcus, just as Jasmine finished her last sentence. "I'm not always late. Just most of the time," he said with a laugh as he slid into the gathering, placing his arm around Jasmine and gently kissing her on the cheek.

"Jasmine, Marcus, Gregory, I would like to introduce you to my son, Dorian. Jasmine is one of the council members and also serves as a Mediator, which is what you would refer to as a judge on the Earth's surface. The one to her left, often accused of being my twin, is Marcus Parreth, another council member who works in our intelligence gathering unit. And the last one, standing next to the beautiful woman he could only dream of acquiring is Gregory, who works with me in the Division of Offensive and Defensive Operations. Thank you all for coming."

"Urieth tells me that you are a professor and scientist in the state of Michigan in America on Earth. How is it you have not joined us sooner?" Marcus asked. He had the chiseled and experienced look of Urieth, with long, sandy-brown hair and blue eyes, along with a commanding tone of his voice. There were no ill intentions that Dorian could sense coming from him. Urieth did not mention the abilities of his guests, so Dorian had to assume they might be able to detect deception or evasiveness; the best approach, in his eyes, would be to tell as much of the truth as he could.

"I was given up for adoption for a time because Urieth wanted a normal life for me, away from all of the troubles you all face. For that I am grateful, because I see what a difficult life some of you have had. My foster parents have both passed on— my mother just a few days ago," Dorian said, glaring at Urieth. "But they were both very loving and wonderful. I could not have asked for more. My father was a researcher and scientist, and when he died from a terrible disease, I devoted my life to study and followed in his footsteps. Truthfully, I spent part of my research just trying to find out about myself, what set me apart from everyone else."

Urieth and the others looked at Dorian with sadness.

"I think I can speak for everyone and say we are very sorry for your loss. You still have family, and in time I hope you will come to see Urieth as a father, if not a friend at least. You are very young. To ones such as us, the short time you have spent above was but a brief moment; however, you should be proud of what you have accomplished, and do not feel as if it has been all for naught. Your experiences will be of value to you in the days ahead," Jasmine said with a loving smile on her face.

"If only I shared your optimism, Jasmine. Events are rapidly unfolding all around the Earth signaling a major change, a coming war," Marcus interjected.

"What news can you share, Marcus?" Gregory asked.

He looked around and lowered his voice. "There have been significant fluctuations in the Earth's energy field. We have reports that two of the prisons of the fallen have been opened and expect more to follow soon. I can also tell you that the Chinese and the Russians will be heading to war soon against Europe. This will have a major impact on the infiltration efforts the fallen have invested with the United Nations. They are vying for a world leader, and this Mullah Xul may be what we have feared; some are saying he is the product of one of the corrupted Angels and one of the Nephilim."

Dorian and Urieth looked at each other and said nothing.

"There is also rumor that the offspring of one of Rapha'el's special guard may hold the key to Asa'el prison."

Urieth's eyes widened. He kept quiet, but it was obvious that he was not happy with Marcus having this knowledge.

"If what you say is true, we need to find this individual before the fallen do; with Asa'el unleashed, the world will become a battleground. No doubt his power has grown over the years," Gregory replied.

"Mullah Xul will have to be dealt with soon if we are to gain a foothold in the coming days," Sonra'el said grimly.

"We have made several attempts to assassinate him, but he has very powerful allies who seem to have some way of predicting our movements. I have my suspicions about why that is the case, but I will remain silent until I am certain of the facts," Urieth said as the wait staff began bringing their food.

They ate their meal and talked of lighter topics. Urieth stood up and made some motion with his hand on his personal display, and the living room transformed as they sat. Dorian's grand piano made an entrance from the back of the room.

"I was wondering if you would be willing to play a melody for us?" Urieth asked with a smile.

"Oooh, Dorian please play us a song," Jasmine said with a big smile, her eyes lighting up. Dorian groaned inside at the thought of performing, but he didn't want to embarrass Urieth, so he obliged. Getting up from his seat, he tapped the keys to determine how well the piano was tuned and the response of the instrument, then began to play. It wasn't long before a small crowd had gathered to listen. He finished a few more pieces to a rousing applause from the audience. Smiling and nodding in appreciation to their gesture, he got up and returned to his seat.

"Quite the performance, Dorian. One would be surprised to learn the piano was not your profession," Gregory remarked.

"My mother was a professional pianist and instructor, so naturally I learned from the best," he replied, pausing to remember her passing.

"That was breathtaking my dear, simply breathtaking. Thank you for a wonderful evening, Urieth. It was so nice to have met you, Dorian. I think we will become fast friends," Jasmine said as she stood up to leave. The rest of the group followed suit and said their goodbyes, leaving Urieth with Dorian to finish up their conversation.

"So now you have met my inner circle of friends here, although I have many others that I value. Unfortunately, it seems that—"

"Wait, Urieth, we should be careful here. Is there somewhere private we can talk?" Dorian asked.

Urieth looked concerned. "Of course, my son. One moment."

He put the room back to its natural state and gestured for Dorian to follow. The two left the Whispering Wind and got aboard Urieth's flying transport, traveling to the enormous floating crystal sphere Dorian had seen some time ago. As they approached the structure, Dorian realized that it was not a crystal at all, but rather an enormous diamond. The colors and lights shimmering from it were mesmerizing. Its surface was cut with many facets to reflect the light with the greatest luminosity. At the bottom of the sphere there was a large opening through which many dozens of beings were coming and going from it.

"This is where we control the central government of Anidon. There are secure rooms in here where we can talk freely," Urieth said. They disembarked their platform and walked into the structure. The ground was an unusual type of stone that appeared to flow like a slow-moving river, displaying information for visitors to find their way. Officials in uniform were coming and going, several of which nodded to Urieth as they passed.

They rode a platform up to the twenty-first floor, where Urieth gave his credentials to the security forces there. A temporary pass was given to Dorian, and the two of them travelled forwards on their platform for a bit until it stopped in front of a set of double doors that also appeared to be made of diamond. A sign upon them read "Commanding Offices for Offensive and Defensive Operations of Greater Anidon. Security clearance required for entrance."

There were no guards outside, only a floating device that was similar to the one Yelnisha had used to get into the mountain. Urieth waved his hand over it and mouthed some words. The doors lit up brightly and announced the two of them as they passed through the entranceway.

"My office is back here; follow me," Urieth said as Dorian was looking around at the see-through floors.

"I've heard of transparency, but don't you think this is a little overboard?" Dorian asked.

Urieth chuckled. "We can alter the floors' colors to give privacy, but after hours we keep them off for security purposes. Most of my more sensitive discussions take place on Verdes Eta. What you see around you is where our basic day to day operations take place. Come inside, have a seat," he said. He waved his hand and the transparent doors to his office opened. There were several chairs inside, a large desk in the back with a floating holographic display of written plans, several potted plants, and pictures on the walls, including several of Dorian in his younger days. Urieth gestured at Dorian to take a seat. When Dorian sat in one of the chairs, it conformed to his body, reclining him into an almost prone position. A floating screen appeared in front of him.

"Do not touch anything, I'll set it up," Urieth said. After making adjustments, Urieth sat in his chair, which moved into alignment next to Dorian's.

"Just relax and take a few deep breaths. You might find the experience to be a bit disorienting at first," Urieth said as he finalized the adjustments.

A moment later, Dorian felt the tremendous rush of force pulling him through the now familiar tunnel. A thunderclap later, they were both on the breece. Verdes Eta was unique in that it was Urieth's own secure space that only he and those whom he chose could access.

The two of them travelled in spirit form to the one and only building on the breeceway, which had the outward appearance of an ancient stone structure crafted by an advanced civilization from long ago.

"We are free from prying eyes and ears here. Was there something important you needed to discuss with me?"

"Yes. At the Whispering Wind I heard a voice in my head. It told me we were being watched and that a Councilman Ashmus was not to be trusted. I was trying to communicate with it when Sonra'el showed up. I don't know what that's all about, but I thought you should know," Dorian said.

Urieth frowned. "I see. I'm not quite sure what to make of it myself. We've had our disagreements over the years, but I do not consider Ashmus my enemy. Ashmus is the Chancellor of Research here, in addition to his position on the council. I, along with several others, have called for closer scrutiny of his research activities, which he has vehemently opposed every time the subject has been broached during the council sessions. I do not fully trust him myself, so I am thankful you have brought this to my attention. It would be foolish for me to dismiss it casually, so I will carefully investigate.

"I trust your dinner was satisfactory?"

"Yes, everything was great," Dorian replied.

"It was nice for us to share a meal together, and I am happy that you have met some of my closest friends."

"There is one more thing I forgot to mention to you before I came to Anidon," Dorian said

"Oh? What's that?"

"I discovered what I believe to be an encrypted message within my genetic code. As far as I can tell it was left for me by Esme. About a week ago, my mother gave me this alien-looking metallic disc; well, more of a heptagon in shape. Anyway, it had these unusual pairings of dots and words on it. She told me Esme gave it to her when I was an infant and instructed her to give it to me when the time was right. Apparently, the right time was just a few days ago, since she had forgotten about it entirely for years.

"When I looked at it at first I couldn't read it. After they turned on my Shi or it was activated, whatever you call it, somehow, I could read it. What we've come up with is that the dots on the object correlate to specific codons, genetic sequences of DNA base pairs that are also linked to these angelic words."

Urieth's eyes widened. "We? Where is the device now?" he asked.

"I left it with a friend of mine, Yuki, who also runs my lab. She's working on decrypting the code for me," Dorian replied.

Urieth looked quite shocked. "I was unaware that Esme'el had placed any message in your genetic code, so I am at a loss for words right now. We need to keep this information between ourselves for the time being, as there are too many variables to consider. I will have Sonra'el place a protective spell over Yuki's home. Whatever this message may contain, it could be information that the enemy might somehow benefit from, so we should assume it does and act accordingly until we know for certain. It may be best for her safety and our security that she goes into hiding.

"With Anidon's technology I am quite confident the message could be deciphered in no time, but I dare not risk prying eyes or questions, so for now we will allow your friend to make an attempt at deciphering the message for us," Urieth said, looking weary.

"I left her in charge of my lab, with the priority of finishing her education. Are you sure you want me to go back there now? I just got here."

"I should like to inspect this object myself, so I will go in your stead. It's best that you continue your studies here for the time being. Given the rapid development of events we need to get you up to speed as quickly as possible."

"More than likely she can complete her education over the next three months, so in that time could you have someone watch over her?"

"I will place several operatives around the University as well as your home. If finishing her education is important to you, then I will comply with your request. We will use the time to prepare you," Urieth replied.

"I can record a video message with the two of us so that Yuki will know that she can trust you," Dorian replied.

"That is a wise decision. Do not share this information with anyone, including Matthias. Be sure that your mind blocking skills are mastered and that you do not think upon it unless we are in a secure location. For now, just continue your studies here. Is this acceptable?"

"Yeah, no problem. Let me know how things go."

The two left Verdes Eta together and said their goodbyes. Dorian headed back to his new home and contemplated the events of the day until he fell fast asleep.

# Sixteen

THE FOLLOWING MORNING, DORIAN FOUND IT difficult to wake up; the recent passing of his mother, along with his concerns for Yuki and what the future held, made it seem as if the weight of the world was pressing down upon him. It was early morning Thursday, four days away from the new year, and a soft bell was ringing in his bedchamber. A photograph from the outside of his house showed Yelnisha's face plastered right up against the imager, distorting her face in a cartoonish fashion. He pressed the option to ignore and closed his eyes. She buzzed several more times, each time giving a different contorted face.

"Okay, okay, jeez." He pressed the communication button on the floating screen.

"Mornin' to ya. Just wanted to see how the new resident is faring on this fine day," she said in a pleasant tone.

He rubbed his right eye with his hand and yawned, showing obvious signs of fatigue and stress. "Good morning," he said politely. "I suppose I should be a proper neighbor and invite you in. But I'll need the code first."

She cheerfully obliged.

"You passed. House, let her in. Please, Yelnisha, no drama today. I'm really not feeling up to it," he said, exiting the chamber.

"Look at you, it's nine o'clock. How can you be a professor at a university if you're getting up this late?"

He yawned again, his eye slits barely letting light in as his mind was fighting hard to stay awake.

"Coffee?" he asked.

"No thanks, I've got a tiny bladder. Besides, if I drank that stuff I'm pretty certain that I would explode. I've got too much energy as it is. Anyway, not here to chit chat, we've got a busy day ahead of us. Lots to do. In one hour, I'll need you to hop on your platform, and meet me at the training field. I've sent the instructions on how to get there to your house unit already. Be seeing ya," she said, with a wink and a smile.

Dorian stood in his robe sipping his beverage, nibbling on some toast. "Thought she was going to attack me again. That wasn't so bad. Maybe Matthias was exaggerating."

After finishing his breakfast, he cleaned up and proceeded to make his way over to the training field, the same one he had visited yesterday.

HIS TRANSPORTER TOOK HIM TO THE FIELD entrance where a security checkpoint was set up, much like one found at an airport. Several small lines formed as the warrior-athletes waited their turn to get in.

"Spectator lines to the far left," the security guard said to Dorian as he approached his turn in line. Everyone around him was wearing some type of form-fitting uniform and doing various stretches and warm ups as they waited to get through. Dorian was wearing a flannel shirt with a t-shirt underneath, along with loose-fitting blue jeans and Converse tennis shoes;

hardly the specimen of athleticism, which is precisely why the guard pointed him to the other line.

Just as he began to leave he heard Yelnisha's voice from beyond the gate.

"Oh, no, you don't. Get back there. He's with me. Let him through, please," she said to the attendants manning the gate. They looked at each other with raised eyebrows and waved him through. A scanner went over him as he passed through the entrance. Yelnisha was stretching out in a charcoal-colored form-fitting workout uniform, similar to the kind everyone else wore.

"I feel a bit out of place here. Shouldn't I be in jogging shorts or something? If I'd known this is what you had in mind, I would have stayed in bed, because I don't have an athletic bone in my body," he complained.

Yelnisha to looked at him as if he had two heads. "Right, you're not in shape? How'd you get that body then? Lifting books and test tubes and whatnot?" she asked, looking over his built physique.

"Seriously, Yelnisha, I'm in terrible shape. I've been so busy with work that I haven't been to the gym in years. This is going to be embarrassing. Shouldn't I just watch or something?"

"Did you forget to change your diapers this morning? Get over it. If getting you in shape is what we need to do, then you've come to the right place," she said, grabbing him by the arm and leading him along. The two went down the corridor, stopping near the dressing rooms for the combatants. "Follow me please," she said smiling.

They stepped into a sophisticated locker room where dozens of people were milling about; some were stretching, and some were in groups going over maneuvers the way a sports team would before a game. Yelnisha walked over to a group of ten people that were huddled together, listening to an athletic-looking female who resembled a cat-human hybrid. She had greenish-yellow eyes with black slits for pupils, and facial features that were closer to human than cat. Her fur was a very fine grey, and her hands looked like a human's—with with the exception of claws. She was wearing one of the form-fitting outfits that everyone seemed to be wearing, along with some type of small device around her neck that some of the other trainers wore. It appeared that she was of a similar species to Zeracon, the head of security.

"Sorry to interrupt, but I've brought along a new recruit that we're going to be adding to our ranks starting today," Yelnisha said with a grin. The group turned their attention to Dorian, who was feeling rather embarrassed over his attire and lack of athletic prowess. He recognized a few of them from his class with Matthias: Xui Mei, the fourteen-year-old prodigy from Changsha in the Hunan province of China; Josiah, the soft spoken, lean and lanky man from Namibia; Sasha, the strikingly beautiful young woman from Domzale, Slovenia; Simon, the funny, young Welshman from Aberystwyth, in the United Kingdom; Emmerelda, the young woman who had been rude to him; and Juan Velazquez of Cartagena, Spain, who at forty-four was the oldest. The twins, Tiddi and Osokas were present and flanked Yelnisha as she arrived.

"Excellent, Commander Yelnisha. Greetings, Dorian. I am Second Commander Lykoi," the woman said in a soft voice. "I believe you are acquainted with most everyone here, so you may want to get changed into something that will allow you to move more freely, in order to withstand the punishment of our exercises. You'll find the skins over there," she said, nodding in the direction of the machine that looked like a body scanner found at airports. Yelnisha walked over to where Dorian was to assist him.

"Here," she said, moving him into place. "You stand inside of it like this with your arms out and say 'measure'."

Dorian did as he was instructed and the device began making a whirring sound as lasers measured every inch of his body.

"Now come over here. It only takes a minute," Yelnisha said, as she stood in front of the apparatus that was creating the outfit for him. A moment later, it was completed. The material was unique; stretchy, but extremely strong. Given its delicate nature and thickness, it was rather heavy, an attribute owed to the advanced technology employed in its construction.

"You can change over there," she said, pointing to the area adjacent to the group, where other visitors were getting dressed behind the solid barrier. She waved her hand over the sensor, and the barrier dissipated, allowing Dorian to step inside. He motioned for it to go up, and he began to disrobe. As he put the form fitting outfit over his nude body, he noticed the group paying close attention to what he was doing.

Josiah placed his hand over Xui Mei's eyes and Yelnisha laughing hysterically. Dorian quickly put on the suit and noticed the backside felt rather drafty, mainly due to the fact it was missing material there. Wrapping his shirt around himself, he waved his hand over the barrier and smiled at Yelnisha.

"Okay, you've had your fun. Can I get a normal suit now?" he asked. Tiddi, who was looking a bit red in the face, walked over and handed him a new one.

"Thanks. How about a little privacy this time?"

"Um, yeah, that was Yelnisha's doing. If you step in again it should work like the others," she said, avoiding eye contact with him.

After quickly changing, he stepped out to a chorus of laughter, as Yelnisha had apparently set up a hidden camera that captured his bare backside from earlier, displaying the images across a holographic screen for everyone to see.

Heat rose in his face. "Two can play at that game," he said with a determined look.

"Um, I wouldn't do it if I were you," Tiddi replied, shaking her head. "Let her have her revenge or it won't end for you, believe me."

He sighed and shrugged. "Fine, whatever. All right, you've had your juvenile laugh. Can we move on now?"

"I need to savor the moment a bit more, you understand," Yelnisha said, wiping away the tears she cried from her laughter.

Tiddi handed him a pair of special shoes to wear "They're fine, don't worry."

He put them on while ignoring the catcalls and hoots from the others around him, and then gave his attention to Lykoi, who was looking rather perturbed with Yelnisha's antics.

"My apologies, Lykoi. This is revenge for an incident from yesterday. I responded to Yelnisha's attack in an inappropriate manner, and she is responding in kind. Yelnisha, I apologize for my part in embarrassing you," he said with humility.

"Bollocks, you sure know how to rob a woman of her pleasure. All right, let's call a truce then, eh?" she said, slapping him on the backside and causing the group to burst into laughter. He held his tongue and smiled at her. Lykoi cleared her throat to get their attention.

"We've got a lot to cover today, so let's get serious now. You are pairing up into four groups of two. Your assignments are on the display. Meet me out on the field in five minutes; make sure you've warmed up. Dorian, you're with me today. I think Yelnisha's had enough fun with you for the time being. Follow me; I need to talk with you about a few things." She dismissed the group, and the two of them made their way out of the dressing area towards the training field.

"I've known your father for quite some time now. He's a good man, for an Earthling," she said with a laugh. "Although I've been here so long now, I'm going to have to start referring to myself as an Anidonian soon.

"In case you were wondering, my kind are known as Kroikas. A handful of us came over from our home planet at the request of the angels here in Anidon. We're not that advanced in our technology, but we make up for it with our skills in Shi mastery and manipulation. The fallen have infiltrated our home as well, and I have seen firsthand the effects of their crimes, so it is my honor to instruct others in the ways of combat against them and their allies.

"Anyway, the first few exercises we are going to do involve getting familiar with one of the two forms of Shi; Melammu and Baltu. The Melammu form is a higher level of Shi and may take many years to manifest if can be done at all. Very few of us can. The Baltu form is a lower form of Shi, one that many use to enhance their corporeal form.

As you may know, what we are looking at for both of us, these flesh forms, are not who, or more specifically, what, we are. These are simply avatars that house our spirits, which are our true form. That form is what you see when traveling to one of the Verdes sites or Erustian Prime—the light forms that exist in another dimension. We can access the spirit energy of that form in this dimension, as well as the one of your planet. Either form will enable one to manipulate matter, enhance physical attributes, gain extra sensory output, and perform thought transference; those are only a few of the many abilities it can confer.

Yelnisha, as well as several others who were present, advised me of your spiritual awakening so I think we should go slow until I know you are comfortable with the training. Does that sound acceptable?"

"Yeah, that's fine, thanks. This is all so new to me. So much has happened in such a short amount of time that it's hard for me to take it all in. I'm beginning to feel as if the old Dorian has passed on. My identity is becoming fragmented," he said with a concerned look.

Lykoi tilted her head slightly and stared into his eyes with a soft gaze. "You've been through quite an ordeal, as I have been told, and I am sorry for that. You are not alone in your grief, however. Everyone in our group has a story similar to yours; they've all lost family and friends and found themselves struggling with abilities they couldn't understand. I'm sure you were unaware that most of the beings in Anidon were born here, and many have never even seen the world outside. All those in our group are like you; aside from your personal tragedies, you all were born on Earth and lived there for some time, an experience which will be of value to us.

"It's my job to try and make sense of everything for you as best as I can. That, as well as keeping you alive. When we go to battle, this training will help us survive. You can be assured the enemy will be well trained in these arts as well, so you had best pay attention. Come, race me to the first marker."

Lykoi arched her back and exhaled, her Shi rising rapidly until she exploded with energy, moving one hundred fifty feet in one second! Many people on the field stopped to watch one of the fastest beings in Anidon move with amazing speed. She managed to run the quarter mile in just under seven seconds, faster than she ever allowed herself to run in front of the humans. Applause and whistles came from the spectators, as well as from many of the combatants who witnessed her skill.

"Whoa, she can really move," Dorian said aloud.

"She's probably the fastest in Anidon. I can only imagine how fast she would be in her second spirit form," Josiah said while shaking his arms and legs to warm up.

"Heh, I ran about that fast when I had a bad case of arsefire; thought I wasn't going to make it to the loo," Simon chimed in.

Tiddi and Xui Mei both scowled at him.

"What? That's never happened to you? Tough crowd here. What you gonna do there, Dorio? Let's have a go, see what you can do," Simon said giving Dorian a slight slap on his upper arm.

"It's 'Dorian', not 'Dorio', you doofus!" Tiddi shouted, her fists clenched, looking perturbed.

"All right, then, no need to get your knickers in a twist, tiddlywinks." He snapped his towel on her behind, then proceeded to run as fast as he could towards Lykoi. Josiah and Dorian both shook their heads as Tiddi gave chase.

*"What are you waiting for?"* Lykoi asked, her voice telepathically entering his mind.

*"Sorry, these kids are distracting me. Be there in a moment,"* he replied in kind, unsure if she had heard his words. Taking a deep breath and exhaling, he began to focus his Shi on his legs, though it was difficult to concentrate given the ruckus the group was making around him. He let out some of his spirit energy and could feel his legs becoming weightless as the energy filled his body. Several combatants off in the distance stopped what they were doing and took notice, as did everyone in the group.

Electricity charged the air as his Shi climbed. Dorian's vision improved dramatically and he could make out Lykoi's face as if she were right next to him. Leaning down, he exhaled and thrust his body forward with incredible speed. As he started rushing towards her the ground gave way beneath his feet. Large slabs of sod went flying behind him as each step became more unstable until he lost balance, crashing in a fashion that resembled a meteorite trail. Laughter erupted across the field at the spectacle. Yelnisha was rolling on the ground, tears in her eyes, along with Simon, Josiah and many others who had witnessed his epic landing. Lycoi stood stoically, her eyes widened with an expression that changed from ease to apprehension.

Dorian got up and began brushing off the grass and dirt embedded in his hair and just about everywhere else. Yelnisha ran over to him, her cackle barely contained with each step.

"Oh my, ahahahaha, did you—ahahahaha, I can't breathe!" she chortled as giggles and gasps of air fought for priority. Dorian shook his head. The others ran over to where they were standing as Lykoi slowly walked towards the group.

"Oh, man, that was a spectacular wipeout! Look at the trail, it's got to be ten meters long!" Simon shouted with excitement.

"Look more like twelve," Xui Mei replied.

Emma silently shook her head with a contemptuous look on her face.

Lycoi arrived just as Dorian was feeling thoroughly embarrassed.

"What did I do wrong?" he asked Lykoi.

She shot an angry glare to the group that was standing around. "I thought I gave all of you assignments. Why are you standing here? This is no time for fooling around! Get to work!" she shouted, slightly baring her teeth. Everyone's laughter immediately ceased and they quickly paired up as the field repair robots set to work at replacing the destroyed section of grass around them. She turned her attention towards Dorian, who was feeling a bit intimidated by her growl at the group.

"What happened, you ask? That is a very good question. It seems you generated far more force than the ground could handle. Your shoes did not have sufficient friction to allow you to travel at that rate of speed over this surface," she said, carefully choosing her words. "I think I will have you watch the others for today. I need to speak with someone, excuse me," she replied, turning to leave.

"I'm sorry Lykoi. I didn't mean—I apologize if I upset you," he said, feeling that he had embarrassed her as well.

Stopping in her tracks, she turned towards him with a soft look on her face. "You have nothing to be embarrassed about, Dorian, nothing whatsoever. I am sorry to run out on you like this, but I need to get some answers before we can proceed. I hope you understand."

She turned and ran towards the exit while the group watched from a distance. He walked over towards Yelnisha, who was overseeing the training of the four pairs.

"You must have really cheesed her off for her to leave like that," Yelnisha said. Dorian looked a bit dejected.

"Simon, lift your leg higher, you flat footed wanker!" she shouted.

Simon, in turn, proceeded to give her the two-finger salute in response. "I keep telling him, and he never listens," she sighed. "So, you're back with me then, eh? Great! Let's start by teaching you some basic hand to hand moves. Now, we're going to take it easy, so we won't use any Shi for this, right?" she said, one eye one Dorian, the other watching the others.

"Sure, whatever you say, Yelnisha. Hopefully, I don't embarrass myself too much," he said, looking over at the area where he had fallen.

"Great. Put up your hands like this," she replied, holding his hands in hers and placing them in proper position. "Now turn your body sideways to expose less of it. Good. Like that. Now, I'm going to rush at you with my right arm and you defend by pushing it aside, and step in to attack my exposed right side," she said. She moved in slowly, demonstrating her maneuver.

They went back and forth for some time, switching between defender and attacker. By the end of the day they had worked up quite a sweat, and Dorian seemed to be catching his stride. Yelnisha was pleased with his progress.

"Not bad there for a newbie. We'll have to work on your Irish to make you a proper man. All in good time. Care to fetch a pint?" she asked, wiping off the sweat with her towel.

"Sure, why not, I could use something to help me relax," he replied. She gave him a flirty smile. "Careful, now, a girl might end up misunderstanding what you meant there."

"I need to get cleaned up first, meet you outside in fifteen then?" he said with a smirk.

"Sounds like a da—, a plan," she replied.

# Seventeen

THE CIRCLE WAS NEARING COMPLETION. SWEAT poured from the forehead of Samir as he, and several others, feverishly worked on the diagrams and pentacles. Conjuring an angel of this magnitude required absolute concentration and attention to detail; failure could spell disaster for all of them. He would not brook any error on their part.

"Ramla, you're doing it wrong, ach. Two lines down, farther apart. Look at Issa's figure. Yes, that's better," he said, as she made the correction.

The young woman with long, black hair and olive skin looked at Issa, who was watching Samir with trepidation. Issa caught her gaze and widened his eyes in an unspoken gesture, as if to say "Be very careful what you say and do". Samir began reciting the psalms while the incense was burning throughout the chamber.

They stood in an ancient underground cavern known as "Campbell's Tomb", located beneath the Pyramids of Giza. Constructed by Enoch of old, it consisted of nine large chambers carved in limestone, with the central chamber having three ornate vertical columns. The ancient order that Samir belonged to possessed the triangular shaped golden tablet that had originally rested in the center of the three columns which contained the absolute name of the creator. It was not without significant discussion and argument that he had managed to get permission to use the tablet. Its presence would, in his argument, help protect the group from the wrath of Malik should something go awry.

The sect did not fully trust any one person with the tablet, so four of their leaders—Rashidi, Msrah, Omari, and Lotus—agreed to accompany it with Samir to the ancient hidden underground lair.

All of the necessary pentacles had been prepared in advance on their respective hours so that the conjuring would not cause him to be cursed. The day of Jupiter and the hour of Saturn were at hand; all that remained were a few minor details.

Samir began reciting the necessary prayers as Ramla and Issa took their places, praying fervently as well. Samir had conjured lesser spirits before, so he had some experience in the matter; however, as he would soon discover, he was wholly unprepared for what was about to transpire. Once the last of the prayers were completed he began the summoning.

"Oh, mighty Malik, I conjure you by the indivisible name IOD, which marks and expresses the simplicity and the unity of the nature divine, which Abel having invoked, he deserved to escape from the hands of Cain his brother.

"I conjure you by the name TETRAGRAMMATON ELOHIM, which expresses and signifies the grandeur of so lofty a majesty, that Noah having pronounced it, saved himself, and protected himself with his whole household from the waters of the deluge.

"I conjure you by the name of God EL, strong and wonderful, which denotes the mercy and goodness of his majesty divine, which Abraham having invoked, he was found worthy to come forth from the Ur of the Chaldeans.

"I conjure you by the most powerful name of ELOHIM GIBOR, which showed forth the strength of God, of a God all powerful, who punishes the crimes of the wicked, who seeks out and chastises the iniquities of the fathers upon the children unto the third and fourth generation; which Isaac having invoked, he was found worthy to escape from the sword of Abraham his father.

"Lastly, I conjure you Malik, by the most holy name of God ADONAI MELEKH, which Joshua invoked, and stayed the course of the Sun in his presence, through the virtue of Methratton, its principal Image; and by the troops of angels who cease not to cry day and night."

The air in the underground chamber became thin and dry, as if a vacuum had removed most of it. Thunder rumbled from within, and the walls began to tremble and quake. The hair of everyone present stood on end as the air became electrified. Lights began flickering, and unusual sounds could be heard echoing throughout the chambers. A humming sound filled the air, changing to a low frequency pulsating wave that reverberated with a constant amplitude and pitch. As if that wasn't eerie enough, colors of various hues filled the top of the chamber, increasing in brightness until they morphed into a white light, which was emanating from a fifteen-foot-tall figure that stood before them. It was Malik in all his splendor and power; a sight which caused the host of humans to tremble in awe of this magnificent being. A golden crown encircled his head, which was also floating above it, spinning in sync with the low frequency tone. His entire form was comprised of light, yet his features appeared tangible. In his right hand, he held a golden scepter that reached almost to the top of the cavern, the top spiked in a circular fashion along with a floating crown above it, moving in unison with the one adorning his head.

Malik's expression was stern; his eyes were flickering grey flames positioned in the usual space that eyes would on a human. As he opened his mouth, the sound he began to make was deafening, causing everyone in the room to clasp their ears, with the exception of Samir, who wisely had worn earplugs. Dropping the pentacles at this moment could cause Malik to be released or worse.

Malik slammed his scepter onto the ground causing it to quake and opened up a small chasm. Samir knew he had better take control of the situation quickly before their chamber was destroyed.

"O mighty Malik I beseech thee; I entreat thy grace that you would show mercy for this monumental affront to your great majesty and splendor for summoning you to this realm. For this, I humbly beg your mercy and forgiveness. Were our position less dire we would not come before you as we do now. Yet our cause is desperate; our hopes dim.

"We humans cannot stand alone against the might of the fallen; at this very hour. they are working to destroy the Earth, the beloved jewel of the Most High," he said, prostrating himself.

The mighty watcher's countenance shifted; slowly his face softened and his stature decreased as he lowered his Shi from an aggressive stance to his lower form until he stood at about ten feet. He began to speak, his voice sounding like the rush of the ocean.

"Arise, son of man. I have tested the truth of the words you speak. Your thoughts I have born witness to, yet what you seek to accomplish is folly beyond all measure, for you do not possess the power to contend with the corrupted ones. Return me to my appointed task, lest you tempt the wrath of the One Above All."

Malik paused and shifted his gaze about the room. "You have been undone. The corrupted stand among you," he said solemnly. The group looked at each other in confusion. Four figures stepped forward from the shadows, one holding a sobbing young girl by the neck. Samir's eyes widened at the sight of his daughter being held aloft.

"Eshe!" he screamed in a panicked voice.

"Ever the dutiful son, Malik, and thy wisdom is great indeed, yet it seems the human has bound you to his will. The ancient covenants cannot be denied. You will provide the location of my brothers!"

"Belial!" Malik shouted, immediately growing to his former size. He raised his scepter to strike the ground in an attempt to disrupt the circle and end his imprisonment.

"Order Malik to be still, human, lest we destroy this one," Belial said, holding Samir's daughter up with one hand as if she were a rag doll. The skin that covered the long bony fingers of his hands was ashen and scaly, as was his face, which displayed his fearsome looking teeth and pointed ears.

"Eshe!" Samir screamed again, his heart bursting at the sight of his daughter in pain. The monumental weight of his foolishness had just begun to extract a karmic payment.

"Quickly, human! My desire to rip her flesh open is growing with each passing moment!" His razor-sharp claws began to slowly slice into her face, burning and cutting at the same time, causing her to bellow out in howls of pain and agony.

"No, Samir! Don't do," was all that Msrah could say before one of Belial's followers, Kludon, removed his head from his body. The head fell to the ground with a ghastly thump. The others, horrified by what they just witnessed and what might be in store for them, began to look for the exits. Despite several of them being experienced Magick users of a lesser nature, they were all quite terrified and unable to perform any useful spells. Indeed, a thick aura of evil emanated from the four fallen, causing all humans present to shake with fear.

"Malik, I command you to cease!" Samir said, his voice quivering as tears ran down his face. Malik lowered his raised scepter and stood still. Eshe was still screaming and crying, annoying Belial, who tossed the girl over to Abyzou.

The demon carefully held the girl in her arms and spoke softly to her. "There, there, young one. Shhhhh. Abyzou is going to make it all better. See?" Her hand shined brightly, and as it did she passed it over the girl's face, instantly healing the burnt and torn flesh. "No need to cry now, little one," she said, staring at the girl with her glowing, cruel eyes. Eshe's crying subsided.

"Continue, human. We would have the information you sought from Malik revealed to us as well. Continue," Belial said, his shrouded face hiding his distorted visage beneath the wrappings.

"Malik, I command in the name of the Most High that you reveal the location of where the Watchers are being held," Samir said, knowing time was short for all of them. The pressure was intense as he was scouring his memory desperately for any spell, anything, that would buy him time or allow them to escape.

"Show us, then, where our brothers have been imprisoned, Malik," Belial demanded. Malik's expression was furious. He held out his hand and pointed towards the adjacent wall and chanted something the humans were unable to comprehend. The wall glowed amber, followed by a flash of light. Suddenly an image of Europe, Asia, and Africa appeared, with an enormous hexagram overlaid on the three continents. There were thirteen dots, one at each point on the outer portion of the lines drawn for the hexagram, one at each point on the inside making the inner ring, and one in the center, in the middle of the Dead Sea. The points were equidistant at seven million cubits. Cheers erupted from the four fallen watchers as the others looked on with dread. The pleasing aroma of incense that filled the chamber was misplaced amidst the dread felt by the humans.

"Release me, quickly!" shouted Malik.

"I think not, human," Belial said, drawing the blade Bernael used in Algeria from the extra-dimensional space in which it resided. Wearing the seal of Solomon, the legendary ring that controls demons and other spirits, he placed the face of it against the hilt of his demon blade, and his eyes filled with flames, as did the top of his head.

"You will not have opportunity to warn your followers, as I have sealed this temple from the sight of heaven," Belial said. He held the blade up and pointed it towards Malik. A deep purplish-black light emanated from the blade along with black lightning bolts which arced all around him. He laughed maniacally as the void attempted to draw Malik's essence into it. Undeterred, Malik stood his ground as he held his scepter aloft. Blinding white light filled the chamber along with a deafening sound as the two forces opposed each other. It seemed to be a stalemate until the other three accompanying Belial lent their power to him. Touching his back and closing their eyes, they all began to chant a spell which increased the power of the void, drawing Malik in with a horrible sound. The blade was steaming as Belial returned it to the dimension it occupied.

"Will it hold?" Ornias asked with a look of concern on his wretched face. Belial held up the hilt and waved his hand over it while silently chanting, observing its integrity and pausing as if searching mentally.

"It holds, my friend," he replied with a smile. The others in his group shouted with glee.

"I have done as you asked. Please, my daughter, return her to me," Samir said, with anguish strewn across his face and arms outstretched.

Ornias and his accomplices smiled malevolently. Abyzou caressed the child's face as she looked at the girl with the soft tenderness of a mother. She lifted the child by her neck and tightened until Eshe let out a cry and clutched at the hand that held her while gasping for air. Her struggles ceased and her body went limp. The harrowing sound of bones crunching were heard as her face turned purple and eyes bulged. She tossed the girl at the feet of Samir.

"I have returned your daughter, human, as you have asked," she replied with cold indifference to her cruel act. Samir's face drained of blood and he fell to his knees as if struck in the diaphragm. He was unable to make any sound as his emotions overwhelmed him, until he finally produced the most blood curdling scream he could muster from the depths of his soul. Ramla and Issa were both sobbing in the corner, unable to do anything. Omari and Rashidi were also unsure how to proceed; however, it was obvious their fate would be similar to Eshe's if they did nothing.

Lotus, who was not particularly keen on dying this day, had been slowly moving towards the triangular-shaped golden plate of Enoch, the ancient tablet that contained the ineffable name of the creator. Seizing the opportunity, she grabbed the tablet and in the process, she inadvertently knocked down the pillar which housed it, drawing all attention towards her. Instantly, Belial knew he had seriously miscalculated by allowing her to retrieve it.

Everyone froze in their tracks. Lotus caught the gaze of Samir, who knew she was not prepared nor consecrated to unleash such a spell.

He, however, was in a position to use its power and widened his eyes at her, hoping to get her attention. The four fallen bared their teeth as Lotus held the tablet aloft, slowly moving towards Samir, who was safe while he stood in the circle. The same could not be said of the others. Ramla took the opportunity to remove her cell phone and capture an image of the wall that displayed the location of the fallen prisons before it disappeared.

Abyzou looked perplexed as she followed the strain on Belial's face. "What does she hold?" she asked in their ancient tongue, unsure if she should risk rushing Lotus.

"The sacred tablet of Metatron from his time as a human. Do not move," he said, responding in kind as he pondered on how to proceed.

"Does she even know how to use it? Perhaps we should find out," Abyzou said with a sly smile.

"Hold fast, Abyzou!" he yelled, shooting a scowl at her. Belial was a high ranking fallen angel; it would be painful to retreat from a few weak humans, but he could not chance losing the information he had gained, along with his demon blade and ring of Solomon. He shot a glance over to Omari and communicated his commands silently to the others with him. All four quickly departed to the upper chambers.

"Everyone, stand next to me," Samir said with a weary voice. A loud booming noise could be heard from above as bits of rock and sand fell on top of them. The spell Malik had cast on the wall began to fade, leaving it without evidence of the fallen's whereabouts.

"They mean to bury us in here," Rashidi stated bluntly. Samir took off the apron he was wearing and wrapped his daughter's body in it. Gently picking her up, he carried her over his shoulder.

"Do not despair, come with me," he said as he moved to the back of the room.

"What should we do with Msrah?" Lotus asked. They all looked at each other, unsure of what to do.

"Issa and Rashidi can carry his body I suppose," Samir said with a sad sigh.

"How will we explain this to the authorities, Samir?" Rashidi asked.

"Fine, leave him then. We can come back for him later after I have buried my daughter," he said, his voice cracking. Standing at the back of the room with his daughter's corpse slung over his shoulder, he retrieved a small spherical crystal from his bag. The crystal ball had a slight luminescence to it. In the center of it were hieroglyphics that appeared to be shifting from one symbol to another as Samir held it in his hand.

"Where did you obtain that?" Omari asked in a slightly impertinent tone.

"I will explain later. For now, it will provide us with a way out," Samir replied as he carefully placed the crystal into a receptacle in the wall. A few seconds went by before they heard a loud noise coming from the opposite side of the wall. As that was happening, large pieces of stone fell from the ceiling as the pounding from above increased in intensity, all signs indicating that the whole room could collapse at any moment. Several minutes later, the pounding from above ceased. The chamber exit was now completely filled with huge chunks of limestone, making it clear the survivors had to leave by another means.

A clicking noise followed by a low rumbling sound came from within the wall as it began to slowly move. Stale air mixed with the scent of the sea blasted them as the wall opened, revealing an enormous underground city. A stairway illuminated by glowing lamps filled with a silvery liquid that looked like mercury stood before them, leading down to a lower platform where a large river flowed. Two statues of approximately eighteen feet in height, each with the face of a lion and the teeth of a dragon, stood on either side of the stairway. Each had outstretched arms holding an iridescent triangular object. The walls lining the chamber were ornately painted with scenes depicting humanoids and humans interacting.

They reached the bottom of the stairs and Samir walked over to a large inflatable raft that was sitting beside the river's edge. They looked at each other and wondered how it got there and more importantly, who was going to stay behind, as it was apparent the raft would not accommodate all of them.

At that moment, Omari produced a knife and plunged it into the back of Rashidi, then quickly pulled it out. He reached over and grabbed Issa by the arm, bringing the bloodied edge to her throat. Rashidi slumped to the ground and began convulsing and groaning as a white foam came out of his mouth. Ramla moved next to Lotus, and Samir quickly jumped back, after having just placed his daughter's lifeless body in the raft.

"The tablet; quickly, or I cut her throat!" Omari demanded with his hand outstretched toward Lotus.

"I wasn't certain whether it was you or Rashidi who betrayed us, but now it is clear. You have doomed us all! Fool! You are responsible for the death of my daughter!" Samir yelled, his sadness shifting to rage.

"There is no winning this war Samir. I did what I had to survive. They would have gotten out anyway. What did you think you were going to do to stop them? What would any of you do? Look at you! Pathetic! I'll ask one more ti—," he said, stopping, frozen mid-sentence. Shock entered his mind as he failed to notice Issa had drawn a sigil in the sand with her toes, quietly casting a spell.

"The blood of one sacrificed, Omari. I was surprised you would be so careless with your blade," Issa said, holding up two fingers with Rashidi's blood on them. Paralyzed, all Omari could do was watch as Samir and the others scoured the area for something to bind him with. Ten minutes later Ramla returned with a dried braided rope about fifteen feet long.

"Help me!" Samir shouted behind labored grunts. He was pushing on a large limestone slab with an iron ring affixed to the top, which was sliding on heavy rollers from underneath. With the help of the other three it was surprisingly easy for them to move the slab to the edge of the river, which appeared to be quite deep.

Samir fastened the rope around Omari's neck and the other end to the limestone slab. All Omari could do was watch his fate unfold as he was frozen in place, unable to speak or do anything. The others watched also, knowing what Samir was about to do, yet they did not interfere with him carrying out justice for the murders Omari had committed.

Samir stepped back and looked at Omari while sighing and shaking his head in disbelief. The memory of his daughter's execution, as well as the realization that his wife might also have been murdered, was pressing down on him. Cursing himself for his stupidity and not listening to Jizam, he began to weep and scream with rage, fueling his lust for revenge. He reached behind the slab that was parked at the edge of the river and pushed with all his might, plunging it into the water. It disappeared quickly, taking Omari into the deep with it. They all stood silently for a moment as Samir began to weep. The three went over to console him, offering their condolences and prayers for him.

"We should leave; we have to warn the others about what happened," Lotus said, her hand on his shoulder.

"I think we'll all fit inside this raft; give me a few moments and I will retrieve Msrah's body and place him next to Rashidi," Issa said as he sprinted up the stairs to the chamber where Msrah lay. Ramla began hunting for something to wrap the bodies in so that they could be prepared for burial. In a small room off to the rear of the platform, she found some linen that was very old, fragile and dusty, but would at least cover them if they were placed close enough together. Issa completed the gruesome task of returning Msrah to the lower level and set him beside Rashidi. Lotus covered the bodies, and they boarded the raft with Samir cradling his daughter in his arms.

"Too bad we don't have the locations of the pris—," was all Lotus started to say when she noticed Samir peer over at her with the look of a crushed soul on his face.

"I wouldn't say that, Lotus," Ramla said, trying not to smile.

"I managed to snap a picture off on my cell phone before it disappeared," she said triumphantly. Samir perked up a bit as Issa and Lotus both looked relieved. The deaths would not be in vain.

❦

THE RIVER CURVED AROUND A BIT AND SPLIT off into four different directions. The current was moving too fast for them to control the raft well, and a rapid drop off caused water to flood in momentarily. They removed as much water as they could with their hands and emerged out of a hidden opening into the Nile River. The underground waterway was as incredible as the Great Sphinx itself, a ten-mile journey that ended on one of the smaller branches of the river. Samir nodded at Issa to paddle up ahead to the embankment.

"Is that your car? What is it doing here?" Ramla asked him.

"I was planning to show everyone the tunnel, and then we would have a pleasure ride back on the raft I left in the cavern. That is why I had Issa pick me up from here," he replied.

The group waited as Samir gently placed his daughter in the car and they all left together.

"Where should we go?" Issa asked.

"We will go to my house first. I need to check on my wife," Samir said, holding back his emotions for the time being.

"Sure. No problem. We can all go together," Lotus replied, looking at the rest of them with steely eyes. Judging from her look, it was implied there was not going to be a discussion.

"What if we come across one of the fallen again? How are we going to deal with them? Most of what I know is very limited. How do you even injure or kill one of them?" Ramla asked.

"There are ways," Samir said bluntly. "I did not come prepared, otherwise they might have thought twice about attacking us. None of us were expecting betrayal, and that is where we failed. You two have learned something valuable in this tragedy. Always consider and prepare for the unexpected. I was so focused on Malik and what could go wrong with the summoning that I failed to recognize the external danger we faced. This does not mean you cannot trust anyone. It simply means that you should not allow yourself to be put into a position of weakness, should the unexpected occur," he said with a weary voice.

"That is good advice. Even though we were betrayed you still need to rely on others. When I had my apprentices, I would often remind them of the importance of community and working together as a group. You may think that you will be better off as a 'lone wolf' but in truth, it is better to work together. A reed by itself can bend and break, but a bundle is strong. Never forget that," Lotus said.

Issa and Ramla both nodded.

"Lotus, that weapon he used, did you recognize it?" Samir asked.

"No, I have never seen anything like that. The ring, however, looked familiar. I will need to consult some manuscripts first to confirm my suspicions. His blade appeared to draw Malik into it, trapping him within. I can only assume it can also collect human souls as well. My guess is there is a limit to what it can hold; the spirit of Malik seemed to be stretching its capabilities. I was able to understand some of what they were saying to each other. They were concerned it would not hold. The question is, what are they planning to do with his spirit?"

"A good question indeed," Samir replied.

# *Eighteen*

AT THE SUMMIT OF MOUNT HERMON, IN THE region over modern day Syria, six thousand years B.C., two Hundred angels were gathered on a plateau to form a pact of mutual sedition. Twenty of their chiefs huddled to discuss the details of their unholy rebellion, sprung from the well of lust. Shemikhazah, their leader, addressed the celestial body with his concerns.

"We have all taken great risk upon ourselves to arrive by mutual supplication at our destination. I ask you all again, is it not unjust that Elohim has set apart the daughters of Eve for the sons of Adam, yet we who have served faithfully have not received such splendor? Why should we not undertake this endeavor upon ourselves, that we become flesh also and take wives to assuage our desires? Should we continue to suffer with passion, thus defiling our spirits within? Let it not be said that Adam did not transgress, and yet, despite his sin, the son of man still found favor in the sight of our Lord. Is inequity to be our lot for this cause? Yet, I fear you will not indeed agree to do this deed, and I alone shall have to pay the penalty of a great sin."

The others listened to Shemikhazah's plea and answered in kind. "Let us all swear an oath, and all bind ourselves by imprecations not to abandon this plan, but to carry out our objective." They mutually agreed and swore together to complete their objective. The die was now cast; their fate sealed with this act of rebellion.

The day turned to night, and the light of the assembled mass shone over the antediluvian town below, some distance from the foot of the mountain. As they made their way down the mountain, the villagers came out to witness the procession of divine beings. Awed by their presence and power, they were welcomed into their community with open arms. Within a short time, the men of the village quickly wed their daughters to the Watchers, with the goal of learning their secrets. All of the others, including the leaders, took unto themselves wives from the villagers, and each chose for himself one. The Watchers began to have relations with their wives, defiling themselves and corrupting the human experiment.

As a result of their union, the women became pregnant; however, since the watchers were not of Earth many of their offspring were mutated, becoming great giants that began to devour all the produce of man. When the humans could no longer supply the giants, they, in turn, began to devour mankind itself.

As it happened, the Watchers followed through with their promise to teach the humans the forbidden knowledge; knowledge that was beyond their capacity to control. It was Asa'el who taught men to make swords of iron, knives, shields, and breastplates of brass, and made known to them the metals that are excavated from the Earth. He taught the forging of gold and silver into jewelry and ornaments, as well as the use of cosmetics for beautification of the face.

Shemikhazah taught spellbinding and botany, Hermoni the casting of spells. Barak'el taught the signs of lightning, Ar'tekif the signs of the Earth, Shimsh'el the signs of the sun, Sahri'el the signs of the moon, and they all began to teach their wives as well. By sharing this knowledge with the humans, mankind was led astray and grew in wickedness, being corrupt in all their actions and motivations.

ONE HUNDRED YEARS AFTER THEIR ARRIVAL, A small gathering of Angels observed their children partaking in sport amongst themselves.

"Let none say the sons of Shemikhazah are lacking in strength!" Barak'el proclaimed after having witnessed Ohya and Ahya, his two gigantic offspring, wrestle with each other.

"Nor are they lacking in appetite," Ar'tekif bemoaned. Indeed, the two alone had stripped the land in that area of Havilah bare of all that it could produce, forcing many of the humans who dwelled there to relocate north to Cush. There were thirty-nine giants in the land of Havilah; the remaining thirteen thousand claimed their own territories across the lands farther east and to the north.

The air was thick and foul where they stood amidst a raised plateau overlooking the valley that stretched many miles north. The sky was overcast with dark clouds, a display which seemed to portend the events about to unfold. Behind the group was a large mountain named Chesed, an antithetical title considering what was contained within. Cut into the mountainside was an enormous channel secured by a barrier made of light, behind which an opaque silhouette outlined a living creature of extraordinary proportions. Loud, guttural sounds, mixed with the thundering of the creature against the mountain walls, could be heard coming from behind the barrier.

The group drew their attention to the stirring from within, and all eyes were on Tur'el as he stood to address them.

"This day, brothers, we have cause to celebrate the creation of a marvelous wonder: a creature unlike any seen on this Earth, save perhaps Leviathan. A magnificent beast indeed; the strength of its limbs greater than one hundred of the strongest who walk the Earth presently. Its claws are able to rend solid granite, and its jaws can crush metal as if made of chaff. The skin of this beast is an impenetrable armor, save for weapons of Magick or high form. Iron he treats as straw, and bronze a rotten wood. Observe the creation of Asa'el my friends; behold the mighty Vorath!"

The barrier was removed and the enormous creature was led out of its confinement. Tur'el flew on top of its back, gently stroking its massive neck. It would not be an understatement to say the sound of thunder was as a whisper compared to the deafening roar of the beast, which shook the ground and bones of all for miles around. Its skin was a thick and scaly armor, with a yellowish-green hue to it that resembled a type of metal between bronze and gold. It walked on four legs that were studded at the joint with sharp protrusions all around. Its footprint was thirty-nine feet long, and it stood just over three hundred fifty-feet high. The ground quaked with each step of the beast, creating a small pressure wave of air. Its enormous tail, several hundred feet in length, moved side to side, proudly displaying the spiked bulbous end which was quite proficient at crushing solid earth. The assembled group of watchers looked upon the creature with awe as it extended it wings to their full breadth—over three thousand feet!

"It appears as the ones found on Reniel, does it not, my friends?" Zohari'el asked.

"In truth, it does, only this specimen dwarfs those creatures. I wonder, does it possess the gift of flame?" Barak'el inquired.

"How does it gain nutrients? It does not appear to be equipped with teeth necessary for consumption of flesh," Ar'tekif asked.

"That is correct," Asa'el said as he slowly rose from his meditations and approached the group. "It consumes Earth and rock, and also gains nutrients from the air and sunlight, through its wings."

They peered in his direction as he was looking up at Tur'el, who had walked the beast onto the ground below the plateau. Each step the creature took was an earthshaking, thunderous boom that generated copious amounts of dust and dirt. The immediate area had almost zero visibility, which was made worse from the tornado-like winds generated by its wings as Tur'el coaxed it into flight out onto the vast open plain.

"How did you create such a terrifying creature?" Kokav'el asked, trembling inside at the thought of it under the control of Asa'el.

"The internal structure required modification in order to allow for survival in this atmosphere. Those modifications increased its girth, stature, and longevity. Indeed, it is an even match for Leviathan, mayhap its superior. It should serve my purpose well this day. Brothers, I would be remiss if I did not give a demonstration of Vorath's capabilities," Asa'el stated with a smile. "Fly to Ephraim in Nod, Tur'el. Show the sons of Cain who opposed us the wages of their ignorance!"

The group looked at each other and whispered quietly amongst themselves, some with excitement, others with grave concern. Tur'el soared high above the horizon towards their quarry some twenty miles away. Most of the watchers had taken flight themselves to witness the spectacle of this dark force in action. Its ominous roar was heard off in the distance and appeared as a dark cloud moving rapidly towards the hapless town.

Within a minute, it had arrived and immediately began to render the town to ash and slag with its breath, which was unlike any fire seen on Earth. The flames themselves were violet-purple in color, and the fumes created from the gasses that ignited the sulfurous flame were a poison in the air to all who were not felled directly by the intense heat it generated. The screams of the humans could scarcely be heard above the roar of the beast which made quick work of the town. The Watchers who followed to observe the spectacle were quite impressed with the might of the beast and praised the skill of Asa'el for recreating this destroyer on Earth.

Word of the devastation that took place in Ephraim quickly spread to the other neighboring towns, and it was not long thereafter that an assembly of humans arrived, offering up their treasures and trinkets as a peace offering to the Watchers, swearing fealty in return for safety. Indeed, Asa'el had a mighty weapon to exert control, which the other watchers took note of. They in turn began to concoct all variety and manner of alien creatures in order to avoid being subjected to the rule of their brother.

Dissension eventually formed within the ranks of the Elohim and they gradually separated themselves across the landscape to avoid interaction and strengthen their sovereignty. It came to pass that many of the Watchers began to feel guilt and regret for their actions and what they had wrought on the planet. They had borne witness to the fruits of their actions firsthand; their offspring used the sorceries and magicks taught to them to wage war against each other in an effort to achieve supremacy. This was in addition to the humans who also fought against one another. Many humans were captured and used as livestock in order to feed the appetites of the giants and their offspring, as well as their unnatural creations. Cries went up to the Heavens for all the bloodshed the Earth was drenched in.

SEVERAL DECADES PASSED UNTIL THE FIVE Satans called an assembly of the leaders of the Watchers to discuss the predicament they were faced with. The word of the meeting went out, and in short order they had all found themselves together again where it had begun, many years ago, atop Mount Hermon. Only now, they were gathered inside of a small pyramid, comprised of granite slabs cut out and assembled by their children who had recently finished constructing the pyramids in several parts of Egypt as well. It was aptly named Shin'ar, land of the Watchers.

Many of those who arrived were not on good terms with one another; territorial disputes had emerged over time between the offspring of the leaders or those who followed under their rule, which resulted in bloodshed and wars between them. The Watchers had lost most of their light, and their flesh had become ashen in color, a consequence of their fall from grace.

None, save the two leaders and the five Satans, were aware of the purpose of the meeting; however, most were receptive to the idea and had little doubt amongst them as to the true nature of this gathering. Shemikhazah, one of the two who had led their kind to Earth, was the first to speak.

"It pleases me to see all of you again, and as such I am reminded of a time when the sons of Elohim banded together under lighter sentiments to sing the praises of the Ancient of Days. Alas, that time has passed, as we have all cast off our heavenly mantle to live as the sons of Adam.

"My brothers, it is clear to me as it should be to you that this undertaking was unwise from the outset. The children of The Creator were never meant to bind to the flesh of the daughters of Eve. Human spirits are weakly developed and as such, an insufficient match to that of our own. For this, and more, we have wrought terrible destruction upon the Earth and upon ourselves. I, like many of you have suffered great sorrow from the loss of several of my children at the hands of others."

Several amongst those gathered stood upright in anger and defiance. Asa'el calmed them down, and Shemikhazah continued. "It is not unknown to me that my sons are responsible for the loss of your children as well. I accept responsibility for their sins and humbly beg your forgiveness in turn. Brothers, we face unprecedented calamity, which you all have undoubtedly discerned yourselves. This planet cannot sustain our offspring and will surely perish if we fail to act. Gadreel shall explain the rest."

A tall figure stood up, almost nine feet, with skin completely ashen colored and covered in sigils which could be seen through his golden robes.

His eyes still shone brightly, illuminated seemingly from behind, the last vestige of his celestial heritage. As one of the accusers, his heavenly task was to bring to light the imperfection in souls; to allow for closer scrutiny and examination of those who decided if a soul was to advance or decline. He was a master of speech and beguiler; on this occasion his oratorical skills would be put to the test.

"My brothers, I come before you today to speak of the coming calamity that will befall all of you should you fail to act. You have lived amongst the mortals for some time now, and in that span we have observed the result of your interference with mankind. Shemikhazah has spoken truly when he remarked upon the folly of taking humans for the purpose of bonding with them; the offspring of that union have been a grotesque mixing of our pure celestial essence with that of lower life forms spiritually undeveloped. Yet, what is done cannot be undone. Mankind is thoroughly corrupted.

"Your children are a plague upon the Earth, as well are their offspring. The secrets revealed to their kind were another severe sin against Elohim, as was having them sacrifice to demon-kind. As a result of these actions, there can be no doubt that judgment awaits you. I have learned on good authority that severe punishment has been handed down, to be carried out by Rapha'el."

Shock and terror fell upon many of their faces.

"What do you speak of, Gadreel?" Shimsh'el asked.

"Oh, what is this look of surprise that I see amongst all of you? Come now, did you really think that abandoning your station and producing these works would earn favor with Elohim? Surely you have felt your grace leave, and seen your appearance change. Your beauty is tarnished, your light dimmed. This was a foregone conclusion. Heaven no longer responds to your prayers, does it not? Wages must be paid for your many sins." The words of Gadreel struck a mighty blow; the weight of shame cast their heads low.

"There may yet be a way to avoid the impending calamity," he said, with a crafty look. They listened intently as Gadreel cast a spell, showing another dimension apart from the one in which they stood.

"My father has found refuge here and currently rules over his followers who were cast out alongside him long ago. He has promised safety and refuge for you there, provided you all swear fealty to him. Considering the predicament, you are facing, it appears to be a profitable outcome, does it not?"

"Chanoch the scribe, send for him," Tami'el said.

"Yes, let Chanoch intercede on our behalf," Sahr'el said with fear in his voice.

"Consider carefully, brothers, as time is running out for you. Do not waste what precious little remains consulting with humans. This offer shall not remain open long," Gadreel replied, somewhat sullen.

One of the Watchers sitting in the back spoke up. "I myself have witnessed a vision concerning a coming destruction of Earth; however, I am unable to ascertain the time of its arrival," Kokav'el said with a dour look.

"My son, Mahway, has also had a vision—a most unusual one of a tablet with many names submersed in water, and all names save three were remaining on the tablet. I have a foreboding feeling of what it portends," Barak'el added.

"Chanoch has found favor with Elohim; he will be granted an audience and may petition for us all," Hermoni said anxiously.

Fear, trembling, and panic began to take over their assembly and they unanimously decided the best course of action was to send for the wise man known as Chanoch, leaving Gadreel and the others to depart in frustration.

Word arrived at the village where Chanoch, also known as Enoch, lived, and he was brought before the council of Watchers. Now Enoch was an upright human, seventh in the line of Adam and well known throughout the land as one who walked with Elohim. Even though he was hidden from the world at this time, the Watchers were able to discern his whereabouts, and he answered their call.

Several days later, he arrived at the base of the mountain where the Watchers gathered to speak with him. The man stood upright before the imposing group, and at two hundred forty years, he was still young in his days, for mankind had a much greater lifespan in those days.

It was Asa'el who spoke for the group.

"O Chanoch, you who have favor with Heaven: Go before the lord, and arbitrate on our behalf that we might find forgiveness for our sins. Draw a petition and read it in the presence of Elohim," he pleaded.

"Who am I, that I should plead the cause of Angels before the lord? Why do the Watchers not bring their petition themselves?" Enoch asked.

Dani'el, a leader of a small group of Watchers living in the South, spoke up. "Heaven no longer responds to our prayers. Our plight is dire; will you not help?"

Enoch paused for some time, looking over the faces of what remained; a dim reminder of the once lofty position they had held amongst the stars. All were silent as he took a deep breath before addressing their request.

"The gravity of your situation is known unto me as well. It therefore, shall be as you ask. I will return when I have received word from Elohim," he said, leaning upon his staff. They stood up with trepidation, wondering what was to be their fate.

After writing out the message the Watchers wanted him to speak on their behalf, Enoch returned to his hidden dwelling and fasted until the following day, spending the entire time in solemn prayer. Afterwards, he journeyed out to the wilderness and sat down at the waters of Dan, in the land southwest of Hermon, reading the petition of their requests till he fell asleep.

A dream came to him, and visions fell upon him until he lifted his eyelids toward the gates of the palace of heaven, where he beheld the wrath of chastisement. A voice came to him saying: "Speak to the sons of heaven, and reprimand them."

When he awoke, he left to find the Watchers all assembled, gathered together, weeping with their faces covered at Abel-Mayya, which is between Lebanon and Senir.

"What word do you bring, Chanoch, O righteous one? For we are heavy in heart and spirit," Asa'el said, with a sunken, hollow look on his face.

He recounted before them all the visions, which he had seen in his sleep, and began to speak the words of truth, and visions of reprimand to the heavenly Watchers.

"I have shared council with Elohim and brought your petition before the assembled host of Heaven. I saw in my sleep what I will now say with a tongue of flesh and with the breath of my mouth, which the Great One has given to men to converse therewith and understand with the heart. I wrote out your petition, and in my vision, it appeared to me that your pleas will not be granted unto you throughout all the days of eternity, and that judgment has been finally passed upon you and decreed against you. From henceforth, you shall not ascend into heaven unto all eternity, and in bonds of the earth the judgment has gone forth to bind you for all the days of the world.

"You will also witness the destruction of your beloved ones and all their sons and all their possessions; you shall have no heirs to them, and they shall fall before you by the sword of destruction. Because your petition on their behalf shall not be granted, nor yet on your own, even though you ask and speak all the words contained in the writing, which I have written. The vision was shown to me as thus: Behold, in the vision clouds invited me and a mist summoned me, and the course of the stars were shouting to me and the lightnings and thunderings hastened me, and the winds in the vision caused me to fly and lifted me upward, and bore me to enter into heaven. And these were the words of The Great One:

"Chanoch, you scribe of righteousness, go, declare to the Watchers of the heaven who have left the high heaven, the set-apart eternal place, and have defiled themselves with women, and have done as the children of earth do, and have taken unto themselves wives: You have wrought great destruction on the earth, and you shall have no peace nor forgiveness of sin. Inasmuch as they delight themselves in their children, the murder of their beloved ones shall they see, and over the destruction of their children shall they lament, and shall make supplication unto eternity, but mercy and forgiveness shall you not attain.

"Asa'el, you shall have no peace. A severe sentence has gone forth against you to place you in bonds. You shall not have toleration nor request granted to you, because of the unrighteousness which you have taught, and because of all the works of godlessness, destruction, and sin which you have shown to men.

"It is you who should intercede for men, and not men for you. Wherefore have you left the high, set-apart, and eternal heaven, and lain with women, and defiled yourselves with the daughters of men and taken to yourselves wives, and done like the children of earth, and begotten giants as your sons? And though you were set-apart, spiritual, living the eternal life, you have defiled yourselves with the blood of women, and have begotten children with the blood of flesh, and, as the children of men, have lusted after flesh and blood, as those also do who die and perish.

"I had given them wives that they might impregnate them, and beget children by them, thus nothing might be wanting to them on earth. But you were formerly spiritual, living the eternal life, and immortal for all generations of the world. Therefore, I have not appointed wives for you; for as for the spiritual ones of the heaven, in heaven is their dwelling.

"And now, the giants, who are produced from the spirits and flesh, shall be called evil spirits upon the earth, and on the Earth, shall be their dwelling. Evil spirits have proceeded from their bodies. They are born from men and from the set-apart Watchers is their beginning and primal origin. They shall be evil spirits on earth, and evil spirits shall they be called. As for the spirits of heaven, in heaven shall be their dwelling, but as for the spirits of the earth which were born upon the earth, on the earth shall be their dwelling.

"The spirits of the giants will afflict, oppress, destroy, attack, do battle, work destruction on the earth, and cause trouble. They will take no food, but nevertheless hunger and thirst, and cause offenses. And these spirits shall rise up against the children of men and against the women, because they have proceeded from them. From the days of the slaughter and destruction and death of the giants, from the souls of whose flesh the spirits, having gone forth, shall destroy without incurring judgment—thus shall they destroy until the day of the consummation, the great judgment in which the age shall be consummated, over the Watchers and the godless, yea, shall be wholly consummated.

"And now as to the watchers who have sent you to intercede for them, who had been before time began in heaven, say to them: You have been in heaven, but all the mysteries had not yet been revealed to you, and you knew worthless ones, and these in the hardness of your hearts you have made known to the women, and through these mysteries women and men work much evil on earth. Say to them therefore: You have no peace."'"

After hearing all this they all became very afraid, trembling with great weeping and wailing. Enoch left them to contemplate their fate.

The five Satans stood silently until Gadreel addressed them. "Look upon yourselves!" he said with disgust. "You who call yourselves Sons of the Most High. How low you have been brought. There can be no doubt that each carries a millstone around the neck as judgment is to be carried out against you. Have you not given thought to my offer?"

"Gadreel is right, brothers, are we not sons of Heaven itself? We have strength with our combined might. There is still time, we can assemble our sons and unite against their forces in battle," Shemikhazah said, in a vain attempt at lifting their spirits.

"Is this then your answer? You choose to continue down the path of folly and madness?" Gadreel asked.

"We should flee as cowards towards subjugation by your master when our power may yet win the day? Well aware are we all of his sin against Elohim; our plight is not that desperate. If Elohim sees our willingness to fight for our children, perhaps He will have mercy on us," Shemikhazah replied, lacking confidence in his proclamation.

"Never would I thought the day would come that I would bear witness to the dissolution and fragmentation of your mind, Shemikhazah," Gadreel said bitterly. "Does he speak for all of you?" he asked, looking over at all who were consoling each other.

"There is no choice, we must follow this path," they replied.

"Very well, your fate rests in your hands. Farewell, my brothers, we shall not see one another again," he replied with a slight bow. The four others—Peneume, Yekon, Asbeel, and Kasdeya—followed Gadreel out, leaving in silent indignation. The remaining leaders huddled together, trying to console one another and formulate a plan.

"There may be little time, quickly, send word to the far-off lands to assemble our brothers and their offspring that we unite for our cause. We must put aside our past differences and come together if we have any hope of survival. Gather Vorath, the dragons, and other beasts at the plain of Cush near the Gihon."

They all sprang into action, swiftly spreading word of the coming calamity, and gathered their aberrations and horrors together to wage war against the host of Heaven. Within two days, all manner of beasts and giants stood alongside each other in battle lines. Six hundred and sixteen giants riding flying dragons made their way to the site, unsure of what to expect. In total, about thirteen thousand giants were present. As they formed into small groups amongst the clans, they began to beat their shields and instruments of war on their chests in unison. The sound was deafening, which brought confidence to the enslaved humans in their company. In all, four hundred thousand gathered upon that plain of Cush, aptly named Dalkhu Girru, or Demon Fire.

Only the Watchers had knowledge as to the strength of Rapha'el and his armies; yet, the giants were proud.

"What force of Heaven has any chance against our assembled might? Let them come! We will crush them to dust and make slaves of their kind!" Taxtag shouted, his voice loud enough to be heard from miles away. The roar of Vorath, however, thundered above every beast and giant, as if announcing to all who was greatest in power.

Enoch had already informed the humans in the surrounding area of the coming calamity. Word had spread throughout the land, and all the villages of humans for hundreds of miles took refuge to the north.

ON THE SEVENTH DAY, THE ATMOSPHERE shifted unnaturally over the battlefield, making it known to all that a response from heaven was approaching. The clouds coalesced, turning blood red; the very air itself became a reddish hue. A volcano in the distance exploded with great force, spewing forth lava and ash, while thunder and lightning accompanied the eruption.

As they viewed the battleground from above on their mounted dragons, the Watchers signaled the warriors below to set up battle formations. The air had become thick and humid, when suddenly, a booming, thunderous horn blast was heard from all around, bringing many to their knees in terror. The dragons reluctantly took flight as the Watchers on the ground made ready their otherworldly weapons.

The clouds suddenly broke with a bright light shining through, and the Watchers witnessed the might of Heaven descending upon their warriors. A terrifying sight struck them. It was not just Rapha'el and his retinue who arrived. Gavri'el, Mikha'el, Uri'el, and Esme'el—the five chief Archangels, along with their assembled warriors—were coming out of the clouds with weapons drawn, their armor shining brightly as if illuminated by a star. They were seven hundred in total, and they were very outnumbered, yet to the leaders of the Watchers below the odds were quite in their favor.

The giants, unfamiliar with their foe, fought with great ferocity, hurling large stones and casting spells at their opponents. The dragon riders met the Angels in the air and struck wildly at them. The Angels responded in kind with speed, skill and precision.

The armies of the Watchers were no match whatsoever, for the well-trained warriors of Heaven, and it became painfully obvious to the forces on the ground, who were witnessing the slaughter of their dragon riders. Asa'el sounded his horn and flew in with Vorath, biting down hard on scores of victims.

Gavri'el, having observed the beast's capabilities, made a sigil in the air and called out for aid. Within a few moments, a deafening roar was heard from the west, and a large dark cloud approached. As the warriors of Heaven did battle with the giants and beasts, the Archangels surveyed the landscape from above, not yet entering the fray. Then, all at once, all five went into different directions without saying a word, communicating telepathically.

Rapha'el, who was in his Melammu spirit form, drew the Sword of Truth, a fiery blade brighter than the sun, blinding all the creatures below as it sliced with energy across a large swath of combatants. The Archangel Esme'el drew her sword, Eternity, and struck the unsuspecting mob below. It was devastating weapon that cut with waves of pressure, creating a sonic boom and knocking scores of giants down, blowing many to bits from the force. The rest of Rapha'el's special guard engaged the flying dragons that were trying to gang up on smaller pockets of the forces of Heaven. The riders were simply unable to contend with their speed. In addition to their physical weapons, the Archangels had numerous spiritual weapons that created fear, confusion and chaos among the beings of flesh.

As the battle raged, some of the Watchers fought back with spells of their own, causing injuries to several of the angels.

Vorath moved in and attacked Mikha'el, dealing a laceration to his armor and spirit being which quickly healed. Gavri'el flew to his side, and the two seized the beast by the tail and threw it over to the west, where it crashed into the ground with a deafening boom, leaving an enormous crater. The giants witnessed the might of the Archangels, and their courage began to falter; not even one hundred of them could budge Vorath, and yet, two Archangels threw the beast as if it were a block of wood. If that did not demoralize them enough, the legendary creature known as Behemoth arrived and landed atop Vorath who was still trying to right itself. The two enormous beasts locked their jaws into each other's flesh, creating rivers of blood beneath them.

The sounds of battle that the Earth had not witnessed since the war of Satan'el, filled the air, and it was becoming quickly apparent to those watching on the sidelines how one-sided the battle was.

Perched atop a nearby mountain, the five Satans stood silently as their allies were being routed by the host of Heaven. Gadreel opened a portal to another dimension, and they all departed in bitterness.

Behemoth and Vorath were locked in deadly combat. They seemed to be a stalemate until Vorath managed to shoot off a powerful blast of sulfurous fire into the face of Behemoth, causing it to roar with great pain. He recovered enough to bite down on Vorath's neck and carry him aloft, throwing him all the way into the Red Sea. The splashdown created a small tsunami, wiping out a few of the towns set up around the edge of the coast on both sides. The creature was not destroyed, however, as evidenced by the water boiling, shaking, and quaking with tumultuous ferocity, along with multiple flashes of light coming from below. Behemoth flew over to the Red sea where another legendary creature was now locked in battle with Vorath—the mighty Leviathan.

The giants were faring poorly also, as they lacked leadership. There simply wasn't enough time for them to put into place any kind of battle strategy or maneuver as the host of Heaven continuously put immense pressure on them. Uri'el cast a spell releasing devastating fire and brimstone onto the armies of the Watchers, while Gavri'el unleashed his devastating weapon, Zamani, an energy whip that crackled with a chain lightning, striking multiple opponents at once. One by one, the giants were cut down until the tide of battle had turned to a foregone conclusion.

Sensing defeat, the giants began to flee in all different directions, while their subhuman creations fought to the last. Many of the Watchers, having witnessed the Archangels rout their sons, became terrified and transformed themselves into ordinary men in an attempt to hide from their wrath.

Having completed their main objective in the battle, the Archangels turned their attention to rooting out the Watchers scattered about the landscape who were either still in combat, or hiding among the humans. In short order, they had captured and bound them all, leaving the remaining work to Rapha'el and his retinue to secure them in prison until their final judgment.

Asa'el, who had fallen to the battlefield from atop Vorath, was plucked by Rapha'el and bound hand and foot with celestial cord, designed to keep him from shifting form until he could be imprisoned.

The Watchers, having all been captured, were weeping profusely and trembling with fear. Rapha'el's regiment sorted them into groups while he prepared each holding cell with a pentacle of binding. Thirteen different prisons for the groups were completed with an additional singular, separate cell for Asa'el himself, for a total of fourteen. To give strength to the chamber, the seal of the inter-dimensional prisons used the spirit essences of two Archangels, Rapha'el and Esme'el, along with five other Angels. By design, should any one cell be opened, the pentacle that bound the remaining ones would become stronger, making them increasingly difficult to open.

Each group was placed on a floating platform and led to different cells far across the landscape. As they were cast into darkness, the Watchers screamed and howled with grief, begging for mercy and forgiveness. With the task completed, only one remained. Rapha'el personally carried Asa'el until they reached the place of his torment, where he was thrown into the dark pit that was the lowest elevation on land in the world.

"How long, Rapha'el? How long are we to be punished?" he asked.

"For seventy generations you will await your judgment. Contemplate all the evil that you have brought into this world, all of the destruction you have wrought, and the betrayal of our Lord. All sin has been ascribed to you, Asa'el. For these crimes, you shall pay the penalty in darkness," Rapha'el replied. With that said, they sealed the final holding cell shut and covered it with sharp rocks. Rapha'el then called the waters to fill up the area surrounding it, creating the Dead Sea.

The rest of the creatures and giants were hunted down until none could be found and the skies were clear. Behemoth came out of the Red Sea, battered and torn; however, the fate of Vorath was uncertain. They had to be assured of its demise, for the humans had suffered greatly at the maw of the beast.

"Go and observe the fate of that creature," Esme'el commanded her lieutenant. He quick sped off to the deep and brought back news of its defeat.

"It lies motionless at the bottom. Leviathan was dragging it off to the deep, holding it fast in its jaws," the Angel replied.

"That is good news indeed. A great victory has been won this day, yet the fate of humanity hangs in the balance. It remains to be seen if their corruption will lead to destruction for them as well. Mankind will continue to prey on one another until they learn to pray for one another," she said with a solemn look on her face, her armor covered in blood.

IN ANOTHER DIMENSION, WHERE THE FIVE Satans had just passed through the temporal portal, there sat a council of elders around their leader, Satan'el.

"My children return alone. It seems we have our answer, my friends," Satan'el said with a look of assurance, as if he had fully expected the outcome. He casually gestured with his hand as he sat with his arm resting on his throne. "It is just as well, for we are not fully prepared to do proper battle with the host of Heaven as I would see fit. When the necessary events align themselves we shall free Asa'el and his followers, and they will consider us an ally. Despite their failure, there is still use for them. For now, they will have to serve their penance. Why, therefore, should I be the only one who ever challenged Elohim and pay wages for that transgression?" he asked, the sarcasm in his voice matching a look of impudence on his face.

"When shall that day come, father, when we rise up?" Gadreel asked, bitterness in his voice over the routing the Watchers had received at the hands of the Archangels.

"There is much to do before that day comes, my son. I have set a plan in motion that will require great patience for all, the fruition of which will take many millennia. Yet, what is time for immortals, ones such as us? My design can be likened to a delicate tapestry, woven carefully and without error, lest a thread be untimely pulled and all is undone. Do not fret, be of good spirits; there is hope for our cause. What Rapha'el and his brothers will have to contend with will be unlike any foe they have ever faced or ever will; of that I can assure you. What you witnessed with Asa'el was an ill-prepared, sloppy troop of angels that displayed poor understanding of the nature of warfare," he said, stopping with eyes aflame.

The atmosphere inside suddenly became very cold. An unsettling vibration permeated their bodies as the light slowly receded and thunder rumbled. Satan'el narrowed his eyes and focused on one of his subjects.

"Have a care, Luri'el—you need be reminded that I know your thoughts? All of you? My battle was fought with far less preparation time, yet producing far greater effect than Asa'el's could ever hope to achieve, shaking the very foundations of Heaven itself!" he boomed. "The outcome will be quite different upon my return, I assure you. Who is it that sits before you and who rots in a prison? Who is it that gives council to Elohim on the affairs of the mortals? Who is it that rules this realm?" he asked to all before him with a burning anger in his voice.

"Forgive my impertinence, my Lord. I should not have compared your greatness to Asa'el's failure," Luri'el replied, putting his head down in shame.

Satan'el looked away towards his five sons. "Come, I have need of you to complete a task for me now that you have returned," he said, getting up from his throne.

# Nineteen

"I am not exaggerating, Zeracon. I know what I felt. His Shi was off the charts and this was not an isolated incident. I was told by a friend who witnessed his awakening that he almost killed everyone in the room. That has never happened as far as I am aware," Lykoi said, standing in an interview room at the Sanctum of Atonement, Anidon's police force.

"He hasn't done anything wrong. I cannot simply interrogate the son of a founder of Anidon without just cause, Lykoi. What do you want me to do? Without proof of wrongdoing, what is there to be concerned about? Perhaps he is simply a prodigy. After all, Urieth is the oldest among us, and he is very powerful," Zeracon said.

"Yes, Urieth is quite powerful, but what I felt was an order of magnitude far greater than Urieth or anyone in Anidon, including the Angels, and he wasn't even in his first spirit form. What if he accidentally kills someone in training? What then? Who is going to be responsible?" she asked, pressing him into action. Zeracon stood for a moment letting her words sink in for some time, then sighed loudly.

"Fine. I'll talk to Dregan and see what he suggests. For now, just keep this between us until I get back to you. Are we in agreement?" he asked, with an anguished look on his face.

"It will be as you say. In the meantime, I will monitor his training closely and keep him away from the others as much as possible."

She held his hands in hers and kissed his cheek. "Thank you husband."

ELSEWHERE, IN ANIDON:

"This is pretty good. What do you call it?" Dorian asked.

"That particular one we call the Ale of Antiquity. It has a sweet creaminess to it, and it uses a four-thousand-year-old yeast from the ancient world, still kept alive. It's quite popular. You don't want to touch that one over there though; that's poison," Yelnisha said, pointing to a blue, milky-colored drink. The two of them were seated in "The Stout Trout", an unusual watering hole that contained drinks from the various ages and regions of Anidon and other worlds.

"So, what do you do? I mean, what is your job here? You do have a job here, right?" he asked.

She laughed a bit, almost spitting her drink in his face.

"Yes, I do have a job here. The first time we met you saw me working, which mainly involves doing surveillance on various people and places on Earth. Sometimes I do field work for the Avavago."

"The who?" Dorian queried.

"They're a part of our Offensive and Defensive Operations Division. Think of it as a military and intelligence gathering department; you know, like the CIA or MI6. A matter of fact, we happen to have operatives in both of those agencies," she said with a snicker. "Mind you, what we do is mostly voluntary; we hardly get paid. Not that we really need to be paid here anyway. Here, try this one," she said with a smirk, handing him a glass of glowing yellow liquid.

He took a sip then quickly drank it down. "Hmm, that was good. Uh... what's going on... here? What in the? I think I'm having an allergic reaction Yelnisha!" he said with panic in his voice as he watched his hands and face balloon up to cartoonish proportions.

"Right, that one's what we call the 'Fun House'. Don't lose your head, it'll wear off soon. What did you think of the taste— pretty good, huh?" she replied, paying no mind to his panic.

Sure enough, within thirty seconds it wore off. "Do me a favor. Next time give me a heads-up so I don't freak out like that?" he said, pushing the drink towards her.

After downing his twentieth or thirtieth (keeping count was getting difficult at this point), he was becoming quite intoxicated, an experience he had only recently become familiar with.

"Okay, whas goin' on now? What did I eat this time? I mean drink. What did I eat this time? Hah-ha, I mean, you know what I mean. What was that las' one I had? Mine feeling pretty good now," he said, slurring and stammering his words.

"Ha! Well, serves ya right. How many did you drink there, skipper?" Yelnisha teased. "Quit acting like you've never been pissed before. You have been drunk before? Right?" she asked, her eyebrows raised as Dorian looked at her with sleepy, half-moon eyes. "Yeah, you're blootered all right."

"I can't get drunk, I mean…Shhhhh," he said, lowering his voice and looking around. "Shhhhh." Yelnisha looked at him with great amusement.

"Mine don't understand, this has never happening. What is this thinking I'm having?" he asked, holding his head in both hands while trying to get up from the table, which caused him to promptly fall over. Yelnisha slid out of her booth and picked him off the ground, helping him back into his seat. A vacuous look was plastered on his face as he stared out the window. At this point walking, talking, just about anything was too difficult for him.

"All right now, time to get you to the four-post hotel, let's go. Here we go, ups a daisy," she said, helping him back out of the booth. With his arm around her shoulder, she walked him outside and carefully placed him on her platform. He slid down and rested on the floor in the fetal position while she flew him back to her flat.

Ten minutes later, they arrived. Her abode was one of the more futuristic types, comprised of three floating obsidian colored rectangles with an aquamarine glow around the edges. It stood about three hundred feet off the ground, giving a grand view of the greater Anidon area. The landing platform in front was quite expansive; it had a front yard with very short grass and a small garden area. Stepping onto the platform caused an energy barrier to became active, preventing her inebriated and sober visitors from plummeting to their doom below.

Dorian was now lying in the fetal position on her front yard, unable to get up on his own accord.

"I'm poisoned, Yeshlina! I was drugged!" he shouted as he rolled over onto his back, arms flailing about in the air, causing her to laugh out loud.

"This is too much, ah. I can't breathe," she said, laughing until she started to wheeze. "I have an idea. You stay right here darling, I have just the thing." A moment later, she returned with a rolling chair and some rope. After spending several minutes attempting to get him to sit on the chair (it would have been easier to drag his carcass in, she thought), she tied him onto it, making sure he wouldn't fall off, then rolled him to the stairs, lifting him and the chair until he was in her house. He was immediately assaulted by her two dogs, Cajun and Curry, a pair of Rhodesian Ridgebacks.

"Thas' a good puppy," he muffled. Their tongues swiped his face from all directions, giving him a good cleaning.

"Get off him, you two!" she yelled. Their tails were swinging with frenzied fervor over their excitement.

"Not all of us are as fortunate as you with your laudy-daw digs. Some of us still have to do things the old-fashioned way around here. All right, here's where you're going to crash," she said, rolling him into a room with a standard mattress and bed.

After untying him from the chair she pushed him from behind causing him to fall face first onto the bed. The dogs, seeing their new toy splayed out, seized the opportunity and jumped on top, nuzzling and mopping his hair up.

"C'mon! Not now, you flippin' manky gits! Trundle your carcasses outta here!" she shouted while swatting at them. That prompted a thunderous and violent departure, with the dog's feet furiously attempting to maintain traction and control on the smooth surface of the floor. Their legs scurried and scuttled, gathering dangerous speed, followed by a loud, crashing noise that came from the living room. She sighed and looked over at Dorian, who was still face planted on the bed sideways.

"Right, let's get these off," she said, removing his sneakers. Grabbing him by his pants at the ankles, she slid his whole body onto the bed and straightened him out properly. After flipping him over on his back she gasped, holding her hand over her mouth as she saw that the special contact lens which normally covered his entire eye was stuck to his cheek, revealing the glowing emerald light that emanated through his barely open eye slit. After carefully picking up the lens, she left to wash it off, returning a moment later to the bedroom where Dorian was fast asleep. Propping his eye open with one hand, she gingerly placed it back in without a hiccup and covered him with a blanket, closing the door of the room as she left. She walked over to her living room area and sat on the couch, silently contemplating what she witnessed.

"If Urieth is his father, then who was his mother? I'd wager a shekel that she's one of the angels. Urieth is one of the Dumuzi, so he must be some kind of hybrid. Well, I suppose that explains a few things. I wonder why they're keeping it a secret here, of all places?" she asked herself, while biting her fingernails down to the nub.

Wondering what to do with the newfound information, she decided to visit Matthias to see what he knew. Dorian was sound asleep, as evidenced by his snoring, so she quietly left and made her way over to her flying platform and set the destination for New Anubus, a spirit center for development and growth.

Several minutes later, she arrived at a large pyramid constructed from a solid surface resembling volcanic rock. The exterior had no visible seams, an engineering marvel in and of itself. Inside the facility were rows and rows of chairs that held bodies in place while they were connected to the djed pillars, a spiritual medium device used in ancient Egypt for the same purpose.

Although Matthias lived and worked in Anidon, his spirit often roamed throughout various dimensional regions assisting and teaching others to learn, grow, and develop. Because he was known throughout Anidon as a humanitarian and scholar, many people sought out his wisdom and instruction. Yelnisha looked to him as a mentor and friend, one she could trust and rely upon.

After finding an unoccupied seat and getting comfortable, she called Matthias on her communicating device. The two agreed to meet on Verdes Beth, Yelnisha's private sanctuary. She found him waiting on the pessipone when she arrived.

"Yelnisha, it is good to see you. You sounded troubled in our short exchange a moment back. I will need to make our discussion brief as I have matters to attend, I hope you understand. What is it you wished to speak with me about?" he asked, as she approached.

"Thanks for seeing me on such short notice. Let's go inside so we can talk," she said. They walked the pathway to the only structure within her sanctuary, a moderately sized wooden house surrounded by a small forest with a stream flowing off to the edge of the property. The grass surrounding it was green, the sun was shining and the air was crisp. It was reminiscent of a childhood vacation home which held fond memories of her family.

The two went inside and sat down. She sighed and began to recount the events that took place earlier through telepathy.

"Okay, I'm just going to come out and tell you like it is, see? Dorian is definitely not like one of us," she said, trying to find the right words.

"Oh, what do you mean by that?" he asked, acting surprised.

"Well, I went out drinking with him you know, and uh, he had a wee bit more than he should have. So, I set him up to crash and sleep it off, nothing out of the ordinary, right? Only thing is, when he fell on the bed he must have hit his face the wrong way, because he had this lens stuck to his face. Like an eye covering."

"Eye covering?" Matthias asked.

"Eye covering. That's what I'm calling it. Some kind of lens that covered his whole eye. Well, I looked down and saw that what was behind it was glowin' bright green, kind of the way the angel eyes do. I didn't check his other eye, should 'a done that. I'm pretty sure it's the same. I got to thinking about when we turned on his Shi, remember that? Well, I would say the math is adding up and giving me a strange answer. What do you think?"

"I see. Who else did you speak to this about?"

"You're the first. I didn't want to go to Urieth with it, who knows how he would react," she said.

Matthias look relieved. "Yes well, that is strange indeed. Perhaps it is best to put it behind you and let it go. It would be advisable not to mention anything to Urieth, or to anyone else for that matter, as I'm sure it's being kept secret for a reason. There's a reason to be concerned about how the others in Anidon may react to that information.

"I am sure you are aware that Urieth has several detractors on the council who would take pleasure in seeing him expelled, in addition to the others who have taken issue with him over the years. I suspect their weak fears may surface and lead to unwarranted action."

She narrowed her eyes a bit. "Did you know about this?"

Matthias looked uncomfortable in his chair. It wasn't in his nature to be deceitful, as he was quite unaccustomed with anything other than the truth. In the interest of keeping Dorian's secret intact as much as he possibly could, he decided it was best to give her a partial view of the picture.

"I was made aware that his origins were different from the rest of us, yes. It is a private matter between Urieth, Dorian and myself. Out of respect for Urieth I ask that you do not think upon this fact nor act on it," he replied, knowing Yelnisha was not one to let things go.

"So how am I supposed to handle his training? He could end up hurting someone you know—if he is what I think he is," she said.

"Perhaps it would be prudent for you to closely monitor him, and avoid intensive training with the others in the group until he has a solid grasp of his abilities and how to control them. I will wait and think upon it further, before mentioning anything to Urieth. Are we in agreement?"

She gave him a long stare and sighed. "Yeah, that'll do for now. Should you decide to confide in me, you know where to find me."

"Tch, come now, Yelnisha, I think you know me better than that," he said with a chuckle. "What you seek to know I am not at liberty to discuss as I was requested not to. I hope you can understand this. Farewell, my friend," he replied as he departed.

She sat for a few moments, brooding over the fact that Matthias was holding something back from her. There was no doubt she was well liked by others, but it was no secret that she was an incorrigible blabbermouth. For the time being she decided she would prod the information out of Dorian himself.

The following morning Dorian awoke to a pair of cold, wet noses probing his ear and other body parts. Like all animals, they held an attraction to him similar to the way humans did. He sat upright with his eyes still closed, a thick fog looming in his head. The smell of fresh coffee mixed with bacon filled the room. Off in the distance, the sound of footsteps could be heard making their way towards him.

"GLAD TO SEE YOU'RE UP THEN!" she shouted with sadistic glee. "You were pished as a fart last night, let me tell ya. How's she cuttin', she asked.

"Like a blade," he responded with eyes still closed. A small smile crept up on his face.

"Oh, look at you, being a proper Oirishman an' all," she replied, giggling ecstatically. "I went and made ya breakfast. Don't be shy, go ahead and eat," she said, wheeling the tray of food over to him. He gently opened his eyes, then yawned and groaned a bit.

"Unh, what time is it?" he asked, picking up the coffee and taking a small sip.

"It's just the right time, in fact, for you to get up, eat, and go for a run. We need to get you in shape. Finish your food first and then we'll talk." She got up and closed the door behind her.

There was a window in the room that was letting in daylight from a distant star. He walked over to get a better glimpse of the town below, hustling and bustling on a busy Friday morning.

After eating and washing up, he walked out of the room to find Yelnisha in her exercise outfit doing leg stretches and pulls.

"Yeah, I'm going to need to digest for a bit before I go off running with you, just so you know. What happened to me last night anyway? I never get drunk. What I mean to say is, I have an extremely high tolerance to alcohol. What was in those drinks we had?"

"Oh, and how did you get this extremely high tolerance you speak of?" she casually prodded.

"Does it matter?" he asked.

"Just having a bit of fun now, don't get your knickers in a bunch. A few of them didn't have any alcohol in them. They use some other kind of drug; one that doesn't ruin your liver," she replied cheerfully.

A beeping sound that Yelnisha was quite familiar with came from Dorian's pocket. "You're getting a call from someone, might want to answer," she said.

Reaching into his pocket, he retrieved the metallic object that was his connection to Uchi away from home. A screen displayed in front of him indicating it was from Urieth.

"Hello, Dorian, it is good to see you. I hope I'm not disturbing anything," he said. He was sitting at his desk in his office at the Department of Offensive and Defensive Operations.

"No, not at all. I was just discussing with Yelnisha here my reaction to the drinks we had at the... what was the name of the place you took me to?" he asked.

"The Stout—"

"Right, The Stout Trout," Dorian finished.

"I trust you were not disappointed," Urieth said with a slight grin.

"Ah, yeah, well, let's just say I need to be careful what I drink here from now on. Can't be too sure on who might try to poison me," he replied, looking over at Yelnisha with a frown.

"Do you want a knuckle supper? I didn't force you to drink anything ya gobsh—," she stopped, electing to stick her tongue out instead.

Urieth laughed. "Try to get along, you two. Dorian, I need a favor."

"Sure, what can I do for you," Dorian asked, as he turned away and stuck his tongue out back at her. She held a closed fist up and smacked it into her open hand in response. He followed with a feigned frightened face.

"Sorry, a favor?" he asked, snapping back into the conversation.

Urieth shook his head and chuckled. "Ah, to be young. Yes. As it so happens, word has managed to travel around Anidon that my prodigal son has returned, so to speak. An old friend, who happens to be a Professor himself at the University here, called me up regarding what he had heard about you. We spoke for some time, and he mentioned that he would like to meet you," he paused. "And... possibly to discuss matters of science and philosophy as well."

Yelnisha pointed at him while covering her laughter.

"Uh, sure, okay. Who is it and when or where do I meet with them?"

"His name is Apollonius. He's one of our council members and a very wise man whom I think you might find fascinating. He lectures this afternoon at The Obelisk of Enlightenment on the seventy sixth floor at the great auditorium, right about the time that your session with Matthias ends. If you would indulge an old man, kindly sit through one of his lectures. I think that he would be happy with that, and perhaps you could visit him at the end for a small chat. I will send the specific instructions to your house unit."

"No problem. I would be happy to speak with him," Dorian replied, looking at Yelnisha, shaking his head in disapproval.

"Thank you, my son, I appreciate it. Oh, there is one more thing that I had almost forgotten. Lykoi has offered to train you personally, one-on-one in combative arts and the use of Shi. She's been a valuable friend, and I did not want to insult her by denying her request," he said cautiously, knowing it might upset Yelnisha.

"Um, no, I don't think that's a good idea, Urieth," Yelnisha interjected, moving next to Dorian. "Here, give me that," she said, grabbing the handheld projector from him and pushing him aside.

"Oh, and why is that?" Urieth asked.

"Well, for starters, I've spent some time with him myself in one-on-one training, and I think we have a pretty good thing going; hate to mess with it you know."

"Yelnisha, I believe you have spent a total of one day with Dorian in training. You have a group of nine that you've been with for the past year who need attention from you as well. Lykoi is not taking over your students," he said, pushing back a bit.

"Yeah, well, I don't think it's a good idea for her safety."

"Her safety? Why would you be concerned about that?" Urieth asked.

"I'm not going to hurt her if that's what you're worried about. I'm pretty much a beginner with this stuff as it is," Dorian interjected.

"You almost killed everyone in the room on Erustian Prime; without even trying I might add," she said.

"Yelnisha, I think that was an anomaly. Once he understood how to control his Shi, there have been no other incidents," Urieth countered.

"He's not like the rest of us, Urieth! I saw his eyes!" She closed her eyes, realizing the can of worms she had just opened.

There was a long bit of silence amongst the three of them, and finally Dorian spoke. "I stand the same chance of hurting you as I do Lykoi. If I think it's going to be too much for me, I'll excuse myself or stop for a bit. As for what you saw—"

"As for what you saw," Urieth interrupted, "I would be grateful—we both would be grateful—if you would kindly keep that information to yourself."

"Why does it matter? There's all kinds of crazy critters here. I don't think he's that much different, even with his—."

"I know you are fishing for information, Yelnisha, but where my son and I are concerned, I wish to maintain some privacy. I hope you understand," Urieth replied, cutting her off.

"Yes...yes, of course. No problem. I hope you both know what you're doing," she replied in a diminished voice.

"Thank you, my friend. I will be in touch later," Urieth said, ending their conversation.

"This doesn't mean we can't train together. You can still teach me what you know in private," Dorian said, trying to lift her spirits.

"I don't think that would be a good idea. Lykoi can be very territorial with things; it's in her nature. She may be from another planet, but the aliens tend to get special treatment here. The last person who got in her way regretted it dearly. No, we won't be having any of that. I'll keep a close eye on you two to make sure she doesn't step out of line. I owe Urieth that much at least. C'mon, time to get going. We can still go for a run today," she said with a dejected smile.

THE SANCTUM OF ATONEMENT:

"That is what she tells me, although I have not confirmed it for myself," Zeracon said, looking like he did not want to be there.

"No, it is good that you brought this to my attention, despite your misgivings about it. We should ever be vigilant if we are to survive.

"What do you have up your sleeve, Urieth? I will have to bring this to the attention of the other council members when we have greater confirmation. She is to train him then?" Dregan asked.

"Yes. I spoke to her this morning and she has approved it with Urieth. Could he not be a prodigy? My wife does not seem to think so; however, I have my doubts about this being some sort of plot," Zeracon replied with an anguished look.

"Anything is possible, Zeracon. She may have exaggerated his abilities. I have a few things in mind to help substantiate our suspicions; however, they require the blessing of the law. We cannot chance giving cause to his supporters. Is this acceptable?" Dregan asked, his steely blue eyes staring coldly at Zeracon.

"That depends on what you have in mind," Zeracon replied coolly.

"When one is on the training field where combatants participate in exercises, things could get heated. Tempers could flare. The environment could be a dangerous place. Nothing that would be out of the ordinary for such a place. Have your wife use this to measure his Shi," he replied, handing Zeracon a small device that looked like a wristwatch. "We'll have our answers soon enough."

THE STREETS OF ANIDON:

"Ten miles down and I'm sweatin' like a knacker in a maths test, and you're dry as the Sahara! It's not fair!" Yelnisha lamented.

"Hey, when you're this good you don't sweat the small stuff," Dorian replied with a grin.

She smacked him across the chest. "Listen, I need to show you a few things before Lykoi officially takes over. Just a couple of things that might just save your ass some time. I know they sure saved mine," she said, huffing with her steps.

"Sounds good. When? Right now?"

"Yes, now. Let's stop over there for a bit," she replied. They walked over to a courtyard in a shopping area to talk.

"So far, I've taught you how to block your thoughts from others and how to read theirs. Now you need to know how to plant a thought in someone's head. To make them hallucinate," she said, looking around.

"You can do that? You people are scary, all right," he replied.

"It's probably obvious, but you first need to be able to read their mind. Once you're in, focus your Shi on the mental connection you have with them, all the while focusing on what it is you want them to see. For example, suppose I wanted you to see an elephant in the street. I would picture it in my mind and mentally project the image over."

"Let me guess, it only works on the weak minded."

"Is that from one of your nerdy fantasies?" she asked, looking at him with a sarcastic face. He shrugged his shoulders.

"Well, in this case you're partially right," she said. "It's not going to work against someone who is a higher trained being unless they're trying to trap you. When you've linked to their mind, they could just as easily plant a vision in yours if they know what's going on and how to do it. So you need to be careful. Also, you could wind up opening yourself up to mental attacks. You have to be quick about it; in and out before anyone knows what happened."

Another pair of runners went by while Yelnisha was watching their moves.

"What is it?" he asked.

"Nothing, maybe my imagination. I'm a bit paranoid sometimes. Just making sure we aren't being watched. All right, let's practice what I just told you. Put a vision into my head," she said.

"All right, you asked for it."

Focusing his Shi on her mind, he was able to form a link. Just as he tried planting a picture, he noticed everything went dark, and a spotlight shone on him. The lights went up a bit to show rows of people sitting in a stadium laughing at him while he stood in the center wearing a clown suit. Yelnisha stood on a platform opposite him wearing a ringleader suit and holding a microphone.

"Too slow," she said over the loudspeaker.

The vision soon faded, and they were back in the alleyway.

"If I get the drop on you, you're going to die. Let's try again," she said.

The second attempt was no better than the first, only now he was a baby seal, and Yelnisha was a polar bear about to eat him. The other attempts were similar; praying mantis and fly, snake and rat, cockroach and shoe, and so forth.

"I give up, I'm done. This is exhausting. If this is what I'm up against, I don't think I'm going to bother with it," he said in defeat.

"You really blew that. You're going to need to make your weakness your strength, Dorian. That's how everything in life should be; this is no different. We'll keep working on it. If you think I'm difficult you should go up against Tiddi. She's a master at all mental attacks, so don't ever get on her bad side," she replied.

"Right, note to self: don't upset Tiddi. What was the other thing you wanted to show me?"

"This next one is more destructive and dangerous. I watched two angels in combat before, one of the dark ones—a very powerful one at that, I might add—and a light angel. They battled for some time until the light one pulled this trick out. I bugged Sonra'el for months before he finally showed me how to cast it. It hasn't worked for me yet because my Shi isn't high enough, but I suppose for someone like you it would probably go off without a hitch. Probably. Hopefully. Anyway, it's called 'The Tripod of Life'. There's several more that he wouldn't show me, 'The Seed of Life', 'The Flower of Life, 'The Fruit of Life', and 'The Tree of Life',' which are all crazy powerful. Each of them make up a portion of the grand spell, 'The Creation of Life', a legendary spell that will probably annihilate everything in creation.

"These are all white Magick spells by the way. You can kind of tell by the 'of Life' part. Dark magic tends to end in 'of Death'. Anyway, you can draw it in the air, or picture it in your mind. Better to keep it mental so you don't go telegraphing what you're about to do. It's just three concentric circles overlapping like this," she said, lifting up her shirt to reveal a tattoo on her solar plexus.

"Now, see this pattern within the circles? That's what you're trying to envision. When you've got that down, you need to imagine lines of Shi following that pattern in the center of your being. Right where I have this tattooed. See? When the Shi is flowing in the pattern properly you'll know it. You won't have to concentrate on it, it'll move within on its own. Oh yeah, you can increase the power of it by doing the same to each arm, but it takes more time, so bear that in mind.

"Now, what you want to do from here is hold out your hand and say *"From the ancient contract, from the law that dwells in time without end, I call upon Retribution against my enemy. Let his judgment strike with a Holy Explosion!"*, and imagine the symbol I showed you on your enemy. You have to use a lot of Shi for it to work. Unfortunately, we have to practice this someplace safe, like Verdes Seventeen. You can try and get the symbol on your center without blowing anything up. Practice that first," she said, checking her watch for the time. Dorian was repeating the phrase so he would remember it.

"So, what exactly does it do?"

"Sonra'el said it had to do with making evil creatures unstable. It targets their energy and destabilizes it. I'm not sure how much it takes out of you, so be careful with this one also. We can practice over the weekend if you want to get together," she said with a smile.

"Uh, sure, that would be great, thanks."

"I've got to get to work, so think about the spell, and let me know if you have any questions. Give me call tonight to fill me in on how your training went with Lykoi. See ya after," she said, putting her hand on his shoulder as she walked past him.

"Sure, thanks again. Hey, how do I get back... wait a sec, never mind," he replied, remembering the device in his pocket. Without anywhere to be for the moment, he decided to jog a bit more around town to get a better feel of where things were. As he ran about, he could feel multiple attempts to probe his mind coming from all different directions, yet it was unclear as to who was behind it. Picking up his pace, he passed some tall buildings and found his way to a clearing where a sign read "Founders Park".

Seven monuments to the founders stood at the entrance, each fourteen-feet tall, constructed of a series of different elements emphasizing their individual characteristics. A placard below each monument described their attributes.

"Heralth is solid granite from the ground up to the waist symbolizing his solid firmament and his efforts in the construction of Anidon. His chest and arms are comprised of iron, and his head of Onyx; a stone containing many different colors and layers, representative of his depth and understanding."

"Chlothar is sculpted of a stone called Berylix, which is only found deep in the Earth. It has the unique property of accepting enchantments, a means of binding Magick to objects.

The stone continuously changes colors, signifying his knowledge of different cultures and races across the cosmos."

"Lucretia is made entirely of diamond, reflecting light everywhere, which is indicative of the love, peace, and humility she demonstrates to others. It also reflects her strength and resilience against corruption."

"Narses is not made of any stone, rather his form is sculpted of an enchanted living fire. The most unusual of all the figures, it stands for his passion and love for Anidon, as well as the power he wields."

"Euanthe is made from a living tree engineered to follow her form. The hands and heart are made of gold, representing her love of nature and her skill in the healing arts."

"Urieth is made of a glowing metal with many colors swirling inside, known as Ocmixthes, which is not found on Earth. It signifies Urieth's ability to rise above adversity and defy the forces of nature itself to achieve his goals."

"Tauria is sculpted from particles of light forming matter. Although she was not alive during this commission, there is no doubt her love and light filled her entire being, and we can think of no better way to honor her memory."

Dorian stood looking over the seven imposing figures and felt a sense of awe at what they had accomplished, in stark contrast to the chaos, violence and mayhem on the Earth. At least that is what he thought until a group of about eight people showed up, gathering around the statue of Tauria. One of the girls from the class Matthias taught, Emerelda, was among them. She knelt down in front of Tauria's statue to lay a wreath and then set up an unusual candle. Her outstretched hand caused an ethereal light to float above, flickering in a bluish-green flame. A few of the others set some wreaths of flowers around it as well.

She looked over at Dorian who was observing the scene quietly in the distance and snarled at him.

"You don't deserve to be here! Get out of here!" she shouted.

He turned around to see if anyone was standing nearby. "Who? Me?" he asked, pointing at himself. "I'm sorry, have I done something to upset you? I've only been here a few days, maybe you're confusing me with someone else?" he replied sheepishly.

A tall male figure, about the same height as Dorian, stepped out of the group and walked over to him. Wearing a long coat with a skin-tight shirt, he appeared to be quite muscular. His sandy-blonde hair was neatly cropped in addition to his beard. Several sigils were tattooed on his body that appeared to have a whitish-blue glow to them. Dorian felt hostility emanating from the others that were there, in addition to Emma and the one standing in front of him.

"What she means is that you might want to think about leaving, junior, before something happens that you're going to regret," the man said, stepping in closer.

"Sure, no problem, don't want any trouble, not sure what this is about, but you all seem quite upset, so I'll just...," he replied, stepping back with his hands up.

He quickly flashed his mind through the group to pick up their surface thoughts. Emma and the tall one, whose name was Jaxon, were brother and sister. They were honoring their mother Tauria's passing as today happened to be the tenth anniversary of her death.

"My mother just passed away last week, so I know what it's like to lose a parent. I'm sorry for your loss," Dorian said, hoping it would have some positive effect. Unfortunately, it had quite the opposite.

Emma flashed a scowl at him. "You know nothing! Your father is the reason she's gone. Now get the hell out of here!" she shouted.

"I'm not going to ask you again. You don't want to find out what I'm capable of," Jaxson said as he began building up his Shi.

Dorian felt the air becoming thin, and time was slowing down for him as his senses became enhanced. Without willing it, his spirit energy began to climb. Jaxson felt the increase from Dorian and took this as a challenge, shifting into an offensive posture.

At that moment, Dorian foolishly attempted the technique that he had just learned from Yelnisha. Unfortunately, Jaxon was quite adept at thwarting such attacks, and his gamble backfired on him. The scene changed, and they were both under water; Jaxson a large shark and Dorian a small baitfish, swimming furiously away from him.

A moment later, Dorian found himself on the ground with his jaw in pain and graffiti covering his face. Lykoi witnessed the attack from above and swooped in on her platform, quickly disembarking with her claws bared, snarling at Jaxon.

"What is going on here! Explain yourselves!" she demanded.

"I don't have to tell you anything, Whiskers. Leave before you take a cat nap," Jaxon replied, trying to act tough.

"Let's get out of here, this day just got a lot worse. Come on, let's go," Emma said, tugging at his coat. Several of the others with her shouted curse words at Dorian as they left, while Jaxon turned and scowled at the two of them.

Dorian got to his feet and brushed himself off, rubbing his jaw that had been punched hard.

"Are you injured?" Lykoi asked.

"I'm fine. Why are you looking at me like that?" he asked, noticing her slight grin.

"You have...writing all over your face. You should clean up. Here," she replied, offering a small moist towel from her pouch. After wiping his face down, he sat on one of the benches for a moment to take in the situation.

"Can somebody please tell me what is going on? One minute I'm looking at these statues, quietly minding my business, the next I've got the Dorian Haters Club in front of me. And here I was just beginning to like this place," he said, leaning down to wipe the back of his neck.

Lykoi sat next to him and took a deep breath. "You picked the worst day and time to come here, you know. I am surprised your father didn't mention anything to you. Perhaps he still does not accept any responsibility."

"Responsibility for what? Was he involved in her death? At least that's what I picked up from the group. What happened?"

She paused for a moment and quietly looked over the seven statues, taking a deep breath. "It was ten years ago, on this same day, your father, Tauria, her husband Narses, and twenty other operatives went to infiltrate an enemy outpost in the land of Switzerland. Your father was responsible for the operation plan, based on the intelligence report he received from Marcus Parreth, a council member here, in addition to his role as the Director of Intelligence. Marcus analyzed and gathered the data, having sent several operatives there previously, including Silvan Ford, who now works security at the research facility. When they followed through with the operation, they were ambushed, and everyone lost their lives, with the exception of Narses and Urieth."

Dorian quietly listened with a stoic expression.

"There were several council meetings afterwards to try and determine what went wrong. When word reached the public here, fingers were pointing all over as to who supplied information to the enemy. It was never discovered if there was a traitor in their midst or not. Marcus, your father, and Narses were all scrutinized closely, but ultimately the public sided with them.

"As you can imagine, the families of those who lost their lives have been divided on what happened. Some cast blame on Urieth and Marcus. I am sure you can guess how those children of Tauria feel about it.

"She was a good woman and a friend, but I do not feel either one is responsible as I suspect there are traitors among us.

"In any case, it was a very painful moment in our history here, and we still are no closer to determining what went wrong. Since that day, there have not been any significant operations against the enemy, which has allowed them to increase their foothold as well as their strength.

"Anyway, go home, get cleaned up, and meet me on the field in thirty minutes. You spoke with you father regarding your training assignment, correct?" she asked.

"Yes, thank you, Lykoi, Hopefully I don't continue to embarrass myself like I have been," he said, rubbing his sore jaw. Setting up his platform, he programmed the destination to return home and departed.

"Thank the Source it ended as it did, as I suspect Jaxon would have been destroyed, and on such a day! Emerelda would have been broken beyond repair," Lykoi thought to herself as she climbed aboard her platform.

Dorian made it home and washed up, all the while thinking about what happened. "Well, that explains why Emma was so rude to me when I went into the class with Matthias. I'll have to talk to him about this. I think it's going to be awkward with the two of us in the same room together now."

ELSEWHERE IN A SATELLITE OFFICE OF THE Sanctum of Atonement, a short muscular man wearing an Anidon security uniform was in a control room quietly making adjustments to several pieces of surveillance equipment that monitored the coming and goings of citizens and visitors. Tapping into the live feed, he played a continuous loop of an empty threshold at the outer gates. Having checked the scheduled departures and arrivals to be certain there was no activity for some time, he sped off towards the entrance, avoiding eye contact with everyone. While en route, he quickly changed into civilian clothes and put on a head covering to obscure his appearance in an effort to avoid detection.

A short moment later, he arrived near the gates and disembarked his platform. Several officers were on patrol nearby, which caught his attention. Stopping a distance away, he held a communication device to his head in an attempt to feign a conversation and not draw unnecessary attention to himself. A moment later, the gate was clear. Timing was everything, as he could not predict when the unexpected person could be coming or going. Leaving was the easy part, it was the return that would prove difficult.

Once he made the necessary hand gesture along with uttering the required words, he passed through the doorway to the outer gate free of prying eyes. An enormous parking structure stood off to the side of the entrance. It held the modern Earth vehicles for those who travelled back and forth to carry out their missions.

He quickly climbed aboard a nearby motorcycle and started it up, taking an extra can of fuel along with him. Having left the structure, he was now in the tunnel. The entrance had disappeared, requiring him to check his arm for the code to the lock. Instead of following the markers to depart, he turned the opposite direction, driving for about thirty minutes until he was far enough away from the entrance to use the device he had procured from the research facility—a tracking locator of dark spirit energies.

The path twisted and turned many times and bifurcated several more before the signal began to increase in strength. It was not long thereafter when he approached the caravan of Arita'el and his followers. They had sensed his presence long before they heard his motorcycle, and all were standing outside of their vehicles.

He pulled up to the imposing group and stopped, then turned off his engine and got off of the bike.

"Whom do you serve?" Lahash asked with an aggressive tone. All of the occupants looked somewhat haggard as they were tiring of their confinement.

"Do not be concerned, Lahash, I know this one. He serves Dantanian. Silvan Ford, is it? I trust you are here to have us freed?" Arita'el asked patiently.

"Of course. Quickly, we need to leave. Follow me closely and do not fall behind. The lock will only work for me and those I travel with," he replied, getting back on his motorbike.

"Wait, human. What of our task? What of Lystad?" Ehasar asked, looking at the others in the group.

"He will be dealt with soon. For now, it would be too difficult to make any move against him in Anidon. There are mechanisms already in motion to ensure his capture. Right now, you all have been ordered to report to Belial in Frankfurt, Germany. Ah, I almost forgot," Silvan said, producing a small silver puck from his pocket. "I was instructed to give this to you."

Arita'el took the object. He held it between both hands and twisted it, causing a reddish-orange glowing light to pulse and travel up his arm into his body. He stood for a moment as if in a trance, then fixed his gaze ahead.

"Let us be away then," he said, his eyes flashing with fire.